I uttered the words exactly as I felt that I needed to, to save my life.

I said, "I can't name the hour. Some time. I started truly not to trust the structure of things . . . I mean this. Doctor Conlon . . . I think buildings could fall, literally come apart and fall! I mean it. I think they can't hold. All the time, I'm living like someone in a shelter underground, for months, with the screaming of planes overhead, and then bombs. Only for me the cave-in comes on all the time . . . in this silence. I can't tell you this terror. I can't imagine where I go from here."

Conlon, looking into my eyes, asked me carefully, very kindly, "Are you all right?"

I was just breathing—glad now that I could breathe, in that room, high in the air. I said, with terrible difficulty, "I can't even say, Dr. Conlon. I can't . . . I can't say."

LAKE SHORE DRIVE

PATRICK JOSEPH CREEVY

A TOM DOHERTY ASSOCIATES BOOK
NEW YORK

This is a work of fiction. All the characters and events portrayed in this book are fictitious, and any resemblance to real people or events is purely coincidental.

LAKE SHORE DRIVE

Copyright © 1992 by Patrick Creevy

All rights reserved, including the right to reproduce this book, or portions thereof, in any form.

A Tor Book
Published by Tom Doherty Associates, Inc.
175 Fifth Avenue
New York, N.Y. 10010

Tor® is a registered trademark of Tom Doherty Associates, Inc.

ISBN: 0-812-51279-0
Library of Congress Catalog Card Number: 92-27462

First edition: December 1992
First mass market edition: July 1994

Printed in the United States of America

0 9 8 7 6 5 4 3 2 1

To Susie, my angel since she was fourteen

"A slumber did my spirit seal;
I had no human fears . . ."

—Wordsworth

1
AM I GOING TO GET BETTER?

It was thirteen years ago now, and for better or worse I know that I was wrong when I thought that I'd never forget it. I remember a great number of the details, and I'm close to certain that if it came to my having to endure it again, I wouldn't be able to—that because of what happened before, I somehow this time would disappear. It stays with me that much. But I don't live now in the real authority of the experience. I can recount the number of days spent in Wilmette's Gillson Park, along Lake Michigan, and the few times that the friendly, good lake air, insulating, was enough to stop for maybe five precious minutes my otherwise unstoppable fear—stop it and answer my prayer, which was also at that time unstoppable. But I'm not scared now, and I don't pray. And if I went down now to the park and the harbor, I'd just grow sleepy, nod off, as the wide sky, water, land—the colors and shifts—all came soon enough to mean nothing, or almost nothing. I wouldn't, as then, stay so worriedly and yet so quietly watching and hopeful.

But I do hope now that I can sufficiently fight off sleep

(twin brother of death) and get down some of the details of it. And I hope I can force to life now some simulacrum of an old prayer, which might provide enough force to get out some simulacrum of a once-true story, the one that thirteen years ago I was certain would live with me forever, but which, in the most vital sense, I have now forgotten.

In the fall of '72, when we'd decided finally to call Vietnam, that strange bullet hole in our nation's history, a hole period and forget it (and though I was twenty-four and hated the war with the complete intensity of my age and of that time, I didn't know about this ending), I had reached a point of absolute crisis. I went to a longtime friend of mine, Johnny Lemaster, and confessed to him the truth: I was next to completely frightened—all of the time—over nothing. It very nearly killed me to have to go to Lemaster, but, all other questions over, I had to have a name, and he could give it to me. He was a medical student, and he knew physicians. I was sure he had answers. If I hadn't been, my position would have been even more unspeakably doubtful. Or more exactly— without a confident reverence for medical, scientific authoritativeness, I would have died, and under very strange stars.

The name I got was Dr. Alexander Conlon. A world-conqueror? An Irishman like me?

"He's the best there is," said Johnny, "and he knows right where you're comin' from."

So both, I hoped. But immediately I felt far too sick to dwell on this doctor's good name or fame. To the extent that he was like me, I was that much sicker; and immediately the mere thought of world-conquest, which did keep sounding in me, if as subtly as Pythagorean dream-music, kept making me shrink to a kind of geometric near-zero. I was afraid to look out and see if I had even an inch of life, afraid I didn't, or that if I did and looked, I wouldn't any longer. Worst of all—and this could not be spoken, any more than I or anyone else can die in a dream—this doctor, this Delphic Oracle, was my single, last hope. So it was just barely possible to think, even for a short length of time, of the first hour appointment.

Also I had absolutely to prevent his finding me insufficiently estranged, freaked out, and his not taking me in. Or our spending even a single hour on the wrong things, or my forgetting a key point. So I actually found the strength to write out a rather lengthy statement; and I took extreme care with my history, though I couldn't believe, past a point, in what I was saying. For the most part I had just to drift into that location of myself at the right place at the right time, and could make no statements at all, nor even think at all about the one I'd made.

But among the things that most helped me in that drift—although I could not admit this to myself—were that Johnny Lemaster was every bit as much my enemy as my old friend and that science was as much my goddamned despair as my hope. It was so good to feel somehow that I might *not* hear what I wanted to hear—for when you're all but completely lost, the last things you want are your own directions or any slight suspicions that, in hope, you're fabricating your own story of salvation. Just plainly calling a hole a hole is a beauteous humble service to what is known as honesty. But I remember the praying too, the murmuring in a nearly total silence, and the looking out from inside my possible inch of life, with next to completely shut eyes, for a friendly sign.

"Peter Roche?" I nodded yes as I entered the office, which was a foursquare box, lit now only by window light coming from above and behind the doctor, who was seated beside a desk, casting a shadow on the floor before him. I looked away. The beige wall paint wasn't the right color for the time, but it was clean even at the light switch and blended with the off-white cloth of the drapes. I could perform normally enough in the moment, making quietly sure that the door clicked shut between me and the other outcast in the waiting room, a girl, who would never look up, just as I would never look back. Then, neither pious nor impious, but exactly in between, as I had to be, I took up my position before him in a chair which awaited me. Then I looked out and saw that he wasn't an athlete, but that he also appeared to be no madman. For an instant, though, I lost all balance and began praying as I never had before, almost vocally begging God, a name I could never really call on if I was to live, that this man here would be powerful and fast enough to prevent whatever was coming—that he had the right arm and hand, even teeth, for all hell's fiends, a number of whom, at night, were advancing on me the second that I closed my eyes.

And I can still very neatly date this crisis of hope: October 17, 1972, one day after the one-year anniversary of my father's death. Back then, however, I didn't like these dates. Birth and death were two things that I had always, it seemed every second, to deny.

"Our friend John Lemaster tells me you've got a few troubles."

"Yes I do." But he was decidedly not impressive, this "best," with a body not really overweight, yet loose-fleshed, soft in the belly, and light brown hair maybe too thin to show all the advance of gray. He wore a very pale blue dress shirt with a flattened open collar, and his eyes and skin lacked color as he sat in the dim light before his window, twenty-nine stories high in the air.

He wasn't much older then than I am now, maybe forty to my present thirty-seven. I haven't the slightest idea of what's happened to him. I don't know what, in the eleven years since I've seen him, he's come to look like. But I believe that I could take it if I heard now that he'd had his troubles, even if such news might erase, in some unknowable measure, the eleven years of distance now and bring me back into the hole myself, to some extent.

But I don't mean coming all the way back again to that actual hushed zero-hour, only details of which remain, when in that small room the two of us began our quiet offensive against total fear. This remains impossible, or incompatible with life, as far as I can tell; and if anything had been really wrong with him then, and I could have seen it, I'd have had no capacity even for any defensive stratagem or even the slightest lamentation. Somehow along a darkening road I had come to utter helplessness, and he was there before me—the last sign of hope. But again I cannot in the fullest sense remember what this was.

"Do you want to tell me about it?"

"I want to," I said. Then, "But I'm not sure what's important. Or I've thought, whenever I could, about what things must be important, but I get incredibly frightened every time I start to say to myself, 'This must be important.' "

I stopped, but he said nothing. So I went on (which he would interpret as a good sign). "And then I tried when I could to think of things you'll be most interested in, but at the same time I said to myself, 'If that's what he's interested in, then I'm . . . I don't know.' "

I'd been about to say, looking at his pale face, that then I'd be in the hands of an intellectual, somebody who thinks he knows something, and I'm as afraid of that, I've discovered, as I am of utter medical incompetence and ignorance. But I couldn't say this because I desperately wanted him to think out a plan and was terrified of interfering, though it seemed there in fact was nothing to interfere with now except more silence.

I averted my eyes from his face, and the window. "I have a kind of history that I wrote, though I really don't know if it's the kind of thing that you want to take any time with."

"And if I didn't want to take any time with it?"

Immediately I admitted, sick-nervous, smiling, "I'd be disappointed."

He smiled back. "I don't see any reason to begin with a disappointment."

But he wasn't writing anything down as we began this thing, as I had some silent hope that he would be. But he never put pen to paper in the whole two years I was with him, though there were ten-minute gaps between patients' hours, and I've always assumed that he took that time at least for recording his impressions—yet I never asked. And if in fact he's kept records, I'd be damned curious now to see them— because there might be things in them I wouldn't *really* want to see. For though I'm nowhere near as afraid now that I was a compelling case as I was afraid then that I wasn't, I still wouldn't want to read that I in fact was nearing the borderline of something permanent or irreversible. Or I wouldn't want really to get the feeling that Conlon was not writing about me but about someone else—to find a story truly incomprehensible to me in his arrangement of the details. Or to read things that maybe would annoy, or possibly seriously anger me, things perhaps about my father and me, or my wife and me, or Johnny Lemaster—whose name came up more often than I'd like to admit—and me.

I took out of my pocket the papers I'd been fingering. Then actually hoping (no reason yet for disappointment) that I was getting us on the right track and that I was saving most precious time, I read him my little piece of work, though I wondered what note he'd really take of anything I'd say.

I read first that I didn't remember a single innocent day in my life—that I just remembered being aware of myself— always. When I was a kid there were times when I seemed to escape, feeling the joy of a beautiful religion ("listening to the girls' voices sing the Latin hymns on First Fridays, looking at the beautiful faces and knowing I'd always believe in heaven") and when maybe I had my small world in my hand. But mostly any grace or ease in my life then derived from victories— victories in fights on the playground, sports victories, which did come. Though by the time I was fifteen I would have a feeling, which never left me alone, that I had lost forever some source of strength, or some grace.

I wrestled on the high-school team, but in time I couldn't make moves. I just would freeze to save energy, and the losses started to pile up so that I couldn't forget them for a minute. I never lived anywhere then, for whole seasons, but in my past losses and in upcoming meets. I kept inviting my girlfriend to come and watch me in the hope that this would make me fight, and I finally got her to come to one event. I got my father to come too so that I would, I figured, be under enough pressure absolutely to explode, and get a victory. And I succeeded crazily in making that day into everything that I wanted it to be—the key day of my life—the test and proof of the worth of what I was.

My father was a famous high-school and college football star, with two brothers who were stars, and it used to be impossible for me to understand how kids who didn't have a tradition to live up to could do as well in sports as they did—though I could envy them their ignorant freedom. I'd even wish for complete stupidity and orphanhood—wish that I'd never known my father or heard his voice—if, even slightly more than they distressed them, such wishes would help my victory dreams.

I stopped—looked off the page, though this instantly disturbed me—and said, "I loved my dad, very much, always. But, honest to God, I can't remember when I didn't have flash-like wishes that he was gone—wishes that would also break my heart as fast as they came."

Conlon smiled slightly and nodded, encouraging me in a friendly way to go on—which made me glad. But then with this there was trouble. It came *immediately,* this kind of friendliness, as a terrible trouble to me and disappointment. I had to turn immediately away again, in fear, from the pale face in the dim light. Voices said—Get your eyes off him. Get your eyes off even his shadow on the floor. And this really is it—this is what I want now to recall—this insane time when every slightest step I took, either toward what I desired or away from it, would register instantly as the first movement of some terror or some dangerous joy that would be nearly too much for my life.

"It's so pathetically desperate," I said to my wife last night. "But for me—even still—it brings the goddamned dead world to life. I mean the way I knew how much to care for myself and yet not to—when I was on the edge, listening to voices inside me—and every second believing what I heard."

She said softly, "I know."

"You know I don't seek pain," I said, "for the sake of pain. It's to get past the unbearable emptiness—all the sentimental lies and the sleep that kill real poetry, the real thing, which—I mean this—can't live if the object world doesn't start to speak, and move . . . some. But I can't really go back," I said.

She said, "You don't have to go back. Listen to yourself.

Listen. It's enough. I can hear you—and know what you mean."

In the beige room, with my head bent down in the low light, I read to Conlon how I had a photograph of my father when he was seventeen like me. It was of him in his football uniform, smiling, with his helmet in his hand. I stuck the picture in my wrestling locker, like an altar niche, and in a way used to pray before it—to work up my pride and get back the energy and grace that I'd lost. I told how I kept going to look at the picture on that day when I'd asked my girlfriend and my father to come see me—one of those days that a teenage boy could turn maybe into the last day of his life—and how I kept imagining myself, as I waited for my match, getting married to my girlfriend.

I stopped myself again here, and said, "Johnny Lemaster was on that wrestling team. I don't know if he told you. I think because he never lost he doesn't remember it as well as I do. Zero tradition." I smiled. "But he knows about the photograph. He even told me, intelligently enough, I suspect, that I might be worth more of a damn if I burned it, though he asked me a couple of times if he could take a look at it."

"He didn't mention the wrestling," Conlon said, "just that you were old friends, like brothers." He looked at me carefully. But I went back to my statement.

I read how the space for me, that day in the gym, was this enormous pure vacuum of light, although the figures—my father, my girlfriend, my opponent—seemed to come so close to me or get removed from me to distances, depending exactly on what would make me feel most afraid. The time of the wait, too, and of the actual match, while always I was in that cold hollow of ice-light, seemed to be set on some clock in hell—moving fast or slow, depending always on what I didn't want. After my name was called—no sound ever more strange in my life—and I came into the center of the circle and heard the whistle sound, I was for a few seconds crazily alive, as if in that glaring void I'd discovered some secret. I even tried a move and almost took my opponent down. But there was no miracle cure, of course no miracle cure, and from the first instant, the truth is, I was down-in more exhausted than I'd ever been before. And only moments into the second period I was on my back, and the referee's eye was down next to my eye, and his hand rose, to come down and end it.

After the meet, I sat alone in the low-ceilinged locker room, a basement now lit with a single bulb. I looked in at my father's photograph and felt the light burn even lower and the ceiling move in more tightly. His picture—the boy smiling, holding his helmet—I started to cry—to weep uncontrollably. I'd broken that line and let something die—that life. I knew too how I'd never in my life be what I wanted to be for a girl.

I said that later I became aware, of course, that there might be nothing unusual either in my losses or in my boy's self-pity. But I was sure there was something peculiar in the way that I took things, something that got me where I was right now. Something in the way that I saw things moving.

I read how by the end of my first year in college I had stomach spasms, which woke with me immediately every morning, without fail. I went to a doctor, and when I asked how long they'd last he told me as long as I had a stomach—a remark which worked like a charm. I soon had to start watching the foods I ate. Then just about all the time, my own acid was eating the walls of my own stomach. And again, I knew that this kind of thing was common enough, but I believed that my way of thinking about it was unusual. I thought, without stopping, about how I no longer had any safe place—about how some enemy was in the gate and was coming in farther and farther.

I reported then on how I came, by steady degrees, to know as things separate, besides my stomach: my neck as it stiffened, and then my throat as it contracted, and then the processes of my breathing and my heartbeat as they became irregular, sometimes wildly irregular. Nothing ever seemed to go away or go backward. Always there was a steady progress, a perfect working out of an intention, which was in fact a fabulously successful irony on my own intention—and maybe on all human intention and hope.

Sometimes, in crazy thoughts, it actually seemed to me as

if disease prayed prayers, and as if they always came true, and that the whole damned world would belong completely to disease before it was over. By twenty, I was dizzy virtually all of the time, though I could still press the top of my skull with my hand and more or less control the vertigo. I studied this way, pressing my brains down, whenever tests came.

I went to another doctor, who showed signs of concern over the prolonged dizziness and wrote out a prescription, to be taken three times a day. I was happy taking my medicine. One of the side effects was dry mouth. I always welcomed it. It came as a sign, about a half hour after I'd swallowed the tablets, that my medicine was completely in me and was at its task, making me right.

Another of the possible side effects, however, was completely unforeseeable cardiac arrest. One day after I'd been taking the medicine for about six months, my heart practically exploded out of my chest. Something like a good friend inside me was suddenly then the most threatening alien presence—some kind of unbelievable fiend, who knew his task too, exactly. With my heart gone almost completely wild, I leaned against the wall in my room and in an instant I placed myself between the position of the compliant bird, with his neck in the jaws of the dark fox, and the initial resistant attitude of actual flight.

Now, more easily, if still anxiously—anxious to get things right—I took my eyes off the page and said, "It's been over two years since I quit taking that medication—but something's still with me. It's a very exact place. In those jaws, not moving, feeling the moist warmth and the hard pressure of the tooth. It's where I keep myself now all of the time, not complying with the sickness, but not daring to move either. And I keep myself exactly here on the advice—which I can hear—the perfect advice—of something deeper inside me than anything I have ever known."

I said yesterday to my wife, as we sat on our porch and took coffee, "Crazy as it all was, A, what's left of it moves me when I come across any real poetry. How to hold what we love . . . so carefully . . . and at the same time letting it go, out of a loose hand . . . because that's the exact dictate of a *voice*. But then what am I saying? That people need to be as afraid as I was? As crazy? Yet I'd trust me over someone who was never afraid."

"I'd trust you," she said, "if I hope that before we're old we'll just be all the time absurd, and happy, with what you know."

But of course the problem of my life is that I don't know anymore. I don't know how I stopped myself, with Conlon waiting, and rested in fact on that "perfect advice," and caught a breath. I can't hear now the small voice. Nor do I really know anymore what it means to believe, for a few seconds, as I did, that my doctor could know the exact place I spoke of—that place in the jaws of sickness—and that he would have a name for it—and that he would know what places one would be likely to go to from there if he did this or did that. I don't have this faith now—nor the magnificent fear, God help me, that possibly my disease might have gone, or might go, even deeper than the saving voice of the small someone inside me.

Now, after years of health, I can sport with the idea that such things as origins and endings are illusory, the idea that no doctor could pretend to know about the place of which I spoke, and that that exact safe location, that point between living and dying, is patrolled by no small someone and is in fact nowhere. But back then I was far too sick, Jesus help me, for this sport; and I was far too sick to be polarized, like the nation.

In those insane days, days of sickness and poetry, I *honestly* (there's the word) would cry for joy in the mornings when the sun rose out of the dark. But I dreaded also, with reverent terror, that the god of darkness would catch me in my tears. I felt an utter fear of death—and an equally true guilty dread over being alive.

But with the smallest, most intense hope, aware as I haven't been for years, of the incredible danger of desire, I kept on reading to Conlon what I'd dared to write.

I said that despite anything that perverse chemical

changes had done to make my medicine work in me now as a poison, my somewhat better health lasted for some time—though also that I worried when my mouth stayed moist after meals. Of course I feared that the movement, the godforsaken progress of the thing was far from over. But, June of '70, several months after I quit my medicine, I graduated magna cum laude from the University of Chicago College and had been accepted at the Graduate School for Advanced Studies—although I felt the demon of disease immediately present at the graduation ceremony. In fact I was sure, in crazy seconds, that the sickness was working with an ever more miraculous exactitude to make my achievements meaningless. But I was married that summer too, in August, to my wife, Allie, the girl who came to see me wrestle that time (Johnny, home from Yale, was the best man). And my marriage was and is happy, very happy.

But from day one in the Advanced Studies Program, where, I said, in my third year I was still preparing for a career in teaching, life wasn't at all what I had it cracked up to be. In fact, in the six months since I'd passed my Master's exam—at the midpoint of my second year—absolutely nothing had been the same with me. Any furies that I might have been able to keep back with career hopes it seemed now were only waiting to make louder and louder noises in an ultimate ridicule of those hopes as they were being realized, and then to come in after me.

I now read too that in the fall of my second year, October of 1971, I came to know about completely absurd, wholly undeserved pain as I watched my father die of cancer.

Conlon leaned slightly forward. He said, "Lemaster did mention that. He could see how hard you took it."

"Johnny was there," I said, "and I'm sure he knew what I was feeling, or some of it." When I'd said this, I returned to my statement.

But before I end now this account of a statement that I no longer possess, I'll say again that I know that my adolescent agonies and my prolonged anxiety, with all the different physical complications—all these things, even with my peculiar way of taking them—certainly don't amount to anything unheard of. Over the last several years I've talked more and more openly with my friends about my hard times, and many of them have said that they've suffered through quite similar things, if perhaps not through so long a stretch.

Yet after a point in such confessions, I begin to feel like a Nam vet, talking to friends whom he respects, but who got to stay home. The final lines in the last battles I fought at that time were drawn far far in. And in that moment in that small, faintly lit room, with this doctor I didn't know, I found it very hard to go on. But the time when I had to talk to someone not-myself had long come, and of course was passing.

I said that it started at night, when I looked into the shadows above the glow from my reading lamp. My nightmare wasn't all there at once—coming ripping through the wall—though I'd seen faces like painted medieval satans with red tongues and the torn limbs of the damned in their mouths. I said that I *knew* now where these pictures came from—right out of the heart of everlasting terror, when the mind is pressed hard enough. For some months now—for me—they were coming alive—pictures—red faces in the shadows of ceilings of rooms, making me lose faith in the simplest safeties we need to live—to walk through rooms.

I lifted my eyes. Conlon's face was now a shadow against the glass and the blank sky. Then I once more lowered my head. With my eyes just touched closed, uttered the words exactly as I felt that I needed to, to save my life: "I don't know if I should scream what I'm about to say—or just barely whisper it—to get it right. I'm trying—Jesus Christ—so damned pitifully here to take some sane path."

Then I opened my eyes. He was leaning forward, looking at me with compassion. And I said a prayer—in absolutely perfect silence—perfect—that when he'd heard what I'd say now he'd have to take me in.

I said, "I can't name the hour. Some time. I started—truly. No words for this. But I started truly not to trust the structure of things . . . I mean this. Doctor Conlon . . . I think buildings could fall, literally come apart and fall! I mean it.

Especially man-made things. Incredible. This is it! The buildings! I'm afraid. I'm so afraid. I think they can't hold. All the time, for months. I'm living like someone—Christ Almighty—in a shelter underground, for months, with the screaming of planes overhead, and then bombs. Only for me the cave-in comes on all the time . . . in this silence. I'm so afraid to say this—my head—it *knows*. But walls—and the junctures of walls and ceilings—and the spans. I can't tell you this terror. But this is it. I can't help myself anymore with this. The whole world. All the time! I can't imagine where I go from here. If I stay by myself, my mind for certain will take the next step into hell. It knows exactly what to do next."

I stopped. Conlon, looking into my eyes, asked me carefully, very kindly, "Are you all right?"

I was just breathing—glad now that I could breathe, in that room, high in the air. I waited a long time, through nothing, and then just touched the paper, saying "I'll read this . . . to the end."

And I read—I was able to read now—how when I first noticed this new, final terror I had prayed that I was learning something of fundamental importance about the necessity of stability in the world—and even that I might be able some day to use all that I was learning, in a story, and that I might say in that story that my fears were the real hidden fears of our time.

But when I learned instead was to keep my mouth shut, or very, very close to shut.

I hesitated for a moment again—but kept my eyes down on the page, not wanting to see at all now the space where I was, or to measure the shadowy light, or any distances. But I knew that Conlon studied me still with care, and this helped me. I read to him quickly now—how before I knew it, in any room that I was in, the walls, floors, ceilings were actually in some horrible goddamned world of black miracle and forgetfulness, where they might simply at any moment no longer do what they always do. I said I fear now all the time that none of these elements anywhere, joists, beams, no matter what the strength of their material, will be strong enough to support weight for very long. And this unbelievable conviction has grown steadily, so that every godforsaken day I am still more thoroughly afraid to be inside a structure, any structure.

Ceilings are heavy on top of me—threatening. I study them with my eyes—the shadows. But everything might be ready. The wind terrifies me, even with small breezes, as it keeps pushing and pushing on things. On the building where I live. Especially at night . . .

"Especially at night . . ." I took my eyes off the paper as I repeated myself. I said, with terrible difficulty, "I'm more afraid of the dark now, Dr. Conlon, than ever in my whole life. I can't even say. I can't . . . I can't say."

I bowed my head again as I said this, and my eyes filled with tears. But I went on.

Especially at night. The wind at night threatens everything I have ever known. And Christ, I said, I am angry. Jesus Christ Almighty, yes, how I want to say to any philosopher who thinks he can play with the structure of reality—"Give this a try for a while, you son of a bitch. Give a try, even for an hour, to a *real* distrust of, say, the post and lintel. See how you like that. Or see how you can stand it. Maybe after you try to stand it for seven months, or for a single hour, I'll trust you when you preach to me about what's honest. But never before, I said. Never on my goddamned life."

But the last lines of my statement were that if I spoke in this aggressive way anymore, something would erase me. That it would come for me and erase me. That it wouldn't let me escape, as it had up till now. That it wouldn't let me open my eyes and see, sometimes, how a few things are still there.

I was finished. But with my tears beginning to fall (sacrifices to several gods), I added, "I'm remarkable for secrets, Dr. Conlon. No one, except my wife, Allie, and possibly Johnny, knows any of these things about me. No one else who knows me can tell a thing. But maybe," I said almost in a whisper, "this concealment is something of which I'm still proud."

He right away moved his chair a bit forward. He waited till I dried my eyes, then asked me, "Why did you wait so long to come?"

Immediately the question brought an answer, a rush of answers, from behind a door that I rarely, if ever, opened. But I was loose all of a sudden, after the beginning had been made and after the tears. The work was actually beginning. My statement had been made, and I had now only the very slightest suspicions of how a first day like this could turn out come midnight, when it would be just me, and a dim light in the dark.

"I simply didn't want to give in. I was extremely ashamed of having to go see a doctor, I'll be honest. But I guess you hear pretty regularly from your beginning patients that they thought they were able to go it alone. I bet this screws up a hell of a lot of people."

I stopped for a second. "I believe pride goeth before a fall—even still." Then I closed my eyes. "But in some moments," I said, "I've sort of dared to think that I've learned something by becoming completely helpless: that I've had a true happy fall. I can actually say that I've placed some hope in this possibility once or twice."

I held up a finger in the air, and bowed my head. "But there's another thing too. I know this now and can say it even if it scares me to death, which it does. I truly wanted to believe that *time* would heal some wounds, at least. I desperately didn't and don't want to think that there may be some force actively, successfully working against me, but I did and do want one to be one working for me—call it time. And I still figure, even though I've come to you, that without pure patience—something the helpless learn one hell of a lot about—I am in enormous trouble."

Then I opened my eyes. "But I suppose humility or stupidity has screwed me up too."

"We have to be afraid," he said, "so we can get to the point where we are no longer afraid, or where fear is strictly useful. You don't want to count on time too much. Things can get away. So we have to distrust—but then trust at the same time. We're going to have to challenge that notion of bad progress—of things continuing to get worse—which has you by the throat. But I share your own sense of a need for čaution. Medicine and time are going to be fairly slow partners here. And you know, of course, that the therapy is going to take a considerable amount of money. The fee is fifty dollars per hour. I've got to tell you this right away, so that we won't begin something we can't finish."

"I have the money," I said, "from my dad." And I thought not only that I was in, but that we were going to finish something that we had begun. I was intensely grateful to my father for the blessed money.

"Good," he said. "I should say too right away that I don't like to treat someone in your condition with drugs. I don't believe medication gets to the root of the problem. If you hadn't had the adverse reaction you did I suspect that sooner or later you would have found the medication inadequate."

This was Johnny's "best," but still I was afraid of the unscientific uncertainty of an empty medicine chest. "I'm absolutely convinced," I said, "that my condition is to some significant extent chemical. The disease gets in and alters your molecular structure somehow. I swear it. It's a stage of this thing. I know it. Mind and matter—somehow they interpenetrate and goddamn curse each other in some kind of a vicious circle. It's unbelievable. But"—and I was now actually praying out loud—"I swear I want more than I can say to believe that biochemistry isn't at the bottom of this. I'm crazy saying this. It's so risky. But I want the root to be something else. Or I guess I'm confessing that I'm glad to hear what you're saying about the drugs. It's gotten to be pure heresy now to say that there's such a thing as a responsible self. I want very much, even if it makes me more afraid, to be a heretic in this regard. Part of me's gotten very conservative. I figure the new thinking of our time truly *could* kill me."

But it was as if I were foretelling something: the untelling of my whole story, with its key points, its connection between the way things fell out and the way I fell. My sister is right now about the same age I was then, and is suffering from symptoms very much like mine. She is being treated by her doctor with regular medication for a disease that at present is called Panic Disorder, and that is attributed to nothing except biochemistry. Science has her quite safe, as well; and, though I suspect she does pray, she is not, even implicitly, encouraged to.

"But what"—I asked him now—"will . . . our procedure be?" I felt again afraid—as afraid as I'd thought I might feel if I ever asked this question.

"We'll talk," he said, "nothing frightening."

"But what'll we say?"

"I don't know yet."

"I'm afraid I've said it all. I've been afraid that I'll just come up empty here and that we'll go nowhere."

"I'm sure you've got a number of things left to say."

"I sure as hell hope so."

"It's very positive the way you've been talking already. The fact that you're making noise is a very positive sign. I get people who can't talk at all. You want to be helped—I can see; and you want to help. I can listen for as long as it takes."

I looked at him and felt perhaps as much longing as any alienated demoniac who ever came raving before Jesus, hoping for the touch or the healing word. So much had been said already. So much dangerous outreach—approaching the brink of salvation.

Before long, however, *because* in this first hour I had let out so many demons whom I had so carefully kept out of sight, I would face a crowd of terrors like none I'd ever faced. I would find myself weeping and bracing myself and weeping and bracing myself whole nights. Or driving off to Conlon's house in the dark just to see if it was there. Or driving down roads where no one was and rushing out of my car to walk and run for hours, then returning to sink against the car door and cry for some sign of mercy to whatever it was that was failing now more and more to keep crushing weight at a right distance away from me.

But now I looked at his pale, soft face and, not knowing what was coming in the nights ahead, happily forgot whatever I might have thought about the possible inadequacy of his power, or the unimpressiveness of his figure, and asked him the next question. I still regard it as the most crucial question I have ever asked.

"Am I going to get better?" I asked, simply—loud enough for us both to hear. But even in the new happiness of those beginning moments, I felt the presence of some trouble.

But he said, "I most certainly believe so."

I could hear him, and I could still see the smile on his face. I now had tears in my eyes again, but was rubbing them away as I broke into a smile myself. I said to him, "You said it would take a long time." Then I asked him another enormous question: "How long . . . is long?"

"I don't like to say," he said, "but I think that we might expect some results over the next few months. But don't expect to be cured by then. It's not unusual for a thing like this to take two years."

I said, "Of course. And you can trust me to keep my expectations within bounds. That's become lately my most advanced skill."

Now too, having read to her every word I've written so far, I said to Allie, "After I'd learned about expectation the way I did—about the arrival and departure of everything moving, insanely, on the pulse—I was ready with this insane heart to *understand* the words—always, in poetry, about absence, arrival, departure—I swear. So beautiful. The beginning and end of the world."

She smiled, and touched my hand.

And Conlon, when I told him I'd keep my expectations within bounds, smiled broadly and nodded. But there were some seconds of silence, and I worried about how many more there might be.

He spoke, however, and I liked the thoughtful quality of his next move. "When you say that you fear that built structures are going to cave in on you, you obviously are not speaking metaphorically—though just as obviously you aren't ducking and cringing at the present moment."

I interjected quickly, "It's as if my mind were out to prove—I swear—that some of the most traditional metaphors, the grounds of poetry, don't come from nowhere—that because of some eternal dictate they, and they especially, will magically, immediately *speak themselves* when you come to certain moments or places in your life; or maybe that the recurring metaphors of poetry have the power of passing from just talk into the mind's absolute reality. But either way, 'The house is falling' isn't just words with me, and I'm not randomly picking and choosing what I'm afraid of, I guarantee you."

"I believe you. People don't make up stories like yours. They couldn't. But there's another question I want to ask you. When you say that you fear that the house is falling on you, do you mean that you really believe that the house is falling on you? Or, even at its worst, is there a difference for you between fearing and believing?"

My answer was certain, though I never knew it like this before, not having known, or perhaps dared, to ask this question. "There is a difference. I'm afraid of it . . . but I don't believe it."

He nodded his head and said, very gently, "That's a large difference."

And in that room, in the shadowy window light, the two of us were extremely glad to have perceived it. I might still, too, with some true understanding, distinguish poetry from both madness and mere words.

But now he looked at his watch and touched it: the first hour appointment was over. He said that he was sorry and rose to shake my hand. But in a businesslike way he asked me if I would be able to send the checks twice monthly and, with his hand lightly on my arm, if I was comfortable with our procedure.

I smiled and told him, "I believe in conversation—and don't fear it."

"Good," he said, and asked me if the hour was a good time.

I said that it was, and we made the next appointment for the following week, same day and hour. Then I even told him that I thought I was in good hands, and he even told me at this point that things would turn. I nodded and proceeded then through the waiting room, still keeping my eyes to myself here, and not wanting to catch any name, if any name was to be called. Then I headed for the elevator which, with its good, friendly lights for each succeeding number, its regular pace through all the unlit intervals, its emergency stop button, its phone, would drop me down twenty-nine stories to the ground.

2
IN THE SMALL DARK ROOM

So a beginning had been made, and though I thought about it as intensely as possible, given my condition, I was able to drive home—so many foul spirits had been flushed out of me in a few moments of faith. I found myself in fact swinging down into the birth-chute at the end of Michigan Avenue happily and riding up with ease onto Lake Shore Drive, entering the traffic flow undisturbed by the number of other cars, the short, calculable distances (changing) between us all, the several loud horns. Things in the October noon sun were there to love: on the infinite blue lake, the last white sails of the year; and along the miles of city parks, the end-of-life brightness in the October leaves.

For an instant, to the left, at Burton, I saw the sculpture of *Hope and Help* in gray stone in front of the Museum of the International College of Surgeons. It was like a pietà or a madonna and child: the man in the doctor's arms, looking up, flaccid, wasting, but with a musculature recalling a beauty worth preserving with a knife. And I felt safe enough even to admire things, to remember the names of famous physicians, even to think of pictures and figures that I'd seen inside the museum: of Asklepios, of his temples; of Hygeia; or of devils and angels hovering with doctors over sickbeds; of the limb-cutting and the staring eyes in Rembrandt's great *Anatomy Lecture*—and all of this while breathing calmly, and in passing.

One of those rarest successions of good songs came over the radio—five, six, seven, eight in a row. So music was king; and expressway driving, too often here caught in the miserable mass jam, was a sweet pleasure; and that noon hour, all the way between downtown Chicago and Wilmette's Gillson Park, there weren't any accidents, or stalling breakdowns. So in my memory I'd keep some rare knowledge of the worth of self-forgetfulness.

Some of the hour remains with me now—traces of the sweet music—even after I've been healthy for so long. But it's safe enough to relax now, to forget myself in a memory of music—as I'll feel no twinge of the steel grip that took its vengeance on self-forgetfulness then. I mean when the feeling of sundown began to punish me for thinking even for a moment that anything was over for me, to turn music to a terror, and to teach me lessons on the final discomposition of the world.

But that day, before late afternoon settled in, the color and massing shifts in the sky were perfectly friendly. In my crazy eyes, the lake and shore, in an October air like peace, knew so well how much they needed each other that they forgot what they knew. The blue sky-dome domesticated everything visible and invisible: everything that was here and everything that wasn't yet here, or couldn't yet be seen. Nothing was afraid of anything. And the sun's real business was to bring to light a tremendous elevating beauty, a beauty capable of lifting me beyond memory and desire. So, far out on the Gillson pier, looking south to downtown Chicago and its world-class towers, now softened by distance into dreams, I believed that all intervals of darkness brought on only a clearer beauty than there was before; and that endings, losses, led only to a discovery of how rightly to begin again.

The Baha'i Temple, which in huge flowering pylons rises over the back of Wilmette Harbor like a dream of heaven, was an incarnation of love, a domed house of prayer, with its articulated exterior power, unashamed and as awesome as any that architecture can produce; and its vast interior emptiness, a disappointment only to damned fools who need to see things all the time, or who never see enough.

But if I went to the pier now, I'd feel dried up, too safe; and if I went to the temple, I'd have to hold open an eyelid with a finger to keep myself from sleeping.

Yet that morning, helpless myself, I had kept an appointment with a doctor who I had to believe was going to help me. The things I'd done during our first hour of conversation were thrilling; and to keep up the feeling, I dared even to go over the high points of the hour with Conlon. And as I recalled every good moment, I watched the one or two clouds in the blue change and break, and Michigan offer its massive, still-blue power as a comfort to a crazy eye.

There was the appointment, which I had made, and kept. The doctor had heard my call and given me a time and was there when I came. I walked back slowly now from the pier to the towering silver-green poplars on the park lawn. I sat under one of the huge trees, unbelievable presences in the October air and light, with my knees hunched up to my chest. I was shaking or crying sometimes, just thinking. I had made a statement, written it out, read the whole of it to the doctor— and he had listened. Without thinking about why, not even for a second thinking about why I had written it, I had written it; and only a few hours before, he had listened to it.

I kept the papers in my hand still and reread and reread them, finding comfort in the thought that the words that were already down had taken me a distance at least, though I worried about what I'd say next.

The doctor's questions got me to reveal things and discovered in me a willingness to reveal more things. After the questions, in fact, I said that I had a slight hope that I was learning something from this experience, that I was actually making an advance in wisdom. I even used the words "happy fall" and suggested that there might be some relationship between what I dared to call my own tragedy and the tragedies of other ages, other places. And I *knew* the worth of my actions in those terrible joyous seconds when to think of them, to think of such things as my making an appointment, my going to see a doctor, my talking to him was to feel instantly the joys and terrors of what I'm calling poetry.

I confessed to him that I'd hoped that some benign force was working in me, that I'd prayed that time was at least partly on my side and that disease—Jesus Christ—wasn't finally everything. And I know that if someone had come up to me then and said that time's being on my side was purely my own fiction, or whispered that disease was the final word for life, I would have had to take him by the throat and put the sweet taste of panic in his gullet, till it had either killed him or worked in him some profound philosophical change.

I confessed to a belief in the worth and meaning of patience, which I said were great, and he—the doctor—had himself said that patience would be necessary for my recovery. Patience and healing. Mere words, I thought, could never make such love with the mind and produce so much there.

I admitted to a curiosity about procedure. I asked a question about it; and when he told me that our procedure would be conversational and that drugs would not be the key to it, I not only made an act of faith in conversation, right there, but I told him that I preferred conversation to chemistry—though I knew as much about the great saving light of science as anyone alive.

But as I sat under the huge trees, and could see at once the magnificent white temple, the harbor, the lake, there were also instant warnings against triumph. A shudder of fear would run through me as a kind of natural response to my thrills of hope; and if any movement or sound of hope brought on perfectly the sickness of dread, it was in the instantly gagged war cry that came with my recollection of those two other questions that I had asked: Would I get better? and How long would it take?

I was never naive. I knew that I wanted certain things to

have certain meanings for me. I wanted my fear, for instance, to make me *know* how much I had to protect the things I loved. But also to warn me against loving too much, and being overprotective. And I wanted any second of joy that I felt to do the same things: to help me to let go of the world I loved and to remind me at the same time of how much I loved it. But at the time, my determination that fear and beauty would make these certain noises seemed nothing compared to the scream in the mind that I heard when even beginning to whisper questions such as Will I get better? Or beginning most tentatively to take any action for myself. I was as certain as death that this terrifying scream *wasn't* any sound of mine, or a sound made by anything I knew, and that it had nothing to do with my determination—and so proved that fear was a voice. I was convinced also to the point of violence, in those briefest moments that I was able to hold a conviction, that we know the soul's destiny and that not just anything can break our hearts.

But I almost fear that if I were in any way to insist on this point now, to go so far as to say that forever our hearts have known what they want, I might break my heart again, get sick—as I may have broken myself before by insisting, although in near silence, or on the borderline of a fraction of an inch, that there was a self in the first place.

But Dr. Conlon had not discouraged this. He wanted me, the self-conscious me, alive, and wanted me to want myself alive, even immodestly, unapologetically to want this. "Identity crisis is recognized as a pathology," he'd said, "and we fight it."

Johnny Lemaster was the one I had gone to for a name as soon as I suspected that my father was dangerously ill. I asked for the best oncologist there was. He told me that the best he knew was Dr. Michael Rothen; and my father, who had suspected, known, for a good time that he was seriously ill, but who for some reason could not say to himself that he was nearing any danger point, finally went to Dr. Michael Rothen, the best—but it was too late.

Dr. Rothen and the surgeons whom he recommended,

also the best, cut into my father, discovered the presence of cancer everywhere and simply closed him. The primary tumor was itself massive and had penetrated into dangerous territory. But what was most significant was that it had long since been metastatic. What that meant, I discovered, was that at some time before, unknown, the disease had progressed beyond the point where any doctor on earth could do a thing to stop it. Why my dad had waited so long after detecting first signs, I couldn't say, though I had delayed going to a doctor myself because I was proud. And what he thought, or how he prayed, when he was informed that he had no chances left, I won't ever know.

Lemaster explained to me the meaning of metastasis. Dr. Rothen's first explanations hadn't been taken in. We couldn't listen—since that kind man had had to say, first thing, that they'd simply closed him. But Johnny was there. He took me aside.

"You want to understand," he said.

"Yes . . . I want to know," I said.

We were in a windowless white-walled consulting room, under an ungodly fluorescent light, and he waited before he spoke—long enough to make anyone suspect that time was strange and dangerous. His dark skin could be seen only in his hands and face, but the power of his body could be read in his flawless, strong cheeks—and of his will in the blue of his eyes, cool under a firm brow and thick dark hair. And to what degree really he knew how hard, that year, it was for me to wait on anything, I cannot truly say. But the seconds' passing was an agony beyond agony, and I suspected that he knew—and felt his power. What would he say? Months of chemotherapy? Excruciating radiation therapy?

"Sit over here," he said, moving me toward some chairs against one of the blank, windowless walls. When he had me placed, he raised his eyes, waited, and finally spoke. "Peter," he said, "we can't help him. He's gonna die."

I looked at him in his white intern's coat—at the powerful body and dark face, the blue eyes intent on me in the fierce light of that room. I'd heard him, but I refused to accept what he said. In the anger that rushes in wildly before the pain of our grief, I wanted instantly to force acceptable words out of him, to force benignancy, humanity if I could—to move him with guilt. "You mean—Jesus Christ—there's nothing you're gonna do—even to slow it down—to give him some time!"

Almost, I'd say, as if to check any attempt at angry hope, he responded quickly, with his eyes now impatient. "We can give him medication, yes, to give him as much comfort as we can when the time comes. But the time, Peter . . . isn't going to be long."

I said, "What the hell d'ya mean, John? Jesus. How long? What exactly?"

"I mean, Peter," he said slowly, ". . . within two months. Possibly a little longer. Possibly not so long. The cancer is well developed in a number of dangerous places. The metastasis has been going on for a long time, and it's now very far advanced."

I begged him, "Please don't use terms with me, Johnny. Jesus Christ. Just tell me what it means—please."

"It means it's spread essentially," he said.

"But spread *how?*" I said louder, "and spread where? I want to know what this shit means. What does 'dangerous places' mean, for Christ's sake? And what is this thing? Beyond chemo? Beyond radiation? Or anything you guys can do to slow it down? I mean, who knows what could happen in time—even next week—the way things are going with the research? I don't want to sound so foolish like this, John—but you hear things all the time. Every day."

"The places," he said, "are the pancreas, both kidneys, the colon, quite likely the lungs, the brain."

"Ohhh Christ Jesus," I moaned, "—how? Two months ago—this wasn't in our lives. God Almighty—one. Tell me how this happens."

And he told me. For if what I really wanted was clarity, he was ready to give me what I wanted.

"A tumor in the beginning, Peter," he said, deliberately, with his eyes again intent on me, "is a normal cell that somehow gets transformed. Somehow the controls on growth and differentiation are lost. Differentiation . . ."

I nodded to show that I remembered what this was, as somehow I did remember from somewhere.

He went to his next point, like a teacher. "If the tumor is benign, it'll show a consistency of cellular structure, and even if it grows crazily, it'll remain encapsulated within a membrane. One of the chief signs of malignancy is the absence of the membrane."

I looked carefully at him—and was especially thoughtful—though I knew too, and crazily, that I'd be punished for thinking at all now—and maybe as hard as for loving my father as I loved him: with my whole life.

"Eventually," he said, "malignancy knows no closure at all."

I nodded, and still crazily was thinking about the distant implications of all that he was saying.

He said, "The malignant tumor isn't at all consistently structured." He moved his body forward. "It's comparatively loosely joined," he said, "and this is what makes metastasis possible." He looked at me more carefully too—his dark face close—and seemed thoughtful himself, and interested. "Metastasis means, then, Peter, basically, the movement of tumor offshoots to distant sites." He paused. "Only malignant tumors metastasize. This," he said, "is their defining characteristic." Then more deliberately—"Metastasis, oncologically, is regarded . . . as the key event . . . in any cancer's history."

I interrupted him, still angrily, if already perhaps in complete heartbreak and hopelessness. "How in hell on earth is it possible, John—how is it possible that something so utterly goddamned chaotic has the power to keep on like this? How in goddamned hell does it stay alive?"

"If we knew the biology, Peter," he said, "we could stop it. All we really know at this point is that a malignancy can penetrate blood vessels, and lymphatic vessels—and that once it's done it, it sends literally millions of cancer cells into the body every day."

I put my head back and shut my eyes tight. "Which it's done in my father's case . . . for some time?"

"Yes."

"And nothing stops it?"

"Something stops most of it."

"Most." I opened my eyes again slightly.

"In fact," he said, "almost all of the malignant cells are immediately destroyed in the blood or lymph, which are hostile."

"But not all . . ." I answered.

"A number survive," he said.

"A number," I said. ". . . Some number."

And softly I closed my eyes again—maybe trying somehow to picture that number. I wouldn't say anything more—nothing now—till he finished—though I was thinking suddenly, as I looked again at his dark face, and his blue eyes, and his powerful athlete's body, how I'd remember for my whole life this white room, the light, and the unbearable shame of having asked him these questions.

"The remnant colonize," he said, "in places where they come to rest. They stick to the bloodstream walls, and then clog. After this they start to separate the cells of the walls of the bloodstream." He showed me with his hands. "Then," he said, "they move out through the gaps they create in these walls into other areas of the body, where they'll establish themselves. After this . . . the history's completely different—and if colonies are established in vital organs . . . as they are in a number of your father's . . . then the prognosis is very dark, Peter, given the shortcomings of our present understanding. Or, to be honest with you, in cases like your father's . . . it is terminal."

"No prayer," I whispered, with my head back to the wall, voicing now the thought that more than any other had been growing in that blinding brightness. I knew too (as in that room I heard every sound more sharply from the instant that the idea of this infinitely perfected horror story took shape) that I would in the future have great difficulty asking any questions, any questions at all, regarding life and death, or making statements. I could feel then, looking finally again into the face and eyes of Lemaster, that I had arrived at another turning point, and that it was the most dangerous turning point yet—in all my shameful life.

Did he say to himself, "You asked for it"? He said to me quietly, "I've heard men like Rothen tell people already maybe forty times, and I've been here only a few months." But later—in our bar at night, with his teeth flashing—he would indeed tell me that I had asked for it. He would cram down my throat the claim that a man like my father was either a fraud or a pitiable fool and that the disease was a perfect response from nature's absurdity to all of my father's absurd dreams and hopes, or last, sad, guilty apologies for dreams and hopes.

Our beautiful wish that some things will endure forever is so often granted by an unbelievable, vicious ironist. The terror of my father's death, of all things the one I wanted most not to last, of course was still with me. The dread would keep on after all the happiness and incomparable beauty of my father's life were gone. It was born and grew, had a life—but would never get sick and die. So in the park, when inevitably the terror vision of those final days came and stopped my insane recollections of my hour with my own doctor, I had to take action—again—for the millionth time. I had to get up fast from the lawn and away from the whitening poplars, now threatening, and walk. In the air, now poisoned—blowing in the huge trees suddenly too bright and terrifying—I moved fast to the beach, over the wide, green lawns, running in the changed light. I struggled clumsily in the deep, yellow sand and spear grass, then made it to the harder sand along the shore, moving quickly in order to feel, God help me, some stupidity in the physical action. I was running, begging some ineffable mercy that I'd find something—maybe in this pounding of feet and the pain and sweat—that could silence the screaming claim that we are nothing—as well as any slight breath of the opposite claim that we were born to live forever.

But I couldn't stop my thinking, no matter what I did. I was exhausted, on my knees, dripping sweat in the wet sand by the gray water—my heart and lungs in enough pain to drown any dangerous voice of terrifying poetry or love. But something in me was bringing back a crowd of thoughts that tore me open, made me sick with hope and fear, and made it impossible to move these thoughts away from my fragile life.

Exactly as Johnny had said, the time was nothing before my father had to come to Mercy Hospital to stay—not even the two months.

"The size of this operation," he said, when my mother and I took him to his room, "has increased three or four times since your mom gave birth to Con in the old building."

He was fifty-three and looked a shrunken eighty-year-old, all his skin bruised or gray-black; but he could still think and talk. He sat on the stiff white bed, tapped the mattress, and said, "Annie, I forgot my razor."

"It's here," my mom said, and held up a tan leather case.

From his small, high room he could see the columns disposed along the top of the bowl at Soldier Field. He said, "It's a good thing they're not gonna let the old place fall down. It has so much history."

He had me place trees in his shoes. In the razor case there was medicine that he had been given by Rothen, with the doctor's orders typed in the usual way on the adhesive slip and pressed on the amber plastic bottle. My mother opened the case and took it out.

"Take that and feed it to the fish," he said, now starting to lie down for what would be the last time.

For the first two days after the exploratory surgery, he'd listened like the perfect soldier for anything like real orders from Rothen, and when he didn't get them, he'd tried to construct orders out of what Rothen had said. But "Uselessness three times a day" was his present interpretation of the slip, and he added bitterly, "with meals."

My mother held his head as she helped him lie back on the pillow. I turned away, when she had him down, and looked over the bed at the medical instruments and gauges which in black and silver were unforgettably sharp against the pale yellow of the wall. But I could see her fit her palm tenderly to his strange, small face. Her fingers caressed the bruised skin—

and my heart broke for everything they stood for in their lives.

On the Gillson beach, I held my own head with my hands as I tried some of the last gifts we have for dispelling panic. I walked, but with zero intention. I kept my eyes open, but looked at nothing. I received the waves of hope and then those of fear without any slight trace of discrimination. I let them all come and go. And rather quickly this worked. For no reason, the disturbance was quieted. I looked for no reason—rather just walked, in the air that dried my skin and eased slowly the hard pain in my chest—and I didn't think. In a few minutes, I was able to sit calmly again in the soft sand and to gaze on the graying coloration of the land, sky, and wide water. Then after a time, in an insane rush, the key points of my morning appointment did come back again in procession—a line which should have disturbed me with its terrible hopefulness. But somehow I could again go over the morning's key points and watch the graying water and sky—and a white sail now moving into the harbor like a swan.

But only now, after all the years of health, can I conceive for myself what additionally disturbed me that afternoon: the still unthinkable revelation that my father had gone beyond even the best medical help—and how much he had come to hate the sight of those doctors.

"If I see one . . ." he said. "If I have to listen to the first goddamned word, I'll shut their mouths. I'll shut their mouths . . ."

The memory of this was far down in me, working on me, but was unthinkable—no matter what else I could consider. Not a fraction of a sound—I couldn't begin to think of a fraction of a sound of it as I walked now in the rising breeze, hearing the squeaking gear of the docked sails, or sat in silence again on the park beach sand. In those hours after the first hour appointment, God help me, I could no more have conceived of a rebellion from the best medical authority than I could have tolerated the eternal victory of Satan in my head. I had absolutely to be the perfect serviceman in the army of my doctor, my world-king. And consequently I have only in some senses forgotten the great worth of obedience, and still can only incompletely trust anyone who doesn't know what it means.

My father and I fought for years, sometimes violently, over Vietnam. "The truth is," I said once, "that as soon as we begin making distinctions between them and us, or making *this* out to be evil, *that* out to be good, we limit ourselves, disconnect ourselves from—I mean this—God, eternity."

"What the hell," he said, "are you talking about?"

I said, "I'm talking about how the whole thing began."

"But now that it has begun," he said, "d'you ever think about how the whole thing's gonna end?"

I said, "So it's a matter of pride?"

He said, "Yes, it's a matter of pride. And it's a matter of courage. And sometimes it's a matter of dying."

Whether he died finally in peace, or in agony, dreading the loss of the last sounds of things, I couldn't say; and if I ever pray again, it will be first for the repose of his soul. There was the godforsaken panic, the terror—in that pale yellow space that contracted finally to the dark dimensions of a tomb. Yet there was also the look called peaceful, which came before the panic, and even after—though it was followed in the end by total blindness and loss of all memory and discrimination. Yet whatever half-truths each of us kept telling during our long battle over Vietnam, we could tell the whole truth in our last conversations, which reminded us of all that we really were, of all we knew—and which brought out even more than we knew. He could still see. He looked for me with the same eager eyes that showed all along that he was my father. In the contracting room, in the shadows, he could lift his hand to my face. I could receive his touch, in ways that helped us find out still more of what our real lives were by making us forget, to some extent, the limitations of what we'd been, a father and his son.

"Shame to waste time half-alive," he whispered in the growing dark. "No time for waste. When I think of you, Pete, I'll die hating most that I was a father, a half-man. Somebody who had to have it his way, when he knew there was another."

"What you chose to be for me," I said, "is what I love."

"Maybe," he whispered, smiling.

And Vietnam made him smile. He worried about me, though. Yet in certain moments, in the last days, he forgave so much and asked for so much forgiveness that it was hard to tell what he wanted me to be, or who he was. It was as strange as his ancient, bruised face on the pillow, in the gray bed light. If also beautiful, unforgettable. But I didn't smile over Vietnam, or make a single complaint about how it was that anything began. Rather I thought with breathtaking pain about the simple difference between the pitiably thin, weak hand that touched my face and the hand I had known before—massive, powerful, beautiful. Without question, I cried most when I was alone because his physical strength was gone, because that particularly, that power that had a history and a fame, even a wild infamy, and that once made him a great star at Soldier Field, was coming to an end.

"One of the great raisers of hell!"—I'd heard this kind of thing a thousand times. And, from virtually every friend or enemy from the old days—"Maybe the greatest halfback I ever saw."

The talisman, the photograph of him uniformed, holding his helmet, smiling, was of a young man guilty only, I thought now, with the two of us alone—guilty only of beauty and strength, and who as my father remained guilty only of beauty and strength—of the fact that he was who he was.

"Disappointment," I said, "I mean I've been a disappointment. Or I fear it. I know what I've done and that you can say you're proud. But I fear, stupidly or otherwise, that I've let you down. I wanted to do something for you; it's been the key thing that's moved me all my life, down deep—to present to you some hard fact that could let you breathe easy for the rest of your life. But I never made it."

No signs of panic or forgetfulness yet, in the quiet, and the low light of the bed lamp. "Three days ago," he said, "I was still defending myself from what I still cared to think of as accusations. If I saw you in trouble, I was accused. I hated to be accused. It's why I was a good father, Pete. I hated to be accused. I hated that, and I loved that you were my son. So much. That's what moved me." He stopped just slightly to catch his breath. "We don't need to be moved now. To feel that we're disappointments. That we stand accused of something. I'm a no-good father now, Pete. I don't care. I figure I was a no-good father often enough before . . . ." He stopped again. ". . . so that whatever trouble you have—because of all this crazy idea of disappointment—you'll ride it out."

But no matter how clear, in the small, dark room he was just a voice, in pain, and I couldn't bear it. I couldn't bear his asking me to forgive him for his goodness, or his forgiving me all my secret intentions, which he said he might have been wise enough all along to understand but could never as a father condone.

"I want *you,*" I said softly. "I don't want this self-forgetting tenderness. I don't want you to forget yourself." I stopped and tilted my head back, to keep my tears from falling, and to look away from my father, now so thin it was past all belief.

"You remember when I was a kid," I went on, looking away, out the window on the city in the dark, "we won 'King of the World' in the Silver Beach fun house—the game in that huge spinning bowl when you push everyone away and hold the middle? You held me with you, and you shouted into my ear? 'How does it feel,' you were roaring, 'to be the King of the World!' "

I began to cry harder and said, "I want that, I want you. I want your hardness, with your hands and your arms beating back the punk heroes tryin' to show their girlfriends and all the sailors with their goddamned tattoos. And you laughin'. I don't want to hear these soft useless good-byes. I know that I'm supposed to feel, when you tell me good-bye, even some relief, some chance. But I promise you," I said, weeping and putting my head down and holding him, "that that's not what I feel."

The sun was bending far down west behind the park, and the water and sky were all gray. The return of dead winter, of the gray ice-lake, was adumbrated in Chicago's October dusk. The city's towers were gone, and the thought came to me, tremendously, that being in one today meant risking my life.

But I said to myself—sick, scared, proud—that the businessman had made it his business to put food in my mouth, not poison. He and my mother had raised me here, in a house nearby, stately, rich in its beauty and size. They taught me to love things. They moved me gently, wisely, into the world of eye and ear, and I went out for big victories.

And that's how it is. Parents tell hopeful stories to their children, rabid with hunger—and so raise them regularly on a line. Period. They would no more tell them that there is no truth, or hope, or good progress of any kind, than nurse them on bad hallucinogens, or razors in apples. They give them a name—and they get them to love. They don't whisper at them "metastasis."

But mine at least were never stupid either. They taught me to converse: to talk, and wait; to live with words, and die in silence.

"This is what we always knew," I said last night to Allie, "just how to talk to each other. Sound off or keep quiet—when the time was right."

She said, "I'm thinking about our own kids. Colleen, the boys—this week. The walls that can go up. The old 'fail any day to tear them down and find them twice as thick the next.' "

"If I go on stupidly," I said to her, "about everything now—for God's sake—the hour of my father's death—the way he spat in the face of medicine. If I'm so *stupid* that I just spill onto pages things that at one time I couldn't whisper alone to myself for a split second and live, maybe I can still say something real about those walls. Say that it's fucking real, eternal devils who build them in the brain. Say that for me, for some hours, in a hospital room, the give and take of talk, the tearing down of the walls, was as old as forever. Try maybe to send today's philosophical world-dogma—that nothing is forever—that the walls aren't the same problem forever—to the hell in ice that it deserves."

But I've remembered now, too, how whenever I thought back then that I'd dedicate to my father the book I'd write (if I could think of writing a single word of it), I could be as terrified by his efforts to do things like talk to me as I was by his incomprehensible and savage death.

And whether I would dedicate it to my father was a question that I put crazily to myself after that first appointment, with the wind rising in the trees in the graying park, and the sun falling behind the houses across the street. Conversation—isn't this therapy a conversation with a point? I insanely asked this too—and as I did, provoked some sound not mine: an alien moan in my brain or the air. And isn't this conversation going somewhere? Isn't it going to get me there? Won't it be to the place that I've known all along? The place where all meaningful conversation begins? Two ways—I explained to myself, desperately—amidst stranger and stranger sounds, like moans, or drums. Two ways to tragedy. You can be too much of a self or too little; trust time too little or too much; drive relentlessly to make a point or let matters degenerate to pointlessness. This psychiatric therapy, this pointed conversation, is nothing other than an effort to steer the middle course, to keep me sane by avoiding tragedy of either type: either talking too much or not saying a word. And I would dedicate this story to my father as he dedicated himself to this same effort, this task of avoiding tragedy of either type. I said so then, remarkably, amidst real growing terror, as I've said it now.

But there were more memories, and there are other details of his end. There was the moment when, for the next-to-last time, Johnny Lemaster came into the room, and my father, after a few of Johnny's questions, suddenly told him to take his smartass face the hell out and not come back.

"The bastard," he said, "hasn't given me anything but a look for fifteen years—since the day he decided he'd never cooperate with anyone among the entire human race."

And in the park, recalling these words, looking up into the huge, threatening trees, with their leaves turning in waves in the wind, I knew that I'd say next time to Conlon (as I hadn't said this first time—this and other things—so there would be more to talk about—maybe things further in) that it's perfectly true that in the tremendous spinning bowl, the fun-house ride at Silver Beach Park, when my father took me under his arm out to the still center where the victorious emperor held sway against all comers, and with his laugh roared to me, 'How does it feel to be the King of the World!' that the last two that he'd thrown away to the rim were Johnny and his father.

But nothing—it was clear to me in the exact second that this unbearable picture came to me—could have been more dangerous than the thought of a neat cause, the thought of the next thing that I'd say to my doctor, the next step out that I'd take with him. The crushing sorrow of my father's end was enough to make me turn away, to make me have to turn away, from the thought that in being himself he was somehow a cause of my misery—and needed to be forgiven.

And worlds beyond the reach of any stain against him, there was the sound of utter agony in his last ravings, the unendurable, if innocent sound—when he couldn't hold down the air he breathed but vomited blood again and again. Under the low, gray-white fluorescence of his bed lamp, my mother would clean him with a warm white towel, touch away the shocking red blood from his strange, small face and mouth, and the pillow by his cheek. But out of the silence in that unforgettable room, the sound and blood would come continually, out of a pain so deep it had to break the heart of the world. And as I watched and hoped in the graying park, while the sun went down behind my old house, this sound came back to me. And I cried out loud, "Oh God Jesus that sound!" Then the sound somehow was audible in the wind and waves. And so of course now—Jesus Christ Almighty of course—there were more sounds, louder sounds, which in fact in that instant made a dedication to anyone or to anything absolutely impossible and for a long, long time brought to a total stop even a whisper of speculation on such a subject. I was silenced—but awake almost beyond belief; and the noises were now so loud inside me and outside me that I had absolutely to move away from the huge dark trees—to get as fast as I could, some hundred yards, quickly, into an open field and pray in perfect silence to become deaf enough to preserve some small fraction of my life. And I *knew* then, perfectly, absolutely, about the possible final discomposition of my world—and of all worlds.

In the end he was given enough medication so that for half a day after a night of terrifying agony he was able to know some peace. His eyes the night before could no longer find us. He cried out for us, and we came to hold him. But then for what seemed an eternity, he could only cry, "Where is the room! Where is the room!" So strange and lost, in that small, dim space, which he could no longer find, he had the panicky look of a ghost—a ghost who fears that his only question comes from nowhere and is heard nowhere.

I can talk about this now—even insist on it, this truth, since I am healthy enough and long enough away from the time. I can ask what my father learned and answer that he learned nothing. If someone were to come up to me now and say that disease in the end is the real "King of the World," I wouldn't need to take him by the throat and change him or silence him. I'm that mature. I don't need my father's arms and hands, which shrank more and more while his stomach bulged with the gross gestation of cancer's monstrosity. My mother after a while could talk about his end also, and my sister, Con, who was twelve at the time, was not abnormally affected.

He made no memorable final statement. He could see the pale walls of the room once more before his eyes last closed, and he seemed less afraid; and during the last half-day of peace, he held our hands for some time and seemed to know us. But he never opened his eyes again, and couldn't talk. And if the loosening of his grip was the sign that he no longer remembered the world, it was in the early afternoon that he forgot who we were.

By six o'clock there was a new sound in his throat. All of us, my mother, Con, Allie, and I, close by the bed in that space, knew we were on the death watch. Time, in the fading light, was bringing on separation and isolation and offering nothing other than a mad laugh at the notion of a dance of its hours. My father's shoes and razor were still there and were an irony, for ironists. But in my utter heartbreak, I murderously

despised—and I can say now too that I will despise forever—
the totalitarian and easy stupidity of irony.

Johnny came, around ten, to see how we all were doing.
It was Allie who signaled to him quietly to leave the room. In
the low fluorescence, the new sounds of the graceless death
rattle still spoke of some last struggle for life. But we all knew
that the critical hour was not far away. Johnny looked back
compassionately at my wife, after which he gave a kind look
to all of us. "If you need me, I'll be close," he said.

When he left, my mother asked us to take each other's
hands and to pray out loud with her. Our voices were too
much for that small place—unforgettable sounds also in that
tight room. But at the hour of his death, I would chant for my
father the beautiful Hail Marys of the rosary—ask the blessed
mother of God, the fruit of whose womb was Jesus, to inter-
cede for him now. In the dark moment, looking at the small,
ghost's face, unstained, moistened now, but lost, I came as
close to complete prayerfulness throughout myself as I was
always at the very core-point of my being, where there is never
any room for doubt. Then a last odd sound made us look
up—and then a new silence.

I asked Allie to bring Johnny, who was waiting still by the
door, though it was close to midnight. He came and had a
strange look. He checked my father immediately for vital
signs, and then carefully a second and a third and fourth time.

But whatever had given those signs, made them so powerfully present to the world on all those many fields of action,
had at last disappeared. Most Holy God save us all forever
and ever. Then Johnny, with what portion of sorrow who can
say, fulfilled his task of looking up to us and telling us, "He's
gone."

And some of this was unthinkable as well, absolutely
unthinkable—though down in, the huge facts of the complete
victory of metastatic disease, of the perfectly fulfilled dream
and achieved end and answered prayer of malignancy, were
bringing their pounding to the siege of the miraculous battle-
ment of my sanity's fraction of an inch. As I stood alone now
in the wide, dark field in the park, the assault was imaged in

visions of gathered monstrosity somehow familiar, ancient, which I in fact could see now in flashes, as saints see the types of hell, if for any one second I closed my eyes. The blessed world of things outside, the world there for my eyes—again I kept thinking and kept thinking—was falling into discomposition.

So, grimmest irony, the afternoon after my first hour appointment consequently, swiftly, naturally, was turning into the darkest night of my life. And now with the sun gone, I didn't think. Promises just came. I suddenly and passionately just promised the god of darkness that for the sake of my children's lives I would never absolutely assert anything, that I would always sportingly make a joke of myself, that I would never tell them any story that would set them on a quest, that I would dedicate myself to nothing so that they might dedicate themselves to nothing. And I said to the god of darkness that I knew he would love my children, when they came, as much as any god in the heavens. And as I got in my car to try to drive to my apartment south in Evanston, I promised that I'd just try to think of nothing with Johnny and Allie and Johnny's date tonight when we went out—nothing—and in the lowest possible whisper, as I turned the car key, I promised absolutely that I would not ask how long before, or even if, I was going to get better again.

3
MEETING FRIENDS

I can still dislike the type of thinking that keeps working hard on the point that our sadness is only an absurd torture. No matter how late-day or mature I may have become, I can reject the notion that what we need to learn most is to get tough—slam the door on sadness, the whining bitch. Or that the most we really can do is honestly, and not sadly, "recognize" the unstable and unexplainable conditions of our existence. When out of the reach of the postmodern critical police, I have even figured that when you hear this "honest recognition" stuff it's only from minds essentially safe, minds basically so tidily together—despite their daring, mature conception of sadness as absurd—that they'll never recognize the true terror of instability because they'll never come anywhere near it.

But maybe I don't want to start espousing causes—because something's been happening in me. Somehow it's been coming on lately with this effort to recall the past. A black magic power in my chant here, it seems, is capable of recreating trouble now in my brain, of bringing in steep mountains, just to put me on an edge again. Such is the wonderful miscreative power of perversion and darkness. Nearly ten years have passed without a trace of the fear—this is not a lie—and yet I can feel it again within the borders of my conscious life. It makes me understand that I should stop driving with the language and back off some.

But I've got to be a writer on the damned edge. I even feel crazily right because I have some of my fear back—like I must not be lying. Because of an utter detestation of sleep (though I don't mean the sweet nighttime healer), I want to tell my story not nodding one time. I want always to be balancing and believing intensely in my balances, or worrying intensely over my balances, my structures, and walking carefully to the end on a very precarious line.

But I want also to ask forgiveness for all the edginess here—and to promise that it won't last. I hate it myself, and the pain is showing this capacity to penetrate at my borders. Yet beyond what I need of structure and worry and care, I need still to come nearer to the powers I can pray to; and the great gods and the holy muses have forever resided on high mountains. And without them our sorrow remains only this absurdity to be "recognized."

"There's a parish in the city," I said to Allie, "called Our Lady of Sorrows. Can you imagine anybody today suggesting that a parish be given a name like that?"

"No." She smiled.

"And all it is—the sorrow they mean—for God's sake—is just this protest in us that nothing is small and insignificant—even, sometimes especially, the radical beauty of the deepest argument against the self. Maybe *nothing* is wrong with the modern version of this argument—which is that we should get rid of the poor self completely—except that it insists upon its own goddamned smallness."

She said, "Maybe, though, you can make small things big without going through hell."

But I have to keep saying, as I've said to Allie, again and again, that I'll get nowhere with this story without my intense hatred of the godforsaken *sleep* of contemporary bewilderment. For me it isn't just words, I literally have fallen asleep for years now when trying to pray or write a story. And story and prayer, both open-hearted, open-minded but also driving, petitioning, struggling on the edge of a belief, give, for better or worse, the most life to me. And I want this fullest life and need it—though I promise that I'm every bit as ashamed over this as I am over my invocation of an edge.

But I might kill sleep for a long time if I could remember how that first day with Conlon I made a beginning and almost immediately afterwards beat a new, significant retreat. As I pulled out of the park toward home, I could think of nothing. I had to keep my promises. If, in those first moments after my oath to darkness, I had thought for a second that there might be, say, two steps forward for every one step back, the god could well have given magic power to the counter-thought that for every one step forward there might be two steps back, or ten, or twenty. The massive dark surrounding and dominating the Baha'i Temple, the House of Prayer, which was lit now like a beautiful white face in an old, dark portrait, dared me even to whisper, to make even slightly audible to myself, something sweet—something like darkness makes light possible, or like the lighted dome was possibly something more than an atom in an absurd sea of darkness. Just try it and see, it said. Just try it and see.

But then somehow, after maybe ten minutes, having watched only the lights turn red or green as I drove home, I could think with some beginning comfort of Lemaster, who as a medical student could describe without mercy the nature of metastatic cancer. He was coming more and more clearly to mind, after I'd driven back down Sheridan to Greenwood (never thinking of Shakespeare's face in Northwestern's garden wall, the *bas* eyes watching over mid-October marigolds and the last roses; nor daring to look up at the wild stained-glass colors of the huge Christ Pantocrator at the turn at Millar). I began even to feel some particular strong safety in the thought of Lemaster. It was as if going to meet him was really the best way now to back off: a compact with lifelessness not to live too much. I could whisper now too that, even on the worst of nights, nights that would end with me keeping my distance from houses as I walked terrified down streets after midnight, the thought of an evening out with friends could encourage me to play the king of secrecy, and so to remain myself.

It was only seven o'clock when I parked on Greenwood, and Allie, who worked then with the resident children at De-Paul Settlement House, wouldn't be home normally till seven-thirty. But the front porch light in our third-floor apartment was on, and I knew that she was already home, waiting up in that glass room and looking out for me. And, no surprise, she pulled a window open as soon as she saw me and called down to me, "Peter, what's the news? Is he good?"

I said, "I think so," as I reached for the door.

But she was already on her way down the stairs, and she met me on the first landing and held me tight to her. "I couldn't wait to see you. I've been watching out for the last hour. Are you OK? Is he good?"

I said, "I think he's very good," and held her tight and rested my head on her shoulder, using it now as a vantage point for gazing on nothing.

I knew that for the night I couldn't believe in love, or the one who loved me, in the same way that I could believe in my opponent, the one who might at times even have been thinking of my murder. Lemaster was my relief now from weakness and shame—for me now the kind of comfort, say, that a person terrified of flying might feel if the pilot's name, when it was announced in the air, sounded nothing like his own.

But the truth is that I could still sense murder, too, though I could never think of it. In deep silence I knew every second how to watch out for a killer, and, unbelievable fact, that the woman holding herself tight against me—with dangerous care in her heart and with her graceful body of a dancer and beautiful auburn hair—was incomparably better for me than the one I wanted so much now to see.

"What are friends for?" Lemaster asked, when I told him that I was glad he'd given me the call. And I said thanks—this time. But at another time—the last time I saw him—I came dead at him and put it to him, jabbing my finger at him. "Did ya ever consider, Johnny," I said, "that maybe they're not always there for offering opposition, that maybe rather often in fact your friends are there to look out for ya in the dark, make ya feel like you're not alone, not so goddamned small all the time?"

But I was under the most savage interdict not to suggest any such thing now. I knew now absolutely that Johnny's consistent position that there's nothing more pitiable and foolish than fraudulent sentimentality and sadness was the one spot of safety for me that night. I knew this as I held Allie and she tried softly to fit herself to me, giving her hands and eyes and lips to the terrible, pathetic task of making love believable.

"Do you know how much I care for you?" she asked.

I kissed her hair and had again in my heart a resonance of the god's most savage drums. I said, "I know you'll be the one who watches me through. I'll count on you more than anybody I've ever counted on." But I knew that by exact order of the drum god she'd be the one I'd find most disappointing: the one I'd violently accuse of the worst shortcomings of understanding, and most want to run away from, as far as from the worst possible shame.

That's the way then that it had to be. I had for my life to retreat from the one who wanted to make me feel that I was *not* alone, or lost in the dark, and who wanted most *not* to see me die—the truest friend, by my definition. And though I'd say that it's also from hell forever, this *is* the goddamned new holiness: this having to believe absolutely in the so-called honesty of estrangement.

"It wouldn't let me look to you, A," I've said to her recently, "—this great special hell's-holy-doctrine of our time. I mean the idea that it's shameful to believe that we'll ever meet a love that could save us. Sin and goddamned death to think of or want such things."

"So incredibly unhappy," she said, with her eyes lowered, "to feel shame over that."

"I know," I said. "I know."

Yet after going to Conlon with my life in the grave, and

making my statement and daring to ask questions and beginning to emerge, and then discovering again how hope can kill too, ravaging down to dead zero, I had to condemn my absurd hope. I needed the voice that pronounced my father dead—although I could no more put it to myself this way than I could say that my father knew the resurrection and the life.

But I could think comfortingly of how Lemaster was a man of our time, and I gave Allie a signal to break from me. I said, "We gotta go, Al, if we're gonna meet Johnny on time."

"Come on, Pete, for God's sake, what's the story?" she said, as she moved a bit away from me. "I want to hear what he said. What's the word on the man? Is he at all *like* you? Do you think that he'll understand you?"

"All I can say now is that he seems very understanding, and that I'm damned glad the whole thing has begun. OK? I just can't say any more right now. I'm pretty sure that I can't say a single word more. OK? Will you forgive me?"

"I just think that you might not want to bottle this thing right off. I just think . . ."

"Don't think of it, OK? Please don't. Just wait. And maybe let's just go. I promise you I'll recount the whole thing before long. But for now, believe me, he seems good and kind, and I trust him and am absolutely certain that I'm doing the right thing. So please don't worry, all right? Don't make me say more."

"All right. But I hate your guts."

"That's fair enough," I said, as I pulled her a bit to me and kissed her forehead—in unspeakable sadness, and in submission to unsleeping terror.

Do Conlon's notes—if any exist—suggest that he understood this tearing pain in the way I did? Or would it be one story against another? I'd be curious to know. When I was better and could listen, his own good marriage of fifteen years spoke to me; and when I described myself to him as a new phenomenon, he certainly followed me and seemed to sympathize with me.

I said that in the old days a man might come to despair if he did something that was considered wrong, or more particularly, did something so wrong in his own mind that he began believing that he could never get back to righteousness. What was called conscience was supposed naturally, or actually with a consistent miraculousness, to be stirred in time if the sinner did begin his journey away from home—toward despair. Conscience was the voice that said reintegrate, get back. And I said that, believe it or not, I could feel all this myself profoundly.

But I told him that now something new was producing in me also a tremendous and powerful sense of wrongness for any slight attempt *to* get back to righteousness. A new piety and a new guilt, even a new despair, and a new conscience—an actual new inner voice which now commands us to *dis*integrate. I said that I suspected that pundits were remarking on this new piety and new guilt and despair and conscience as they had on the fact that not only are we no longer Victorian prudes, but are now hopeless sinners if we haven't fucked around enough and fucked often enough and long enough and inventively enough. In me, in fact, it had now become a terrible sin to seek Paradise; it seemed as if at the Gates of Eden there was now an angel pimping.

"I'm not just playing intellectual games," I insisted, "I'm an actual good child of the rebellion. One of the good little boys and girls who very piously think of Western religion as the fucking Whore of Babylon."

"You've felt tremendous pressure to conform," he said, "—so much that you're afraid even to let anyone hear you complain."

"Yes. Exactly—even to hear myself complain, in my own head."

But obviously I wasn't the full, true modern man, since simultaneously, with hells both up and down, I was both light and shadow—as perfectly the son of my old-time father as I was the son of the new age; the patriot who had also learned to hate his country; the Vietnam Age boy, not one of the later variety. And I can still manage to say, even now, that I do not want to be cast into the outer darkness just as badly as I do, and that I do want to sit in Paradise, at a perfect still-point with my father, as much as I want, piously, to fucking blast him there between the eyes and run.

But Johnny is the modern man, or at least the Johnny that I knew then was. He had no sinful interest in Paradise. Opposites, those supposed halves of some original whole, light and shadow, had no appeal for him. The idea of reintegration was trivial to him; and it seemed natural to him, and right and easy, to see the world as nothing but an agglomeration of small misfits.

"Behind the mask with the smile and the mask with the frown," he said to me once, "you'll just find a couple of odd-looking truths."

Yet it was Johnny who was the beautiful, champion wrestler. He had speed and power, great hand and arm strength, full coordination and an inexplicable thirst for victory that seemed perfectly both insatiable and satisfied. Unaccountably, too, it seemed that for all the great life in him he took no interest in the story of himself, ever, and that in fact he had no interior. It seemed that Johnny, like a perfect proof of meaningless energy, really just *was,* and that his complete thirst was perfectly simple, animal.

A profound, dangerous curiosity regarding the source of Johnny's never-sleeping power and full grace has always been a motive of mine. I wanted to get a right reading of him then, and I still do. I can say now too that if my new piety and guilt and dread of despair made me seek him that night, indeed made me feel that the only thing that I was allowed to consider then was that he was now the right patrol guard for my miserable borderline of an inch, my last interior, I wanted at times to murder my friend, the man from absolute nowhere, as much as he wanted at times to murder me.

But even now accusing him of such an intent (and so far away from his face, so many years away) gives me only a very wavering, uncertain satisfaction. He could easily have been innocent—more innocent than anyone I've ever known; and my story of myself could be as wrong as I sometimes feel it's wrong even to attempt to tell a story of him.

I think now too, as I could and did that night in remarkably sweet if also necessarily hushed reveries (which I hope may make my deep love for him more understandable) of our younger boyhood, when we had days on end of adventures that I'll remember tenderly for the rest of my life. And whoever the gods are who allow the sweet manic before the terror of depression—the aura before the seizure—they did allow me also a little time of forgetfulness in an evening out with friends, and let me dream as I drove down Sheridan Road and the Inner Drive (my eyes, however, almost never looking up at any of the buildings rising over the shining streets).

And if I might have known from the aura what would come later, the dream, as I say, was incredibly sweet. It was of an early morning one summer, when we were ten, and Johnny'd come running up into my room, all excited, shaking me. "Petie, Petie! Ya gotta get dressed quick and come on. I saw this place yesterday. I gotta take ya. Ya won't believe it. It's this secret place up at this private beach. It's all secret, and there's this lagoon and birds. Ya gotta see it. Nobody's ever seen it. Come on. Come on!"

There was just time to put apples in our pockets as we ran out through the kitchen and jumped on our bikes. Johnny could pull up the front wheel of his bike and ride along balancing on the back wheel. It wasn't easy then, the way it is now with the lightweight bikes that are made for it. Nobody I knew could do it except Johnny.

I remembered us heading up Sheridan Road toward the mansions, up the huge green cathedral vault of elms with the breeze at our backs, pedaling furiously and gliding, gliding, and pedaling like madmen. And Johnny saying, "Petie, it's so neat. The birds and this river and this lake."

But it wasn't easy. We had to ditch our bikes near one of the park beaches, make sure that they were safely hidden, and then make our way for a long time along the shore where there were the fortress barriers of boulders and iron walls and barbed-wire fences that the rich people put up so no one could walk along the sand there and break into their privacy. It was like entering France over German barricades.

I said, "How'd you ever find this place!"

He said, "I don't know. I was just goin'!"

That was Johnny too, every day. But he said, even though no one alive could take a fence the way he could, "I hate the fuckers who build these things," when he was straining high on one of the rusty iron walls. It was unusual for him, very unusual to say that anything bothered him. So I remembered it.

When we had climbed the last fence and came wading under a dark pier between some monstrous green-bearded pilings, with their smell, there was a wide, beautiful beach, cut in the middle by a thin stream that ran down from a broadening, dark pond which was bordered with huge pines that ran up both walls of a steep, high ravine.

"This is the outer part of it," he said, when we came up from the beach. "Be quiet. Follow me."

There was a path along one edge of the pond, and we took it till it ended; then we waded in till the cold clean water (the dark color of the pines, till we held it in our hands and it was colorless) came up to our necks. We dog-paddled for quiet to the other side, where a small dock led back to a path that cut that side of the ravine, running among more huge trunks.

We were scared now that someone might have heard us or seen us, so we stayed behind a tree and didn't move till Johnny finally lifted his hand and pointed up the path. He whispered, "Wait till you see."

But it was beautiful already, with ferns and rich-colored rocks and green golden light which came down from way high in visible shafts, a sign, I used to think, that God was there. Before us mossy bridges, fancifully built of dark planks, receded in a series, and in the dusty light showed how the path crossed and recrossed the ravine stream.

Johnny signaled. We went on, crossing three bridges, then a fourth, which led to a wider, salmon-colored cinder path, with rails and steps, which rose to flat ground before a high wire fence, crowned with dark ivy. Johnny said, "It's right here. But be careful. I think the fence could electrocute you. I got a shock when I tried to climb it. But maybe there was someone watching me, and maybe he's not here today."

The fence did have a strange black wire in the ivy, maybe for a current—but beyond it was the most beautiful pond I'd ever seen, with deep green lawns around it and yellow and purple and blue flowers in terraced beds and a gray columned and hemidomed gazebo with words in Latin—I knew from the Mass and altar boys—*coelum* I knew, when Johnny pointed.

Then he pointed to the water. Coming in pairs, out from a high cover of cattails where they'd hidden, were four white swans. I'd never seen these birds in real life. I didn't know if they were real or just birds in storybooks. But they were here and as beautiful as I ever could have imagined. Slow and graceful, floating—like our hearts in some wonderful sorrow.

Johnny whispered, "Wait. They'll come around close to us. Then watch 'em. Watch their faces and their eyes."

Carefully he touched the fence to see if it was safe, and there was no current—so we put our hands in the chain links and our eyes up to the holes and watched the swans come. For me they were signs of the grace that descends in tremendous high cathedrals, in shafts of light, mysterious as places I entered when I heard the girls' voices singing on First Fridays.

They came as close to us as they would. Johnny said very softly, "Look at their eyes. They don't care about anything— not anything. If you don't scare 'em."

I looked at him. He was staring at the swans. He knew so much more than I did about everything. I was so proud of him. I was proud that I knew him. I felt that if I stayed with him I'd always be OK. But then it happened. The current came on and ran through our hands and touched our faces. It stung sharply and deadened. It made everything terrible. We jumped away and turned to run. Someone was coming up the path behind us. It was a man—on our side of the last bridge— twenty feet from us. He wore a dark shadowy hat, and there was nothing for us to do but listen to his voice when his face came up from under his hat. He was dark-looking and ugly, and his body seemed to have huge bones, that were wrong. He said, "What d'you think you're doing?" We didn't answer. He said it with anger: "What do'you think you're doing!"

Johnny took me tight by the arm and started to move us

to the side of the path. The man came within a few feet and stared right at us. And Johnny, while he had me going, right back in the man's face, said, "Fuck off, Mister," pushed me, and ran with me around him.

We both took off down the cinders and over the first bridge as fast as we could go. We heard him behind us, but not so close that we'd have to be afraid. He wasn't running; maybe he was old. He shouted, "What's your name, smartguy!"

Johnny stopped for a second, turned and shouted, "It's Nobody, smartguy!"

Then we ran with our heads down, through a place that was dead for us, till we came back to the outer pond, which we took with a loud dive and a fast swim, then out our path and over and under things that in our hurry cut us now and hurt, till we were far enough away so that we could slow down and breathe, and head toward home.

In the car, I smiled thinking of this, and could even have let tears come; it was safe enough then, along the lines that I was taking. I wasn't driving, rather just gliding in the city night, saying nothing to Allie—not only not looking at any object but not trying to celebrate anything that Johnny ever did, just letting the memory come, and thinking that I'd be safe with him. Yet now, after everything, I cannot help thinking right this second of seeing him again. And saying to him, "See, you *were* a hero! You *do* bring into the world things greater than anything an uninspired life could ever comprehend."

But still then I went easily down to the Northside bar, really watching just the lights turn red and green as I passed on (though for a second I caught a glimpse of the gigantic pair of angels at the entry to Mundelein, pointing up and holding the cross-crowned world and the stars and the book, and the gray building on their shoulders). And if my sweet boyhood dream was allowed to run its course, it disappeared as we pulled into the Northside's parking lot, though I *could* recall, even now, I swear, a smell from the aura. But then with the slamming of the car door and the cool touch of the October night air, I came back fully to this evening out with friends;

and when we entered the warm dark of the bar, with just the sconces and the low lights over pictures of old sports heroes, there was the safe noise of the crowd and dull music that stimulated no desire.

Allie and I sat by a side window, under a clock. I began looking out, which could have been an extremely dangerous attitude, but the furies remained satisfied, because I was searching for signs contrary to hope. So the room then was standing still, and the night would stand still.

Allie—her first words—asked me, "Who's with him tonight?"

"Somebody different, I suppose," I said.

"And so what else is different?" she said.

I smiled, still looking out. Johnny's car pulled in, and I looked up at the clock. "Remarkable," I said. "Right on time."

"Johnny, as it were, on the spot," Allie said.

And then there he was, walking in with the new, beautiful date. The young intern from nowhere, brightly alive, with bright eyes and color in his dark cheeks, an open leather jacket—and all his muscular force called up as usual, noticeable like weapon flashes in his movements, quick and alive—and the beautiful woman, the new somebody different, moving very agreeably with him, just because that's what can happen.

I wasn't disappointed. I felt immediately relieved. I was taking comfort too from seeing Lemaster's date—brown-haired, pale, beautiful-bodied. And I'll step aside a moment and say that this became and remains a significant comfort. A sort of dark plus, or positive negation, like an addiction which helps to distance some painful reality.

Who was she? Barbara Dern, as it turned out, wasn't just another of Lemaster's beautiful dates. He'd been with her for several weeks then and lived with her after that for nearly a year, till he went to California. And she has a place in my history, as I'll show. Also she's just lately, or her image has just lately, been involved in the actual making of this history—as I have been in need again of a certain kind of comfort.

I could say that to Allie's "Glad you're home, Pete,"

Barbara, with her shadowed eyes, black skirt and sweater, and long, polished nails, suggested a kind of "Come on in, Peter, to the place where no one remembers who he is." Or I read this (whatever that says about me) in the light of her pale skin and soft lips, against what I saw in her light brown hair. I would like the despair in her laughter too. And what happens is, at some points now, when these words stop and I sink with the thought that I don't know where in hell I'm going, my mind will drift aside to her beauty—for the sweet difference—and to get the long, warm kiss and be held and comforted in the bed where, good old joke, we never sleep. So she's often there in the gaps as I write and think now. She's there too as a retreat if I feel the need to back off: a soft-eyed sweet dark mystery, one I can fall together with and with whom I can roll like pornography easily to agreeable and hopeless, if never sad, conclusions.

Johnny introduced us, and Allie smiled. I shook Barbara's hand and said, "Nice to meet ya, Barbara. But, ya know, this guy's absolutely no good."

"Ahhh," she said, leaning against him in the mellow light, "I might have to fall in love, then, after all."

"Please don't say it," Johnny said. "Please for sweet pity's sake."

Allie said deadpan, "OK, I won't say it"—which got a good hard laugh out of Johnny and gave me a cue to play host, which I felt that I could do. So I took everybody's orders, and went to buy a round, figuring for a second that I might have enough friends here in the dark even to get me through till I slept.

For the next few hours I didn't remember what day it was, or the jeopardy I'd placed myself in, going with terrible hope to see a doctor. We all were just drinking and making no sense together, and if I noticed that Johnny drank more than the rest of us, I didn't care. Barbara was taking us to strange new places with frank talk about family that she'd left behind and drugs that she'd used, and it was fine for me to be completely erotically charmed.

"At school there was this doctor." She laughed. "He

made me set up this kind of endless series of appointments so he could come on to me. But if I told him every week I was sick, he'd give me the nicest medicine. And he never charged me."

She told me that she'd done ether once or twice with him, but that that was the end because she "didn't wanna die in some odd color, or any shit like that," which made me laugh.

She talked to Allie too. "There was this guy," she said, "who I dated before Lemaster. He tried to 'bring me home' to God . . ."

Allie said, "Can we call turning to Johnny a strong reaction?"

They both laughed. And so for hours it went on. But then of course at some point I got suddenly too relaxed. Punishments for such changes, too, came palpably like a presence.

I heard Johnny say to Allie, "Nothing. Nothing ever ends." I thought that he knew something, if he was getting louder and now—I could tell—was maybe a bit too far gone. But when Barbara stepped out for a moment, I began like a complete fool to picture closely, of all things, the words cut in stone around the Baha'i Temple dome: about the heart as the home of God, and the stronghold of love and justice, and the oneness of the country earth. As if I could tempt the gods who would never, after my having made and kept an appointment with a doctor, have allowed me to pray a single word out loud! I saw between the giant rising temple buttress prongs, among the endless vegetable filigree and crosses and stars—insignias of all the world's religions—the cut words I knew so well from many hours up on the high steps, where in the breeze, looking down at the harbor and the blue, open lake, I *was* moved sometimes to audible prayer! And I knew immediately how I would pay for thinking even a moment of the sweet religious opiate, which carries with it a punishment sufficient unto itself, deadly as the drug's—a penalty just for hope!

And how in hell could I be thinking of something so hopeful as those cut words? The dark bar was crowded with late-nighters. The atmosphere, the dull music, was so good now for not thinking, but I couldn't help ruining my peace with comforting thoughts. I kept hoping, thinking that the end of my therapy would be to come to some place of quiet and prayer but where I'd definitely *remember* the terrible presence of the gods. I'd remember it because the gods would recently have come to me in my sickness. But I'd feel in this different, safer place, that they had now lovingly let me out of their shadow. So it would be some place for vivid recollection, but intensely peaceful—neither too close to nor too stupidly far away from the terrifying end of my small life.

But then the unbelievable rush of shame and self-disgust that came with such thinking! I got up and went to get a tray again at the bar. As I stood there, Johnny came up behind me—a perfectly timed insult to my absurd and sickening dream of the oneness of the earth. He grasped me by the arm and turned me to him. And I felt (fully contrary to everything that I'd believed for hours) that he was exactly what I did *not* need! So more intense panic—that there was no help in this man from nowhere—a panic which brought with it the rush of the wings of furies who for the moment would dance around every word we said. He ordered a vodka. He said, "So Conlon advised, 'Just stay outa mirrors. Just avoid the glass. Best thing for the self-image.' "

I smiled, God knows how or why. "I think he's the right one for me, John. He seems to understand me." But it must have been that at this suddenly confused moment, in an ultimate perversity, I was rushing to die. I couldn't believe, even as I did it, how far I stuck out my neck—how I set myself up for Lemaster even as I felt that I needed to run as far as I could from him.

He wasted no time. He looked at me steadily, oddly. "Fine. Just so long as he doesn't take an understanding attitude toward what's killin' ya."

Quickly then, to stay alive, I erased almost all of myself; and to keep Conlon safe, for me, I dissociated him from myself as fast and as far as I could. I said, "I didn't, and absolutely couldn't, say that he was sympathetic. But don't forget," I added, trying to coax some sympathy from Johnny, although

I knew I would not get it, "that you're the one who said he knew right where I was comin' from."

"Yes I did," Johnny said, "but I figured you'd know I meant he had a good eye for someone's comin' from the wrong place."

"Which I did figure," I said, "or I couldn't have gone near him."

"Did ya talk about your father much?"

"Not yet—just a little bit."

"Yeah," he said. "And did ya lie to him much?"

"Not that I can think of," I said—and pushed myself back to oblivion rather than say to Lemaster: *Don't push me.*

"I wish," he said, "that I knew that meant No."

"I told him honestly what I expected," I said. "I sort of exposed my hopes." And there I was again, placing myself in more danger than I needed to—so much danger, in fact, that even the gods should have said, "Enough! Stop!"

But Johnny kept things going. "Did he tell ya to keep on hoping for the same bullshit? Don't misunderstand me, Peter. I'm asking as a true friend—which I know you know."

Yes. I knew. But again there was something in me that almost declared, suicidally, "Ya mean bullshit like the hope that I'll get better sometime? like hoping and waiting for the better time to come so I can keep on living?" But I fled to agreeability, and gave a different, and equally true indication of my feelings. "I'll tell ya," I swore, "that if he had told me to keep on hoping for the same old things I couldn't have stayed. That's absolute."

Johnny said, "Good again."

But then as we started back to the table, and as I was making myself as agreeable as it took to avoid the suicidal act of defending myself, a pathetic question came to me, and with it the feeling that in the shadows of the ceiling, the end of my life was coming with the dark birth of a collapse. I asked, "Do you go to his house?"

He said, "I've been," and looked at me curiously, and loosely, no doubt more than half drunk now. I could see it.

But I went on. I couldn't help it. "Where does he live?"

Smiling for me now like the Nobody who is Legion, he answered, "Ask me again and I'll tell ya the truth."

I asked, "So where?"—knowing now that the night was lost and that I'd pay for everything I'd said and done.

He smiled and shot down his vodka. He made an absurd face, and I laughed, even with the departure now of all the sweet angels who abort the birth of hell in the dark corners of a room.

He said, "He lives, Petie, in a crooked house on a crooked street. And in secret he finds No Fucking Purpose in what he does. He finds No Fucking Use. In secret he hates all use and fucking purpose. He dances naked and masturbates and picks his nose all day and makes funny faces and fucking nonsense sounds. He says, 'My house embodies No Fucking Ideas! I hate the useful arrangement of things in some supposedly useful order! Nothing causes anything here! No goals. No logic. No word order. No fucking words. No fucking stages of time. No story. No beginning. No fucking end. This is the fucking Mars Hotel. This is a pussy.' "

And I was laughing, shaking my head, no matter what I felt, as he left to go to the john, and maybe to stop at the bar to pick up another Russian brainwash. But I couldn't look. Yet I ran crazily over my theories (murderous, jealous things which keep me dangerously awake) regarding this person who indefatigably whispered no prayer in his soul to anything ever. I considered my suspicion that he wanted to be my father's son (his own father was a drunk who, until he died and left him alone, beat Johnny regularly to hell), which I took from the way he hung around our house all those early years, and from the way he wanted to wear my father's football jersey, which I wore, and would not let him wear.

For a second, the "repressed," the wonderful secret intentions and unrealized potencies of darkness, moved and groaned in the corners and the far extensions of the spans of the room, and I almost cried for him. Then for my life I had to look at objects—the sconces, the framed athletes and playing fields, the pennants—then to look away, to look, and to look away again. Jesus—I almost cried! So damned foolish!

But I was saved by thinking how he'd never cry, never on this earth cry for himself. And the theory that he hated me, because he loved Allie, who loved me—I left it gladly in the same nowhere with my tears that didn't fall. And this kept the bloody red teeth and tongue of the devil above the pressed tin of the ceiling, even if I did see that Johnny—he'd been gone now some time—was bringing back with him a small glass of clear liquid. I suffered too for thinking that this was his nectar and for thinking that confession to the postmodern priest was still confession to someone who had a hell to send you to.

I'd talk about sports, I decided. But I had no chance. I used the wrong words.

"I wish to God . . ." I said.

He said, "What?"—staring right at me.

"I wish . . ."

"What?"

"I . . ."

"What?"

I said, laughing, "Fuck you. I wish to God I could see myself play a sport pure and simple."

"What?"

And I was laughing, even absurdly happy, because he was still looking right into my face strangely. I said, "I hate your guts, Lemaster, I truly do."

He said, "Fine—just so long as you don't start thinking that's what I was born for."

By now the women were listening, and Johnny sat back, sipping his vodka.

Barbara said, "You boys having fun?"

Johnny said, "Yeah. And did you know Peter was a Jew?"

"I've noticed contraindications," Allie said.

"Not every Jew is intelligent."

"I'd like to give him an examination," Barbara joked, and touched me warmly on the arm.

"No need for microscopes. You see," he said, "it's very simple. He's a devout worshiper of Big Mo. An event comes and our boy here feels the presence of Mo, and believes the outcome of the event will be a sign of Mo's favor—or disfavor. Mo the Schmo has abandoned him, for all his prayers, and let the other side carry the day—shall I say—a number of times. But our boy knows about something inside him, a leetle homunculus, and he believes that Big Mo will never let that die. The world is full of meaning for our boy here. And should our boy ever come to see that it is full of shit instead, he is sure that he would be deprived of all his vitality. So I say, especially because he really only wishes he could believe all of the above, that our boy is incontrovertibly a Sheeny."

Allie just smiled at me, shook her head and said, "Shalom."

And Barbara said, "I think at midnight he becomes a Cherman doktor."

"Just a friend of nature," Johnny said.

"Just a fiend and pervert," I said, and laughed, but looked out the window to see how much open space there was for me in the dark night. That's how simple and terrible this was, even if I was out with friends. Any move was wrong now. Any anger. Any flight. I couldn't even laugh too much.

Johnny said, "Nature calls her friend, or fiend"—rose, and left the table, smiling, giving me a friendly slap. Allie left with him. To say what?

She'd once said to him, when we were in college and things came up: "You know as well as I do that the name for what you do to people is hurt."

And he'd said, "Too simple. Too simple, and you know it."

But I couldn't think. I could barely remain now under this low ceiling, the tin buckling after too many years, with all the life and pressure. I knew that I'd have to go soon.

And yet—so strange are the powers that be!—there was a free moment now, with Barbara. Of course she was right there for me, as I needed her! I could write it now in a stream—a seamless dream. She touched my arm again with her warm hand and said, "Isn't he unbelievable? It's not funny."

But with her I didn't have to look up, or out, or away. My eyes could take comfort in her shadowed eyes.

She asked me very sweetly, looking closely at my face, "What are you thinking?"

I told her, "It's strange as all hell on earth he's becoming a doctor. I want just to ask him why he's becoming a doctor. But I'm sure it's not my business to interfere with his life."

I stopped, but I was opening up so easily with this girl who was smiling at me—that I even told her, "There's something in me that's afraid of these kinds of questions."

She said softly, "So he'd have us feel—but to hell with him. What's getting you to become a teacher? Tell me."

And of course I could talk perfectly with her—converse with gentleness and patience. I said, "I think that when I began grad school, two years ago, I was sure maybe of a number of things—most of all the simplest: that I could interpret pretty well the words I read and could maybe give the meanings to people who didn't know what was goin' on."

She was smiling warmly. "And now?"

"And now," I said, "I'm gettin' pretty badly lost myself."

She said in her softest voice, "I think I'd love to take a course you taught."

I said, "You'd be very welcome."

But then Johnny was there, and he bent in front of me and gave Barbara a kiss on the mouth. And I knew that before I left—in order to find out if he had any right to be, or whether he was really what he appeared to be—I'd ask him why in hell he'd decided to become a doctor.

Allie came back and didn't sit but took her coat from the chair, with a pleading look; and if I had a sudden fear of how much remained of the night, of how many hours there were before dawn, I knew that it was time to leave. Everyone knew. So we all without saying anything were just standing and taking our coats. "Oh yeah," someone said, "work tomorrow." "Don't say it." "Kill joy." Then the girls were gone on ahead, and Johnny and I were putting tips in the bartender's glass.

But when we were walking out, even while we were still

in the shadowy, low, and threatening bar, where the lights only lit the dark wood and left junctures in shade, I certainly as hell did go where I had no business. I said, almost as if a number of things were proven, "Honest to God, John, why doctor?"

He stopped and turned. "What?"

"Why really are you becoming a doctor? What for?"

He smiled at me, gave me another friendly tap, and said, "Because I like to study the differences between what people hope for and what they get."

I laughed, shook my head, and knew, as I stepped out the door into free space, that if the time really demanded it I could kill him.

But now the evening was over. I caught Allie and hurried us. I could hear Barbara, just a voice, saying, "Hope we do this again soon." Then nothing more.

But when I had taken the key out of the car door and was holding the door for Allie, with the world getting ready to come down, I felt Johnny's grip on me again—the leather of his jacket against me—and then felt myself being turned a bit as he put his other arm around Allie and kissed her.

"Didn't get much of a chance to say good-bye," he said. "Hope I see ya again soon."

Allie said quietly, "Hope so."

She got in the car, and Johnny closed the door for her, looking in to smile a good-bye. Then I could feel his grip on my arm again, tighter, and myself being turned, harder. He started to say, "As a friend . . ."

I jerked my arm free. "Ya know, you got a habit of grabbin' people."

He said, "Ooooh," and laughed again. "Ooooh. Ooooh."

And I said, "Don't tempt me."

He walked away laughing. "Ya better hope I don't, old friend. You wouldn't have a prayer in the world."

4
MAKING LOVE

As he headed away I almost took a step after him. I started to shout something, but in the dark I was ashamed and afraid. Then also, rocking, unbalanced, I was ashamed because I was afraid, and regretted not telling him everything I thought. But I couldn't. I just opened the car door on my side and got in, burning, but also thinking about how I had vowed I would not think. Allie (and I loved her) had something to say—though I knew that it would be better for me if she had nothing at all to say—if she would just keep quiet.

"If he's not the worst thing for you at this point," she began, angry, and with a sad, worried look, "then I'd like to know what is. What was all that about anyway? Was he eggin' you on or somethin'? He knows exactly what you've been going through and where you were today, but he thinks he can play his funny games. Nobody has the right to do that. Nobody. And I don't give a damn if his tongue got loose because of the booze; for him it's a truth serum."

"I actually think sometimes that he's tryin' to kill me."

"Peter, does agreement help? I know I'm your wife and I

love you and I'm worried all damned night and day about you—so I'm naturally the least reliable witness in the world—but does some agreement help?"

I said, "It helps," and, as afraid as I was, I still thought for some seconds that, with such a comrade-in-arms, I might begin a revolution for my right to exist. I started the car and headed for home—feeling for some odd moments actually relaxed. Then over the radio there came a couple of relaxing love songs, and Allie came close to me, took my hand and fitted herself in under my arm, letting her red-brown hair fall across her face.

Then she looked up into the dark in front of her. "Peter, can you tell me now about how it went with Conlon?"

I said to her, "Yeah, I believe I can." But, God Almighty, as soon as I said this, I wanted to get her out from under my arm, get us apart and put an end to any hope. I wanted this even though I loved her and every second kept in mind, somewhere, our own promises to each other—which were very different from my hopeless vows to the god of darkness. But unbelievably, Christ, the road at night back then would sometimes suddenly lift for me right off the surface of the earth and lead up to a kind of nightmare precipice with nothing after it even to fall to—far higher than any safety—something out of a childhood terror dream. And rapidly now the Drive was beginning to lift like this. It was so God Almighty unreal! But I still held Allie against me, though actually forgetting in panic what I'd just said.

But as I was about to pull the car off the Belmont exit, to get out, walk the parks or streets, her voice came out of the silence, asking, "Is he anything like Lemaster?"

I hadn't thought. I said, "Now that you mention it—no. Now that you mention it, I'd have to say no. Jesus. Johnny knows him well, too. They're friends. He talks to him. He goes to his house."

And as I spoke, the Drive came back down. The spectacular illuminated Thunderbird at Addison stayed perched atop the huge Alaskan totem against the black trees—like an answer to a prayer. And the revolution, the fight for freedom

from Johnny and from the sacred obligation to put an end to
my life, rolled on for a few more minutes, while I recovered a
bit of my dangerous first-day enthusiasm.

After fourteen years of marriage, Allie, in the next room
now, still moves with me in the spirit of vows we haven't
forgotten—if, in the inquisitorial Age of Division, I could
never be forgiven the pathetic oddity of this kind of antique
way of talking about what we've got.

We've discovered somehow in ourselves through time
(never too friendly but no determined foe of our vows, either)
that the secret is patience. On our part a desire, a vow, a
perduring refusal to accept collapse, and on time's, it seems, a
demand that we actually do learn to accept unending changes
and to wait till we are given what we want.

Allie knows now too that I'm getting scared sometimes as
I seek what for me is real poetry. She knows it—and all the
other grim goddamned ironies. And she disagrees in part with
what I'm doing. She believes the simple imagination makes
extremes of experience unnecessary. "You just can't live without this faith, Peter," she's said to me. She doesn't, though,
want me not to rediscover what's beyond me or not to pray
again or not to write. She listens when I tell her about the
difference between where I am and where I want to be—listens
to me and gets me to listen when she says I can write a book
and not necessarily hurt myself. "We *can* know what to believe
in before it's too late. That's called *life.*"

Perhaps with her as a helpmeet, her husband (the late-
twentieth-century Chicago boy, who didn't go to war, and in
the Prairie State sure as hell never found mountains or deserts)
might in fact come unharmed to some spot safely out past his
worst moments. Or to some point out far enough so that
without terrible danger he could say a word about such moments—but where his helplessness would still be a living
memory.

What I remembered, some months after I'd begun with
Conlon, when I was in such a place, was how waiting in silent
faith, just barely praying, can become an absolute necessity.
How the absolute demand for silence is a perfect indication

that to be yourself you cannot *be yourself*—that the gods would tear you apart for the sin—the noise. But for me in this place the memory of falling walls was so alive that I had an answer for anyone who'd tear walls down. It was still a place where, if I couldn't be myself, I *had* to be myself. And I'm calling it again the place where I discovered the beauty of poetry, the tension of the still center and the whirling rim, great as everything—and where I read poetry, if necessarily sometimes in agony, the poor wrestler's misery.

Allie, God knows, isn't naive about heartbreaking stupidity and the feeling of triviality. She's had some terribly difficult years of becoming what no woman born before 1950 expected she'd have to become, that is, the new woman. She almost lost herself in the ordeal once, if the truth is going to be told, trying to do more things at one time than was even close to possible.

But not everything for the two of us has been trivialized finally by modern awareness—by postmodern mature "recognition." There is again our odd antique attitude toward marriage and vows, and I can add the odd antique attitude that we share toward raising children—toward the family (sickening word). We look at our kids (and we see ourselves in them as, married, we see ourselves in each other—so it's all dangerously selfish—but we don't give a damn) and we say, with the most complete, wise and, for a second, edgy, panicky sincerity there can be, that if anything ever happened to them we don't know what in hell we'd do. We say this while we know we can't push or hold them either; and all of this together keeps us passionately involved in time—an entity purely mythical, in fact, only for those who never even once ate manna or never very much had to have the truth. So Allie knows that even the good things—simple, hopeful—can be as frightening to say as the bad things. But for us both, no matter what happens, there is also always patience.

"Marriage is definitely hell," we agreed one afternoon, swinging on the porch, and we laughed on and off for a solid week—till for a moment marriage was sort of heaven. So in these things it goes. And if we truly believe in the old forms that we've chosen for ourselves, we do by marriage just mean constancy—profound constancy so that, God help us all, there will be depth and not triviality (this word I've learned from Wordsworth, for whom it was the most perfect signal for nightmare). And if she's forever more sane, Allie could smile with me when I said that the retardation of pace, the slowing of the rate of change necessary for constancy only can come with *fear* and *need,* and that fear and need are at the heart of the language of being and sorrow, in which words connect with things, and in which thingness, being, and sorrow are the mountains where the muses sing.

"You'll make me say then, Peter," she said yesterday, "that what's missing in a world that's not afraid is the poetry."

I smiled. "I won't make you say it."

And in regard to constancy, and raising children, I have kept *hoping,* dangerous as it might be. There's no complete hiding of it. Also I'll say, or maybe I'd better just whisper, that I've only half-kept my dark vow not to tell stories to my children. I told them once that the grandfather they never saw ran eighty yards at Soldier Field for the National Championship and that he flew thirty-five missions over Germany as a bomber captain and that when they told him that he could go home he didn't, but in the most dangerous skies in the history of warfare he flew to the end as a fighter pilot in a plane called the P-51 Mustang. I showed them pictures. Something in me was saying fill their hearts with it. Make them proud of where they come from. But I was scared, or remembered what it was to be scared; so as fast as I could I made nothing of it and easily wore out their short patience by never answering the first question.

When, after our evening at the Northside, we got back home to Greenwood, the light had gone out in the stairwell; and arm in arm in the dark we were clumsy going up the stairs. But I was able to say a few things, even small-talk a bit about Conlon.

Allie said, "So he's different?"

"Yeah. I think he's gonna try to keep me who I am—believe it or not."

"So he hasn't suggested divorce yet?"

I said, "Give him time. Give him time."

And the small talk was enough almost to keep the walls where they were and the vertical dimensions of the stairwell what they were. But the feeling I had suddenly, as we passed the spot where we'd met when I came home after the appointment with Conlon, now all dark, was that I had no more business entertaining questions at this point than I had then. I was immediately warned in fact that if I allowed any more time for this—for questions about Conlon, about procedure— I'd come to see how I had even less business, perhaps far less business, permitting such a beginning now than I had then. The walls and ceilings of the stairwell began to say, in fact, that I might pay for every vanity I'd ever entertained in my life. I asked Allie, as we came to the second landing, if she could wait for the rest of it. I whispered to her, "Maybe still, A, I'm afraid to hurt it with my mouth."

But in utter perversity, a question came up in my mind; and it was, in so many words, whether marriage, or one like mine, was possibly a legitimate, true poetic metaphor for a good human life or history. Though as I felt for the keyhole in the dark, and turned the key in the door, and switched on the so-called kindly light of home, I hurled this question to the farthest distance that I could—which gave me a little more time under a stable roof.

In our bedroom, in the low light of our bed lamp, there was a gardenia—which had borne two beautiful, richly perfumed flowers; and an alarm clock with digital numeration and a light of its own—a good thing for me on a number of occasions, both before this and in the dark nights that came after.

The bed was an old four-poster we'd picked up in a secondhand store. We'd liked the rich, dark but not heavy wood and the subtle warmth of the enclosing, classically cut posts and boards. And this second I can see Allie kneeling beside this bed as she did occasionally then to say night prayers. True. Her father, a very beautiful and kind man, had told us that every night before he went to bed he prayed the Memorare and that it kept him and Allie's mother confident through all their difficulties for over twenty-five years. He'd whispered this in our ears as a last suggestion of advice, in 1970, in complete sincerity, as he gave Allie away to me at the altar.

I've thought that a night prayer, a gentle petition on the borderline of sleep, could I pray one the way he did, would bring far better ends to my post-ritualized days than their own straight passages over the line. And that whispering an amen before shutting the eyes may be one of the best ways to kill trivialization—though I'm always ashamed now that I'd want to kill trivialization in the first place. And if that night after the Northside I'd said out loud a word of the Memorare, a prayer that we be remembered and protected—I might have had to take flight to the never-disappointing aid of complete suicidal forgetfulness.

The wind was rising and beginning to make a small noise in the bay window behind the bed: an unquestionable omen. Something was approaching now, no matter how cautious I might have been about keeping all my supplications silent. I lay down and looked into the high shadows over the light of the low bed lamp; and I knew, as Allie took a beautiful sheer nightgown from the closet hook, that I was going to be punished again, and soon, and possibly more savagely than ever, for coming from where I had come from and intending to go where I believed I should go—and of course right now for going to visit the doctor and for making the statement and asking the questions and, for an hour or so, considering the doctor's presence a sign of hope.

I'd almost fought with Johnny too, and I couldn't keep my mouth shut. Jesus God—I wished there were some drugs left for me. The alcohol I'd had was only making worse my miserable vertigo and my sick worry over the wind's pressing harder against the weight of the building's walls.

And if only just arriving, everything in me that I wanted to repress—the real diseased fear for the world—was here once again—all of it, in the wind, in the rattle of the air in the window. Also, though I kept running and running from the thought that my last card had now finally been played, I did think it nonetheless. And I'll just say here that I'm thankful, no matter what I say I want, that I still can't really describe this kind of moment—or that I can repress the memory. In fact I have enough of my fear and misery back to know that I'd take no moral criticism from anyone who didn't know first of all the great worth of repression, for I remember that I had immediately to use the most brutal secret police on the thought that I had in fact played that last card.

Allie, very gently, but almost as if she were trying to make me feel the full meaning of sadness, put her hand on my arm and called my name, choosing this moment, exactly wrong, to break the silence.

She lay down next to me—in the dim blue light of the clock face—with her hand still gently on my arm. "I know," she said, "that you don't want me to say anything more—but I'm gonna risk it." She began to speak more warmly. "Peter . . . I love you so much . . . and I know you." She turned on her side to look more closely at me. "I know you, Peter. I know you're really afraid now to hear what I'm saying. I understand. But I'm telling you Lemaster was lucky I wasn't armed tonight, because you don't need his shit either." She touched my face now, tenderly. "That guy isn't at all what you think he is. Please don't feel bad, OK, but he's not the great free spirit you make him out to be, not even close. I don't want you to worry about him, all right? Whatever he is, it's not your fault. And you're on the right track with Conlon. But we won't talk about that."

She gently touched her forehead to mine, lowered her eyelids and whispered. "You're gonna see that Conlon knows what he's doing, Pete, and you're gonna get better. You'll see. And I'll be here with you all the time." Then passionately she placed her hands behind my neck and held me. "This scared-to-death stuff," she said with her voice breaking, "is gonna stop sometime. You'll be yourself again. It'll take time. But that doesn't mean it won't happen. It means it will."

When she finished, she was crying, but she very gently was running her hand up and down my arm. She kissed my shoulder and softly pressed herself against me, wetting my neck with her tears and touching my chest and neck with her lips. But all of this could only fill me with a conviction of condemnation and strangeness, and could not stop my reading of omens—though the warm press of her mouth had a calling power still as she brought it down again and again to kiss the skin that she'd wetted with her tears.

We hadn't made love for more than two weeks. In bed at that time—and even describing me gets ridiculous and disgusting—I was a pitiful, absurd complexity and contradiction, often either huddling in a fetal crouch, with my back turned to Allie and working on my memories, or, alternately, planning and planning for my future—although the rethinking and the planning all went on almost completely mechanically, sort of like sucking, as I carefully huddled and crouched. I was living and satisfying my desires while retreating further and further from ever really being born. So nothing could have seemed worse to me than an actual living partner—someone who would make me move and live here and now, not someplace else. And the sympathy for me that I now felt coming from Allie, at a point when coming to life seemed the surest way of ending up stone dead—the understanding and sympathy that asked me not to run like mad from a world that I saw beginning everywhere to collapse—seemed to make even the slightest loving gesture absolutely impossible.

But still Allie, taking off her gown, naked now in the blue light, in the wet from her tears and from her mouth, was slowly and passionately moving her kisses over me. She was wetting me with her tongue to move still more hot caresses in smears over my neck and chest and had her face half pressed against me so that it was distorted in beautiful passion. And I knew. I knew that against imprisoning weight, forcing it, all the times she'd been tender to me were there—from the first when she was fourteen and came with her girl's kindness, like the one angel I would ever have, to help me better understand the story of Paradise. And Christ knows, she wasn't just an angel face either, or just what I called daylight, with her auburn hair falling over her shoulders—and a dancer in fact—so wild at parties that people would laugh that she wasn't really like that, or that they didn't know what got into her when the music started.

Nonetheless I knew as well, as I actually began then to answer her and kiss her arms, her breasts, her face, lips, hair—and I remember how I was even thinking this out—that I absolutely could not play any old poet's game and extend, even slightly, any praise of her; for what they would call the beauties and charms could only amount, if I were to dare to count them, to a number of terrifying inadequacies. And my thinking of these inadequacies would, I knew, encourage the absurd horde of banshees around and in me—who needed no help. Yet Allie's kiss, her wet, tortured mouth, was able to kill off enough danger so that I could actually begin to close my eyes.

But who now in this nightmare farce was beginning things? One of the most remarkable, and I'll say again ludicrous and disgusting phenomena of this worst night of my life, was that even when I had absolutely to keep retreating, I couldn't go on with this lovemaking unless I was the one starting it. Jesus Christ Almighty! If I could have laughed at myself as Johnny could laugh at himself, or could have made moves as Johnny could, moves in response, always in response to what was beyond him, to what he was not, or was not yet—I'd have been what? Less ludicrous and more mobile? At least.

He'd laugh at me. "It's absurd," he'd say. "You exaggerate and let what you think is meaningful accumulate till you're paralyzed by the pseudodrama of your life."

And I was only my small, ludicrous and disgusting self when, after she'd begun things, I froze up on Allie again—till after a time she just held me lightly and then turned away and began heading off to sleep. Her turning away, though, actually gave me a moment free of fear and got me more fully aroused, made me creative—in a sense which may be as real as Johnny's after all. And in this now creative mood, with the ego on edge, ready to start something, I looked at the line of her hip and thigh, beautiful naked slender body—I could say it—"So beautiful"—and I could run two fingers lightly along her skin and call her back to this now definitely strange business. Of course if she had cared about these damned beginnings herself, things never would have begun, no matter what I wanted. But she was willing softly to come back out of a half-sleep when I touched her, and she turned to me. There was no more than the clock light and the soft glow of the moon, but Allie, in the dark bed, letting me possess her like a jewel in a case, looked as beautiful as I had ever seen her.

But again, even in this warm reprieve, I was blocked. I couldn't say to her, as I wished to far far down in, that her beauty went deeper than all the sadness I'd ever known— couldn't speak even while the angels of darkness were gone off a distance, to wherever they go. It didn't matter how fast I might say such a thing to her, the fiends would be just as quick to come back. Yet, somehow, I was beginning to forget my sadness when I touched her delicate white neck and knelt and held her two shoulders in my cupped hands and bent to kiss her. I put my mouth then to what I could have called even in that moment her perfect breasts, full and beautiful, gracing her slender white body. And with kisses over and over, like a chanting, I said my prayers after all to the great Madonna of the Misericordia—all guilt and shame of any kind, for some seconds, forgotten, and no miserable approaching sense of the absurd or trivial.

So for better or worse we were for some seconds like our deepest dreams of what moves the world. There was resistance and escape; but I could feel her weight and she could feel mine only as the condition of our experience of freedom—as what was necessary for conjunction and lightness and grace. And with all these joyful feelings we were coming to what I do know is also, alongside our sorrows, at the heart of poetry forever. Then I entered her—when she let me; and we began to learn further the meaning of ecstasy and discipline—and the sweet interplay of the two, which I would say, even now, is the real and great condition of human joy.

But then the discipline could always in this situation involve such a contradiction for me (and for any man?) that I would have to use any strategy I could to keep myself from

coming to the self-annihilating end that I wanted beyond all
else to come to. Goddamned pride, or odd miraculous pride,
or pitiful pride enters in, then, on the brink of ecstasy. It's got
at least this place. So naturally, proudly, pitifully—just listen
to me describe it—after the number on the clock light once
caught my eye, I began in a kind of slow rhythm to look at it,
and then quickly to turn away from it, and then again to look
at it, and then again quickly to turn away from it while the
numbers, at my desperate urging, moved on: 11:31, 11:32. I
even thought strategically, sarcastically, in whatever way it
took, about what prayers might be good for this occasion—
and could suggest that maybe telling beads might work! It's
that absolutely, perfectly funny and sad.

But with my eyes wide open, I began to look now again
at Allie's face, and as I did, I knew again why I couldn't, at
times that evening in the bar, even begin to look at her. She
was going off in her pleasure, and sometime, not too far away
now, she would let me know that I could come along with her.
So I could forget my godforsaken discipline. But now, as I
kept looking at her face, I couldn't be with her and feel Right,
or feel that I was being called to any Paradise—though with
her head thrown back and her eyes closed and lips parted she
was erotic enough to be the best dream girl of any other man's
best dreams. Instead what I felt when I saw her face, and was
in her, was perfect incompleteness—sad, ultimate incompleteness. Not only no grand and great feeling of being Right but
all the isolating dread of a young man trying to retain his
power when it is going, swiftly departing—as it was. I was
losing it. Now quickly going soft. What strategy then, when
everything good gets more distant? What restores grace and
power at this point?

The answer came. And it came exactly when I needed
it—a perfect answer to an urgent prayer. I made Allie into
Barbara Dern. Immediately, too, when I had Barbara in my
arms, I could gaze completely at her sensuous lips with light
but noticeable traces of a red gloss, and feel a great surge of
confidence and power. And when I heard Barbara's voice
whisper, "Kiss me," and I kissed her, it was more than

enough. But in addition—such wonderful, comforting addition—there were her beautiful, dark-shadowed eyes which could turn back all the numbers of a banshee charge and which gave a new, good name to variety—at least as convincing in its magic power as any well-worded celebration of great beauty's charms in any old poem. And passionately, with a perfect feeling of completeness, I kissed Barbara's eyes over and over and over. Then, still more, in the blue light of my own bedroom, in my own bed, there were her pale arms, golden-braceleted, and her hands, gold- and emerald-ringed, and her long fingers, with the long, sensuous nails, red-polished.

And with her charms and beauties, she called me and brought me in till her arms could hold me safe from all intrusions of darkness or crazy fear. Her breasts, full, warm, gave me the power to sing, as old poems say, loud and long. So minute after minute was passing now on the clock; and I could look at it, no quick turning away necessary, and watch it, and even move it faster, if I wanted—or wait for it, if I wanted, in perfect faith. In this undeniable fairy tale, all dangers kept their distance, as I called Barbara's name over and over and enjoyed refreshment from her generous nipples, which I kissed and sucked with absolute delight. It was all true—miracle of miracles. The damned fairy tale was such a distance beyond irony.

Of course, also, I could not call Barbara's magic name out loud because as much power and grace as it gave to me, it might take away from Allie. It might stop Allie, who was not yet as far out as she wanted to be. But I knew instantly that I might myself make a sacrifice for her, as well as bring an end to my own guilt. I began to whisper to her that she could make me whomever she wanted to make me—though when she first heard me say this, she began turning her head from side to side and whispering "No." But I kept on saying that she could make me whomever she wanted—and she at last no longer resisted. She was moaning and giving me signals, and I whispered, as perhaps I had wished to as long as I had known her,

"You can make me Johnny if you want to make me Johnny—it's all right. It's all right."

She was brought so close now that, perhaps, she could only moan louder when I said this. But for whatever reason, her signals were calling me louder and louder, so I made ready to come along with her. Yet to do it now, I had to have Barbara again, and when I had her again, I needed her to change for me, to wear a costume and make it a masquerade, with no selves remaining what they were—which she did in perfect cooperation. Then she offered me friendly drugs too, giggling "not sweets for the sweet but *la roche pour la roche.*" And as she dragged on it long and sensuously and passed it to me with her eyes closed, I—perfectly with Allie as she came to hers—came to my desired end.

And this wasn't all. Ironies succeed ironies. It had been two weeks since Allie and I had made love, and would be at least two more before we would make love again, so there's almost no doubt that this was the night that she became pregnant for the first time. But I say this now, after all, because I have the completest faith that my thirteen-year-old daughter is no joke on us. She is Allie's child and my child and no one else's, or no more anyone else's than any of us is inevitably alien—which means she's just a full complexity, no simple irony. Her hair, because of nature's memory, is the beautiful auburn. Her face—I could make a blazon of her young beauty and offer her life with full confidence as a good reason for my marriage. But because the word "marriage" has become now one of the chiefest of obscenities (and it does sicken me too), I would make everyone look at the way she dances when she goes to parties, look and see what her mother's given her, at the way she moves. It's in the spirit of our vows: joyful, because in devotion Allie and I never made too much of how far we had to go away from each other, betraying each other to give fire to our moments.

Further, that I lied to Allie that night is, in a sense, insignificant. When it was over, she was half-turned from me, sort of laughing and crying at the same time. I lied to her then, that it was as good to have had the bit of light we had as it was to have had the darkness. I could be lost in the mood but always see too that she was still there. And it was a lie for me also—it would have registered as a lie on a lie detector—to say "Yes," as I did, when, almost bursting into tears, she asked me if I still loved her. "Do you?" "Yes. You know I do."

But this too was, in a sense, nothing much. For far more, perhaps infinitely more significant, I could say, than any of these things was the fact that a few moments later we were laughing straight out and that then I did love her and that my "Yes" then would certainly not have moved the lie detector.

But I won't say any more of this kind of good, "safe" thing, for it starts to come back to me now, although still not to the danger point, that around midnight, postcoital depression (fine term) began the transformation of what would seem the last million hours of the night.

I've been avoiding things—carefully. Because of those traces of my old fear, I've been very carefully putting off my account of the worst revenge darkness ever took against me— for all my expectation and desire and broken vows. But I will say now that after Allie fell asleep and I was enjoying a few moments of a sort of necrophiliac sentimentality, lifting her hair and arranging it again on her shoulders, it started coming on. Allie lying motionless, dead asleep, may have had more power against this return or rebirth than Allie wide awake, telling me that she loved me and that I'd get better before too long and that Johnny wasn't really what I thought he was. But the steady growth of fear, that hour, would overwhelm even her still, composed beauty. I had to leave her—get out of the bedroom to the porch. Immediately now, too, the thought of the regenerating power of disease and of where and when it might be born again, makes me fear whether the best wisdom, if even discoverable, could finally amount to anything against it.

Yet, despite my sister's case, and every fear I have, the fear even of attempting to make stories, I must work in the faith that some good comes in time. I must believe that it can prevent the assaults of midnight upon the lives of those I love, and on me—if I must suffer again to win such faith, or for playing some hero, the thought of which truly sickens a mature mind. And in any case I will not put off any longer now the account of what was maybe the absolute crisis of my life—which began when, as on no night before or since, I could not sleep.

5
A MEMORY OF SORROW

I'm the end of this story, and so for all I might know, I can't say for certain where it's going—though I'm sure that the disease never ended in me. I know it's only in hiding—that it's always remained with me somewhere. And the crazy correspondence now between what I'm saying on my pages and what I'm actually feeling—it even has me praying—asking, as if it could happen, that I'll return to that point where I could rediscover the absolute need I once had for everything to work out. I told Allie, "It's like the fantasy of some veterans to return in safety maybe to some nightmare bend of the Mekong so that they would know in a way they did once that we've come to the point where *only* peace, *only* peace, can rule the world."

She nodded thoughtfully—uncertain, if understanding.

And while what really lies around the river's bend might be just the panicky conviction that the only story that doesn't end is modernity's *Heilsgeschichte*—the story of the world's final dividing and falling apart—it's my hope (I'll say now) that what will be revealed instead is some unaccountable power in silent prayer.

From where I am now, the possibility that all construction is irremediably untrustworthy is still remote enough.

"The buildings, A," I said, "don't tremble."

"Will they have to?" she asked.

I said, "No. They won't have to."

But alone now, maybe with the help of some dark angel come out of long hiding, I can see myself that midnight, sitting by the porch window, rocking in a chair and taking what had to be tremendous comfort from the regular rocking motion, while I kept my eyes and ears open for the first sign of a cave-in. And I know that as I looked out and saw a number of lights still on, I thought of the whole world that, for reasons it wouldn't even consider, would never feel this fear of mine, or have to keep any kind of lookout like this—and of how much godforsaken knowledge I would sacrifice to be brought back to that innocent, unafraid world again.

A doctor—but I wouldn't think—a doctor—somebody who is actually there—somebody who sees us and takes action, offering explanations for the movements of disease. He could make it so I wouldn't have to use my senses for this kind of insane surveillance. But I refused to think of a doctor. Because of what he was supposed to be and might not be—and I wouldn't think of Rothen—I would not think of Conlon right now. I wouldn't. And Allie, lying in the bed now with her arm reached out—especially after she'd spoken to me what she hoped, mistakenly, would be actual healing words—I simply couldn't turn to her for any comfort. So I wouldn't try that either.

But now Johnny, my opposite, I could see him with his arm raised by a referee. I remembered, under night flares of thought, how Allie saw him win, and how my father was there, and how I had to sit there with my face down in my hands, having desperately put my life up as a wager that my arm would be raised too, but having failed.

And as I sat rocking, I was brought back further to my terribly hopeful meditations before that wrestling meet, and to the recollections particularly of how much I wanted Allie to be mine, and of how much I wanted my father to see me carry on that tradition. But as I sat rocking and watching for anything, any monster face of ruin, that might come suddenly bursting through the ceiling, it was only for moments, thank God, that I could think of these things. I couldn't be making things worse with thinking, not and live. For if the old physics of angels was a dead cold lie, its nightmare opposite was coming perfectly true—and the devils and furies, as the night went on, were perceivable in the cracks, making the cracks wider, working and successfully bringing down the world, which no angels other than in dreams ever came near to holding up.

I reviewed once more a history that I'd reviewed many times before—though that night it could be perceived only in flashes in the dark. I thought for the thousandth time of how I trained for that meet, having already, from the first day I knew of it, made it the most important day of my life—as only a teenage boy can. I saw myself putting more and more weights on the bar, hoping I would get somewhere, working religiously every day against a greater weight. It was the saddest, most intense discipline. Me alone in the attic with the dust and the weights and the bar. And almost nightly—I thought it with such sick misery, as I looked around me, rocking—I wrote messages to myself on the wall next to my bed. I told myself with colored markers and pens that I *would* win, that I *would* turn things around. I had marked the dates on the wall when other turnarounds and beginnings were to take place. But, in some of the first battles of my war against irony, I had erased all the dates that turned out to be disappointments after all.

But with this meet coming, obsessively I kept up the message writing and took to sleep slogans like "Pride Is Life"—and threatened myself on the wall with being "Nobody" and "Nothin'." I was sure, too, that there had to be an interdependence between grace and power, and that even Jesus, if he was a man, got a great deal of help before his holy sacrifice from remembering that he was also God.

I said once to Conlon, with a torn heart, "All I wanted, when I was that kid, was just to have my name mean something, so I could just have some feeling of worth. And I mean worth in the way the old poets meant it."

"How did they mean it?"

"I'm sure they meant by it," I said, "the feeling of that measure of self-love that we must have before we can be capable of any self-forgetfulness. They're always careful when they speak of our 'worth'—because they know that any self-love, any trace of egotism, is also an immediate threat to self-forgetfulness. But they'll insist with beautiful power, say, that kings make their men feel their own worth."

"To which," he answered, "I say 'Amen.' "

I said, "I've always thought, too, even when I most admired Johnny, that, down far in, a sense of worth is a *sine qua non* for the saints of selflessness, the Johnny Lemasters, as much as it is for egoistic sinners like me. I've thought it—exactly as I've thought that no one could play games with the structure of reality (and I'll challenge the greatest saints East and West) who once had had the structure of reality play games with him."

The match would come at noon, and that time and the date were scrawled on my wall in blue: Noon, January 11, 1966, with the words "This Is It"—a sight that sickened me as from my pillow I looked at it that morning. Immediately, no matter what I had thought for so many months, I couldn't even begin to call this the most important day of my life, though instinctively I took a long, long shower, making myself as clean as I could. I took a long time brushing my teeth, though not so long that the mist would be clear from the mirror—so when I began to use the electric razor on what few whiskers I had, I needed to clear the mirror with my hand. When I saw myself, I let the shaving go and looked at my face. And though I wouldn't then have asked myself a question like "Who in hell am I?"—I was wondering about my green eyes—what they were for—what good they were—and if they had beauty. Or if I was handsome—if the girls thought the hard lines of my face were too hard, or frightening?

I caught a glimpse of my shoulders, and I needed to study them once more, definitely, to see if they were powerful enough to win the match that was almost here now, just a few hours away. So I toweled the mirror all clean; then, stepping back, I could see my body to the knee.

I recall very well now that on the porch in the dark, that night after the Northside, tears started in my eyes as I remembered how these arms and shoulders and hands were not going to be enough. But I know I fought the tears back immediately, gripping my chair for a second like steel—convinced that an even more fearful price would be exacted from the one who thought sometimes—I said thought like a complete *fool*—that not just anything can break your heart.

But this was the night that I'd learn to read, learn poetry, structure! I would see war with Homer and Virgil (Virgil who went not just to Homer but to true hell for his words)—*see* the merciless rejection of the pleas of lost souls holding heroes' knees, the scattering of horses, disconnected heads eating the dust, terrified boys and old men receiving with wild eyes the sword-point of utter violence, young and old soldiers dying worlds away from home, the bright colors of grotesque disembowelings, good men left to the alien mouths of carrion dogs, ripped faces and genitalia.

But also the beauty in the pain when that unbearable poem ends calling Hector, for the last time, "tamer of horses." Unbearable beauty. The heartache that leads to Virgil and makes him steal away from the burning city, and then to Dante, who moves out of hell's pain with Virgil and on to the gates of Paradise. And to believe it—to understand and *believe* in the pain and beauty—and Paradise.

I want now so much to name some of the wrestlers on my team—maybe to let them know, if they ever read this, that I haven't forgotten them and that I think of them always with respect for what they did when I knew them. There was J.J. Rossinni at 112 pounds, who twice every season had to face the same one opponent he could never beat, but who never lost to anyone else, and who was the best student in our year, outstanding especially in Latin and physics—so we called him the Doctor. And Donnie Home at 128 pounds, one of my best friends back then, passionate and argumentative. But he was always the first to laugh at himself, and in Donnie, as long as I knew him, I never detected a single sign of unkindness. He had good athletic ability, and good strength, but always, I'd say, he won the matches he won because of his courage. The last I heard, maybe '68, he'd gone off to points unknown— South America—following a girl whom he'd met at school. And Jim Ehrling at 145, who came right before me at 154. He was from a pretty rough neck of the woods, and all the time I knew him, I never knew what Jim did when he went back home. I heard years later that he got in trouble with a gun, though when I heard it, I was surprised since he was always so kind to me, and quiet. I always used to figure that if Jim beat his man he'd leave the mat charmed for me and I'd beat mine. How good if that had worked out.

Then at 165 there was Johnny—the best—the brilliant orphan who J.J. said once was "great because he doesn't care," which made Donnie say that "he doesn't care because he's great." But that was Johnny—provoker of theory and debate.

And finally I'll mention the giant, the Ajax, John "Marty" Martin, who once bragged that he could beat a certain man in ten seconds—so he waited till there were ten seconds left in the match to make his big move, and failed, and cost us the meet, and got himself kicked off the team because his game was so obvious that the coach could tell—but got back on because he was such an amazing, 260-pound power-house and he gave the whole team a feeling of strength whenever we took the floor.

But if I saw any of them that night on the porch, with the wind gathering in the dark, they were only accusers condemning me for thinking so much and losing so often. I remember a ghostly Donnie Home who asked, "But did he think so much because he lost, or lose so much because he thought?"—which made a Johnny spirit laugh. And I could hear what I overheard Marty Martin say once to Johnny about me: "I don't know, I don't know. It seems like he's only gettin' worse and worse."

But all such things could come only in brief flashes, visions revealed quickly under night flares, as I rocked and watched, looking out sometimes at the lights of the city beyond, taking comfort from the standing presence of what I could see there and at the same time fearing to look at anything with hunger. So I felt repeatedly that I had to gaze instead at the structuring of the small porch room I was in—at the white plaster walls, all shadowed, and the double-set window frames on three sides, and the shadowy ceiling *because* they threatened me; and contemplate the building's roof and the floors beneath me *because* they were going to cave in. I did this until the gazing and contemplation became undeniably suicidal. But this kind of sacred modern quest for my own end, for the ripping apart of my self, would then provoke its sinful counterresponse—a betrayal—for the sake of life—for my life. And I turned around again and again until second after second I was standing alternately before some Destroyer and some Preserver—neither of whom I could call by name.

An hour before the meet there was the weigh-in. In the gymnasium basement, we stepped up to the scale to see if we could enter a fair fight, one that would be determined not by how big but by how good we were. And something that I envied and would envy forever was the way that somebody like J.J. Rossinni, the Doctor, could raise his fist in joy when the scale showed that he qualified for a test of how good he was.

And that night on the porch, as I rocked and gripped my chair, I envied this as desperately as I'll envy anything as long as I live—though I could express absolutely zero wish for it. I recalled in extreme distress, with the eternal metaphors of terror coming in seconds as close as possible to a successful usurpation of what is—furies prying violently, peering into the world—that my own fist-shaking when I stepped off the scale was always pitifully subdued and false. I could feel myself raise my hand slightly and falsely when I got off that morning under that low basement ceiling and made room for Johnny— who of course qualified and made nothing of it. And as I thought of this, I felt a shame as large as my inexpressible desire for a courage that would just for once be enough.

We ate, we ate too. I was always amazed at the way the others could gorge themselves when they had to wrestle in an hour. But even I liked the honey, which always went around at this time, because it never made me sick and was supposed to provide good, quick energy; and it looked like it had a kind of magic potency—though nothing short of ambrosia, I'm afraid, could have been magical enough to make me ready for a test of what I was worth. And on the porch I wanted bitterly to mock myself when I thought of my sucking on the honey bottle, as if I had a right to it like the others.

But when I thought of what I went to for nourishment when I couldn't eat, I almost let my tears come again, for what I did was take up the picture of my father. I thought this was the only way. If I couldn't ever win by forgetting death—though I wouldn't have put it to myself this way—I might win by remembering it. So I made myself desperately responsible for keeping something burning, the tradition, that I said would certainly have gone out without me. And if there was no magic food for me, there might be enough energy coming from miserable shame to get me to where I wanted to be.

And Allie, out there, watching too. I still believed that the worth of my life depended on my winning a victory before her eyes. So I used her also to put myself in extreme jeopardy, in the hope that something different would happen along the edge of my life. I'd win the world for her and drive down into it a *pax romana* so deep that it would bring an end to time. So God help me, I couldn't let her see me have points put up against me or be bent to the floor and pinned and have the referee slam his hand down and signal that I was finished.

But Johnny! Johnny was always a winner. He wouldn't ever be finished like this. And God knows he wouldn't ever consider such a morbid, self-jeopardizing strategy! Never insisting on a direction, he never needed a turnaround. I could see him, though, kiss Allie by the car door—smell his jacket, and feel his hand on me. I could remember him coming up to me back then too, in the low gray locker room, and my feeling his grasp on me. But rocking in the dark on the porch, I could no more call him an oppressor than I could escape his oppression; and I could not ignore now the motion of a presence in the shadow on the wall.

"What are you starin' at?" he said in the locker room.

I said, "Nothin'."

"Nothin' my eye." He put his hand on me and moved me away from my locker. "What in the hell is this?" He reached in and took out the picture of my father, our age, in another numbered jersey. He said, "You don't need this shit. You'd be a whole lot better off if you just burned it."

I said, "Maybe it helps me."

"Helps you for what? For freezin' up and waitin' for somebody to break ya down. I'll bet it helps ya for nothin'."

"How the hell would you know what's gonna help me? You aren't me. You don't understand me. You're pretty sure you do. But you don't."

He said, "I've known you all my life, Pete. I'm tellin' ya, you'd be better off if you just plain burned this thing."

And sitting on the porch, as I heard this again, I came as close to believing it as I came to believing that the presence in the shadows was opening now a lengthening, black rift near the ceiling—which was as close as the reality of hell to the heart of poetry and the world's truth. But, because I was too afraid before the meet to make a pointed remark, I said nothing about the fact that Johnny himself was examining the picture carefully and that he in fact took his eyes off it only once or twice the whole time that he spoke to me. And if there ever came a moment when my thinking that I had this kind of thing *on* Johnny would have resulted in the severest punishment and the fullest exhaustion of all my capacity for evasion, it was while I sat rocking in that chair on the porch—awaiting now the hour and approach of only God knew what, and discovering, with the walls and ceilings failing to keep from my imagination a cracking in their shadows like a mouth, that the most intense prayer may be the one offered at exactly the same time the act of praying has to stop.

I said nothing either when Johnny tossed the picture back into my locker as the Coach, who had just come in, bringing slowly before us his loosening body and tired eyes, clapped and called us up to sit before him for the pep talk, in which he would threaten us with disgrace and so motivate us by making us need frantically to rebuild ourselves, and to which Johnny would pay zero attention while I would listen carefully—as I would listen still under the poised weight of terror in the wall's shadows.

"All right," the Coach said, as in the low room and dim light he started walking back and forth. "This is it. You know this. You know we haven't come this far just to turn back or stop. You know if we win this thing today we break out of a tie for first. You know we have only one meet left. It's with a weak team. We're gonna win that. So as far as I see it, TODAY is gonna prove how much you want the trophy. And ya GOTTA want it. You have GOT TO WANT IT."

He stopped and looked at particular people down the line. "Home! What about you, Home? Do you want it? Do you know how much you need it?" "Yes, sir." "Jakobson? You?" "Yes, sir." "Rossinni?" "Yes, sir." "Roche?" "Yes, sir." But, as always, he left Johnny alone. He stepped slowly back to look at us all. Then, after a silence, he suddenly screamed, "WELL YA BETTER GODDAMN WANT IT!" Immediately then, in a quiet, fierce voice, "Because if ya don't want it, you're not gonna get it, and no one's ever gonna come by and hand it to you. Not once in your whole life—believe me. So it's you and nobody else. One way or another you're gonna know who to thank."

He paused for maybe ten seconds, and went on again, his eyes sweeping over us all slowly. "How long is *nothin'* gonna last ya? Ya wanna know? I'll tell ya how long. It's not gonna last ya at all. Do you know what I mean? Nothin' is gone in no time flat. Do you know what I mean? DO YOU KNOW!" We shouted, "Yes, sir!" He said, "I CAN'T HEAR YOU." So we screamed, "YES, SIR!" He said, "That's better." He paused. "Do you wanna know somethin' else? Do ya? Well I'll tell ya somethin' else. I'll tell ya how long a victory here's gonna last ya. I'll tell ya how long a championship's gonna last ya. DO YOU WANNA KNOW!" "YES, SIR!" He looked at us all down the line, and, in the now completely quiet basement, he said in a low voice, "A championship, boys, is gonna last ya forever—that's how long."

He turned his back to us and looked up at the ceiling—at the lines of heat pipes. After another moment, he spoke again, still turned away. "But there's a problem," he said. "A problem with the fact that victory isn't the only thing ya get when ya go out there and that you're not gonna be wrestlin' with your girlfriends when ya go out there." He turned to us again slowly. "You're gonna meet an opponent when ya go out there, and he wants that trophy too and all those memories that last forever. Think about it. Think about it, every one of ya right now, before it's too damned late! Your opponent out there wants what you want for himself. He wants you to go from somethin' to nothing' and to be kingpin himself of this whole goddamned thing—with you nothin'."

He put his head down, waited, then lifted his head and looked at our faces again. "But I'll tell ya somethin' else. I know you guys, and I know your opponents are *wrong*. I know that what they think's gonna happen is NOT GONNA HAPPEN. I know it because I know you want it more then they do. And all I wanna know now is HAVE YOU GOT THIS?" "YES, SIR!" "All right then, it's good. We're ready. Today's a beginning, a beginning of something that's gonna last forever."

He said, "Let's put our hands together." Then all of us rose in the low, dim light and put in an arm for a spoke, and a hand for the hub of the wheel, except Johnny, who only vaguely leaned in from the perimeter. And when the Coach said, "Our Lady Queen of Victory," all of us, except Johnny, who wouldn't have responded to this at gunpoint, shouted, "PRAY FOR US!" Then the Coach said, "I'll see you on the floor in five minutes," and walked out and left us to think about it for ourselves.

Fewer lights now were visible across the street from where I sat on the porch, but I couldn't look long enough even to start a count. But that I had no trophy, no memory to last me—no blessed, stupefying memory of any new beginning—no feeling that a prayer for victory had resulted in anything—

made me feel for a very unusual second that I was *better off* because I had nothing: not as stupid.

But this sudden absurd feeling, a self-defense I'd used countless times before, coming in this spasm, was only preparing a new and far more potent burst in the progress of dread. In a second I knew, as I never have since, that I'd have given anything for any victory that would have made me stupid enough to be able to turn out my light and go to sleep with the rest of the world. But that kind of victory—and I cannot describe here the pain and terror—was exactly what I did not have.

And with only minutes left before the meet, after all the weeks, after a lifetime, I turned back to my locker and began looking furtively at the picture and thinking to myself of marriage. I was sick to death with nervousness, mixing up all the things the Coach had said, and that I'd felt, crazily in my head.

Johnny came up to me. "Feeling inspired?"

I said, "I hope so. I think so."

He smiled. "I was doing my best to keep my ears closed without sticking my fingers in 'em. But I couldn't keep all the shit out. I had to hear some of it. Yes, Sir! So I'm feelin' sick. I just pray to Mary it's not a beginning of somethin' that's gonna last forever. I'm so worried already about my opponent. But I want it so fuckin' bad, and I know how much I want it—so even though my opponent wants it too, I oughta be able—Mary pray for me—to eat the fucker alive! Jesus Christ!" He laughed, taking hold of my locker door. "Come on, let's take a break from all this shit and go do some grapplin'. And you, you complete dumb shit, listenin' to him! Take it from me. There are no important days." He jerked my locker door shut. "Let's get outa here."

And as I sat rocking in that chair on the porch, I could see and even feel him do this, and see us walking down the dark tunnel toward the bright light in the gym. And I began actually to cry out. "Oh Johnny, you bastard!" I said, rocking back and forth now very fast, gripping the chair seat so hard that I would injure my hand. "You bastard, I could use you. I'm thinking of you. I promise I'm thinking of you. It's not a lie. I promise. I promise. Oh God please. Please let this end. Johnny, you don't know. You don't know until you've had days like this how important days can be! Did you ever see in your walls, you son of a bitch, what I'm seeing here! If I look, red faces peer out of hell; and if I think too long, they make the joists beneath the skin of the ceiling break through it like cracked bone. You. You were never what I was—one way or the other. You never *needed* the world to be an illusion. You never *needed* it to be the truth. Beauty. Fear. You never needed. Nothing. You could mock the Coach, but did you ever believe one minute that the room you were in wasn't going to hold! Just try it some time. Just try."

But now an unbelievable roar said, "No—just you try!" And in the next moment, almost complete panic spread over me—so bad that I needed to find ways to keep myself safe that I'd never found before. Frantically, I began to chant my dark promises, moaning over and over that I wouldn't think— things getting better—no—assert nothing. And then, as it seemed a true, great safety, humming the fragment that I kept hearing—There Are No Important Days. And finally chanting and humming—There Are No Important Days—There Are No Important Days—There Are No Important Days—was what I did believe, or so very nearly believed, was alone keeping the room from crushing in on me.

And now, at whatever distance it is that I'm standing, as I think back on myself walking down that dark tunnel, J.J. Rossinni and Marty Martin out in front of me and Johnny beside me, I'm not sure at all whether I can or cannot play with the idea that there are no important days. But as I rocked back and forth, with red furies waiting to cleave the ceiling the second I looked too long at anything, I had absolutely to chant There Are No Important Days—it kept up the world. Yet never were opposites more vitalized. And although the voice of hope in me (the voice that in a different world of possibilities would have roared back in anger at the dark that this was the *real day, the important day, the turnaround!)*— although this voice had to maintain perfect silence, there *was* an angry conviction in me that it was a dead cold lie that there are no important days. And if I could just regain this tremendous conviction—housed back then inside a fraction of a fraction of an inch—I might bring to an end the problem of sleep and build a structure that wasn't falling, that wasn't a lie. I might roar out against the dark that There *Are* Important Days—that there are beginnings, that they are children of time, and that because of them the world—as it must—gets better.

At the end of the tunnel, Marty burst through the swing door, and the crowd met him with a tremendous noise. I could see him raising his fist in the light, and J.J. doing the same. Then I could feel the pull of the forward rush of the event and that I was beginning to run out into the noise and light myself, with Johnny beside me. And I felt now incredibly sick, and guilty, because I had all my past and all my future, in place, ready out there to greet me—my father and my girl—all my memory and desire, the faces that would make me fight now as if my life depended on it, but plants in the audience.

I raised my hand in the air too and clenched my fist and shook it as the crowd, in the huge vacuum of the gym, roared its approval. I tried to make sure that my feet moved not clumsily over the floor as I jumped and ran out onto the side mat to warm up with the team. But my eyes were looking then for Allie and my dad. I was carefully scanning the crowd till I found them sitting together near the center, the old king and the maiden, he in a red sweater and she still in her green winter coat. They were waving; and I waved back, but then lowered my eyes, so that no one would catch me, and brought myself to the business of getting myself ready.

And as on the porch I sat and waited (God knows, not making up the language of the terrified heart as it pushed now so incredibly near to madness in the walls)—the story of the meet came on. I could see again the opposition, already there. It came back to me, like poetry understood in the simplicity of tears, how at times each of us looked over his shoulder to catch a glimpse of the one he'd have to face—all except Johnny, always Johnny, who never had anyone in the stands or across the mat that he gave one damn about—and who never shook his fist for himself or for anybody. In moments like these, he always seemed especially just to be there, utterly careless of his past or future, and I was always so ashamed because of it.

Yet I will speak out—I must: on that day I noticed clearly that he saw my father and Allie and that he looked their way, more than once. I'll report with all the satisfaction, the self-disgust and shame that go along with an act of vengeance, that after his match he did what he had never done before. Twice he raised his fist in the air and shook it, in the direction of the center of the stands. But really I mention this more for what it says about me than for what it may or may not contribute to a story about my old friend. And as for me, I had my eye turned regularly to the 154-pounder whom I was going to wrestle, whose name, Tom Fair, I'll remember as long as I live.

But more came. More, when I saw this Tom Fair pushed by furies into the light of clearest memory, where they knew he'd shine—his pale, cold face, his cropped blond wrestler's hair as unforgettable as any of the *ideae naturae* of hell and pain. I remembered how desperately I began to wish that I'd been defeated in the challenge matches. The desire to have had my own preliminary victories taken away, to have gotten killed in the beginning and never to have been anyone, has made me think ever since, too—it's made me know, as poets know—that against the glories of selflessness, or the idea that it's wrong to be somebody, must be set the real ignominy of cowardice. Do I efface myself for God?—or simply because I'm afraid to live?

But then if I was purely afraid, there was still nowhere to run; and with the ungodly meet-buzzer filling the great empty volume of the gym with a sound like an air-raid warning, I had to take my place in the row. I stepped up clumsily, with cold feet, trying pitifully to remember now some moves that might work when my time came, and then in fact remembering those preliminary victories and taking what comfort I could from them, even as I regretted them—though nothing could stop the clock now from moving more quickly the more I dodged.

A full hour passed before my time came. I have never

known what happened to that hour. I know that although I was trying to keep myself as secret as I could, I kept a subtle eye on Tom Fair, peeking up to see if I could read him, read anything in his hard, square face, and to watch him when he rose to take his final stretches. I know that I looked over just to see that Allie was still there, her face, and that my dad was still there. I suppose too that I could say what J.J. did and what Donnie did and Jim, when they went out there into that circle. But if time ever raced by, and if, for better or worse, I ever learned the terrible meaning of speed (so important too for poems, which live and move in the world's limits!), it was when that instant hour rushed against my heart.

And as I sat by the low porch light, gripping my seat in utter desperation, refusing to look at the reflection of my face in the window glass, I thought How Long Before It Comes? There was an absoluteness in my fear that I beg will remain for me now essentially incomprehensible; for if I cannot completely make this book, or be totally awake, without this absolute feeling, I cannot with it either, as certainly I would be gone. And back then—if somewhere some voice of mine was most definitely screaming, "Oh God, how long? How long until whatever it really is will come?"—I was somehow able *not* to hear myself screaming such things. I still, with the shadows above me assuming the lead weight of death, was only mumbling what I had to to keep away the thought that I had once, with an unmentionable desire, expected a turnaround and that that turnaround had not come.

The instant my name was called, all my expectations at once reached their greatest intensity and went absolutely cold dead. The difference between what I'd hoped for and what I was now getting (I put it to myself in Johnny's words somehow as the wind, rushing over the top of the elms, hummed in the glass that enclosed the porch) right with the event became infinitely great! The crowd was roaring for me—hands clapping, in that endless blinding volume, voices cheering and approving. But I wasn't much more then than the tired ghost of someone already dead from exhaustion. While the noise was so terrific, it seemed to come from a distance that could never close. And across that mocking, infinite gap, almost too beaten now even to be ashamed, I looked once more to find the faces of my father and Allie, whom I would never, in this world, please now as I had hoped. They were there, but they weren't there. I saw the red sweater—it was there—the green coat—a hand waving, a fist shaken encouragingly—but all now so terribly far away—so far (that word the poets use so heartbreakingly, I know, to change all mathematics, all time, all distance, to the measure of our disproportionate sorrow!).

Tom Fair, the adversary, with his eyes on me, gray, and his sandy blond hair, was coming right up to touch me. The referee, who had called our names, once we had come into the center of the circle, was giving us our instructions. "Take the standing position in the first period . . ." Of course it was a sport, a game; so we shook hands and even wished each other "Good match," "Good match"—a salutation that I could barely speak, with my tongue all dry. But with my hand in Fair's moist hand, I was somehow able to decide that if I was going to die, it would be a wild fiery martyrdom (as good a disguise for fear as there is), terrible with screaming and agony, or that my ghost life would have all of the wild energy of despair.

The referee set us face to face. He set our arms and hands into the right beginning positions, so that our heads, each set hard against the other, were enclosed in our arms. I could smell Fair's life, so close, and feel pain already with his moist skull like a fist pressed against my cheek to bruise me. Amidst all the shouting, the hysteria, I could hear Johnny say, "Be easy." I could see him as the referee turned us a bit so we'd be in the dead center of the circle. Then the whistle sounded, and I couldn't see Johnny's face again before I felt the shocking pressure of Fair's strength and heard his strange-familiar voice whisper in my ear: "You're no good, Roche. You're goin' down."

And what sounds would come to me on that night, after I'd made, as cautiously as possible, a first move toward getting myself taken care of, seemed to be sounds that only moved me back and back—that knew how to move me back. And possibly *because* I was someone who was crazy enough to want a world of bright angels, the strategies of the King of Darkness took his forces right down to the center of my life where with psychosomatic genius they knew exactly what to do, and did it. I could hear Fair's voice perfectly. I could see his face—as I sat rocking and, for the sake of my life, refusing to imagine anything else—any kind look or sound.

"You're no good." I couldn't hear that I was good—no sweet voice of Allie, who has said to me now, "I only thought, Peter, that you were beautiful. I never cared. Maybe I was just a girl, who didn't know. Or maybe I knew better than you."

And whether now Allie's kind words bring me forward or backward is a bit uncertain—truly. But on the porch, high over the darkening street, there was no question. The only thing that I could safely think was that if there was good news for me anywhere, ever, it was a lie. When it came to my worth, I had then desperately, for my life, to act only as the complete unbeliever—though I can still say now that at other times, when I wasn't so sick, I could look forward to getting a reverse on my extraordinary assailant and having him down, the knife at his throat, and asking, "How does it feel to know that *you're* no good—that the dead man is *you?*" But I was perhaps exactly as far from that position as possible as I sat on the porch and knew the building as Judas knew the dismembering darkness of the mouth of Satan.

After the starting whistle sounded—and the referee's word, "Wrestle!"—so little time, so little time elapsed on the high scoreboard clock before I was overpowered. And in the night, with so much of the memory coming so quickly before me, I wondered who brings such powerful wings to world-destroying images of terror! Even as I needed objects so much that I cannot begin to tell it—needed the stability of *things* before my eyes—I wished I'd never opened my eyes or ears in this world of objects. Not if a window's glass only showed me my own ghost face—and above it the fanged, bloody-mouthed reflection of my pitiful death-fear.

But I kept myself safe, somehow safe, by thinking without any slight trace of sadness—as I thought only seconds into the match—that I shouldn't hate what Tom Fair breathed into my ear: that I had no worth. And how I looked forward even to the handshake at the end of the match, to admiring Fair, to being his good friend someday, and enjoying the great release of admitting that he was better.

But in the circle, somehow, smelling the cold skin of him, with the salt taste of his sweat on my lips—I couldn't believe it—but I knew something was coming. Fair was only pushing me back to set me up for a sudden, surprise pull forward. Then he did it—and I was ready. I didn't lose my balance, but got low and pushed him so that he lost his. He was falling. In that glaring vacuum, I could hear the crowd roaring tremendously for me—closer and closer. Fair's powerful, pale cold body, with the smell of my death, changed then. He was smaller. I almost whispered in his hear, "You son of a bitch, you're goin' down." But with the tumble-over we'd moved all the way out of the circle—so the time stopped on the high clock and there was again nothing. Then, standing outside the circle, on no legs, breathless in the empty air, I was glad that I hadn't said a word, and that I didn't really have to take Fair down, and could believe that my dad, Allie, the roaring crowd, would know that I'd showed enough courage.

The referee touched us and put us back into the circle. The whistle sounded close in my ears. Then Fair—before I knew it—was back, gaining, *right here,* while I was losing all energy—the energy I complain idiotically can't live in a world without faith. He dropped with too much speed, got one of my legs and gripped it hard at the knee. With unstoppable strength, he lifted the leg high up—so immediately I was a freak, one-legged, hopeless, about now to fall. In no time I was down, with Fair's cold weight and his smell and sweat on me, and I saw the red electric 2 come fast up high on the score-board.

I heard the Coach's voice, screaming. "Roche, for Christ Almighty's sake, don't just let that happen! Jesus Christ!" I saw his angry face at the edge of the circle, as I was trapped and broken down.

And that's the way it was. So quickly Fair had me down.

I could rise then only to my hands and knees, and he was working already to break me down further so he could turn me over on my back and finish me. But now desperately, on all fours, I had my arms flexed rigid so he couldn't break my head down and cave me in. But he had me turned in such a way now, so that with my neck strained to the uttermost—I could hear the blood pounding—and my head arched back, I could see my father and Allie right before me, close, within reach. So I had to squint my eyes because I couldn't go on if all were dark, but also couldn't look out into the light.

And with a belief in magic that had to be complete and simple, I braced myself in the porch, stiffened my arms and injured, inflamed my hands resisting the room's falling in on me, and arched my neck to keep up the structure of the dark, fragile building in which I was. My eyes had also to be squinted; for if I didn't look at the wall, the wall might disjoin immediately, in defiance against things that we never even consider expectations, things like our awaiting our next breath—and if I did look at it, I'd see that it was moving already, or I'd make it move.

But thinking of this, I'm not sleepy now! I'm writing this with speed—with a sense of possible structure, a sense of the possible connection between time and time. For a moment, I can write fast, feel how in the gym, with my eyes squinted and my arms planted and neck arched back, I kept myself safe from a pin, and how in the state of utter exhaustion, I was certain that this was all I could do. I could hear the Coach's loud voice trying to shame me. "Where are you, Roche! Where ARE you!" I saw Allie's and my father's faces—he was nodding encouragement and holding his fist tight—and for a moment all of us were locked eye to eye.

I could hear Johnny yelling, "Move! Move!" I wanted then somehow to hurl away the weight of my life and stand up and get free from this grip of Fair's. But I saw now too on the clock high in the ghost light over the crowd that only fourteen seconds remained in the period. So I could wait it out. It would be over. There would be more, but then it would be over. Then I saw thirteen seconds. And if the Coach was yelling "Ya gotta hurry! You have Got To Hurry!"—I stayed locked in agony on all fours, safe from the pin till the period's last seconds ran finally down to zero, and never got my point for an escape.

And in the dark on Greenwood, I thought, here's a history! The gargoyles of the fearful, static mind reverse—turn back and penetrate the unprotected walls. Self-defense against every spirit in the air is at last just the petrified gaze of Blake's crawling Nebuchadnezzar, that spooked caricature of the ego. I know it! But I know as well that to get the ego off its knees there must be a victory. What do they know—the philosophers of murder! Why should I listen to anyone else when I know that some tremendous victory down in, some ultimate belief in the profoundest stability and measure, is necessary for movement, for grace? Only victorious God, in all his worth, can be Jesus, and only the King of the World the clown. Only all the world can dismiss all the world. Take away the measure of self, the victory, and you don't move. You can't. You just hold on and beg for forgiveness. I knew it in hell.

Only I couldn't whisper it. I could find God again only in selfless blindness and silence. Having waited motionless so long in the agony of fear, on all fours, on my own, I came at last to the point where I *had* to wait motionless and do *nothing* on my own. Such a history! The balance of the world in my walls. Have the world so you can let it go, and let the world go so you can have it. This is the grammar of joy and terror, of loss and victory—which I do know now—as the world for me is coming alive at times with its poetry—at odd times—just watching my daughter and her little brothers, talking to Allie—in quick rushes.

"I hear you," she's said to me. "I couldn't . . . do the same. But I understand what it means to you. You know I do. Just . . ."

I said, "I promise you, I won't go all the way. I can't."

And if, as I drove the Drive today, this grammar of the soul revealed to me, under a light shaft driven through varying gray clouds, a sudden island of incredible blue color out on the lake, and for a second brought to life for me the harbor at Belmont, and sails like familiar stars, and branches of park trees rocking in the wind, I know that I can't go all the way with this. I'm certain that just as, with the dawn still too far off, I had to get out from my porch that night, and away from the completest truth, into a safer space, all this now has to remain safe, and the story (because madness is *not* poetry) has to be incomplete.

But (and I've said to myself that I've come through my own Vietnam War—that I'm not a coward!) I stayed with it that night till the end of the match. I could remember still how Fair immediately, after the second-period whistle sounded, reversed on me for two points. The beast was all over me. I was one of the sons of Laocoön! I tried to crawl out of the circle to get away—to get out to where nothing could happen. But Fair, with his arm gripped tight around my waist, kept me in; and the referee, who'd moved to his knees in anticipation of a fall, warned me to get back and wrestle or he'd penalize me. "You've gotta stay in, son. You've got to stay in."

What time did the high clock say? I don't know. But a moment was coming soon which would mark the end for me of the chance for a graceful life, a moment which would teach me, for better or worse, how to read the thousand paintings of the angel with the sword at the gate, and why time can be called a disease. The voices in the crowd were yelling louder than ever, expressing in their way the misery that goes with the imagination of dying.

I couldn't hear Johnny at all. Then in that endless cold light, my eyes began a last frantic search. I was looking a last time for the red and the green. But I couldn't see them at all when Fair broke down my arms—which of course were not enough—and which, as I had known from far back, for all my writing on the wall, were never going to be enough. I could see no one as my face, and mouth even, were pressed violently against the mat. The disgusting smell and taste of the rubber vividly come back now—and the disgusting yellow color, which was pressed into my eye.

My head got lifted, or violently scraped, off the mat, as

Fair first shot his arm under my now unbraced arm and over the back of my bent neck and began to turn me over, having driven his other arm up under my crotch and gotten me completely into the machine of his hold—which meant the end. There would be nothing left but sorrow, no hope. But with not even a chance of escape, I wanted now even more to see my dad, who, no matter what else might be said, believed in beauty, and in lessons learned in fear, as Johnny—and I offer no explanations—just could not. My father was what for me had to be true. And Allie was my intention, my marriage. So I wanted to see them. It turned out to be my one wish then that did come true; for Fair, when he at last had moved me to my back, also drove me around so that I could see them out of my left eye, underneath the belly of the kneeling referee, when I arched my neck in a last effort to keep my shoulders off the ground.

But immediately I was squinting again when my shoulders finally collapsed under the unbearable cold weight of Fair's strength and the referee began his count to three. Then the complete, final, double misery—in front of the two of them, in front of Johnny—when the referee at last slammed down his hand. I closed my eyes, and not in prayer but in complete shame.

Yet on the porch I still had them open, looking so briefly to confirm my undying hope for a standing world. And let all the damned contemporary philosophers before they begin their speculative dismantling of things, of the pitiable self, maybe just feel this for a single miserable hour! Let them have the hand slam down on them and then for one hour have everything truly become an exigency for them instead of one of the safe surprises of their mere speculations! Fucking abstractions! Fucking idiot ignorance of terror and sorrow!

But right now again, Jesus, I want only to get out of this. I don't want to get angry. And that I can make no real claim to understanding in this matter is clear from the fact that I'm making any noise at all. If I knew really what I meant, I'd be silenced. But I'll just say quietly, very quietly, that if it was obvious, severe insecurity that made me, on the porch that night, want space to remain space, I had the faith briefly that there would be such a mercy. And if it was glaringly obvious death-fear that made me want especially a safe territory for myself and a lasting safe time for myself, I also believed, in those moments when I came to blessed, complete helplessness, that my name had a small measure of worth.

But I could *never* ask for such feelings of confidence to last, nor know how much of the night had passed when I could no longer endure waiting under and on top of and in the middle of a nightmare—nor when, more terribly than at any time, I knew that I had to get out—get out of the building, and away from it, as from the speeding peripheral devastation of a bomb. I was so unbelievably afraid, with my self's own petrifying Medusa, my face, still visible in the window glass, and with every conceivable sound, the quietest aching of timber or electrical hum, starting waves of acid fear—a burning lake rolling in my own godforsaken head. And still I was promising over and over, even if I kept squinting at the walls, that I would take no action for myself, chanting also whatever needed to be chanted about no importance, no decision, no hope, no doctor—no doctor—because I was at the door to hell—where the fear that the world is falling becomes the actual grinding hinge of a conviction.

But I knew decisively, wildly, that I had to take action, in hope, because my life *was* somehow important, and it would be lost if I didn't act. I rushed then in silence (through a place, as I now read it, where Virgil led Dante, though the poet of hell had to know it by himself!) under the porch lintel and back to the kitchen, turned on the light and opened the telephone directory.

I ran my finger in wild sinful hope down the columns, using my eyes as the kitchen still cooperated and held. And I found it. There it was: Conlon, Alexander—211 Cherry, Winnetka. Thank God I didn't have to call Johnny for it.

Those words of Johnny's on Conlon's house. I'm reminded. Just hours ago I read the words of an architect attacking architecture, the form-giver, the creator of hierarchical and symbolic structural unity (and so a blasphemy against sacred division). The architect hates architecture—the art that's motivated by an underlying belief in the unified self— and so false to today's posthumanist circumstances: the disruption, disjunction, rift between space and action, dispersion of the subject. Jesus Christ! Johnny rules the whole goddamned world! And I would absolutely have had to call him if I hadn't found the name of my doctor in the directory— though hearing Barbara's voice, if she'd answered, might have helped for a moment: made darkness comfortable for as long as a pathetic, useless sigh.

But (and I could whisper that this too is for the good of the whole world) I have to say now that Johnny, my friend— and this was not the only time—showed signs of compassion? understanding? when he saw me later, after the meet. And this tenderness, no matter the cost to me to think of it, is there to remember forever.

I had showered longer than anyone, standing the whole time away from everyone else. They were shouting, celebrating because the team had secured the title. But nobody bothered me, and a good number were already gone when I came back to my locker. I went on slowly then, so that before I was dressed I was alone. I just sat in the dim basement light and silence, and stared at my locker, not lifting the picture—until finally I was compelled to. I reached in—and as I turned it up and saw my father as a boy, in uniform, I bowed my head, then broke down weeping. I sobbed profoundly then and couldn't fully stop when I heard a noise behind me.

It was Johnny, and he came up to me without saying a word. He knew me from far, far back. He knew what this was about. He knew the writing on my wall. He knew about the deletions. He'd made a joke of me forever. But when he put his hand on my shoulder, it was very gentle. The way he took out my coat for me and replaced the picture and closed the door had in it, I know in my heart, all the grace of human kindness.

He told me, "You know more, Pete. The Doctor doesn't know shit compared to you. It'll be you who's gonna write a book someday. You're somebody the Coach can't figure. Come on." He got me up and steered me out of the low dark toward the door. Then he added with a smile, "Of course you'll lie on every page—give everybody the same shit you've always given yourself"—which got him laughing.

I felt better, so much better, though utterly confused, when I laughed with him. "Goddamn you," I said, laughing, as we walked out into the bright main corridor of the school.

But before we could really talk, he looked up and just said, "Gotta go" and left me—which may, though, have made it easier for me to join Allie and my father, who, I could see now through the main door window, were waiting to take me home.

But I couldn't for a second think of any of this in the kitchen. With the electricity humming closer and louder—loud as hell—I wrote Allie a quick note: "Had to get out for a while. Don't worry. I'll be back." I made my way down the back stairs of the apartment, avoiding, out of a perfect respect for the darkness that I was defying, the front staircase where Allie had raced down to meet me so long ago. But getting in the car again and driving made me think of the whole day—so I didn't dare turn the radio on. Yet I headed to where I wanted to head—I had to—and if my brain was too near exploding, I could see some first obscure illumination over the lake as I headed up Sheridan Road, across the harbor bridge under the now unlit Temple. I didn't dare to look long at the deep-shaded, misty park or at my mother's house or to think of anything specific now, at this point. My silence was a supplication—to the power that I was defying—for this moment of release. And the perfect sincerity and full reverence behind my prayer were, as it turned out, understood, and were enough—and they won me the time to get to Conlon's.

And when I got there, I could take simple comfort from the actual standing presence of an ordinary house near the Village Green, with a yard and a car parked in the driveway. It was all in truth that I wanted to do—just to see if it was there. I didn't gaze overlong at the house's features—if I couldn't help seeing that the front was the familiar face: the windows and doors like eyes and mouth—which didn't, however, shame me or make me afraid. And though I knew profoundly the enormity of what I was granted in that moment of release—just to see the house there—I actually thought also of what would from a normal point of view be regarded as the pitiful nature of such small satisfaction, and I began finally to shed tears for myself.

But crying, shaking my head back and forth, saying no to I didn't even understand what, I felt again that there was mercy for me and that I was even being given now some few rights. I could still think, quickly, that exactly this kind of confident notion might lead to some inconceivable dangerous happiness, and so I tried to suppress it. But some gentle granting of mercy let me continue to cry, as the sun came closer to rising. And the feeling that I had been granted some few rights didn't leave me, so that when I had flushed myself out with my crying and was able again to breathe properly, even comfortably, I looked at Conlon's house and thought, all the furies for the moment departed, that my recovery would not after all be beyond my truest patience. And remarkably nothing came after me for thinking this. So it seemed, importantly, that something at least was over and—I prayed as hard as I believed I could—that maybe the departing darkness had made some kind of peace with the arriving light.

6
ARMAGEDDON IN THE MIND

It wasn't only one night in hell. A number of nights that week, my fear was almost equally insane. But the third crazy midnight was not as bad as the first, and my confidence began to grow as the days passed. I needed little tests still as the week came to a close, but by Sunday I could stay home all night, and on Monday, with the second appointment the next morning, I had some confidence that I had gotten beyond at least one crucial point. I still could just sleep with Allie and not make love, but it was easier to hold her in my arms. I could talk to her a little, even in the dark, about how it was important for me—and I was allowed to recognize that it was important for me—to have this success in coming to a second appointment.

"It's not as if I've done anything, though," I said. "It's really because I haven't made a single move."

Allie was careful not to force any issue herself either, knowing, on the one hand, how important it is that we believe in the good of some work and in some successful action—but, on the other, that whether there'll be any good results can depend sometimes on our first doing absolutely nothing. Also if she had a dim feeling or two that she was expecting, her instincts might have told her not to expect too much. Her mother had tried for five years after a stillbirth, but had not been able to get pregnant—until adoption papers made her easy and Allie's brother Jim was conceived—which I think we all know is a surprisingly common story. Allie was also in a way getting pretty well prepared for all the patient, careful work that would come when her own daughter was born, as she tried very carefully, for me, not to force a thing.

"Just let things happen," she said. "Don't worry about watching over it. Just let it come."

But if she had a few happy suspicions about herself, she had a right to them; and I felt then, as I suspected dimly that a few good things might be going on in me as well, that it wasn't utterly wrong for me so to suspect.

And yesterday, I felt that there might be a chance for me here, on these pages. When Allie asked me how things were going, I complained again, bitterly. "It's a damned battle. You know, A, how much I don't want to do what I'm supposed to do. The unbelievable duty to reiterate that there's nothing except what late-twentieth-century philosophers say there is. Honest to God, to hell with that sermon! Poetry's either heaven or hell or a feeling of uneasiness that it's neither. Otherwise it oughta shut up and close shop. It's music—and if it's not extremist, what the hell is it? An expression of satisfaction with the ordinary? But maybe I feel now like I could inhabit the mental middle ground—I mean the place where we ordinarily live—without forgetting in complete idiot fashion about places a little farther back in the head."

"You mean the middle ground where you teach the poetry you say you can't read? And get paid for it so you can pay the mortgage on your current address, which you never mention?" She smiled. "I'd like to see it."

"I could have started a book back then," I said, "when I was crazy. And it would have been wild. But I never would have lived to finish it. So I know it's deadly crazy to *want* to be crazy."

"And you want to finish."

"I want to finish . . . in the place where . . . you know . . . I came out after I was crazy. I think . . . It's a hard place to find . . . but one understands there what the hell words mean."

Exactly when, however, and for what reason, my recovery really began (and the same can be said for the disease) is as difficult as anything to say. Alone now, I feel this, and feel how with no date and no cause, it's impossible to tell a story— to keep the soul afraid enough not to sleep. (And isn't sleep, honest to *God,* the problem above all others that our *ère de soupçon,* blinded by its own violent program, fails to consider?) It's as impossible for me, in fact, to keep things going with factitious notions as it is with no notions at all. But I shout this to keep the prod on—to get me to tell as much of the truth as I can and give my story as much life as I can— though the enterprise has certainly not been always honest— none *can* be—and has also been given over on a number of occasions for an easy stimulus from a dream of sleeping with Barbara.

But the birthdate of the subtle feeling of my possessing of some few rights, and of the first stirrings of a kind of revolution in me, can at least be set like a July Fourth—the night after the first time I saw Conlon. And with the events surrounding this July Fourth, my story has begun. I've wanted to say a prayer for this story, to entangle prayer with it, though I still can't really. If prayer is the heart of poetry beating in the body of the world—if it's both the blinded, kneeling silence of self-annihilation and the selfish roar of wide-eyed desire for things to go our way for a minute or an inch—then I can't do much more than name it in my sleep. But if I were ever to see Johnny again, I'd be ashamed even to complain. I can hear him say, "You call praying a natural state of mind. But you're a liar. There's no such thing."

On the morning of the second appointment, a considerable amount of the park's elm-yellow was gone. As I drove up one of the crests on the Drive, looking ahead to the city, I saw not much in the long miles of fields that disturbed a community of dull gray and brown—with the undifferentiated mass of the lake reflecting the low gray sky and the buildings on the Gold Coast quiet in the gray light and rain. Nothing was announcing itself—no horns, no speeders—and I listened to a soft music that made no significant protest against the monotony. But beginning to understand maybe, in some very secret place, the quality of joy in complete patience, I had no objections. If the rain made me think some and turn on my lights, I forgot almost completely the distances between me and everyone around me. I saw the nameless Indian signaling peace at the Traps, and even as I remembered the sounds of target-shooting guns, I didn't cringe. That someone would say peace or that someone else would shatter targets with guns didn't hurt me. Perhaps my pitiful need for a secured identity made fewer demands where there were no bright colors, no lines drawn and there wasn't any war.

So I wasn't worried, as I headed off the Michigan Avenue exit and into the shadows of the huge buildings—all truncated by a wide fog up in the air—that the sound of the occasional light thunder would set anything off in me. As, some minutes later, I walked through a clean office-building lobby, porcelain-tiled, pushed number 29 on the elevator, and then watched the lights come on with that good steadiness between the floors, I was afraid—but miraculously less afraid than when I went up the week before. In the waiting room, listening for someone to signal to me that it was my time, I could very nearly give hard consideration to the number of differences between this week and last.

I had no statement now. Yet I wasn't worried that I'd have nothing to say. I was ready to speak openly with Conlon about all that had happened since I last saw him, and I didn't care exactly how we proceeded. It would just move along the way it would; though I thought, while I read a news magazine, of Johnny and his dad, and me and my dad in the bowl. Then I heard the inner door open, and I saw someone walking out, and I was ashamed—but I didn't hide myself and through the silence of the ten-minute interval could keep my eyes on the page.

Then Conlon stood in the doorway. He was—right there—the same man; and I felt now that the ordinariness of his round face, the thinness of his hair, the barely traceable touch of city in his voice, the slight age-color and slightly turned alignment of his teeth, and all the things that my eyes and ears had gone after before, were not now dangers to me. And he didn't have to check any card to see who I was. He looked at me and said, "Peter," and signaled for me to come in and have a seat—all of which was powerfully relieving because I did have at least one new fear: that our memories might fail and that it might not seem at all as though we were picking up at the same place where we'd left off, or even that we'd met before.

We sat down in the beige room (lit with an overhead light to help the window on this grayer day). He said, "Let me guess. A number of absolutely terrible days since last week. All week you wondered who the hell I was and what possibly I was gonna do for you now that it's gotten down to it."

This was a good start. I felt so without any miserable reaction, or even much of a suspicion of one—though I didn't lose respect at all for my danger.

I said right out, though I knew that it might worry or bother him, "The first night, around dawn, I searched the phone book crazily for your name. When I found it, I went to your house, just to see it. I'm sorry. Two other nights I had to get out, just to see if buildings were still up."

He said, "There might be times when you'll have to call me. I don't think you'll feel the need as much now—but I don't want you to worry about it or be ashamed of it."

This made me feel very good—and again without a reaction, or a threat of a feeling of one.

I said that still it was things like the presence and endurance of the construction of houses that I wanted to see. "Just to know if things were there and standing."

He asked me if at any point during the week I had "gotten closer to believing rather than just fearing that construction like this couldn't stand up." He asked me if I could always still "judge the fear." This made me feel all right about his memory of me, and about the possibilities of our picking up things where we'd left off. It made me feel all right enough to begin slightly to forget how much I needed memory and continuity.

I said, "I think the difference between fearing and believing must be great—even when the distance between the two gets extremely short." Then—as honestly as I could—"But I was more afraid of how close I was getting that first night after I saw you than I've ever been. . . . But I think . . . that the closer I came, the more clearly I knew how significant the difference is . . . and how wonderful the force must be which preserves that difference. So yes—I could still judge the fear. Maybe better this week than ever. And—if I don't want to presume—if I God Almighty promise I don't want to presume—I think this all came down after I saw you because my coming to you, in itself, was even better calculated than I suspected for making me find out really who I am."

"Tell me more about what coming here means to you. Do you think you know now what you're looking for?"

"It sure as hell's not simple," I said. I was still afraid to do it, but I was sure that I could speak of that exact location, that zone between living and dying, and of the war in me that made it the only safe place.

I said, "It's not just that I'm seeking to preserve myself. I want to get torn apart almost as much as I want to get saved. I've got this feeling that if my doctor stands for what I stand for, that that only makes two liars. But it's because I want so goddamned much to stay alive that I want to get taken apart. I want, just like everybody else I guess, but with this intensity I sure as hell have never known before, to stay the same *forever*—or at least for some part of me to stay the same. Yet at the same time—and I know all this is unremarkable and old, but I feel it like a raging war in my head—I want to be relieved of every false hope I've got.

"I think sometimes that a baggage of false hopes is about the whole makeup of my life. Yet when I begin to strip myself down, I become murderous in my self-defense. And honestly I hope that you'll stop me from defending myself in some harmful, crazy way, but at the same time that you'll tell me that it's OK—that it's OK to have a set of hopes, especially hopes like mine, because when my hopes are stripped down—I want you to tell me—they have the look of essential sanity. So—and I swear to you I'm letting out an absolutely dangerous secret—I want you to be a good authority for me.

"I've gotten incredibly angry—I think you've seen this—just thinking about people who spew out crap like 'Maturity means living completely without authority.' Only fortunate fucking babies, I want to say, who have no goddamned idea how much authority they live under all the time, could spout crap like this. Let me think of it—I caught a little item the other day from one of today's gospels. Something like 'The search for coherence is a disastrous and cowardly defense against the nothingness that alone exists.' That's *the* religion. I swear there's only one way a statement like that could be made. *Ex cathedra* from the mental easy chair. By somebody who knows nothing about the nothingness and even less about disaster or the nature of self-defense."

"And you *do*—and you're proud of it—like the war veteran?"

"Yes—but then I think—or all the time I think—of things like the unbelievable shame of our political behavior—trying to spread America all over the world—or of the possibility, or fucking likelihood, that it's the mind's desire for authority that sets me up in the first place for all this fear about how much time I've got and about safe distances. I think I'm an expert on this possibility, or call it a probability—that is, that I am where I am exactly because I don't agree with that fool. Then with all this damned false-American world-kingdom shit I'll start thinking maybe of the Buddhist monks in Vietnam and really honest to God believe—believe in tears—things like the only authority is an incinerating fire. I know that it might seem staged or something. But the two sides in this controversy are goin' at it in my head like Armageddon. And I'm praying for peace every second of every minute."

"You want, though, to win the battle especially against people who from your perspective are making facile statements about nothingness. Your very painful experience is a matter of pride. It makes you think you know something they don't."

"Definitely right. Even worse, it makes me feel like I know something I'm *happy* to know. But I swear—I mean—I went to Johnny to get a recommendation for a doctor—and this was the second time. He recommended a doctor to me once before—for my father—and it was a doctor who only found out for us that there was no point in hoping. It's as if I was seeking safety, when I went to Johnny again, as if I thought he'd send me to somebody who'd get me to dissociate myself from my kind of hopefulness."

"So you do listen to voices that say 'Tear yourself apart.' "

"Honestly—although I'm really praying like crazy for the exact opposite result. And with Johnny it has always been as if I were the damned Bible, or Aristotle or something, and he's this Darwin who kills me. But he's got the truth. I mean that's not that far off—I go to Johnny just as some people have gone enthusiastically (which is fucking incredible to me) to the idea that the entire movement of life's past and future is random— as if somewhere there *were* still a dangerous authority left to kill! But for me it's like this conscientious quest against my grain. But I do it. I do it."

"And strong Johnny had the truth about your father, and his cancer. Have you ever wanted to be Johnny? Ever gotten angry, say, about people who spew out crap about healing?"

"If you want to know, I'll tell you. First—and I never would have said this last week, I promise—I hate to death the look of any Freudian shit, even though there's maybe a hell of a lot to it, because it makes me scared you've just been reading a book. And second, I've wanted to be Johnny in some senses all my life. And third"—and I was rolling a bit crazy now—"I whispered in my wife's ear the other night, as we were making love, that she could make me Johnny if she wanted to. She was shaking her head no, but she came as I said it over to her a number of times—which I think makes her pretty much like me—only not as crazy. And fourth . . . But this is a story. It'll take a few minutes—or maybe a lifetime."

He smiled. "Go ahead, short version first."

I smiled—but stopped; a sudden terrible emotion would have brought me to tears if I hadn't fought it. I was ashamed—because I was thinking that this story might *be something,* which also made me afraid—afraid that I could think this. But I began. "Across the lake, there used to be a park—an amusement park—called Silver Beach—in St. Joe, at the mouth of the river. We went sometimes in the summer.

"One time Johnny and his father were with us. We'd tried about all the rides. Then we were in the fun house—where one of the rides was a huge bowl that seated on the rim I don't know how many people, maybe two hundred, and that spun— once everyone was seated around the rim—so fast that almost no one could move off it—though a lot of people would try maybe to turn their bodies or limbs in odd ways."

I stopped. I could go on only with my voice dropped low—just above a whisper.

"The ones strong enough, who could get free of the rim, and fight their way to the center—they could enjoy it out there—on this flat circular plateau. But, you see, the victory was never easy—because there were always more strong guys out there than the little circle in the center could hold. So there was a game . . ."—I used a finger to dry my fool eyes— ". . . this game . . . called King of the World—trying to win and hold that place.

". . . We sat next to each other on the rim—Johnny and his dad, and my dad and I. It had been such a fun day. We were all happy and laughing. Even Johnny's dad—and he was a mean man, I can tell you. When the bowl started spinning we were all laughing."

Suddenly something almost amusing occurred to me, but I put my hand on my brow to keep the light from my face.

"Johnny and I—we were maybe ten years old—we couldn't move at all. The thing started whirling like hell. But then my dad—he just *took* me under his arm and started to make his way off the wall. I was this little Ascanius, and my dad, by God, was off to found Rome!" I asked him, "You know what I mean?"

He laughed. "Yes. But remember, just the short version."

This made me laugh now too, so I wouldn't cry. I said, *"No way* he wouldn't be King of the World! There were tough customers there—military guys and young hard guys trying to show their girls. *Lots* of 'em. But no way. We took the center. My father with one arm sent every one of 'em flyin' back to hell and gone. He literally hurled them. And I would have loved it, except for the fact that Johnny, with this look in his eye, started coming out. Then his dad took him under his arm. I can see the veins in his dad's neck and Johnny holding on to him as they moved out. They came up right to the rim of the plateau, and looked up, and tried to get up on it. They were struggling. But my father with one hand and this huge laugh, sent the two of them whirling off into outer space, awkward, like all the others. I can still hear it. I can still hear my dad laughing and roaring in my ear—'How does it feel—to be the King of the World!' I can hear it, and sometimes it does this to me—just makes me cry. I don't know. I'm not sure I even want to know what all it means. The shame. Shame and pity. So let it be. The damned fool tears may help you see that I'm not lying anyhow."

He waited and smiled. Then—"So in this heaven on earth, where it's perfectly still, and things don't change, and no one gets to you or touches you, it's more frightening than hell."

I said, "Well put," and laughed, as my finger trembled at my eye.

"So the answer to your father's question about how it feels is 'Not So Good.' "

"The answer to the question is not so simple—not so simple." I breathed, now that I was delivered of this story, a full breath of relief. "Jesus—the other night when I was hitting a freak-out point, I thought that even if you were his friend, you really weren't like Lemaster. I felt like I'd been let out of a torture chamber—that you were his friend but weren't like him. So the hell with him. The serious deadly hell with him."

"So we have a Lemaster who has a strength that you admire but also despise. Excuse the Freudian cliché—but how would you say that for you Lemaster and your father are most importantly different? I'm asking this because I still want to know why, in what sense, it's Armageddon in your head."

"If I thought that Johnny were anywhere moved by love, I swear I'd be terribly uneasy about there being any truth or strength anywhere—the last true man gone!—though I'd be happy, triumphantly and dangerously happy. I'd think that everything had gone soft—but that this was good. He means, sometimes, that to me. My father, on the other hand, was a very loving man. But he could show me the terrible distorting power in desire. He believed in his America, his religion, et cetera. He could be ferocious. But he could also be what Lemaster, I think, could never be. He made me believe in love—which I think sometimes may be why I'm here! Lemaster sure as hell isn't!"

"So Lemaster keeps safe for you the things you value—by destroying them before you destroy them with too large an investment of hope."

"Yes. But more, I think of my father, who hoped for so many of the things that I hoped for, as standing at ground level for what has *got* to be true. But because what he hoped for and I hope for about where the world is going, what life's for, what's good, might *not* be true, and because saying that it *is* true might be what? a Disastrous and Cowardly Defense Against the Nothing That Alone Exists—I turn to Johnny."

"So it isn't just anything Johnny destroys. It's what? The things you're certain are essential for life. You don't think your sense of how the world moves is an option—just as it's not an option to live in a building you don't believe in."

"Yes. But I turn to Johnny again also because my father really did show me how distorting and violent desire can be. We came to blows once over Vietnam. It was brutal—one of the worst days I can remember—if there were also things about it that were extremely good. Because after terrible experiences of fear I get a feeling of conviction."

"Like the veteran who knows . . ."

"Yes. I believe more fully then, when the world is falling apart, that everything that my father and I hoped for has *absolutely* got to be true—true, or this Nothing that some people think they know so goddamned much about might win a battle they couldn't even guess the seriousness of."

"Your experience is more real than their thoughts and words."

"Yes. When the world is falling, I'm even more convinced, in fact, by myself than I am by Johnny. Sometimes I see him as really just ignorant and lucky."

"Doesn't appreciate the terrible fragility of being."

"No. And he'd hate what I'm about to say. And I feel miserable saying it. But I believe that I at least understand, when the world is trembling, what others have said about powers or gods, or that I get religious, or have at least a sense of the sacred and possibly miraculous—although I'd be afraid to say God's name in a final and complete manner—just as a nihilist should be afraid, I'm sure, of a final and complete commitment to his dear nothing."

"Probably so."

"But I still respect these people too and constantly and reverently repeat them, and so say things that I wish weren't true, because of how much they may know after all about what is true and what isn't—and also, when I've been afraid, I've made promises to something like a *god* of nothingness as sincere as any I've ever sworn. I expect that some of them are promises I'll keep forever—though I take a dangerous delight in imaginary scenes in which I cut in pieces the new hero, who believes in the 'nothing that alone exists,' with questions about whether he ever really believed for a fucking second that the world isn't going to stand. But the hopes are so painful as well as comforting. And God knows how my father and I fought over Vietnam."

"But maybe it's pretty tough, Peter, to go after your father when you and your father are so much the same." Then he smiled, and stretched against the window, breaking the tension for us. "Of course it's also tough not to, when you're so different."

I sat up straight and breathed deeply. "You got it. The story of my life. Or at least part of it. You didn't see Lemaster this week, did ya?"

"I did."

"He tell ya about what happened the other night when we were out together?"

"He said he was bored to death with Barbara and that you and your wife were a large relief."

I tried to calculate the truth—or lack of it—in this. "He tell ya we almost got into a fight?"

"He said he had a few too many and that he maybe said some things."

"I asked him where you lived and he amused himself by telling me you lived in a kind of modern analytical insane asylum, which, I should have told him, would be habitable only for people utterly incapable of going insane—like philosophers, and other bloodless types. Then I asked him why he ever decided to become a doctor. He told me he liked to see the difference between what people hope for and what they get!"

"He told me he said things he couldn't understand his reason for saying. He said there was something about you that made him say things."

"I think sometimes I'd like to kill the son of a bitch."

"It sounds like sometimes he might deserve it."

"But he doesn't give you shit like this."

"He doesn't, but I could see where he might."

"If you told me it was OK to hate the bastard, with all my heart I'd feel again like I just got out of a torture chamber—but it would make me scared because—Jesus—I don't want to be talking to myself here, hearing you say just what I want. But what do you think of him? He's your friend, too."

Conlon put his elbow on his desk, and rested his head in his hand, and stared thoughtfully at the floor. "I think . . . that in several respects he's not what you think he is. He's maybe a good deal more compassionate and vulnerable. He might have a drinking problem. I'm worried about him. How's that?"

But now I was hearing, from someone whom I had for my

life to believe in, that maybe Johnny wasn't the fountain of pure energy I'd always thought he was. Of course I suspected that he was never free of troubles. But I didn't want to hear that. And I can say now that although I don't know what's happened to him in the thirteen years since he left for California, I prefer, at least half the time, to think of him still as someone who not only would never cry for me but would always laugh right out at everything I needed to take seriously. I wouldn't mind it either if Johnny had an irreverent story about what's happened over the years to Conlon.

"But really, why?" Allie has asked me, "why do you court this kind of pain? Or why not think of laughing in *his* face?"

"No," I said. "That wouldn't work. It just wouldn't work. Something in me still can't laugh at what he says. Can't ever, maybe."

And the moment Conlon said that he was worried about Johnny, I asked a question that brought us to what a part of me will always say is the real authoritative Lemaster. I asked him, "Honestly, did he never even mention to you that he was a wrestler?"

"Never. I was surprised when you mentioned it—though certainly I can see it."

"He was the best I've ever seen."

"Is it that that makes him so formidable in your mind? Why do you suppose this matters to you as much as it seems to?"

I thought a moment. "It's the need to see that the things that you hope are right, and good, have some kind of championship power. Wrestling was something like sin and death for me. I never thought of it like that when I was in it. But I knew that for me winning was some vindication of everything that I had decided on, or identified with; and that losing wasn't just seeing the match go, but everything that I believed in, or everything that I was."

"So you're talking about something like original sin— some kind of deadly hyperawareness of who you are."

"Exactly. I'd always been self-conscious, but after my losses I began, as I've said, to lose energy. Grace. I'd say the fear of the loss of safe distances between me and things that could come down on me and hurt me, like buildings, rooms—began *then*—and that the clock began to tick for me then, or tick for me in such a way that I could hear it.

"When things were at their worst the other night, that wrestling match was haunting my mind. I can't describe how much I'd put into that thing. It was the largest, most dangerous emotional investment of my life. And then there was Johnny, who first announced that he didn't believe in God when he was ten, or anything else when he was eleven—not just winning but winning with an ease and power that made me envy his entire life, *including* his upbringing."

"He's the wicked one who prospers. And this makes you wonder about how anything is energized—or given grace."

"Yeah. But you've also given me this stuff that I don't want to hear—about how he may not be prospering. I've had my own suspicions about this and I hate my goddamned suspicions. His greatness—and I have sobbed thinking of *it* too—the courage and the beauty and grace—has always made me utterly ashamed of myself for entertaining any such comfortable notions about him. But now that it's all brought up, I guess I could say that I believe Johnny and I are both like half-sons of my father."

"Yes."

"But never more than half. I always had the place, and he always had the power to hold that place against the world. Neither of us ever got what he always needed, or thought enough of what he already had. But I can hear Johnny, if he ever heard this, telling me to drop dead—and laughing while he says it. And if I hate him for that, I love him and respect him, even at the cost of my precious life.

"But when I think of how he said to me in the last moments before that match that there are no important days, and I think of how important certain days have become to me now—the day I first came to see you, today when I've come to see you again—and so many others, the day of my marriage, the day my father died—I want to say to him that I've had a successful beginning now and that I want to see it move to a successful end and that I don't need to give over to him my precious *life,* no matter how guilty it may be for me to hang on to it. Saying that there are no important days may be the right thing to do when you're not down to it, when you're trying just to relax, or just playing philosophical games. But when you are down to it, saying that there are no important days isn't the right thing to do at all—I promise to God."

"Saying, you mean, that no particular results should be expected—that no particular day marks the beginning of a change for the better?"

"Yeah—that—and . . . well—while I can't pretend to know what level of experience is most valid, I do know that there are very different levels and that there's one where all I've ever hoped for—regarding the possibility of healing in me and in the world and the absolute worth of that possibility—must be true, and statements must be point by point false which suggest things like the desire for coherence is a cowardly defense against the nothing. I mean it. I mean what I goddamned say."

"You recognize a danger for you, though, in making statements like the ones you're making. Do you think that you're placing yourself in jeopardy saying these things now? I don't want you to misunderstand me. I don't think there's any reason for being afraid to make them. I think in fact that what you're going after is the discovery of all that's unnecessary in your suffering. It should, after all, be perfectly possible for you to entertain the kinds of thoughts and counter-thoughts you do entertain without feeling that you're on the battlefield at Armageddon. Your thoughts ought to be able to come out as art, maybe, or good philosophy—if you can forgive my saying so—and not degenerate to mere games. The feelings, yes. But the suffering, no.

"But you have these figures in your life whom you think you have to imitate or outdo at their own games. Did you ever think that it's not necessarily your business to be a great athlete or a great heroic preserver of the traditional good or a great *diablo?* Because you're not any of these things, you're afraid the world is falling down around you. Did you ever think that the world could be more yours if you entered it as yourself?"

I nodded and half-smiled.

"You don't have to be a saint. And you don't have to be a sinner. Maybe what you're best at is seeing the worth of both sides. I don't think an equitable mind is necessarily paralyzed either. Nor do I think it's necessary to be in the state you're in to be religious—even if you're after sainthood—just as I don't think that Shakespeare had to go mad to find out what King Lear was or Macbeth was. And I sure as hell don't think you owe your life to your father or your friend. Also I don't think your hopes are unhealthy—just so long as they're not inappropriate. I have a feeling that you just may not have been the best wrestler around—exactly in the way you're not blond, or six feet eight—and that it probably wasn't the best idea for you to hope to be. It's a good idea, Peter, not to forget the destructive power of unrealistic expectations. It's better, too, to start with love or passionate interest rather than guilt or a desperate feeling that you have to get yourself right."

"I like to hear you say these things. I say 'em to myself sometimes—especially the stuff about the wrestling. It never helps enough, though, just to hear yourself."

But as I looked at Conlon in the even light against his window, I suddenly took crazy advantage of the more relaxed feeling I had, and said, "Really though, too—and I say this even as I agree with what you say—I think of the wrestling as being so much like life, and so not one of those things about which you can say, well, I'm simply not good at it. I can think too of my father's cancer as this death-machine that just didn't get dismantled in time. I think of the time thing, and the pressure, the urgency, getting to the *right* place *when,* which associates for me with my situation now. Have I gotten here on time? And here, I'm starting with guilt, I'm sure, and with the desperate feeling that I've got to get myself *right.* I don't want to end up lost to the world, repudiating doctors, the way my father did when it was too late. I don't want it to be too late for my life—though just saying these words could get me back into an adventure that I've begged God to bring to an end."

Conlon was now bending and unbending a silvery paper clip. Was he frustrated? Angered? I meant only to tell him what I felt. "About Johnny and my father: I couldn't talk about either of them last time. It would have put too much fuel on the fire. Everybody has heroes. They're my heroes. Maybe all that I've learned is that nobody should have heroes. But I can't believe that. I can't believe that somehow it isn't good for me to have this passionate admiration for my father, who was decorated fighting for his country. And then for Johnny, who'd never fight for any cause but who does just as much to make my admiration profound—even while he's splitting me in two. I don't know, maybe it's my job to go crazy for a while—not stay sane like them—so I can feel things enough to tell the story. Maybe that's my basic task, to go crazy and tell a tale—to rediscover poetry for myself. How else in Chicago— the city that's like the world after God died? Really, how in hell else can a good little North Shore boy—no wall, no windy plain, no burning ships—who never went anywhere or heard a shot, do it except by going mad? Only, Christ, just saying that this is my Vietnam makes my mind scream, remembering that I *can't* lose, any more than I can pretend at this moment to win."

"When you say story? Tell me."

"I mean basically my own success story—here—although I can't allow myself to cheat on the story line—or on what makes the story go—which makes me think, God Almighty, of Barbara. You say you know her."

"I do."

"Bored by her?"

"Not exactly."

"Me neither. As a matter of fact—Jesus—I can't believe I forgot to mention this. In my head I had her in my arms the other night while I was telling Allie she could make me Johnny. So it was perfect—the two of us turned on by some-thing completely different from what we'd chosen. Another old story, I guess. But, honest to God, against Barbara, and all that kind of stuff, I want my marriage. Just as I want the end of this disease. But this disease I swear *wants* to stop my marriage—I mean the way it sometimes won't even let me hold Allie in my arms, or listen to anything she says to help heal me. It's incredible. But it's not as bad as it was a week ago."

But now Conlon had to smile at me—and looked at his watch to show me that we had only a few minutes left. "Do you want some parting words?"

"You bet."

"Come on home from the war. There's only so much that anybody needs to see. You've won your way home and you don't need to stay on. You can go *home*. You don't need to repudiate your choices. I've heard your wife's a very fine and beautiful woman. Go home to her. Your life isn't wrong and it isn't small. I'll grant you that your hypersensitivity has made it what it is—for better or for worse—but now you can say to yourself that for better or for worse it's been remarkable enough—and, yes, remarkable for its courage. And if I'm telling you things that you do want to hear, you don't have to be afraid that for that reason these things have got to be suspect. Such a fine story and image. You in the bowl in your father's arms, the question. I'll remember them. But don't let poetry tear you apart."

I smiled and took a deep breath and felt embarrassed as I stood to go—as if I were being given a medal. But significantly (though any compliment on any story I've ever told is immediately painful and disturbing for me), far down in, I felt very good, and wasn't afraid—even as I saw lightning and heard thunder crack and shatter the atmosphere—that I was completely undeserving of my medal, or that I had no guaranteed right at all to my recovery. And when I left Conlon, I even thought I could go home—though I knew it would be some fair long time before I got there.

7
PRESERVING THE UNION

To be told there was nothing wrong with heading home again was—no question—more good than not. Yet with the light rain still falling and that occasional thunder, although it was maybe moving away now, I had to think some again and turn on my headlights. As I pulled onto the Michigan Avenue entrance and had to watch the varying distances between all the others out there and myself, I was, if only very briefly, thinking how one short hour's reprieve had a week ago brought on nearly unendurable division and pain.

But when I was out moving again on the Drive (where, with the changing weather, the presence and absence of objects will alternate so spectacularly that no one who takes it, summer mornings to winter nights, could fail to be impressed—even to the depth where his dreams are born), it was once more just that dull gray everywhere, with distinctions so soft that there was no lake or sky, and in the light rain thinning now to mist, only a very quiet spread of gray-brown park.

So all the varying distances began not to matter again, and I forgot even to turn on the radio for any right kind of sound. I thought then, too, that the second appointment had been made and kept and a third made—and was able safely to consider myself as situated in a good spot: having to depend on the kindness of somebody not myself, and believing in him and finding him compassionate.

I saw myself then as a long way, almost at an opposite end, from any kind of sainthood, not having, like saints, to get rid of the world, but, with the world completely loosed or exploded on me, having instead to get it back tight again. But I could figure that the very careful, nonstop prayer which I prayed in silence for the success of my doctor, for me, was maybe as acceptable as any wild thanks of an ecstatic, and that what wisdom I had about the saints themselves needing some measure of safety and self-love might not be worthless.

But now too just driving easily in the rain was worth about as much as all that possible wisdom; and when I saw the exit sign for North Avenue, Lincoln Park, I simply got off, just looking maybe for an easy drift through the winding in-park streets, which at that hour would be close to empty. It was very good to forget, too, as I did some then, that I had my damned life to save—or how a few days before, I had almost lost it. And I drifted along for some time, since I really could just sail over the near-empty drives, colorless then, under the wet, bare elms, and with only a few brown leaves, now sodden, in the gutters. I didn't need to see much, so I turned the wipers off and let the mist just gather on the windshield.

After a time, though, when the rain stopped, I did pull over, at the far south end of the park, on a quiet street of city mansions, behind the Cardinal's. I sat back, breathing, without fearing that I might later be unable to breathe, or fearing either to look or not look at the beautiful, dangerous mansions (as in night-panic I'd had at times immediately either to open or close my eyes). I got out and began to walk and taste the cool, moist air. I felt too, with growing confidence, that I still had a right to think about all the comforting differences between this week and last. Also I couldn't be accused of abusing such a right, as it was only for moments that I thought about these differences. But my consideration of them still made the walk good.

Then the walk became a search. After a turn suddenly familiar from years back, I was *looking* for something as I kept on walking in the softening mist. And in a moment, it was there in front of me. In a cleared ground stretching out past the still green lawn of the Museum of the Historical Society, erect, with a foot stepping out over the statue block, the great wrestler's body of Abraham Lincoln was a solid dark mass, an unforgettable black sublimity against the open gray sky-lake beyond. Maybe the name had stopped me when I saw the sign out on the Drive. Whatever, though, had gotten me there, I was instantly ready—to see this monument. I wanted in a boyish way immediately, almost unmindful of any threat, to say that the things that we don't forget about him, about Abraham Lincoln, the things that we make stories about—the fanatic honesty, the mystic desire to preserve the Union—were *any day* as tough in the center as the unkillable germ of sick fear!

And right now, this second, as I say this, I think I understand maybe how it was safe, and even how it struck me as miraculous that it could be as safe as it was, to feel the admiration I felt in the second I got up to that body: the human figure staring ahead, concentrated, wearing the three-quarter-length coat and vest and watch-chain of the time, walking from the presidential chair with its eagle-winged back and the raised *e pluribus unum*—the kinds of things which at that time, with Vietnam still raging in the brain, could by themselves make me too afraid to say a word.

"And that was it, A," I've said to her now. "I felt the freedom to love these things come like a miracle. I mean it—miracle. This was the thing—that it was incredible to me just that I was safe enough to do something like love a man and a country."

"I remember you coming home that day—telling me you were glad you didn't get caught."

"It was such an amazing feeling, just being able to admire something—anything."

But I stood there, on the wet green lawn, *not* angry and patriotic—rather now almost begging for the completest simplicity. Or to be able just to say maybe that it was better that men like this sometimes walked out against the gray and were heard over the world's noise. I say this even though I haven't lost any measure of respect either for the idea (and I remember putting it to myself exactly this way at the time, as I read the famous words of his address on one of the memorial globes which punctuate the ends of the wide half oval that embraces him: the stone enclosing wall cut with his name, birthdate, and death date) that it might always have been better for any nation conceived in any way and dedicated to any proposition whatsoever never to have been born at all.

And—this second—I come near to tears, recalling how with no one around but a poor sleeping homeless drunk, prostrate, wet on the stone bench that runs under the name and dates, I began so quickly, seemingly unprovoked, to cry like some kind of fool in that park, standing before that figure. I was sure, as I haven't been in years, that nobody had any business existing anywhere, and *because* of this I believed all the more passionately that Lincoln belonged right where he was—in that place against the sky and lake.

I knew I was getting dangerously incautious again, in this mist, with only quiet thunder; and immediately I sensed the need for more careful restraint. But I had not indulged any dangerous, stupid victorious patriotism. I could still believe too that there was nothing wrong, or punishable, in my letting come that beautiful release that now continued more fully as I cried, thinking about Lincoln and the things for which he stood. Not throwing caution to the winds, then, I nonetheless felt safe speechifying, crying in a mumble for nobody, that he was the one who taught us how to count—trying to make eighty-seven years sound like a long time. I thought out loud too, in a kind of choking passion for the benefit of the gray park and the poor drunk sleeper on the bench, that he might have been the only one ever in the presidential office (because he was a damned poet and maybe the saddest ever there—and only healthy men are now electable, God Almighty help us) who had any idea how long that time really was, eighty-seven years, or how pitifully short, or what a goddamned inch is or a mile is or an hour is when you're stuck out and getting tested in the world.

As miraculously safe as I still did feel too, I believed I could whisper that there was somewhere an America worthy of unmeasurable, inconceivable devotion, as he said. Of course—Jesus—of course any number of things could be said against him. But this is, I know, where I was. I was thinking in tears, like a fool, that just as you've got absolutely at some point to leave your mind alone, you've got also to be able to say with conviction, down near the inch, that there is honest greatness—either that or put the bullet in your own head. And I knew that I had to maintain an inconceivable devotion to something somewhere myself, with my head as close as it was to being torn apart.

There had to be for me some uncut simplicity. Down in, I had to have my name and an extraordinarily simple home, and for minute after minute in this place to extend my identity in an uninterrupted line—my little Biblical generations. I needed the news there to suggest with some real regularity that time was on the side of my mind's little country. There couldn't be gaps there, no breaking of the devotion that might begin some godforsaken analytical discussion of my simplicity. 'And in that faith let us to the end dare to do' and 'Malice toward none' and 'With firmness in the right as God gives us to see'—I *couldn't* laugh at this stuff. I had to have this, myself. I had to have this without laughing.

Yesterday, as I recalled some of this to her, Allie said to me, "I say things to you, Peter, about your happiness—to try to keep you safe. I believe you can learn as much from happiness as from anything else. But I know that getting to the word 'miracle' isn't as easy as just listening to it."

"You know," I said, "that I'd rather die than say that words—that any words I say—are really incomprehensible this side of pain. That all I had for learning was my experience and not my mind and my goddamned soul. Or why not just murder somebody to find out what that little word means? But getting to the word 'miracle' isn't as easy as just saying it, either."

When I got back to the car, I let my head sink to the steering wheel and, with my face and mouth now distorted against the wheel, was sure that my mostly accidental pilgrimage in the rain, this drift toward a memorial figure in a park, would be forgiven. It had to be forgiven, because this need for a country in the mind is nothing other than life. I was convinced of this, despite the dangerous, beautiful mansions, with their trimmed, dark green ivy glistening in the mist.

But I was at a point where I could every bit as easily turn and rediscover my anger at the simplicity of my father on certain matters. And I mean to suggest, when I say *every bit* as easily, the same feeling of safety from punishment, and to get it clear that this immunity, just like the remarkable freedom to be simply patriotic, hadn't yet degenerated into a healthy stupidity.

With just enough health, then, I could, and perhaps in the same way can now, turn and disregard all his night missions over Germany (and I can see now the beacons peering into the dark as eyes for the Luftwaffe, and hear sirens and roaring antiaircraft guns; and see the flames of falling American planes) which must have had hours of supreme simple righteous devotion and which were arguably as necessary as anything I ever had to do—even when my world was so far torn apart that I was completely in need.

When I was still younger—sophomore and junior years of college—before I knew what it meant to have to be completely self-defensive *as well as* utterly self-denying—I could easily forget about what he did, the remarkable number of flights. I could say things to broaden "the generation gap." I could tell him he was finished and feel as if I were doing him some good. "If it kills you," I said once, "that I'm not you, then you might think how if there's anything sacred at all, it comes only before values like yours assume the damned throne, or after they leave it."

Of course I was really doing all this to myself—and was continuing under the mansions to do it to myself, sickly, even as I needed as much as ever to leave myself alone, to let the gaps heal and go home. But miraculously, in the car, in the returning rain, I felt that I could safely think of my father gone, of America gone, of my self gone.

And as I felt so safe, I just went on and started thinking about that Christmas dinner, four years before, in '68, when my father and I actually began to shout and then push each other, take up our fists. It was unbelievable. It was, that night, as if I were a sickness myself. I went after him like a cancer. And again, in the car, I was like a disease in the way I now contemplated that time, tearing myself apart as well. So I couldn't say much about Johnny as I sat there, wanting so much to observe the differences between what people hope for and what they get (between what I hoped for and what I got)—even as I needed for there to be somewhere, safe inside the last fraction of an inch of my sanity, exactly that perfect righteousness and that inconceivable devotion to an unquestionable good which made possible what my father did in night flight after night flight. ("But for the love," Johnny once said, "of nothing. Or for the few faces in the same plane—for that hour. That's all.")

Yet *because* things were getting better, I could be a disease. Because the differences between this week and last were not discouraging—because they put difference on my side—I could afford to be religious.

The one rumor, though, that I've heard about Johnny since he left for California—that he never got married, never had any children—reminds me that I'm writing primarily for people who at least have to think like mothers and fathers, that is, who absolutely cannot afford, when it gets down to it, to think that life has no story or that if it has one it's a bitter farce. And if I could send my father to hell during the Vietnam years and send myself toward some perfect zero of annihilation, I was and probably always will be, for better or worse, more of a patriot than a saint.

But I could see us that Christmas around the main table, run out to fourteen feet for well over twenty people, which my mother and my grandmother and aunts had worked on all day—with the tremendous carved birds and the nice eye-catching spread of all kinds of other meats—ham, beef—just hot—and the gravy boats and bowls of red cranberry with hot bread and yellow-white butter, and all the colors of the vegetables; and everyone reaching and getting what he or she wanted, two, three times, or however many more it took to get ridiculously over-full.

And a feeling of what I can call true honest communion came with this completely unashamed show of prosperity, this good fat unashamed wealth, which nobody, no matter what the damned point in time, or how old he was, said a single word against. The drinking was good too; so sadness was off. And although the noise was constant, there was all along a kind of wonderful rhythm in it: conversation, good talk, exploding laughter, and then quieter new beginnings. And always more of the same. So it was beautiful Christmas—no matter what else. And we were all along in one of those places where—again I hope we can claim—we learn something that's more important than what we learn when the conditions aren't the same.

But then, Christ, an old story too—after a number of hours we'd maybe just gone too long—so someone had to say something about the war that started a whole new thing going. Right away then the give and take wasn't what it was—that was Vietnam—and some of us began sort of sizing each other up. And in the car too, in the shadow of the soul-killing, frightening satisfactoriness of those beautiful, high mansions, I felt a kind of religious anger again, or as much of it as I could, given the fact that I was hanging much closer to an actual nothingness than I had been back then, when I was still just furiously playing games.

I answered my uncle, who'd said, "The only thing wrong with the war is that we're just not winning it," that "It wouldn't kill us to lose one"—which caught my father's attention and had my uncle just staring for a second.

I said, "The most dangerous thing about us is that we think the world is our God-given regal domain and that consequently we're never supposed to lose anything. I think that until we lose something we're gonna be basically untrustworthy. We feel like we've gotta keep things going—keep up the string. We oughta just forget about ourselves and let everybody else be."

My father put down his glass and looked me in the face. "Ya start forgetting about yourself and letting everybody else be, and you're gonna end up jack point nowhere."

But as I was sitting in the car after the second appointment, I thought I wouldn't have been able to go after him then the same way I did that Christmas, even if he were alive and had all his strength. I thought too of how he looked three years later, having lost finally over a hundred pounds—of the way he couldn't find my face, even though I placed it in his hands; couldn't find the walls of that last small room, for all his frantic turning of his head. I knew that all the things he needed were exactly the things I needed—and needed especially as I sat there at the end of the gray, sodden park, hoping I would make it.

As we sat at the warm table, with the snow gathered in the leaded windows, which looked out on Gillson and the lake in winter darkness, I somehow was willing to end nearly every effort at self-protection he wanted to make, no matter how deeply understandable such an effort might be, or truly important for his life—or for mine.

At that time not old or wise enough, I could stop counting the long runs at Soldier Field and the heroic string of air victories, the lifetime of honest business. And if I could never completely, radically deny, I could still disregard even his tenderest desire as well, and all mine, and my passionate admiration and love for him, which were and are as deep as my life. Positioned safely enough, I could put off all this. And in the park, I could now for moments believe religiously that if it weren't for all these things, his great victories and even his tenderest desires, I wouldn't have suffered what you do when you come to the end of the line of your own misery.

In the quieted dining room, aware now that I was talking alone, I said, "The number of things that we can't stand about the people, the country of Vietnam, shows about how bad off we are, how far we are from what we love to think of ourselves as. I mean we absolutely hate how silent the whole thing is. Those people aren't saying things that we can understand. We don't know what's in that jungle. We don't know what's around even one corner—except that it's gonna be somethin' with some incomprehensible intention, dangerous as hell even if it's a kid or an old woman. And because we're not even close to what we say we are—believers in freedom, government of the people, by the people, for the people—we'd like to take care of every person and every green leaf in the entire place, put an end to every living thing. That's what it is now. Or that's the mood right down in there. Let's not lie. Let's not lie about what gets us over there and over everywhere. We're money men, and we measure our advances in inches and miles and hours and days that don't have anything in 'em but money men like us."

My father, who hadn't for a second taken his eyes off my face, just said, "Maybe I oughta cut your money off. Give a new meaning to the generation gap."

I felt the thrill and fear of such a close meeting and said, "Maybe I could extort it from you, saying your interests in me are too vital—be your little Israel. Maybe I could say you'd lose me. Maybe it's worse for you not to keep things going than it would be for me to be broke."

"I'll tell you what you are," he said.

I said, "Go ahead."

"I'll tell you what you are. You're lazy. The world's imperfect. The government's imperfect. And you'd rather give up and die than stick to the task of making things work. People like you hate politics because you're bored with your own survival. You're an end-of-the-worlder who'd like to have it happen now so you could stop doing anything."

And in the car, no matter what the influence of gray, or of the window mist now blurring more borders in this dangerous, wealthy place, I could see him again on his deathbed, in the dim room, after he'd forgiven me everything that I'd ever done to hurt him. "Forever, Pete. That's good now—that it's simply forever." And I heard myself again almost begging him not to forgive me—because I was wanting so much for his criticism of me, the-end-of-the-worlder, to be true.

But in that gray, rain-smeared light, I thought of how he had come to repudiate doctors, of how he himself had run and hid possibly from the work of keeping himself alive, waiting till it was too late, not taking care of the spot on the back of his neck. And just as surely then as I could feel that there was somewhere an America worthy of what was called the last full measure of devotion, I could think how I said in my father's face that I wasn't his anymore.

Breathing freer in the gray light, I felt healthy enough really to move some this way or that—felt that I could actually assert or deny, and with an understanding of the power of assertion and denial almost as good as I had had when, at my worst crisis point, I couldn't move an inch one way or another, or play at all with yes and no.

So I just thought of how I said, that Christmas night, "The end of the world is gonna come because of people like you!"

And of how he answered, furiously, "But I suppose that doing nothing is being alive—that *that's* our business! Well I do *not* believe that! I believe that if we're intelligently afraid we'll do things and care, and that if we do things, for God's sake, and care, we'll see the values at some point that make life worthwhile. And I say there's damned good reason to be afraid in the first place because there are people in this world that could and would, or will, kill and suppress millions. You like to think that we're doomed because we're so filled with our own purposes. But I'll tell ya it's because we're not anywhere near as filled with our own purposes as they are that we're in serious trouble—and not tomorrow."

Everyone at the table was afraid now, staring, silent. I looked at him, afraid of and thrilled by what I was going to say, then took a drink and said, looking right at him, "I've thought that all the things you think are true are *not* true. I've thought it as deeply as I believe I can think anything. And this is part of it. I've believed that the most wrong thing that we can do is insist that this goddamned world is the main thing to be defended, and that it's got to be defended by good old America, and that it's got to be defended in all four corners all the time. If we were honest, we'd say we've got no business doing any of this—because we're nothing."

"That's it," he said, pushing his chair back from the table. "That's exactly it. Honest. When does honesty become sick self-hatred? Are you gonna say that criticism of the United States is *never* sick? That at *no* point it ever becomes diseased or rather that at no point it *can* ever become diseased? When's it gonna stop, is what I wanna know. Or when does it *have* to stop?"

I said, "If we were what we said we were, we would let it stop nowhere."

He said, "That's sick. That's sick. You can't just let things happen. Even Christ got angry in the Temple!"

I pushed my own chair back and said, "Yes! And now I'll tell you what's what—seeing how we're in the business of telling each other what's what and who's what. That's your Christianity, which you also say you live by but you don't. What Jesus Christ got angry at in the Temple was nobody else but you. And you know it! You know this. That's why you're angry and hate to hear it—because you know it's true. And if you really had to be an American or really had to be a Christian, things whose reputation you like to suck on, you'd be scared to death. You'd be so completely disorientated you'd think the goddamned solid world was falling in pieces. It's all just King of the World, Dad—that's what you're playing. But until that game ends, you can blame yourself for any Armageddon."

And in the car, and now, at such times when, for better or worse, some movement is possible for me, I could think of him when his solid world had in fact gone to pieces, of the feeling that he must have had, as if he had really seen or heard the unstoppable missile—and known that This Is It—that this is the real nuclear warhead—that the end of the world is unstoppably now. I could feel it and say as I did when I stood up at the table and put my face over it even closer to him: "Religion isn't what you think it is. The truth is that as soon as we start making distinctions between them and us, or making *this* out to be evil, *that* out to be good, we limit ourselves from, I mean this—God, eternity."

He was standing now too, leaning across to me, with his huge fists pressed down on the table, and with his eyes, never empty of compassion, as violent as I had ever seen them. "What in hell," he said, "are you talking about?"

I knew coldly now that we were very likely coming to blows, which would be something all new. "I'm talking about how the whole thing began."

Then with his face tortured with anger, and his right hand lifted off the table, he put it to me, "But now that it *has* begun, do you ever think about how the whole thing's gonna end?"

I said, "So it's a matter of pride?"

And he said, "Yes, it's a matter of pride. And it's a matter of courage. And it's a matter of living or dying."

I said, "That's a pitiful coward's mistake."

Then he seized me by the shirt, up near my throat. I felt a surge of strength and confidence unlike any I had ever felt before. With a sudden wrestling move, I wrapped my arm inside and around his, broke his grip, and then had him and actually pulled him to me. I said in his face, "If you begin all your thinking with the thought of your own dying you're more hopeless than I suspected."

I let him go, contemptuously, but he came around the table after me and threw all his weight into me and with his powerful hand smashed my head back against the dining-room wall. I lowered myself then and tackled him and lifted and smashed him back into the table, which cracked under his weight. I stood there over him with everyone screaming, not believing what was happening. I was completely stunned now too, and I saw that what I had begun one second ago, in amazing confidence, was one of the most radically terrible things that I had ever done in my life. I knew that one more move might bring on some unwanted end that couldn't ever in either of our lives be changed.

He was rising now. He came at me with his fist, which he shot at me, grazing and cutting my cheek. I was shocked again and as miserable as I've ever been, but I had something in me brutal enough to overcome all that sick feeling. I raised my left arm before my face to protect myself, took back my right, and came up with it to drive a blow to his jaw and neck, which snapped his head back and brought him to his knees.

And when he was down, I had words for him. I screamed, "So am I the big king now! Is this what I'm supposed to be! I'd rather be nothing than this! It's no good for me. Nothing is right. Nothing is ever right!"

I turned and passed my mother, who was speechless and sobbing and looking at neither of us. I said to her crazily, "I've never been more sorry, Mom, over anything in my life. I'll make it up to you, if it takes me forever." And then I left.

Allie and her family that Christmas were on the other side of the city, with relatives, but Johnny was in the Northside, spending his Christmas with a date. So, though I couldn't believe what I was doing, and wanted desperately to stay and undo what I'd done, I pulled out of our driveway and drove off, heading for the tavern, even as the thought of going made me sick. And driving in the Christmas snow—a white peace which I couldn't look at—and listening to some angry music of that time, I very oddly began to think of myself as stuck out alone in the incomprehensible jungle that I had described. I was actually in it: counting hours and days, or, when heavy fire started, seconds and inches, in which my life might still be safe. I could see myself, unknown to them, coming up on Vietcong whose position I knew and taking care of them; or outsmarting them, if they trapped or surprised me; or saving friends from them; or meeting any violence they might show me with utter courage and then violence of my own—ultimately silencing the foul noise they made with tearing firepower.

"Thank God you weren't there that night," I've said to Allie, "—the insanity. Then thirty seconds later I'm thinking the opposite. Winning the Medal of Honor in my brain. But at the same time I'm doing this, I'm feeling this unbelievable need to detach myself from the world—like a saint."

"You went to see Lemaster," she said.

"Yes—at the Northside."

And though Johnny was no more a saint than the god-damned dog that gave its name to cynicism, he was careless enough about where the world was going so that I could carry on a conversation with him. So I went to find him at the bar.

And after the second appointment, sitting in Lincoln Park in the rain, I wanted him again, no matter what had happened the week before, in our near fight, or what I'd just been feeling. I miss him now, too, no matter what happened ever between us. And I'm thinking again of how my father incomprehensibly cast him out in those last days at Mercy.

At the bar I tapped him on the shoulder. He seemed glad to see me. He looked carefully. "What in hell happened to your face?"

"Would you believe that my father and I just celebrated Christmas with a fistfight?"

He sat me down and introduced me to his date, touched the waitress walking by and ordered a beer. His date was a blond nursing student. Her name was Chrissy, for Christmas—I remember—and she told me that she didn't think I'd get a scar.

When he heard that we'd fought over the war, Johnny said, "Nothing like an absurdity to get it going. My father used to come after me because it was Tuesday and he wanted to keep up what he'd started on Monday, and on back, and on forward."

So we had a laugh at the expense of fathers, and Johnny said he wouldn't exclude mine from the list of the dangerously ludicrous. "Your father's got hopes," he said. "He's a hoper. I'm not sure if my father didn't have the same problem, or if he didn't at least start out that way. But yours is definitely a hoper. I'd say even a high hoper. So the fact that he slashed you doesn't shock me—seeing how you're a born disappointment."

"Thanks," I said, laughing and choking on my beer.

He said, "Don't feel bad. A hoper like your father looks at me and says, 'The only thing worse than a disappointment is somebody who's too damned worthless to know what a disappointment is.' You can put that in the book some day. But remember: if you keep going the way you're going—exactly as your father's son—I'm gonna let ya have it. I won't take your shit. I'm gonna cure you of all your useless intelligence. Maybe I'll let you write your book first, though—it might be a good useless book. But after that I'm just gonna wipe the shit out of ya."

So we laughed some more. Chrissy was very friendly and attractive. She and Johnny did help me forget where I was and why I was there and what the day was. But I'd reached the Northside only an hour before closing time, and two or so beers down and it was time to go. Johnny said I could sleep at his uncle's, where he was staying until time to head back to school—but as soon as he said it, I knew how much I had to go home. I knew that even if Johnny might do me some true, serious good, the last thing I could afford would be to leave what was broken at home unrepaired. So we said good night, Johnny laughing, wondering if he should wish me luck. But when I got in the car and pulled away, I could get some feeling, after all, of the white peace of the fresh snow.

The radio was carrying Christmas music. It was a high-school choir now, with one girl's beautiful voice singing how all our hopes and fears were met in the dark street in little Bethlehem. Unremarkable, except for the girl's voice; but given where I was, and why there, and the time, the sound had a deeply powerful effect on me. It made me want everything—want Johnny, want my father, whom I loved more than anything, want us all, together, in extreme peace. After the second appointment too, in the mist, I could feel it again freely, the need for some extreme resolution, some world peace, and not just the terrifying balance of power that I knew when any slight move might mean my world would collapse.

And that terrible, beautiful Christmas night, passing General Sheridan rearing snow-covered in snow-light, I thought that without such a one and those guns in his saddle, there could be none like Lincoln, no mercy for all—if for a second I could see the stallion's huge cock as painted red with Indian blood. And I wasn't ashamed of or embarrassed by the words cut in stone at the Temple Shalom, the House of Prayer For All People: "Have we not all one father?" or by the capitals of the temple columns—vegetable, bestridden with wings, penetrated by the amphisbaenic snake, covered by books, lit by the seven-branched candle—which held up the arches and cornice of this fantasized desperate, cutting, measuring image of the fantasies of the sadness of Ezra and Nehemiah.

Even this far back, I was so moved and "touched," insane. And at the quiet snow-covered turns in the road, with the music playing, it was Christmas: at St. Andrew's under the Greek cross; and at the turn of the Sacred Heart, at the Convent where the figure in the shell exposes the flaming heart with his fingers, or at the Grotto, where the figure's arms spread as he stands over the spilled cup and thongs, and the light catches also the twelve promises made to Saint Margaret Mary Alocoque—that there will be the receipt of grace necessary for this state of life, that communion on the nine consecutive First Fridays will keep the hour of death safe from loneliness and pain; and at Calvary, at the city's end, with white snow gathering in Gibbons' urn, and in the letters of the names, on angels' wings, in stone flowers; and in Evanston, at the Pantocrator—whirling stained-glass God of countless colored stains—softened (a word I take from the poets, so in love with and so ashamed and afraid of things) in the snowfall, at this last, quiet turn before the Baha'i, where the bridge and harbor lights caught the snow that fell from the beacon-lights shining high up on the magnificent temple in the dark.

And now I remember how, when just before midnight I came up a softened, white street toward home and saw that in the dining room a light was on, and that my father was there picking up, there was an incredible peace for me that I valued and understood. I had come to such a point of good understanding—which in the car that day in the park, with him gone, was an even more intense condition. I knew even better then—and I hope against sleep and every kind of deadness and stupidity, that I will know again, with that truest intensity—what it means to achieve peace.

He was alone, bent over something, whisking it into a dustpan; and the unbelievable sudden temptation, when I came inside, to walk past, off to my room, was a weight that almost kept me from him, just as his temptation to keep his eyes on the broken glass and not look up, I could see, also very nearly ruined our chances. But no matter what ever happened, we always, always, wanted each other more than we didn't. So against all the dead weight, he put down the dustpan and broom and got up and turned to face me. I went up without saying a word and took him in my arms as he looked at me. I whispered to him, "I love you more than ever," which made him hold me tight and say, "I promise I'll never try to hurt you again as long as I live. I promise I never will."

And leaving the south park, heading for the Drive and home, I was able to promise freely too that for every flower I laid upon the altar of one god, I'd lay another on the altar of his opposite—and I understood again, as well as it might be possible for me to understand it, the miraculous impelling action of the twin divinities of fear and beauty.

8
THE GREAT AGE OF DIVISION

I hate sleep enough so that eventually, I think, things will open up for me and I'll get to where I want to go. But if it weren't for the hatred, I swear, sometimes I wouldn't have even half a damned prayer.

I've had to leave the book for months, to keep other things alive, and I've gotten nearly completely stupid again. Jesus Christ, I think about those places that make all the difference in the world. Those spots where you feel you have the right or the strength to assert or deny, but won't forget, even for a second, the magnitude of the distance out of assertion, or of the distance in of denial. Places where yes and no mean so much that the color of a flower or its motion in the wind can teach you how to read the best things ever written— and vice versa. And I don't give a flinging goddamn about what I'm supposed to be saying in this incredibly prolonged age of miserable irony and division—the spots are there; and I want to get to them to save my damned soul, which, however, I regularly enough can only keep active with this detestation of sleep.

And again *yes,* I want to be in some place that's not too healthy, because believing only in health is like believing only in love, for God's sake, and never in loneliness, or only in happiness and never in sorrow, and I can't think of anything stupider or more incapacitating when it comes to storytelling, or loving.

The progress, the definite drift of a story, is still, for me, expressed so well in an image of true, danger-beset healing (if gestation and growth can say a good deal too); and I hate sleep, Jesus, and the dullness of our idiot age, or anything that stops me from getting to the spot where I can tell the story I need to tell. And after some good movement, of course, I'm feeling this setback now, and fool drowsiness. So I'm angry, which doesn't give me enough of an impulse to get a story going.

But now with nearly a whole day having passed since I started this chapter—hours since I've written a word—if I'm murderously demanding a composition of place (the hard focusing on specific locations that is recommended for keeping spiritual meditation awake), I do see myself heading home from that second appointment. I can feel again now (as I keep going in after words that will match with shades of experience, or experiences with shades of words) at least a small something of what it was to walk up those stairs on Greenwood. See the varnished wooden banisters, shining more brightly as they rose into the light above—and know something of how, as the weeks went by, and a third and fourth and fifth appointment were made and kept, I began to feel less and less that the building was in any danger.

I know I didn't need either, then, to keep the walls up by driving off questions about the meaning of marriage (for instance, how much, without marriage, would we fail to know about who we are? or how much, without it, would poetry have lost in joy and sorrow?). And what I want to say now, listening to Allie downstairs working, keeping after the children, *is* that at that time, beginning to recover, but remembering perfectly how a little time before this I couldn't hear a single good word she had to say without falling prey to terror,

I knew the worth of a loving partner who would keep calling me out, sensing as best she could what the right times were for dropping in a good word.

"When Conlon just listens," she said once, "You know things are still going on. He doesn't need to pretend there's some huge significance in what you say. He probably puts about as much stock in it as you do. You'd come out feeling sicker than hell if he started going 'Ah hah!' or some such thing. I mean, I've wanted to know what kinds of things he's got to say—but mostly because I was afraid he'd be constructing some kind of case. I think that he *hasn't* is a sign that he's really good—that he knows what he's up to."

She'd missed her period by then too, for the first time ever; so we had a pretty sure sign now that those first strange feelings that she'd had were what we thought they were. And with a child now in mind, I began thinking about what things make the world a safer (but not too safe) place.

It was tremendous, the relief that came to me when I could say, out of the earshot of the radical furies of Vietnam protest, that I sought some final patriotic devotion, if only to some inconceivably small mental America. But telling my father that I didn't believe in a thing he believed in and that if any kind of thinking was going to bring on the end of the world it was his kind, had come also as a very powerful relief; and remembering it was a relief even after his unbelievably savage death.

I had a feeling, which came with balancing my hatred and love for the world, my father, and the country, that I could make my child at least more ready for living here. I would sometimes imagine myself rocking the baby so that it wouldn't cry, whispering maybe some good low sounds in its ear that would let it know, without ever really saying anything to it, that I was always there. But I saw myself beginning to make clear sense in time too and telling the child stories, raising it as intelligently as I could while radicals who stayed radicals (ZPG buttons staring nails at baby carriages—what a time!) would have to end up childless or, secret tyrants that they sometimes are, with pets—although I was far too smart then, beginning to live life like lines of poetry, to believe that there was the first thing wrong with abandoning in silence all desire for a posterity in this world.

But I know too that raising children is like doctoring, and that working patiently to help move a healing is the same as writing a story, although Johnny Lemaster would I'm sure find these large assertions ludicrous, and *despise* the sound of these words on parents and children. And it helps me to know this—I'm relieved to say.

But again, it would disturb me if, in whatever notes he kept, Conlon said something about Johnny and me that told a different story from the one I'd tell—perhaps something about my finding reasons, in my thinking about Lemaster, for ending my life. This just isn't it. Indeed the difference, which Conlon and I spoke of, between my fearing that walls would crush me and my actually believing it, might well have depended, or at least half-depended, far, far down in, upon my never really seeking Johnny out for my deepest hope's demolition—for the final undermining of my life. There was always, I would say, some higher, safer reason for my going to him.

And when I called him six weeks or so after our little disaccord in the Northside parking lot, it certainly wasn't to erase that crucial difference between fear and actual belief, or the good difference that I could see in my health. Odd as it sounds, I wanted just to have him confirm for me, as I was making progress in my recovery, that there's great *use,* for the very purpose of making such progress, in wanting at the same time to go nowhere. And I'd say there's a very large difference between seeking a friend out for this reason and taking too many sleeping pills.

Yet it was with a sudden terrible feeling of heartache, after I got off the phone with Johnny, that I thought of what I'd told Conlon about the spinning bowl, and Johnny hurled away with his dad in "King of the World," and then of how the last thing maybe that my father did in this world was hurl Johnny away again. I was so ashamed. But I recovered and felt good thinking that possibly Johnny just proved that you *didn't* have to be the son of God, or my father, to be Jesus. As well as sons of God, world-bastards like Lemaster could teach us how to find peace in the largest possible silence, merely by being the bastards of nothingness they were. But I wanted to see him too just to say (as maybe I do again, after all these years?) that I was sorry for what happened.

And right now, thinking of what stories I would tell my child, rocking it in my arms, I remember a very beautiful night—mid-September beauty—when I did hold Colleen in my arms in my chair. It was long, long before she could know a word of what I was saying. Some eleven months after I'd begun with Conlon—mid-September of '73—which would make her only two months old. But as I rocked I told her, or thought out loud for her, about Johnny and me and my father and Johnny's father. It was again that story of the bowl, which I continued to think of so often back then—and so think of again and again now. But when I whispered it in an infant's ear, I wasn't at all ashamed. Rather it was one of those nights when I was in the deepest heart of some place where my memory of helplessness, along with my true and present understanding of radical patience, had kept sunrise and sunset still holy. A place where the merciful gods gave me room to act and speak—where I actually began to write a poem, where I *could* write one: right there where terrors were turning to the most joyous convictions. What would Johnny, the man against fathers, say about this night with Colleen? It was so different a thing. I don't know, if he read of it here, what he would say then about this book—which comes with what grows out of these returns to places that simply haunt me.

But all of this was long after he and I went too far—broke apart our friendship for good—that night when I went to see him again. It was the evening after my seventh hour with Conlon, I remember; and that day, with no reason yet to be ashamed to be alive, I had moments of beautiful advancing confidence.

In Grant Park, the deep snow was again a perfect white spread of quiet. The peace of it actually readied my heart for the advent of any color or the slightest sound. As I unlocked my car in the bitter cold, and saw General Logan in the saddle reared high in black over the names of his battles, I imagined (and could think that if I really knew not much more than most about the facts of the Civil War, I might have been close enough still to its history) the sound and weight of black, steaming horses and blue-uniformed men breaking some snow-white silence over a hundred years before—and Ulysses Grant and others among Lincoln's avenging angels planning the day's work for the Union. And the lake, now an undifferentiated gray mass, and really always an image of what the citizens of the City of Weight sense might lie beyond their borders, whether joyful, or painful and lost, was the right ground again for the poetry of the drive past Lincoln Park and up Sheridan Road, through all the memories of the War—and I could see Grant now, unchanging, heading south, high in the cold wind at North Avenue—and on to the end at Calvary.

Life in the Advanced Studies Program was improving too; and I was involved now really in the "great task" of beginning to fight a little for my self. I'd even walked the day before down the Midway—from the Fountain of Time and on past the mile of medieval towers, which I could criticize for their ahistorical inappropriateness, admire still for their beautiful expression of a love of timelessness (if this made me laugh again that maybe in Chicago the only real hope is the lake and a touch of insanity) and not fear for their falling—to the eyes in the iron helmet of the Blanik Knight and read, without a dread feeling of loss, and without a pious snicker, the cut words "Jesus, not Rome."

So on my way home, after the appointment, I let the radio music work a bit for my pride; and the book was something that I thought, for a moment, I might dedicate to my wife and child—though I then got rid of that thought as I felt that I needed to.

But I could listen now to Allie—and I was coming out some when she called me. So when we were showering and dressing, getting ready to meet Johnny, I could work on a reminder she gave me that he wasn't what I thought he was—that the idea that he had no intentions was naive.

"I promise you," she said, "you can watch out for him

without feeling guilty." I should say too that the other day I asked her if she'd given Johnny any thought lately.

"I have, actually, yes," she said, "and I haven't changed my thinking: if it weren't for your theory of him, which makes him into this hero of utter denial, he'd look a lot more ordinary. He may have won all his wrestling matches, Peter, but his denial of the worth of everything, as you'd put it, was possible because he didn't have the things you had and, more importantly, couldn't see what you saw, or feel what you felt. So he might not deserve all the credit for disinterestedness that you give him. Understand that he wanted to take things from you. I promise you, he did. The time you fought him, I thought you were at your absolute worst. I couldn't believe it. I hated to see it. But there was a moment when I could have hit him myself. I wanted to say I'm *sick* of apologizing for choosing something and having it and wanting to stay with it. It's amazing the way he makes you feel this. And what is he?"

I said, "You do hate it. My going back to these things."

"I never would, if your going back helps you see that when you reject Johnny Lemaster, 'and all his ways,' because you want to *live,* you're not some second-rate soul. It isn't easy to say no to him—but God knows it isn't wrong or stupid."

"No doubt."

"I keep thinking of your daily life, Peter—the person everyone sees and the person you are. I don't want you to forget this person—least of all because this might be the recommendation of a devil you've embodied in an ordinary man named Johnny. And what does he know about all these years? Your work? Your life with your children? The five hundred recitals? And five *thousand* games? The countless nights with other kinds of people—people whose names he's never even heard? I'm your friend. I share your vision, I promise you—no matter what I say sometimes—maybe right down to the last sentiment on sorrow. But something about him, or the way you think of him, makes me want to remind you of your own basic happiness. And what if he laughs that you whispered those words to Colleen? What if he thinks it's absurd to care or believe like that?"

I assured her that I shared her vision too—and that I hadn't forgotten for a second the satisfactions and happinesses of our lives. Her own years at De Paul and now with the handicapped at Providence. It was just that Johnny didn't share the same faith. That was exactly it. That, and the fact that sometimes maybe sorrow *is* the only thing that can convince us that this world isn't everything.

After that night when I whispered Johnny's name in her ear, I never asked her what the words "You can make me Johnny" had meant to her. And of course I never mentioned my Barbara fantasies, which I figured were all normal enough, given the essential damned strangeness of human nature. But Johnny had told me that tonight it would be Barbara again, and as I dressed, I wondered how I'd feel, given what actually did get said and what did happen. But I cut it off, as I've basically cut it off ever since—though, as I say, I can still see Barbara's beautiful light brown hair and shadowy face in the gaps and take comfort from lifting her chin and bending with my eyes closed to that beautiful moist and reddened mouth. So sometimes the book moves on. But at the bright top of the stairs, I put my arm around Allie and descended the darkening well without fearing the vengeance in the walls, and I could think about marriages as emblems of the sweetest combinations of motion and stillness. I got out of the building door, too, without having to kill a quick thought about the inconceivable worth of devotion and fidelity.

And in the car, I could talk to Allie, talk about Conlon, Johnny, nearly anything, as we swung south into the city, which showed us briefly from the point at Calvary its huge lighted night towers.

But there were quiet moments as we moved with the green lights down Sheridan toward Loyola. Then reading the name "Loyola" made me think of another time with Johnny when we were kids—as young as you could be in those days and still ride the train down to Wrigley Field for a game. And at Loyola I've thought a number of times—all right, this is exactly what the new, honest philosophers mean when they clamor about how many different things a word can mean.

For when I think of Loyola, I almost always think of the saint, or almost always when I'm here, in the spirit of the Drive, which for me has on so many days monumentalized the same events in religion or war that our history books say have shaped the world, chapter by chapter (if also I see here spread out junk, dirty paper scraps blowing in the wind into the architectural face of commercial hideousness, and known how completely the poor, the racially repressed, are driven off this road—like the Indians driven out of sight forever under Sheridan's horses' hooves), Ignatius Loyola, the fanatical brilliant counterreformer, founder of the Jesuit Order, and his brilliant *Spiritual Exercises* (now fodder for contemporary structural analysis) who found in the absolute zero of perfectly devoted obedience the fullness that ignorance calls repression. Or was it just the thrill of the thongs?

"LOY-OLA! Next stop Lllllloyola." So it came out of the conductor's mouth, nearly lost in the roar of the EL and the amplified rasp of the PA. A tall, old, scrufty man in a long gray coat, all wrong for summer, came on carrying a cardboard box of Bibles, New Testament King James, including also the Psalms. He came up to us with the train stopped, and he gave me one and I took it and said "Thanks." But when he offered one to Johnny, Johnny said, "I don't believe in God."

I remembered Johnny's crew cut, his tough muscular body, for which adults despised him, and his baseball cap on backwards so he could cool his face, catching the wind in the open window of the train. The old, dirty man didn't care. He walked on, smelling drunk. But I'll never forget how a fat woman who sat next to us with her children, a boy about our age and a girl a little younger, got up and took the children away to find new seats—and how Johnny laughed.

But this was the first time I'd heard him say this! I'd never heard him say he didn't believe in God. I couldn't believe it. But he made me laugh too. And I was still laughing when the train pulled out and Johnny put his face back into the window to catch the wind.

So: LOYOLA. I saw the name written on the station house and then looked toward the blue light-sign of the

Aphrodite Cafe, and drove on when the light changed, letting the memory fade as Allie and I talked about Loyola, the university, and Loyola, the basketball champions, the beautiful team of '63, and where they all might be now.

And so it went, down to the warm, dark Northside, where we sat at the same window, under the lighted tavern clock. But I wasn't looking out for signs contradictory to hope. This was different from the last time. I even felt with some incipient, dangerous pride that I really wasn't ever physically afraid of Johnny and that this idea of my not having a prayer in the world wasn't quite as true as he thought it was. Or that there was a chance, maybe, that as I had done to my father, I could roll Johnny down with a spirit or a simplicity from somewhere out of this world.

So I sat there in the snug barroom, by that same window, actually holding Allie's hand and talking to her about whatever came up—if now perhaps also against the beginning of some fear that I shouldn't do any such thing at all.

I heard an awkward screech of brakes and looked out and saw that Johnny had just come to a halt in the lot. I gave Allie a little laugh and shook my head. But if I knew then nearly everything that I could about the danger of hope, the danger of discovering my rights, or of daring to show my face, I figured that I could answer him if he made some smart remark like I believed in even less than he did.

When he came in, wearing a blue T-shirt under a dark sport jacket, and with his teeth flashing in a smile, he appeared sharp enough and certainly ready for me. And Barbara reminded me immediately of the comfort that, after the last time we had been together, around midnight, I had to take from absolute nothingness.

She was wearing over her breast a golden leaf with sapphires on a white cashmere sweater, which softened her beautifully and brought out her pale blue eyes and shadowy face. I thought that if Johnny really found her boring, then he didn't need any escape from any troubling *something* (some secret wish for the self) but was just what I thought he was—

right at home with nothingness—familiar and comfortable with, and even unexcited by, Barbara.

He was perfectly convivial. He said a friendly "Hel-lo" to Allie and bent to kiss her cheek. As we sat, I saw that he wasn't sober; the signs were there, sharp as he may have been. He ordered a vodka. But I began quickly to feel careful about making anything of his drinking; I wanted immediately to take no comfort from thinking what I sometimes thought of him—of his most secret intentions. I didn't want to start anything. I had not, after all, left the place where the question of his interest in me drives so deep that I can only barely ask it.

But for hours the evening was fine. We drank, ate good junk food, laughed together. I was even thinking that this was how it would be when I was fully healthy again. And Barbara again was charming. To my mind, she offered to the world the lotos in the land where it's always afternoon. She was able to make me laugh—even as she made me sure that I believed in nothing.

Speaking to me about her writing for a class in poetry, she said, laughing, "I'd run my ideas by this freak friend of mine who used to *name* rather than number his pages when he handed in papers. Shit like 'Sunshine,' 'Kama Sutra.' Last page of the paper always: 'The End of the End.' So I used to write up these utterly off the wall papers. None of it made sense to me (maybe that's why I liked poetry). But the teacher—this guy who hated his wife and talked about her in class—had me thinking I was Susan Sontag."

And she had the table laughing about the gods, the doctors, Johnny's other friends—teasing that to a man they'd sacrifice divinity for a mortal woman (and, maybe looking at me out of the corner of her eye, she did mention Conlon—if to say only that "he was picking out the music at this party—great music").

But exactly as I go back now, not just anywhere, but again and again to the Northside, and wander in my mind through the low dark crowded room with the sconces on sports heroes and listen to the juke and look out the window from the warm booth under the clock, I found myself again, after those few comfortable hours, back in the ancient battle with my friend and foe, whose drinks I did count. And I'm sure I knew that with Johnny the old trouble would return, no matter what I say now, or thought then. I even knew, maybe, that the night would come exactly to what it came to. For fear and the love of beauty do go to the same peace and trouble like hunger to food. Or maybe like a drunk to his tavern—which is what? pitiful routinism? or again the poetic brilliance of our sorrow, which can't sit down where it won't get the right warm poison?

But it seemed just to come, the trouble—if not with the suddenness of the unexpected. Allie and Barbara were talking ("Really, you've known him . . . ?" Barbara asked. "Since high school," Allie said)—and there was a lull in my conversation with Lemaster. Then, with his eyes over his glass, which he held like a priest, Johnny said, "Things still going smoothly, Peter, with you and Alex?"

But maybe I was the one who started it. I don't know. I said, "It's frightening to think how well sometimes."

He sipped and said, "I wanted the best for the best." Then he finished his drink and looked me strangely in the eye. "The most believable for the one who needs something to believe in."

But I thought now with a rush of stupid, dangerous confidence, or coming violence, that I actually *could* answer him! I said, "I don't think that's all bad. You know damn well, John, that it helps if your patients believe in you too."

"Then what are you frightened of?"

"I'm frightened of offending the god of despair—you wouldn't know anything about him, would you?"

He smiled. "My best friend."

I looked at him in his dark jacket and blue T-shirt—at his smile—and a still deeper aggressiveness became possible for me. I began to let my suspicions carry me on a bit—my theories that he would kill me if he could, that he would be my father's son, that he would take Allie, that he was just lucky he was the wrestler he was, just born with a talent—and that he was no more free of hope than anybody else who was covetous, and even capable of murder.

I said, "So you say," and drank, and put down my empty glass. He just smiled. Then suddenly, no doubt too confident in my own visions, I said, "I think that in the center of everybody's mind, John, there's a watchman—I've *seen* mine—who keeps patrolling the core—no matter what philosophical bullshit he may have to listen to. He's the one, if you don't know what I mean, who holds your arm down when you might raise it against yourself with a knife. You can learn something about him from seeing doctors." I hesitated. "Even doctors like the one you're going to be."

He gave me another strange, maybe drunk look. "You oughta be glad I'm not the little life preserver you've cut me out to be. If it weren't for my *not* giving a damn, I might feed you some more of the bullshit that's got you where you are. The little man. The homunculus again. Shit. The disease of pursuing what you pursue."

"It's occurred to me," I returned, "that you recommended Michael Rothen for my father and Alex Conlon for me. So it's occurred to me that you do give a damn—though I agree that there may be some trouble for me in that."

And after all these years, I think now that if he had ever pursued the same things I did, it might have been much worse for me. He might really have put himself before my father's eye, or Allie's. I don't know. In California, it seems, he's done nothing of the kind. But who knows? There's been only the one word.

I said, "Of course, though, as you know, I seek you out because I believe that you *don't* give a damn. That gives me a sense of peace—or freedom from guilt. It aligns me with something that I think is far safer sometimes than safety."

"Jesus Christ—we're back to the same thing you were into with your old man! I recall some of this crap from after that fight you had. Huge double moral condemnation: damned if you do live, damned if you don't. And doesn't this remind me that maybe the only person more full of shit than you was your old man!" He turned to the waitress, ordered a vodka and, laughing, said, "The *only* thing I'm proud of, as far as I can tell, is that I find people like you two incomprehensible."

As soon as he said this, everything in me was ready. God knows how I'd known, or how I felt what I felt, but sure as hell I moved out now with that same kind of beyond-this-world aggressiveness and power that I had when I went up against my father—a surge which like life feels good and guilty, a shame.

Immediately it was very nearly too much. I said, "Do you *ever* think, Johnny, about this war we're in? I voted for McGovern but had this weird feeling of sacrifice when I made the mark. Did you *ever* have a feeling of terrible sacrifice? Do you know what I'm talking about? Did you ever count our dead and seethe with anger? Did you ever have a slight sneaking suspicion that, if only in one or two claims out of a million, the conservatives might be right? Did you ever have to admit or deny? And who the hell *are* you anyway?"

He took a long sip of the vodka, and with the glass in both hands under his chin, he said, coolly, "Not you."

At the time we both weighed about the same. For a second I was looking him over and sizing him up. The amount of exercise I took crossed my mind. But beyond this, with my strange confidence, I was sure that in any confrontation here, any at all, I could give at least as much as I took. I thought of those words—goddamned commonplaces—on the cowardice revealed in our search for coherence or authority. I said, "I hope you don't mind, however, if I make progress toward keeping myself together—even if that might seem to you disgusting *amour-propre.*"

"Yes," he said, "but who the hell *are* you, anyway?"

I watched his mouth widen and teeth flash.

I said, "I've read your book too, ya know, Doc—very forcefully written. It's a story of utter vengeance against our dreams, if I'm not mistaken."

"But," he said, "have you read it with mercy, pity, peace, and love?" He kept smiling. I could see how high he was. "That's it too, Petie—you're lazy. You could write the book on fucking inertia. You're an expert on immobilizing weight. You want weight, some *body* with a fucking name, Peter La Roche, in that center of things you're imagining you'll write your book on some day. But you come to me for an occasional lift. Why? If you want to hear me say I don't care about fucking America one way or the other, I'll be glad to oblige."

But for a second he'd put on an intense, serious look. Then he smiled. I saw his teeth again, as he said, "But I want to be *there* for you, La Roche—when you want help."

Then (and when I think of this I feel such immeasurable regret) he looked at me and said, slowly, "And if I ever hurt you, I'm sorry."

Allie glanced over, having caught this unbelievable sudden kindness, and looking surprised. And Barbara smiled our way, as if to say—or so it appeared to me that she was saying—I'd offer you kindness no matter what you came for.

Allie said, "How many has this guy had?"

Johnny said, "Actually not quite as many as he needs," and went to the bar to buy another.

But immediately, brutally scoring his drink order, and now spoiling for something, I felt the pleasure of calling him a *liar* to myself—saying that he'd love to see himself firmly in the fucking center of things. I felt warm because of the women, and because of this, perhaps, was hard against any slight suggestion of condescension on Lemaster's part. Who was he to tell me who I was and what I needed and who was full of shit, or even who needed kindness? When he got back with his drink, I came out more, rolling with my miraculous confidence, picking things up immediately where they'd been left.

I asked, "But isn't it really lazy, even tragically lazy, not to care, as you say, one way or the other? I've been accused of not caring enough about how things might end up; and I've got this sense now—like none I've ever had—of how wanting to influence things, even wanting it slightly, of how caring *at all,* can be so weirdly dangerous that one step in that direction might ruin the whole shape of your life."

He smiled. "I'll bet you do."

"Yes, I do," I said. "I sure as hell do—but I can wonder

still if there isn't some incredibly important political task that we've been given. And goddammit, Johnny—seein' how you're busy at no such task—if you're not more gracelessly selfish than anybody you accuse of being self-protective fucking dead weight. I can confess now—and this is weird as hell—that seeing how there are forces trying to spread themselves out over the whole damned space of this globe that we might be disastrously lazy if we let 'em."

"So you wanna go into the air with guns!" He was smiling still now, as if he'd seen everything there was to see about me, and found it ludicrous. "The liberal is fighting against himself because what he really wants is to be like Daddy and go into the air with guns and knock outa the fucking sky as many enemies as happen to make the mistake of coming along."

I said, "Listen to the man of peace!"

But Lemaster looked now almost bored. He said, "You're keeping the same secret, Petie, as all the other frauds who'll go Republican when this popgun bullshit is over. That's the political task you're talkin' about. So, yeah, you feel funny when you vote for George." He smiled again. "Only I know somethin' you don't wanna know."

I saw for a moment Barbara's golden pin on her soft breast and her cheeks just colored rose under her pale blue eyes. She turned to talk to Allie again, maybe to pretend not to hear what was going on, to get us off it, but kept her legs turned to me, and I wanted their touch, so I actually made a slight move. But Allie looked at the moment very, very beautiful to me, with her hair glowing in the mellow light—more beautiful than I'd seen her for some time. She seemed only half to listen to Barbara and to watch the direction our conversation took. And I had a feeling that I knew why she watched— or that I could come up with a theory.

Johnny said, "What you don't know, my friend, is this." He took a long drink and held his glass again in two hands below his chin, as Allie turned her head from Barbara and looked our way. "What you don't know. What you don't know, my friend—is that you love me too."

When he'd said this, Allie turned back to Barbara, and I

thought maybe that I could say why. But I wanted to answer Lemaster. I said, "You think I'm a lot more stupid than I am, not knowing what you've meant to me."

He looked harder at me, lowering his glass. He spoke then as if he knew the end of my story—as if there couldn't be any other. "You'll always love me, Petie, no matter what I do, or what I did, or what you remember of me. In fact, you'll always love me exactly for what I have done to, or for you—only you don't know how much. But some day I think you will. You'll know that my intentions weren't what they seem. I've never wanted to hurt you."

Allie was turned our way again, and I thought she wanted to put in a word here and build some defense for me. I could think she was with me. And still dangerously I cared for my convictions, for my belief that we have some rights and some political tasks, even as I cared for what then was happening in Allie's womb.

I said, "If you loved me, John, given my present situation, you'd take back what you say about the disease of pursuing what I pursue. I mean what are friends for—sending people off to get help but suggesting at the same time that nothing makes any difference? I can't stop myself right now. I want to own a little property inside my mind. I want the day to come when something there is mine. I think we *need* to lose—maybe even at some time to come close to losing all—but that we don't *need* to lose *all*."

He smiled unblinkingly then, staring, sniffing a laugh.

And frustrated to the point of despair, I said, "I swear that you'd know this if you'd lost as much as I have—which I promise you you have not. There's a point . . . I mean, forgive me, but I goddamned want you to confirm something. Not everything. Not everything, John, needs to be lost—and the something that remains . . . Somebody even told me you have a heart. I've been told you're not what I think you are. I tell *myself* you're not what I think you are—though that scares me. But I want you to admit that something somewhere is important—and goddamnit—worth fighting for—protecting, maintaining, even expanding—worth working for. Something like the idea that life is good or that there are days when we make significant beginnings."

Allie and Barbara now both were turned to us, and I could feel the warmth of Barbara's leg against mine but had my eye on Allie, who was watching closely, I would say, to see if Lemaster's next move might really get to me. Allie could never forget what it was like finding me once before sunrise, crying for mercy in the dark and begging in an extreme cautious whisper for the sun to come up. I said to her in tears, "I can't even *begin* thinking of trusting the buildings, A. The punishments come that quickly. I can't even start to think there's anything safe in this godforsaken life. I can't start." And she held me and repeated, with the greatest caution, "Give it time. Give it time. Give it time."

"Friends"—Johnny smiled—"just for comfort? I don't think so." Then after an odd look at his audience, "The idea, Jesus Christ, the idea, the idea—that you're supposed to let your friends just take comfort in what they're thinking, or in what they believe, is fucking crazy. It's cra-zy. Crazy. It's more pain in the end. If there is an end. It's good . . ." Then he looked directly at me. "But I don't mean harm, for Chrissake. It's good to take from friends—not just give."

But it was now, terribly, that I had the chance really to make use of my new, small freedom from pure dread. He was down and vulnerable now because of one drink too many—so I actually stuck my finger at him in the air and began to jab it some as I came at him. I asked him, jabbing my finger, almost touching him, "Did ya ever consider, Johnny, that maybe friends aren't *always* there for offering opposition— that maybe rather often in fact they're there to look out for ya in the dark, make ya feel like you're not alone, not so goddamned small all the time? Or did ya ever think, say, about preserving a friend's life? Did ya ever think, old friend, that that might be a good idea?"

I had a shocking warm feeling that Barbara was deliberately moving her thigh into me—and then definitely her thigh was there with a slight motion as well as pressure. It was unmistakable and unforgettable, like the last words of an unbelievably compelling story. But I was still watching Allie's eyes as she watched Johnny and me—because I was becoming further and further convinced that what I wanted—though I was torn apart—was to make as much of a rightful claim as it was possible to make for my life's territory.

"Inches," I whispered to Johnny, "precious inches of life are what I'm asking for."

And right now—for this second—I can feel something of that need for territory, almost as I felt it then, with all the keen mind I had along the dangerous edge, as I want to throw in the teeth of all the pious moral critics who think otherwise (and whom I love like fire and silence) that it's not all bad to want some light to shine in your life! I can feel how the outward movement of this actual statement-making is like making the very first move—a good, dangerous move right at daybreak— in the tensest war zone imaginable.

But Johnny said to me then, coldly, "It's only when you're *not like* the old man anymore, not like that generation of toughguy barroom brawler World War hero assholes that you really don't want the old man to stay fucking dead. Do ya get that, Peter? I learned it when I was too young to bullshit."

He stopped, looking now as if he was going finally to say something that he'd kept a dark secret for a long time. "Your father, ya know, got angry as hell at me one time. It was over nothin'. I can't even remember. I can't. But in the argument he came after me. I told him I didn't believe in a thing he stood for—that the clearer his thinking came to me the sicker I felt. I didn't even know all that I meant by it. He'd caught me with some booze—it was good ol' high-school booze-stealin' time. We were raiding your place—without your even knowing it— so I felt like shit. I was a little drunk already. He just looked at me like he wanted to kill me. He told me that as long as I had no character I'd be as worthless as I was then. I just lost it—I don't know—for some thousand reasons. I said to him, 'Fuck you, if you're gonna give me your incurable disease.' He was gonna hit me, but he walked off. Maybe he was just scared."

Under the low barroom ceiling, I said, almost rising,

furious, "There are as many different feelings, Lemaster, as there are goddamned fucking different days. But sometimes we just know things. I can't tell you what it is for me to say the things I'm gonna say to you. But for starters—one more word of contempt for him and I'll reach for your fucking neck."

He answered me with a new fierceness, as if begging for something, "And I'm gonna tell you this, Petie. Your old man was either a fraud or a pitiable fool. I thought this all the way to the end, when he died. The disease—the disease—call it just the last honest answer to all the false hopes he ever had, or all the holy joe apologies he offered you in the end. But you know this. You know it damned well—because you were saying the same things yourself. You were asking me all those questions about his metastasis because you wanted the answers I was going to give you. That's you. You know this. And you know that it's good I don't give a shit where you are now."

In no time then, though I remember some faint touch of Barbara's on my side and a last look from Allie, I took his arm and directed him up from the chair and said to him, "Outside."

He rose with me but was laughing. "Ooooh. Outside! Peter Roche—cock-roach—wants to S-t-e-p O-u-t-s-i-d-e!"

But if he was laughing only to hurt me, in the bar, with people looking, I lost no confidence. The simple weird power which I'd had in the fight with my father came on. The strength was *there!* And for a change I had *his* arm, thrillingly, and I actually moved him out toward the back lot while he kept up his sarcastic laughter. Then the second we came to open space, I hooked my leg behind him and with brutal violence I tripped him over it, so he wouldn't laugh, and I could keep on living. And though the girls came up now and pleaded with us to stop, there wouldn't be any stopping, not till enough of something had happened, whatever it might be.

And if I am ashamed to say how the memory helps me to write these words, with speed, I recall enough now of the power that came on in my gut and arm, and of the way I looked hard for a spot in his face to strike him back down to the concrete. Achilles ripping some victim limb from limb, making his dead mouth eat dirt, leaving his severed skull a sweet bowl for indifferent birds—I can understand, partially. I can see the face that I haven't seen in so long (God forgive me—did I scar him?) with the look that has always made me so ashamed. The mouth is almost here, the lips that kissed Allie by the car door. I can see the face come up defenseless enough against me. I can hear my maniac self. "Who the fuck do you think you are!" I screamed as I drove my fist right toward that drunken face. And I landed the blow with utter success, ripping the skin off his upper lip so the blood came fast all over. "Who the fuck is 'Not Me'!" I screamed so loud that a young black bar cook opened the kitchen door of the tavern to see what was happening. The girls were crying now, too, and they asked the man please to come and help. But my indignation was burning far too brightly then, its savage light holding hard this friend and enemy of mine—whom I hated and loved from a time so far back that I could never say when it began.

And he was laughing, with the blood in his teeth, telling the cook now to "Take a fuckin' hike, Sam," and saying to me, with his red mouth laughing, "Petie, boy, soooo sensitive, you can't have the guts for this. You'll never have the balls, Petie boy. Good devoted boy. Born in shit. Dedicated to shit. Afraid it won't last, even if it kills him. Afraid he can't keep it. Killer shit. Full load of SHIT!"

But with my eyes on nothing but his laughing bloody mouth, I bent my knees and dropped my hand down to bring up my fist with my whole body and take it to his teeth and stop him.

This is what was coming—now that I was healthy enough to pray again for my own life's intentions and to think again of my history. I drove up my fist, with my full weight, into his mouth and finally did stop him. And it was nothing other than what maybe all my thinking life I had conceived it would be. The terrible guiltless moment and the possibly endless guilty aftermath—just like the inconceivable miracle of being born. He lay there fairly senseless, and I was standing over him, shouting, "You're wrong! You're wrong, you fuck! And you can go to hell and stay there! Stay there forever, you fuck!"

Then in my triumph I walked away crying—to catch Allie, who'd already run crying to the car. And I was as relieved as anyone would be who, to prevent his own murder, had killed something he'd loved even more than his own life.

A SERIES OF 9 REVELATIONS

I have been in some other places I'd like to find again—on the altar, for one, when I was on my knees and rang the bells, believing absolutely that Father Gleason had called Jesus Christ into the bread with his words (so a place where metaphor was fully realized—where the hard world was transubstantiated for the heart) and then having the feel and taste of the sacramental host in my mouth. And I start every time here with these attempts at prayer and with some effort at hard aggression against sleep, just hoping that I might know again something like the life that comes with such humble kneeling expectation—which, I promise, I knew even more vitally in extreme terror, hoping for just barely more than nothing.

I have done something with the words—with the incantation. But the innocence that chimed with the beauty and power and hope of the Mass naturally got lost too much along the way. And the experience of terror, I still have to say, left me fundamentally cautious and dull, despite the fact that it had a taste and feel even more powerful than holy communion.

But to have Johnny down and bleeding—to have wiped the intolerable smile off his face, and at the same time to have known completely, in unbearable sorrow, that his smile was what made so many things live for me, is to have been somewhere. And to have known such triumph and sorrow mixed, at a time when I had been for so long walking the thinnest line between living and dying, but had just come to a wider zone of safety—is truly to have seen fear and pity for the eternal friends of the heart that they are.

Helplessness (a word of course conveniently missing from the tough modern lexicon) makes you know that if anything saves you, it won't be yourself. It makes you truly, absolutely patient; that is, it makes it impossible for you to live without a faith in silence. And nothing that is not-you, and that comes out of the silence to save you, can be trivial for you. So in my helplessness I knew, with every slightest and futile attempt I made to change things, the enormity of what was in me and with me, but was not me. When I was patient long enough and believed in healing, and was healed, I knew for a while too the benignity of this silent not-me. And its great angels, as they let me live, sang to me and warned me and made me weep in the bitterest shame when, losing all faith and patience for the moment, I hurt my friend Johnny Lemaster.

I was crying to Allie in the car, "What did I do? Jesus Christ! What on God's earth did I just do!" But she only cried herself, her face hidden in her hands—which should have been enough for me forever. Enough, as I heard the angels' song of warning: the music so terribly beautiful that it gave worth even to the sin that brought it on.

But honest to high heaven, now that I'm trying to move on again, *off* the safe middle ground of my life, I'm wondering if I've got even to murder someone before I can find that second Eden—the place that poets know is discoverable on the other side of the self's worst sins. Would I have to kill him before I'd cry out for baptism? Or before this dead city could become again for me the body and blood of God—which is exactly what I want?

My marriage—I know this—comes to moments that offer

from the muse's hand a miracle flower: the delicate art, the astounding color, the sweet smell for the air. Allie's face, like a portrait with its light set against the darkness of human pain, can come to me with the message that the wait here is never worthless. We talk about the ways things come and go and where we'll be in the end—and the drive of the marriage, seeking the deepest passion in every coming and going and in the end, is like the drive of a story. Lives set against pain and as valuable one to the other as a rare diamond—we treasure them. And in all honesty, we don't—so that we can always go nowhere as well as somewhere, or just end the drive, and sleep together.

"God help me," she'll hear me say. "So many years— with the *wrong woman*." And I'll hear her say, "It's gotta be hell, man"—and hear her laugh and feel her warm kiss.

So it's wise and dangerous love we have, and I could say a word again about how love is taught us by all the gods of dark and light, and is sung in our ear by the muse of poetry. But what could be more certain than that Johnny Lemaster would say that the wisdom and the set of expectations that I work with ruin the only chance of living anybody ever has— even if finally I do just want to sleep in peace at the story's end, or if I want to make him its hero. He'd say my life and marriage aren't dangerous enough. And certainly Penelope and Odysseus, the husband and wife enthroned in Ithaca over the pool of blood—no matter how necessary were their actions, or how long and profound their sacrifices and reconciliations—is something he would have as little sympathy for as possible.

But if only he weren't laughing at me—if he cared at all that he put such a sharp cutting edge on my hatred that our long, long friendship had to be severed—I'd make the deepest sacrifices for him. I know it. Or if he'd admit that he *couldn't* forget what I did to him but wanted to avenge it—as I would, as any ego would—I could have a conversation with him that might, after all our failures, succeed.

I might tell him that he'd been a silent partner in my marriage forever. "My passionate desire for good moments,"

I might say, "for turnings, significant days—and a good end: I wouldn't know this desire if it weren't for your trying to break me apart. Your trying to kill me, John, shapes my life, which would be shapeless without your deadly smile."

And he might give me that deadly smile and say, "Glad I could be of use."

Then I'd say, "No. Not that either. I can't think of it that way either. I could never really make *use* of you. Because, see, you make me know that the truest mercy begins with our learning, far down in, how our desire is the worst of our crimes. So I'll *forget* my conclusions if you want to tear me apart."

And if he needed me now, even if he did try to kill me and ruin everything that I believe in, I'm sure that I'd come.

I still can't understand why my father expelled him at the end, or the way he did it. I've guessed of course that at times my father wanted Johnny, and not me, to be his son, or that he wanted me to be the power that Johnny in fact was. Johnny's rejection of him and his undeniable strength must have been, coupled with his disappointment in me, a complete bitterness for him. But I should say too that it *helps* me, thinking through such painful things, if I can call the antagonism between these two heroes a world-principle (light versus darkness!) and see myself, in my painful position as "disappointment," as an especially well-qualified reader of the world's history.

"Really, poets *have* to be born disappointments," I said once to Conlon, "so they can want crazily enough for things like the battle between my father and Johnny to have everlasting meaning."

He asked, *"Do* you see it that way?"

I said, "Only if it makes me uneasy—otherwise I'm ashamed to think I'd make that kind of claim."

But if I saw Lemaster again, I would ask him about my father and him. Yet what he'd say is anybody's guess. It's been so long—so long that we might find a meeting so odd that even he would wonder what in hell life was.

I asked Allie what she thought might have changed in him

since that crazy time. She said, "When he's not with you, he's never what he is when he is with you, or that always used to be the case. Maybe all these years without putting on his act and he's forgotten how to play it. I'm certain he ran from you, so I suppose he had changes in mind."

I said, "Honest to God, what makes you say that? What makes you think he would run from me?"

"Let me put it to you another way. I never met anyone who didn't know something about pain. So my guess is that he's done what we all do when we're lonely. He's searched for love and found it, or not found it and wondered why and suffered, all in ordinary ways. He's no doubt battled with anxiety. And I'm sure that to an ordinary degree, with ordinary weakness or bitterness, he's been good and bad to people, depending on their effect on his position."

The two of us are just like everybody else. Clearly what Allie knows and what I know have to be different, seriously different. A good part of the marriage contract—I'm not just trying to be smart—has to do with changing your vision of the past to meet your partner's. And I've needed for my life to see how ordinary Johnny is—the way Allie does. But Allie would say that my history is good too—an extraordinary history of the insane heart. And I know that what I had after that last night with Johnny was something of a mad poet's strength of vision, since some days after, it helped me to read in tears the story of Joshua's blowing down the walls of Jericho: to feel the poetry inseparable from the Bible's story.

I could feel it all, too, this crazy strength of the poet, when we pulled out of the Northside parking lot, after the fight, with his blood on my hand, and my blood, from where his teeth had cut me. The power came comfortingly, terribly, with that victory that I'd been waiting for all my miserable life. Under the high buildings, I drove and looked around with no vertigo and dead cold knew that I had no vertigo, though immediately I was sick at how much was wrong with the way the whirling in my brain had gotten stopped—at the idea that peace for me could come at the expense of Johnny's greatness. But I remember that as I turned on the radio I could actually look around—and see how Allie was looking away from me, giving me the signal clearly enough that for her there was something terribly sad, maybe even unchangeably sad, in what she'd seen.

Her face was pressed against the window glass as we passed Mundelein's shadowy angels. And the moment was one of a series that night that brought me to one of the best visions of things I've ever had. My triumph and my pain, and in Allie's face the sorrow over Johnny's and my inability to overcome our differences—all these spelled out for me a meaning about what's right and wrong, about pride, that I could read with my mind and understand for seconds in my muscles and nerves. I wasn't just some thing of disjointed limbs. A new bodily grace, after so much grotesque, miserable awkwardness, was there. It was appreciable, and it made a way for a moral conviction that I could believe we have a right to but are granted only when we've come a journey that we might never make twice.

But just two days ago, on the Drive, I passed the small obelisk to Swedenborg (a touch of insanity, standing happily before the trees and the sand and the wide water), and I remembered how oddly and passionately I thought that night, in just a passing second, of FDR's remarks (a president's words!) cut in this obelisk—words on the location of conscience in the modern world. I remembered how I thought then too of Blake's *America,* a poem, or a history from below the flesh and bone of sanity, which I could read then, I knew, because I was driving every moment between Lake Michigan and the burning lake in hell. And how when I saw the second Indian at the Traps, with his squaw and the wrapped papoose and the dog, and saw the beauty of his brave's body in the white light in the dark, his eyes watching and caring, I loved poetry in the human form—as I thought also of the Corn Dance, the Hunt, the Cutting of Trees.

I had the most powerful feeling too, between the sounds of the wind and of the waves pounding the shore, that when we got home I wouldn't need, like the last time, to murder myself or mask Allie and change her to make love, but could come on with my own power and then die of simple natural causes, and never think too much. The music sounding on the radio kept putting me in the right rhythm too—though I was sure that it was right because I knew that I had just done something completely, incalculably wrong.

There had been a turnaround that night as well. I'd beaten him, so I'd be more stable; and the right, smooth changes now would cooperate with this stability. Because I'd beaten him, I could be easy now with myself and stop hating him. I knew it all. But the image of Johnny came immediately to remind me that any turnaround of mine would and should be in the end a turn toward nothing. This is what he does to my history. Everyone needs someone, a friend, a brother, to make such tremendous things clear—though very few are as fortunate as I've been.

At the St. Andrew's turn, sweeping widely in the bend over the dark water, I thought too that I could write my name and the date on a wall now and say something good about naming and dating. And then there might be Johnny again— like the murderous flood before the rainbow, or the purging fire before the last return. He *is* my history with Allie. I've known, always, that in the center he's what makes it what it is. He takes my time out of my control and drowns me or burns me. But in the end he doesn't prevent the great covenantal bow in the sky. Rather, he gets it ready. I know it. I know too that Allie understands what he means to me, even if he means something different to her; for when we're right together, we settle our differences. What's different between us doesn't go as deep as what's the same in us, or at least not when what we're thinking of is the prayer we both pray for the writing out of the book of our lives.

There was also, that night, my magnificent, liberating conviction that if there'd been a wrestling meet the next day, I would have had none of the sick feeling of not wanting to qualify or step into the circle. I can feel something again too of the way that wonderful belief and freedom helped me look up the staircase on Greenwood and walk into the increasing light without thinking that I was offending any dark power by noticing my progress. It made a difference too, I could tell, in the way Allie and I walked up. We had a better, more graceful understanding of the steps and of the varnished banisters; and everything around seemed more comprehensible and even beneficent.

I heard Conlon saying again that I could go home from the war to my wife—that I'd fought in a war, that it was over and that I could "go home in peace." I heard him and believed that, coming back from one of the utmost limits of tolerable danger and fear, I had some claim to think I knew all about war. Allie and I were like a GI and his girl in an old picture from the day the war ended.

Her breasts were beginning to swell then too with the pregnancy. Near the third month, moving past one of the danger points for miscarriage, she was showing nothing but good signs. Superstition, it seemed, didn't need to build any desperate defenses; the quietest prayers were getting answered well enough. And I could think of it—think of how things were going our way. I spoke with her too about the hours, even the progress with Conlon.

"Even physically . . ." I said, ". . . I can feel it . . . like backing away from a fire."

Then, standing with her on the first landing, with the high staircase walls actually out of my mind, I went a crazy step further. I said softly, "I may have passed a point now, A . . . maybe . . . the first real step beyond the worst part."

Immediately then, as we turned and rose higher on the stairs, she leaned into me and pulled one arm even more tightly around me while she reached and touched my face very carefully with her other hand. She was crying for reasons I knew well enough—for reasons of mercy, sorrow, and love. I could see it in her tears. And that moment was another in the series that brought me to a stupendous understanding of my life—one that was its own assurance that time here is only to be counted like clock time in a game.

I heard her say plainly, out loud, as we rose slowly into the light, "I know that if we keep on believing, Peter, it'll all be over. I know there's an end, if we believe in it and hang in."

The words were good for me, and I could think so and take them in.

She said quietly, when we'd made it to our landing and in the bright light I took out the key, "I hated what I saw tonight . . . so much . . . but if, because of it, some large change is over . . . and we can start over . . . for me it would be something that never happened. He's maybe just out of things now. I hope. But I *know* that no matter what comes up or comes back, you're going to be all right. I know it."

In that moment, in that light, I could see where her hopes and fears came from, and where all hopes and fears come from. Free now, but alive with the most vital memory—the close memory of buildings teetering on the verge—I was situated safely but at a close enough distance from both unbelievable sorrow and a frantic vision of the terrible dangers of joy. Everything was alive to me, inside and out. I could see where Allie's anxieties and joys belonged, how they would run and turn in lines of poems. I could enlarge her feelings, with my sense of proportion, until they were wide enough to reach beyond any present state of being. And, in another moment in the series, I felt a happiness and love that I knew were good proof of the final stupidity of being afraid.

"So many things never amount to anything," I said, opening the door. "But this time, this feeling of freedom, comes at me now like I don't know what—the first American face into Dachau."

We entered the apartment arm in arm. I could tell that I wouldn't contract again into a pitiful fetal crouch if she touched me in a first movement of lovemaking. I knew well enough the pathetic history of all the small moves of our nights, or my nights, but I hoped that this sad history of paralysis would change, along with all the other things that had to change. She was so good to me. "I can wait," she would say. "Don't think I can't wait." All these years too she hasn't asked and has asked, as she best sensed what was good for both of us—always, always that way.

As we walked into the bedroom, with the low light soft on the beautiful bed, I was thrilled. I sensed a structure of the world so powerful that it wouldn't ever let me sleep—as long as I remembered it. The bay window reflected the blue clock light and the green of the flower's leaves, and I *knew* that life moves as an interplay of exactly those forces which I'd learned, at the shortest distance from my own death, to fear and need and reverence. It has all been said before. It's the Jews in Numbers and Ezra and Nehemiah and the Prophecies. But for me to have it, and yet be safe—to have the near and vital memory of falling walls threatening me in the dark, or of the sunlight bringing me to dangerous tears in the morning, and yet have good walls and night peace and the delineating, coloring sun—as much as if I were stupid—was to be everywhere and nowhere.

I knew too, as we moved together in the bedroom's semi-darkness, that I wouldn't have any care for the clock, even if the blue numbers on the panel gave me something to think about as they half-lit the room—coloring with that beautiful blue haze the rich green and white of the gardenia, and showing us our bodies mixing with each other in the blue-lit shadow. The history of the world wouldn't for that hour in that place need any devil's engine to move it along, for still I was sure that I wouldn't have to call up any foreign face to give sufficient energy to sad lovemaking. All of this too *because* I wasn't scared to death anymore—*because* I'd learned so well from helplessness and patience that there must be something other than myself to count on, or that it's best to let go, or that letting go is exactly what keeps alive the life one treasures.

"I love you," Allie whispered to me, as she opened my shirt and softly kissed my chest with her wet lips. "Love you . . . love to kiss you."

I lifted her then slightly in·my arms; and, if only for seconds, the grace that this dancer in my arms would give to our weight would tell me something about a lightness in the body and set it in the mind against our sorrow. And I would understand the message about lightness as well as can be—*because* of my coming from where I had just come. Balancing on the edge, with my father telling me to live and Johnny saying that nobody had any such right, moving with extreme caution between the beautiful, terrifying voices of one god and another, getting to know them by the tremendous real power of their threat, like the actual limb- and jaw-strength of jungle cats that one had only known from a perfectly safe distance, or pictures, was again to learn the lessons of fear and reverence as they had to be learned.

And to know what it meant to be just free of this oppression, just free, so that my first words and thoughts about it were a kind of first light breaking out over precarious, if holy, darkness. To remember perfectly that my situation still was one in which things absolutely had to work out, but clearly never would if I said that first word or thought that thought even a moment too early. This for me is the writer's edge: that place where the words are written with perfect hope and perfect caution, and where the difference between noise and silence both thrills and terrifies the heart, but where you *will* know and say out loud that if there is no hope, there is no life worth protecting with sealed lips.

After Allie and I undressed each other and were in bed— the sheets soft, with a warm-colored flowered print, softened in the clock light—I touched her cheek and she turned her mouth to the palm of my hand and kissed it. She took my hand and began with it herself slowly to find the spots we wanted to find. Those spots, though, came up everywhere as we went. It was so good—as good as it can be.

Life's not been unkind to us either. There have been other times when we've had something *like* this. I've been thinking again and again now of the first time we made love, in a beautiful cream room downtown, when the histories of our whole lives, the poetry and wisdom, slowed us and gave a pace to what we did—we were so lucky when we began. And of some times recently when with patience and good luck we've gotten to some places we've never been to before—one, not long ago, when I was whispering, "Don't be afraid. I want you to keep going. Keep going. Find what you've never found. Find it."

But so very rarely have I had, right there to set against the best joy I can possibly know, the tremendous feeling that just living is an unbelievable crime, or such a complete sympathy for what we cannot understand, not just what we can. I wanted her, Allie, and only her in the warm blue light, but I knew that she was so much more than I could ever know. I wanted her arms and shoulders, the feel of her hand, its weight over my hand, the closed lids of her eyes, her mouth. I wanted her words. But beyond this I wanted to let her know that every word she ever spoke or would speak was food for me: that I loved everything she'd been or was then or would be. Let the changes come. And I thanked what I'll call God for the great chance to be afraid of dying and then, maybe for hours, even days, not to be.

Still, too, Johnny's otherness, at that hour, was far enough away. After the triumph I'd had, I didn't need to be him or to offer myself to Allie as him, and I wasn't, as far as I could tell, anywhere sickly whispering his name. But it was more than that. I was maybe released enough from my own insecurities so that really I could be more than myself, or all of myself, and simply not think of him as a dread, thrilling name—rather just entertain him, the stranger, like the best host that it was possible for me to be, to have him bathed, clothed, fed the best portions, his wounds all touched with oils.

But, now over three weeks ago, when I wrote that last sentence, I scribbled fast and enthusiastically, before I went to bed, notes telling myself that I would finish this book. I told myself, even if I thought that it wasn't a good idea to tell myself, that Allie and I ought somewhere in the end to come to that same place where we were after the night that I'd torn Lemaster's mouth with my fist—the highly tendentious description of and song for which I leave in here because I believed in them when I wrote them, even if I can't read them now, with my eyes gone blind in pitiful torturing sorrow and rage.

That I'd actually see Lemaster and Conlon again were

thoughts that I'd had since I wrote the first pages of this book, now maybe twenty months ago. That I'd actually find things out from them that would undo everything I've said here lay at the heart of a curiosity that clearly I suspected was dangerous. My observations on Allie's movements whenever Lemaster was around aren't simple. I knew always—forever—that there were questions I didn't want to ask. I knew something when I whispered in her ear. I've always sickly whispered his name. Always. Always irony and division—and metastasis.

I've thought a good deal, over many years, about what it means to be a host. When I wrote the words of that last sentence above the line, I thought that I'd open this book up truly to the present, that I'd actually now write a letter to John Lemaster and that I'd include the letter in this book—but as it turns out I didn't need to write him to find out what he's like now and where he is. And I'm sure that there's more in the present than even writers dedicated to "The Great Now" want to know, although I hate to say this with all my life. But, whatever may have happened now to my straining intentions, here, I'll cleave this chapter with a line rather than end it and start anything new, even if I've got to let in the absurd sorrow and frenzied rage. I simply know that it's more accurately reflective of my marriage and my life to do this than any divorce would be. This isn't a modern idiot's tale, even if, after all, I've found the cannibal book now to eat every word I've written.

On a Friday afternoon, two weeks, four days, ago (it's now, I think, Tuesday, late afternoon), I went to find an old high-school newsletter that had mentioned Lemaster's appointment to a San Francisco hospital's staff. I'd kept it some six or seven years. As I remembered, it had the hospital's address.

In the secretary, one compartment beneath the pigeon-holes was locked. I couldn't see the old newsletter, and I couldn't find the key. I've heard now from Allie that the key was hidden in a book of Emily Dickinson's poems, a book I'd given her for our tenth anniversary. And I asked her in a fury if she, who knew that Lemaster was dying, planned to tell me if she ever found out he'd died. For when without that key, which Allie had hidden some days before, I just snapped the weak lock of the compartment drawer, I found out, among other things, that he is dying right now, in another San Francisco hospital. The information was contained in a lengthy letter, addressed from Lemaster to my wife, which I found wrapped in the newsletter, in an envelope marked only with her maiden initials. This letter, which in fact runs an eraser stroke over all the neat chalk that I've put up so far, I've taken over and still possess and will include here, if maybe for no other reason than that it does fit its jaws to any purpose that I somewhere might have had.

Dear A.M.,

I am lying in a hospital bed, and you come to my mind. I can't care about the effects of what I say. I have a cancer that has invaded the pancreas. I've lost my sense of humor over it—don't laugh over anything. Nobody needs to tell me about the time I've got. I might rather just leave here silently. But I have a few things to say to a few people. I love you. You know that. You know I always have. I haven't spoken to you in years. I don't know if you know anything about what I've done out here. Never married. Never found anybody like you. I never thought much of choices, but I'd have chosen you. Or I did, but you didn't choose me. Lying in bed here with maybe three months left, I've been thinking hour after hour of the times we spent in bed together. I'll give a good report on you in the afterlife. But let me save my sweet talk till the end.

I hit booze out here pretty hard for a few years, heavy drugs too. Even needles. I lost two jobs over it before I got some help. It was as bad as it gets. I was homeless for about six months. Spent two days in a gutter with an open knife wound. But maybe it wasn't as bad as this. I've always shied on oncology. I remember when Peter's father died. I wanted to talk to you alone so badly. But I distanced myself. I hated Peter's father, maybe for reminding me that my own father died of shame. Or maybe it was just me. Maybe when my father died, I died of shame and came back shameless. I thought things about P.R. Senior. Do you believe he once very passionately compared me favorably to Peter—right before he told me I had no character. Maybe I'll need to be forgiven for what I've thought of him. And P.R.—there are times when I want forgiveness for that, too. Some times, yes. But you know how I am when it comes to your safe, sweet Jesus, though he and I in those early days of heaven had a friendship. Maybe it was because sometimes we both hated God.

Why am I saying all this? I don't know. I'm just saying what's coming. So I'll tell you again that I love you. That's what comes, hour after hour. When I think of how back in high school you gave me your virginity, I'm happy. But that crazy week before you got married is my most treasured memory. I see the room, the bed, that bath. I think of the passion, which you may say was just for those five days, though you know it wasn't. I know your words still have me in them when you speak. Whenever you say 'I love you,' you know you've said it somewhere else. When you see one person you see two. At that wedding it was as hard and strange for you to say 'I do' as it was for me to hear it. The two of us made that wedding insane. But I'm going to stop. If I have three months I'll be lucky. There's a lot of pain. I think of you to help it. If I could hear from you, I'd know I was right making this last bit of noise.

John

She denied nothing, except that she ever even once told him that she loved him. "Never. I swear on my life, Peter. Never once!" We'd locked ourselves in our bedroom, and I stood, still holding the letter—like a weapon I'd wrested from a killer—while she sat on the end of the bed crying. "I was suddenly so afraid . . . so scared . . . my getting married . . . I don't know. I did the craziest thing I could think of. Thought of the one who'd made me as sad as I've ever been! God save us—please! We do things . . . say things . . . that we despise ourselves for forever. All our lives."

I screamed at her, shaking the letter in the air, "You loved it! It made you happy! It made you happy!"

She was sobbing. "That's not the name. Not the name for it. No. No matter what he says. It's no surprise that he'd use his deathbed to hurt. Who would say what he's said just before he died? It's a lie. All he wanted was to stop the wedding. He never had the slightest affection. I knew. I was glad. Believe me! So glad! It was the relief that saved my life. Neither of us having any affection. It being this strange nothing. I despised him for wanting to stop the wedding, too. That's all he wanted. But I felt this crazy compulsion to be with him—to do the same, before—I got married. But I never thought of it as a danger to my getting married. I know that sounds like a lie. But it isn't. It's not. Please believe me. I'm so sorry. Oh, God. I'm so sorry."

I made no step nearer. I brandished the letter in the air before her. I screamed, "How'd this get here—unstamped!"

Then she put her face down in her hands, and moved me into a new world one step further, with a last revelation. "Maybe ten days ago. After you left in the morning—Conlon came. I didn't know him. I'd never seen him. He gave it to me, told me who he was, what the letter was, and left."

10
· THE WEDDING

The way things were going, I had actually intended to go back at this point to my wedding. Honest to God. Or perhaps that had been my intention for a lot longer than I knew. But maybe I've had for a long time also a hungry, sick suspicion and have been secretly sustained by the possibility of a terrible ironic unfolding, one so perfectly demolishing that it would forever save me the task of hope and prayer. "Maybe," I've said to myself now, "I've always known—or I've gotten what I've always wanted."

The wedding now, though, as that unkillable bastard puts it, *is* insane. And my history isn't just emotionally irrecoverable, it *is* someone else's. This is in fact so damned weird that I can't say it. And it is *not* what I want—even if I hate passionately the thought of my ever dying without having made the terrible discovery.

"God fucking *damn* you, if I *hadn't* found out!" I said to her, "if it had been a secret I never knew!"

Him standing there with the ring (now a pure cultural oddity, and no longer the emblem of the eternal unbreakable relation between thingness and love). Him standing there as best man, with the bride his secret passion and partner. All of it to be revealed after the passage of now absolutely absurd, divorcing time. No integral, responsible selfhood—and so no poetry, no sorrow—only easier and easier betrayal. The final legacy of dullness.

But this story right now doesn't scare me. Don't misunderstand me—it makes me want to kill. It makes me want so badly to murder that I think that I could do it. And I know for certain that I could have done it if I'd found out at the time— actually turned the lights on on them—in some unforgettable room. But the betrayal and infidelity truly do not get me far enough beyond stupidity.

"All it's done," I said to her, "is goddamned break me. The anger is a complete fucking idiot. So thank you—finally—for the pure goddamned miserable weariness."

In the old days, coming out past the shadow of terror, I knew that it was by trying so hard to keep myself together that I'd gotten into trouble—but also that the trouble was so serious that nothing could deny me mercy. It was the oldest story of all—a fall and a salvation. And the first move out, after the coming of grace, was into good love. And love was so much the right place—in the best sense so good and sweet for me in the muscles and the brain—that it blessed the move.

So I'll give them credit. They've taken the hope out of my story. Modernity's bitter sleep is what's left after all. And that's it. That's it, I know.

Before that Friday, living in that old love story, I knew that marriage keeps us together but also keeps us open till the most unconventional, real, and crazy loving moments we're going to get, finally come—our moments of loving grace. I knew this—even if I'd also had my life threatened for placing a second's worth of hope in marriage. And I might say that I was always praying that I could show sometime how marriage does its work. Maybe no such prayer is possible now.

Or is that the real laugh? Tell me now, for Christ's sake, is the idea that we'd ever stop our prayer for love, or our mumbling of our attempts at such a prayer, worth very much?

It's the earnest recommendation of our honest and courageous goddamned century that we do stop. But what's that
worth? We've been told that our prayers for love, the order of
our words, our story-shapes, push life around. Our condition
is purely schooled, we're guaranteed; and we can be taught so
that anything can break our hearts. So I want to punish and
kill because I went to a particular school, where we prayed
certain distorting prayers. If I hadn't gone to that particular
school, I wouldn't mind if I saw Allie dialing his number or
closing her eyes as she took his cock in her mouth. We're told
that the prayer that this would never happen, or that, if it ever
did, the wounds would at some time heal, is not a prayer for
life itself. We're told that this is absolutely certain.

But even the incredible bitter taste of all this shit doesn't
work right now for me. The alienation isn't enough. The sorrow of it takes my breath away, but it doesn't bring on a
strong enough protest against my living and dying without
meaning, without love.

It was a deadly, heartbreaking romance that I was writing, and it had moments of great promise. But maybe it's
really over. Vietnam is out of reach; the late sixties; the early
seventies; that picture of the kneeling prisoner taking the bullet in his shocked brain, the shot of the monk sitting in his
body's fire aren't accessible to dull, semiparalytic confusion.
The zero hour, the so-called dark night of the soul, can't
successfully prepare someone for love when his head has got
pictures in it of his beloved with her fingertips so carefully
tracing his enemy's lips, and sounds of a whisper, in a secret
room, asking for everything. So he doesn't go. He's left with
a story that might only work now as a murder story. But it's
too late for that now too, since sweet metastasis is on the
move—doing its work like a modern-day cannibal critic.

But still it's something that I *could* do. I could use my old
dreams for eating, keep up at least some kind of directed work
by cannibalistically dismantling myself, following the limited,
ironic critical program of my time. Which I do—though I
wanted, with prayers just beginning to form on my lips, to

renew old ways. I wanted to come back home after a deadly quest, and find Allie waiting, the way I did before.

But I can't stop seeking now the absolutely most destructive details of the thing. I've imagined myself coming upon the two of them in every stage of their progress. I've heard every word. I've looked at every gift that was given, and seen how it was received. I've heard the requests and the thanks. I've plain out asked Allie too, over and over, if she did this or did that or any other thing.

"God Almighty, Peter, please—please Christ!" She was crying. "Let me forget. I don't want to remember. You don't know—you don't know what it means to want to forget—till it's all gone. I had it forgotten. I had it *forgotten!* Please stop!"

And I said between my teeth, though I hated too what I was saying, "You *don't know* how much I despise the idea of my dying in ignorance—the pitiful thought of me buried a fucking fool, lying there a fucking fool for eternity."

And I carry out my inquest with a mind in fact totally at work. I can't give it up, no matter how stupid it is. I keep over my own pain a watch that would satisfy the Prince of Darkness. So in this phase I am exactly the modern cannibal—the one who dismembers and eats the best hopes he's ever had. And that would be it; my new action line would be obsessive surveillance with the passionate anti-hope of catching everything I believed in, *flagrante delicto*. And the great liberation would be divorce.

We haven't slept much. Again and again we've sat for hours cross-legged in the bed, or sat in the car, talking. That we're talking I'm sure is good—even still. The intensity that for hours on end can win easy victories over sleep shows that we have a prayer in the making.

"I swear, Peter," she whispered to me last night, with almost no voice left, "that there's this in it. There's the fact that I grew up and became wise with it. You say to me there's a place where you know that the only thing you can do is love. You tell me how you know, when you're there, that this is the only way—or you die." She touched my shoulder as we lay together in the dark. "I think I know what this means—what you mean—because I walked into the trouble I did. I swear it, no matter what I may have said at other times—about learning from grief—that it can't be that we have to learn everything from grief. I say that because I saw soon enough how close I came to losing everything I have. Everything—for nothing. That's what I'm afraid of."

And we won't just fall off, keep silent and let time have it. We're both afraid enough so that we'll keep up the fight, and we'll win enough of a victory so that we'll gain some kind of beachhead. What's there after that? We'll see. I don't know. I've got to stop the incredible desire to punish. But (and visions of Barbara return) the desire for revenge—the desire to send to some kind of deep hell the ruiner of my life story—makes me want at the same time, like an Orpheus, to seek her in the halls of the dead. Only she's not there, and I won't have to go. Maybe that's what's wrong! I *won't* lose Allie. I know that she loves me. So I can't write a triangle tale or murder story because I'm just not afraid enough, which is to say I'm too fortunate and stupid.

But I can see her. I don't see often enough, in the way I want and need to, the people and things around me. Before I saw clearly enough his physical presence, I needed my father's body to be diminishing, for the power in his hands to weaken until, discolored on the white sheet, they became the most frightening, heartbreaking sign of his dying.

Allie's hands are not large, though they're beautifully long-fingered. Her nails are always gracefully trimmed, always subdued. Once in a blindfold party game she took into her hands, one set after another, the hands of an entire roomful of people and identified the owners—naming correctly nineteen out of nineteen.

Still she has the slender figure of a dancer, with breasts that come to a beautiful roundness. If she were photographed, she would have no need to turn or hide anything in shadow or under her hand. Her face is white with shadows, and now beautifully sad-eyed in repose. Her lips, neither thin nor full, might receive some light coloring if she's dressing for a night out; and when she smiles, they open on the white of her teeth and the darkness of her mouth and throat beautifully, with an attractiveness that has never once failed for me. And is there anything in this that is more than a sign? If she were wounded or torn, would it break my heart just because that's the code for heartbreaking? Why is she beautiful? Why? Her gray eyes under rich brows, and her hair—the dark auburn now cut short—and always the dancer's grace.

But when I think of her in some room with him, five days, I want to go there to make her movements hideous. I die to scream out and see her limp off like a shot dog. I want to see her taking steps backwards, trying to hide her nude body with her hands, and her face tortured. I want to slap her face and send her to the wall and watch her mouth bleed. Is this heartbreaking? Is it? Or is it just a set response to a set of signals? Or a mere preference? If I were afraid enough, if she'd left me for him forever—I wouldn't ask. Or if I ever did harm her, truly harm her—or if I had come up with a weapon and put a bullet in his head, not just threatened him but done it. But I'm still too stupid. I just lose my breath and feel a pain that *almost* makes me ask if I'll recover, but doesn't because I know that in asking I wouldn't have absolutely to proceed *incognito* in the odd moments Legion sleeps.

But her life is here too. And with my heart broken as it is, I'm alive enough to need deeply to say her name, Alethea Maria McNeal, and that she was born on the North Side of Chicago, January 22, 1948, at St. Joseph's Hospital, and that she moved to Evanston when she was seven and there discovered the lake. Her home on Sheridan Place, a huge gray stone castle, stands on the bluff; and all through her childhood she had a view of the water, the sunrises, the sails—a closer view even than mine. And her family is so kind. One sister, two brothers; and they've always kept close, which I love. Her mother a rough, laughing, beautiful pianist; her father an eccentric millionaire bookseller, who might have prayed Yeats's Prayer when Alethea (the healer) was born, for her life has been close to an answer—though she's had some strong opinions, and spent some time with the stranger, and married me.

She went to school with the nuns at the Convent of the Sacred Heart—a name incomprehensible to the dividing, minimizing idiocy of our time, but something that I know Allie understood. She was loved there and remembers loving best a Japanese nun, Mother Kenoka, who taught her in the first grade and again in the high school, in fact in her last year.

She was a beautiful high-school athlete. She could shoot the eyes out of the basket, which thrilled me so much. In spring, '66, when we were seniors, I saw her hit sixty-three on her first turn in a twenty-one game. It was in her back yard against the captain of my high school's team. He never even bothered to take his turn. But again—again—there's something I know. Jesus—so Christ! *fucking* painful. I'm sure that it would have been then—right about then, with Lemaster. I know it because that game was so near the time that I'd asked her to come see me wrestle—right at the date. I remember. And the more I think of it, the more I'm goddamned certain that that's why he walked off so quickly when he saw Allie and my father waiting for me in the car. So, good. Fine. What are the important days for me anyhow? Honestly, what is my shocking, incomprehensible life? What of my feeding ravenously now on these details that kill me? I bring the story back to them over and over. That's my new intention. And I'll come back to this particular disaster a million more times now and bring all the facts and ironies into an idiot collision for the sake of some goddamned enormous gratifying ruin.

Her college years are now for me years of secret-keeping. I never thought of them that way before. I saw her at Northwestern, studying mathematics and sculpture, but spending more time on social work, hours and hours helping high-school dropouts with math, and their lives, showing remarkable wisdom but always too innocent for great secrets, certainly keeping no secrets that might shock like a mutilated face.

But I asked her two days ago if there were letters, and she said there were. I asked, sent? received? She said both. I said when? How often? She said mostly over a semester's time in senior year, and very few, though there were one or two others before that—one in first year and maybe one in third. I said, sent or received? She said received, but maybe a brief note sent in third year.

I asked for more—for what they each said, what he said, what she said.

I asked screaming, "Did you two ever mock me!"

She said, her head down, "Never—I'd *never* give him anything on you."

I asked her, "What'd he say about me? What did *he* say?"

She said, "He knew he'd better not say anything. But I'm sure that what made him pursue me was rivalry."

I said, "What makes you so sure?"

She said, "He would imply things. I could read the hatred between the lines. Even in remarks about the stupidity of the Chicago school of thought, and about good people, about the weakness of caring for causes and even of my loving my parents. It was sad. And I was blown with frustration, right when I was with him, that you believed your own dignity was a pathetic fiction and his the main truth!"

"But then what's the complaint about me, goddamn you!" I shouted. "What's its name! Why can't you just spit it out and let me just goddamned know it! Go ahead and say it! I'll hate you—I swear it—if you tell me that there isn't one. I'll hate the goddamned soft lie. The shame of pathetic ignorance—Jesus. But you knew too that if I'd known, I'd *never* have come to that altar. I'd sooner have died. You *knew* that! You risked that! And in the fucking dark you go and kill everything that I am! What made you do it! What made you let him put his goddamned cock in you! Oh Jesus. It won't ever change. Never. The pain of this shit is so intense. The gift of yourself. Complete. Your virginity. God all fucking mighty! Anybody but him! Why did you fucking murder me! Don't lie. Don't say that it was nothing. I want to know. I want you to tell me right goddamned now!"

"Peter," she said, "please don't. Please! I swear to God I can't help you if what you're looking for is some word that will kill you, or end us. I never gave myself to him because I loved him. I promise you I never said the words or had the feeling.

You want me to name what I did. But I can't help you. It was excitement, maybe, or surely—and maybe my own death wish. I don't know. Maybe it was mostly fear. I know that it wasn't love. And it was not an expression of feelings against you, or even a trace of distaste."

I looked at her with disbelief, but she went on. "I was afraid," she said slowly, "when I began with you, that it would go so deep I wouldn't get out. It was real, Peter. I had incredible fears for myself. Maybe fears that the ordinary world would go. But I didn't fully understand. I didn't really know how much I was afraid. I wanted something to end my dreams. Something real—that could get me free—of my beliefs.

"He came over that night, which I promise he had never done before and did not do after, not once. We walked down to the lake, to get away from a party crowd at the house. He put his arm around me because it was cold. But we were seventeen, so it just got for me to be something more—simply because of what is. Please don't torture yourself. Don't put yourself in hell—I beg you. That's what got it started for me then—with him. That's all."

I turned my head away, but she touched my arm.

She said, "He talked about freedom. He said I needed to be free of everything, everything like the party up at the house, the people, my parents and family. Then he turned to kiss me. I put my head down. But he moved me with his arm and hand. I know how you hated that too. And yet when he talked about freedom and compared himself to you—and I know, Peter, he came when he came because he saw where I was with you—I got afraid of love. I almost hated it. It was this new feeling in me, though maybe I could say that it had been coming. And I just stayed in that grip of his—which was supposed to be freedom—until it had all happened and was over."

I had something to say, but I couldn't speak—couldn't. I just let her go on—which she would do till she'd persuaded me to believe something.

"Then," she said, "I just ran in tears up the back stairs as soon as we got back, and I cried until I heard birds in the morning, I remember. If you knew how I felt . . . I thought I'd never get back to my life . . . to what I liked about myself. I hated myself. But there's this sick charge in this. So once, twice with those letters, and then in that week, I was working like a madwoman to ruin myself. I frantically built this wall around myself and made it as high and as hard as I could—I mean I wasn't looking, just piling up this barricade. The frenzy was so insanely narrow—if I *always* knew, *always,* that I could get out from it."

I looked at her now. "There was no happiness in it, or pleasure—you want me to believe there wasn't any passionate happiness—your goddamned happiness!"

She put her head down, weary, silent. Then slowly, "The same as you, I can't just blame him, go after him—without feeling guilt or pain. I didn't love him—but—yes—there was a happiness in it, a kind, the thrill of being that wrong. And I'm sure I'd say to him—just for speaking of him the way I have to you—that I'm sorry. But God, that's not the whole story."

"I can't believe," I said, "cannot—that there wasn't love—that there isn't love."

She said, with a slight smile, "Never—not love. Not for a second." Then, "You want to make me the great disappointment of your life. You want me to ruin the whole story. I know you. I've heard you. But I won't. I'm your wife. I love you so much you can't kill it. Nothing can kill it. I swear to God, you know it. And you have to live with me. You have to forgive me. We go too deep. We go too deep than for any insanity to end what we are."

She touched my arm now and held me. She put her head on my shoulder and cried. "I want you to understand me and forgive me. I know forgiveness . . . is the thing you're looking for . . . I swear you could find what you're looking for if you forgive me. And I promise you'll find me when you look for me—never anybody else."

As I write, she's sleeping in the next room. Our bedroom, with its new things and old. The old bed, with a beautiful new white spread, and the old clock on a new glass table. A room that fills with light when the sun comes in through its many wide windows.

And I've thought, too, in plunges like dying, how there is, as she says, some chance for my life in forgiving what came out. I've already started to do it, too—though I have dull feelings that she may be wrong. And then I stop forgiving and let memory and desire work on dull murder scenes that don't improve my faith or understanding. I've killed him with a bullet that punctures the center of his forehead, with a bullet in the mouth. But it stays dull; for even if I can never in my imagination get him to beg for mercy or apologize, and this frightens and infuriates me, I can't really plan any ending of his life. So let cancer have it! Let cancer make a liar out of him and have him screaming for some help or hope. The metastatic disintegration is exactly what he wanted, for Christ's sake— just what he was sure the world was, beyond our words and ideas. The demolition of the self makes love and poetry impossible—and just so, let the beautiful alien disease take out the structure of his fucking brain.

And let my father go with him. To hell with life. Lemaster is me as son; he's me as husband—Allie and my father both preferring him when it gets down to it—and me preferring him myself, for that matter, when it gets down to it. Or at best, things become so intolerably divided and diminished that nothing is complete, or even credible. With him around, no one's able to tell the truth. Everything we say is a lie.

I promised my father that I felt no trace of relief when he was going; and I was overwhelmed, so overwhelmed, but I was also Johnny in part and I wanted my father gone. My father said he loved me, but even on his deathbed he wanted Lemaster. The violence of his exiling him burns into me like fire his ineradicable disappointment and anger. Allie promised for years and years that she loved me, and she told enough truth to keep our lives happy; but her white dresses don't win me over the way they did some weeks ago.

He dwarfs everything. Nothing, when he divides it, is big enough for faith. Disease rips things into small pieces, and disease is Lemaster, the final word. But I can't even say, "So let him see how he likes it!" I've got too much love and respect for him! Christ, I really should murder him. That would be a perfect last chapter.

But Allie, oh God, I can see you. I see you now as rarer than ever. I think of you as going in time, in some room not ours. I think of your safety, the days of it, the inches of it. And I forgive you. I forgive you! Christ, who am I not to! But I want to be in the right place. A place where I have to forgive you or die. I want to feel the pain of what you did to me as something I could neither lie even slightly about nor stand another, even indiscernible measure of. Then I want to make love with you, after some long, incredibly tense patience, on the first day of some restored health, and come out to you, the real healer, as the blessed creation came out to the first morning light. But Goddamn you. You did it. You made our wedding as insane as he says. Or I should say as incomplete. I have too much respect for insanity to grant that bastard his term.

And what was the complaint? You won't tell me. I asked you why you called him one week before our wedding—what it was in me that made it such an overpowering need—and you won't say. You prefer to protect me. You tell me there's nothing to know. But when someone does something as large as what you did, there's got to be something to know.

I didn't expect perfection. When I sat there in a daze in the hours before we married, my mind was overwhelmed. The thing was so powerfully weird. The tremendous size of it all created a silence that made any slight discordant sound as dazing as the magnitude. As we sat in the sun on the patio behind my mother and father's house, Johnny asked, "So how strange is it?" His voice, coming out of that perfect silence, had a power that made me feel that everything was imperfect, even profoundly flawed. But I laughed off with tremendous ease all the idiotic remarks about how much of a spread or a line we were going to get. Six months. Till the honeymoon was over. We were so far from a joke. We had loneliness cut back so far that we *were* the king and queen of the world.

You know how I think. And if I'm not damned, I could have read Spenser that day. Remove Lemaster from the silence, and I could have read Spenser because you and I had things as close to the dream wedding as Spenser had them in his dreams. And I say this knowing that I was moving toward a sickness that I'd been preparing for all my life. How should I say it? The rich dye of the hour stained out as much of my red terror as was ready to bleed.

So it was that, before I found the letter, I thought our marriage was the place to come to after I remembered, for the first time in years, the night after that fight with Lemaster: the joy of it, the feeling of coming to life after making the best possible peace with death: the complete joy of meeting you there and making love, as we did that night on Greenwood. And you know I spit at a modernity which couldn't read a line of Spenser, which would run with its goddamned hands over its ears, hearing "This day is holy; doe ye write it down,/That ye for ever it remember may." But the history I had of our wedding is so shredded now that I'm ready to give back to Lemaster his word—"insane"—utterly refusing, however, to grant that he'd know what the word is worth.

It could be called a day that we really had made ours. I knew that some deep humility was necessary for asking the powers-that-be to set aside a date for what we wanted. I had that much intelligence—but, if I'd said, "You need to be very careful when you ask time for a day to be all yours," I could imagine what Johnny would have said. Maybe: "You have to be a complete fool to talk to 'time' about anything."

Until recently I could still think that we did ask carefully and that we got our wish, and that getting it was, in some very crucial sense, enough. But now what? This is so ludicrous I can't stand it. Another tidy irony. I remember thinking that the wedding had enough power in it to remove from the calendar that other great planned day, the godforsaken day of the wrestling meet. Maybe nothing will heal some wounds. But what a joke now! I know it's modern and enlightened to think of the gift of one's virginity as nothing much—as something that ought to get lost in a sufficient number of other premarital sex memories. But I don't think that way. And those five days before the wedding! I scream: Where Did You Do It!

Where!—because it matters now to me almost like death, almost seriously. You say "Places. Just places." I demand to know Where! Goddamnit—because maybe I'd like to go look and see if those places are still there, and maybe take a torch to them. Who knows? And I want to know desperately what name you called him. Was it a nickname? or just Johnny? or John? or did you not need names? You say, "It was so long ago. How can it really matter?" But I say that for me it's right here and now and that it really matters, if, however, still not enough.

It takes faith to do the things we need to do—to raise children not to be too stupid or too crazy, to stay together year after year—enough faith so that we won't give in to the dividers, the ones who say that nothing is the same in any two places or at any two times or under the sway of any two languages. I had to be married in a church. I could understand this. I loved that we invited people and that they were coming, to the place, at the time. We needed to say that what we were doing was good any place, any time, and that the language that moved us, moved us in the heart.

And yet Goddamn you. Jesus Christ, how I wish I'd caught you! I'd have ended something then. But it went on. We went to the church at noon, ready to be "made one," with you in that white dress which was as simple to me in every sense as it was in its design. Cotton, not satin, it is something that I've actually seen for years, even blind as I am. But obviously I see it differently now. It works for me now as a pall over rot, a death pall in a dream, which means I am as far now from where I'd hoped I'd be at this point as I could have thought ever. Yet I still believe you when you say you never loved him. And I'm dead cold certain that I always will believe you, though I perhaps need not to, if I'm going to see you as I must before we die—as for me the rarest of all beautiful souls.

There were festoons of flowers at the end of each pew. Also bouquets of rich roses and peonies, pink and white and purple—the bridesmaids' hands were filled; and they had crowns of delicate white baby's breath in their hair. The altar was decked with deep colors, and rich whites, though nothing was overdone. And uncountable white petals would be strewn everywhere between the church door and the waiting limousine. Allie's hand and her mother's hand had arranged it all. And I had enough sense to see the colors and shapes—rich compositions against dark wood and white drapes and shadows, or hanging in the air—and to let them work on me like the music, which came strangely and beautifully from a flute.

I'll mention too that in a second, from the side door where I waited, I saw the then dying Mother Kenoka, who was also a teacher of poetry and music, a gardener of roses— mention it again for sorrow on sorrow. For the now utterly disastrous fact remains that I stood waiting in the side door with Lemaster; that I handed the ring to him in a small hard blue jewelry box; that I hugged him after he'd looked at it and read the inscription inside the hammered gold band, Browning's "Grow old along with me" (And when I think that he could even touch the ring, the golden shining object which poets place on the hand of the enduring self, I want to rip out his heart!); and that he whispered in my ear—I know now— something like "I wish I could be you."

Bitter ironic farcical shit, and the difference in meaning that everything takes on for me now is incredible. But of course I'm still not tired of grotesque scene-making, imagining such things as holding his head, trembling, in a toilet, and snapping his neck back only to put murderous words in his ear, and then killing him, watching his red blood staining the water. I've defended myself at my own murder trial countless times already. And I've asked myself, wanting to spit blood, how that goddamned week she had time for it all. But more, I swear, it's just a case of my having no history any longer— though God knows I'm glad as hell I'm not going to die a fool. The thought that I'd be so pitiful sickens me no end.

We made our vows, wrote them ourselves. But what in the name of anything can I do with them when I have this vision now of Lemaster standing there, watching Allie, maybe catching her eye? Religion makes things large enough; he makes everything too small to live with. Allie's coming to the altar with her father—that good but intense man giving her away and whispering in our ears that days ended with the Memorare were good days, useful against oblivion—"Your mother and I—all these years, honey," he whispered, "it's never failed us."

I can't say anymore that these things are what they were. Eliot's beautiful words on memory's use: "For liberation—not less of love but expanding of love beyond desire, and so liberation/From the future as well as the past"—we had them in our vows; and I might in one past have understood them, but they and all the things we put together to provide ourselves with comfort, to help ourselves be strong enough to give ourselves away, seem things for the poet's wasteland, not a church.

Even a saint needs an hour, and the fucking son of a bitch won't let me have an hour. That kiss by the car—it wasn't too much; and now it's everything. The hour's his. Goddamn *life*. And the kiss in the church, which I felt brought me back and in a way let me ring the bells again. And yet, all right, the way it all was supposed to end loneliness—I had it in my mind for this story for some time. The filled pews, the flowers decking the time and place, the promises, the words, the kiss and blessing, were supposed to prepare an end. I confess it. I confess it for the sin that I'm sure I always knew it was. Marriage is *the* sin against the twentieth century. But God Almighty! Her body still had the smell of him! And he stood there! She said, "I do" with a self-consciousness to which mine can't even begin to compare. And mine, as I say, only needed a touch of noise in an awesome silence.

And my father out there. Who in hell in this world was he? Who was he when he died—when in his hand everything ended? I *was* complete sorrow. I *was*. I don't care what I've said. But what's the point? Literally careworn—for what? Or can I figure a way to drive out Lemaster myself? I wish to God I could. There are no words for my saying how much I wish I could.

When I danced with her at the reception—in a beautiful rose-colored tent on her family's wide lawn, overlooking the water—I took her by the hand into a circle made of friends, family, family's friends. We had four hundred people. And if the dance had the look of a thousand other wedding dances, it was different for me because it was mine. I had in the hour something for my pitiful human wounds. I had the best possible friend, not an enemy, in my arms; and if the beauty of the time lasted just several minutes, there was in it an actual triumph.

Yet in those moments in the rose tent, with the evening lake behind, wide and deep blue, it seemed that nowhere, not even in the center of our minds, were we making use of any force. I can't say this right, but we were winning more of the world with some gentle, sure kind of righteousness. The circle around was for seconds again and then again completely charmed. In certain steps I'd pass with her out of the reach of any odd sound obtruding on our brief silent communion. And when we *were* embarrassed, felt looked at, self-conscious, and, I guess I could say, stained again, we had some way almost immediately to get clean. I don't know, maybe just because we'd been there once, we could get back to that heaven again.

I'd look and see her face, with her warm eyes looking back. Her smile kept me feeling light in my weight, which may be the best human feeling there is—along with the joy of movement in measure. She said, "I'm so happy, Peter, I'm frightened." And the breath of her whisper warmed my ear, opening it so much better for the music.

The touch of our hands was also so light and warm that our bodies declared in that ring, I'd say, a sort of world peace, which worked on the hands of all the people of the circle, so that they clapped, and the clapping sound let us know that whatever happened, happened for us. And honest to God I can say it. I was so fulfilled in the moment that if, in the long hell-hours not far off, I was allowed to think at all, I did think of my marriage and this dance in some very key seconds—in crucial seconds when I was allowed to fight for my life.

But of course now, unbelievable, I can see her after several dances—with me, with her father, with my father—leave the circle when Lemaster came in. She walked off very quickly and strangely past the close-packed crowd out of the tent—I can see it—when he came up to where we stood. My pitiful stupidity! Jesus! And the real meaning of the moment is obviously in this departure, or in a new understanding of his unforgotten, now brutal remark: "Did I do something wrong?" A line for which he perhaps now really needs to die. He even had a smile. It's so completely absurd.

But in protest, if not for my life, I have to insist that what was in her mind was everything that had moved her life, everything, not just him but also me—and everything that had ever torn or healed her heart. And I ask in dead cold sincerity—can it be possible that she saw him as her real, last destiny? Is it actually possible? Only my extreme stupidity got me married, but if I keep in mind real possibilities, I have got to say that Lemaster cannot be All Right—because there's more than the need to tear down: there's the need to build, and build more and more beautifully. And the last and truest history will be revealed only when the nature and destiny of desire is totally clear.

If I saw him now, what would I see? He's beyond all doctors himself now—absolutely zero business to be done for a cancer-ruined body. I know. So would he say still that there are no important days? none that turn things importantly in a new direction? Does he need no truths now? no lies? no good? no evil? I needed him once to mock everything I stood for, to make a complete joke out of my name. Dying alone at the other end of the world, wouldn't he need me to call his name? He sounded in some lines of his letter almost like a human being.

And that he is one of course has been Allie's theory all along. It's why she always warned me against him. She said to me the other day too, when she thought that it was safe, that there were times in the first two years after we were married that he'd called her. She said again that she was sure his motive was the destruction of everything I was. With violence and shocked-out misery, I asked her if she'd spent even a single second with him alone since we were married. On her life she promised me she never did, that she got rid of him quickly each time on the phone and never called him back. But then she sat me down, both of us in chairs before the windows in our bedroom—and told me there was one thing further that she hadn't said.

She looked out, and waited a long time before she spoke. Then she told me, "The last time I was with him—and I swear to you, Peter, I'd rather die than hurt you with these details— but that time he said something to me." She stopped as if she didn't know whether she should say what she was going to say. Then, with her voice breaking, she said softly, "He said, 'I could get rid of him.' He laughed when he said it, but then he said again, 'I could.' And I know that, if only for that moment, he meant it. I mean really meant it. And I stayed with him. It was so weird—if I also knew that, where it mattered, my revulsion kept him ten million worlds away from me, and no matter where I was then, I had an ark intact for you and for whatever of me was left."

"So you built your little ship of death," I said.

She said, "Of course—and it was tight as hell."

I smiled.

She said, "It was only possible—my insanity was only possible for me, Peter, if I believed that it would never *truly* hurt you or hurt me at all. There absolutely had to be safety for what we were. And I knew that there was this safety. I knew it. But I tell you, he didn't want me to know this. He wanted to see me capable of unbelievable things! Or at least, for a beginning, capable of smiling at ideas. I took it to mean also that he wanted to see me capable of suicide. And I would call Johnny Lemaster Satan, only somehow he's *not* that interesting. It's maybe more accurate just to say that he's a bad human being."

"Which you can say now," I said, "without remorse?"

"I can tell you," she said, "that there was a brute in him too. I had the feeling that he could hit me. But this too you just stand and sort of look at, and wonder, what in hell am I doing here? If you ask me what I remember first, other than what I've told you, it would be that."

I said, "When my father was dying, we tried to forgive

each other everything. I didn't know what all there was to forgive and he didn't tell me all, but I'd have forgiven him the rest—I know it, no matter what I might feel now.

"His last days, in that room, he sometimes made me want to close off my senses and become a monk. In a way he made me want to die. And as it turns out, he was also nowhere, wanting Lemaster as a son, just as you wanted Lemaster for a lover and just as I wanted to be Lemaster instead of myself. But I forgave my father for driving me out of the world, making me want to disappear; and if I weren't so dull and shocked, maybe I could forgive Lemaster for driving me back in, for making me want so much to stay intact. I don't know. I vaguely feel it like a calling, but I'm so beaten up. I can't even hate. I'm asleep, Al. Even the violence is dull. But maybe if I saw him before he died, or wrote, or something—I honestly feel it like some weird, damned calling."

She said, with no smile, in the clear light, "Peter, why don't you just let it all go—all of it? Maybe the fatigue you feel is a sign that you ought just to forget it. And again—again— do you have to have the kind of total conviction you seek? I don't want to be another tempter for you, I promise. I know what I've said before, but I don't think that you need the *last* deadly edge to live, or write, or to love me.

"I *swear* to you, I kept that letter simply because I feel it makes a claim on my decency and humanity. But I still don't trust it. This is horrible to say now, but I think he wants to hurt us still. Of course I've thought of writing, but I don't know what to say. Feeling you're being manipulated by someone who's in the last stages of cancer is too much. And there it is. I've got him forcing people, even at the end. And you've got him possibly willing to admit for the first time that he needs something. Maybe we owe it to him to leave him alone—to let him die in peace."

Her words have been working in my mind for three days; and I can't get rid of my feeling that I'm called, nor my trust perfected. I've been thinking obsessively of Conlon as well— the one who had in my hardest time to be my world-king. I've begun to wonder again if he has ever come to any grief. Also

I've wondered very seriously if he had any idea of what had gone on between Allie and Lemaster when he was treating me. And what the hell did he think of his recent messenger duty, if he never knew the first thing? Or, if he did know what was up, and still served as a messenger, what kind of a friend is he to me?

I've asked around now, and I've been told that the Privacy Act of 1972 gives me the right to examine my medical records. That would mean that I'd simply have to request a copy of them and I'd receive his notes. It perhaps would mean also that his story will be sanitized, because of the law. But that doesn't cool my desire for it when that desire comes.

11
THE DOCTOR

Two days ago, for the first time in nearly fourteen years, I called my old doctor. The large difference between what I wanted him for now and what I wanted him for then struck me with a blunt weight. I was also immediately brought back, for a moment, when I called—and more powerfully than I've been brought back by any of my desperate, frenzied efforts. When I looked for his name, something of what it meant to me once to find that name printed on a page came back. The fact that he was still there, still actually in the same office, gave me a mixed feeling of comfort and sadness. And if the sadness was new, because in the past I couldn't have him even slightly pathetic, the comfort reminded me of those briefest seconds of respite years ago, when after I had dialed, with the first ring, with the sound of that voice, the gods let me feel that my last chance might be a good one.

The sound of his receptionist's voice specifying and repeating the day and time (next Tuesday, again Tuesday), and just the answer to the call, engendered a response all through me—and for the moment I could read it closely. "Science could save my life" was a thought that came to mind, and that I knew could only have come to mind back then in a flash, but which I also knew *would* for seconds flash out, in those hours when I was some kind of tight, miserable location for the truth. That great need that I had for authority and the absolute dread of saying audibly that I'd found it; and Conlon's saying that we'd proceed just with talking, after I'd built up the courage to ask what we were going to do; and the fear of taking the slightest action, when I needed more than I ever had in my life to act; the fear of hoping even for a single thing—all of this, with the call, or in the silence after dialing, in the first ring, in the sound of that voice, came back. And I can say that I still wanted him not to have come to any grief, though I think of him now as some kind of sickening go-between and have for him even more furious anger than I know—though I might give a report on its possible dangers for me.

But I thought all afternoon yesterday, with an extreme tender and intelligent sadness, of a very different appointment—one that I remember perfectly was in the afternoon of July 19, 1973, the day before Colleen was born. It was an hour when I talked to Conlon about patience and healing, and I thanked him for what I knew. We'd had appointment after appointment over that string of months, and he'd just let me tell my story hour after hour—which helped me so much to sleep at night. There'd never been orders to follow, just his very quiet lead. But there was enough progress to make me patient, and I mean patient enough for me to forget for long times on end what I needed.

Without him I wouldn't, some days, have been able to stand up or breathe. The simple necessity of authority is like that. Sometimes it's have it or die—no matter who thinks differently. So his being there again and again is a fidelity for which, even still, I owe him everything. He was the doctor, quite simply, who helped me believe that when I opened my eyes the sun would still be shining on the same world. And as I progressed in that faith, I won the strength to relax and wait. I began to operate under the assumption that somehow in this murmuring universe my name had not been forgotten and that good work would be done to save it. This is what I mean by patience, and I know that in some situations clearly, and perhaps in all situations whether we know it or not, we have it or we die.

"You gave me the chance"—I said to him—and I remember right now how it was with tears burning—"the chance to be patient while I got better. Maybe loving this, wanting to love this, is what makes me crazy in the first place. But I won't forget it."

I told him too how I thought that patience as the perfect silent prayer was maybe the key to the beginning of all stories—as it made possible a healing, which then showed us an intention, and a direction, and an end. So I thanked him with profound sincerity for helping me become a writer. "Truly, you have, as much as anything I can think of in my life." And all this again was right at the time that my daughter, beyond the reach of any lie that I might ever tell, was about to come into the world.

Just driving the Drive that day was also remarkable. And I promise, it wasn't because I was more sharply on the lookout that I knew that the distances between me and the other cars moving along the road were safe. It was simply that the time had come for me to enjoy one good hour under the summer sun.

The joy that I felt then made the long wait for it almost worthwhile. Distance just didn't come to mind. The idea couldn't survive in the air that down by the lake in sweet July brought the heat of the sun to everybody—out on the water, down on the beach, sailing along the Drive.

For miles and miles, it was just the games. I saw good tennis, even a sweet slow backswing on a fairway at Waveland, and hardball, and softball (sixteen-inch, Chicago's home game), and beautiful Latin soccer and black hoop—with everyone out there enjoying moving with the ball. They were keeping it in play while time passed in the sun, and looking forward to the sweet fatigue that signals that there's nothing more to do except laugh, drink cold beer with your friends, and go home.

In that dry warm air under the wide sunlight, I was able to think, too, like some mad romantic, that all the fear that I'd ever known was only preparing my soul to move out among beautiful things come summer. I knew how for thousands and thousands all down the city beaches, the sand would be a perfectly warm bed—and how then the blue water would kill off the dry, sandy sleep, but also bring new kinds of self-forgetfulness. Along the road, the newer buildings were shining high for me in fiery glass-light; while the gray stones of the old facades were a brake on change like wealth. Both old and new were beautiful along the Gold Coast, with so much peace in the air.

The fact that architecture for so long didn't know that it could change, and then that it did change, was something that I could actually read, and enjoy (with Mies my bath leaving me clean under the nails), rolling alongside the miles of green parks, which backed the built world clear off so that infinite blue could come right to the city's eye. And I could say to myself that care is a danger but knew that my care for this place, for this one vital composition of land and water and sky—that my worry over these structures, gardens, the purity of the incredible water, gave me something that would be waiting when I recovered my life. Something large enough to take in my history of terror at the inch line.

And there was this very beautiful story in the fact that, beyond the reach of anybody's speculations, my daughter's life was forming and growing in the dark, giving a good name to what we can't see. And just as the world's formations and changes had so much poetic power for me after chaos had for so long threatened any positive move of my mind, the actual coming of her birth was even more intensely wonderful because it shone out against one of my dying superstitious terrors: that if I had any hopes at all for my child, any, I would do it harm, even deadly harm.

I did write a poem for her when finally she came safely to us. But the poem—which has a great deal in it of a world seen as a beautiful daring book—would for a number of reasons be impossible for me now. The book that I've got now will maybe try to bring children along in the world by recommending that parents tell lies. I don't need to say that in my lovemaking with Allie at that time there's an oddity for me now even greater than the oddity that was. Lemaster really *was* there, in my place, which kills my heart. And if this makes me edgy enough to think of ending his miserable life, I'll say it again: the world doesn't form or change any more spectacularly for it. And I'm just going where I'm going.

———————

But it's over now, *completely, so completely*. Two weeks ago now I went to see Alexander Conlon; and two weeks ago—and so *of course* this new breaking line—I finally called Barbara, whose face and body had been coming constantly into the gaps between my words (though I tired of saying it), and who luxuriates before me now in every silence in my life, and who has for me the power of an absolute conclusion. If I can say that I got no answer when the phone rang and rang, I'm sure that that doesn't matter at all.

Further, of all the uncountable suppressions of things in this book, I suppose now that among the most interesting and significant may be the fact that I made so little of Barbara's having mentioned her acquaintance with Conlon and his saying that he knew her and did not find her boring—though I can't even really believe myself that these things were suppressed, rather than just let go. There never seemed to me to be much of a noticeable item in such things, as she mentioned him in an apparently insignificant context and he only responded to a question that I'd asked—though I never forgot that she'd said he played the music one night, and can recall perfectly now, if there were endless bizarre and deadly dreams that I woke from back then, that I'd had a dream not long after this of the two of them dancing together before me grotesquely. But I think now how remarkably some piece of new knowledge can make pieces of the past return from near oblivion and begin to form into a story.

They danced together before me grotesquely. He played the music. I didn't know that he knew her when I first saw her, and when I first saw her I was drawn to her and made long love to her in a fantasy. But let the cannibal tale, in all its viciously tendentious fury, have it that I went to her now because Conlon at one time came to know her very well in reality—or because the end that I really want, and want not to wake from, is my nightmare's end.

Two weeks ago yesterday, when I went to him, I felt sleepy and stupid on the Drive—dull like the December day outside. I imagined myself bending to taste Barbara's lips, closing my eyes and forgetting my life. But the need wasn't that strong, and I could say even that my dull feeling was like what this taste would be if I'd ever really had enough of her lips and, for them, had really forgotten life, marriage, structure, joy, terror—given up everything for nothing. I could think that this would be modernity's promise fully realized—with everything made simply as small as it was—and with sex, after some stupid little destructive fire had gone out, missing the hard shape that it gets from desire; or that it all would be a chapter straight out of an idiot book on midlife crisis.

Yet with sudden great power, before I moved up into the Michigan Avenue exit, the enormity of this actual return visit came at me. The towering buildings now rose over me out of sight and darkened the street. And as I am still who I am, I remembered—as I took a last look at the shore—how once, if I wanted not to disappear, I had had to walk down that shore with absolutely zero intention, just letting the sand and the water, the wind and a dead sky hung over a pool from the Ice Age, be what they were.

A loud horn made me quickly mind the road, afraid I might run a tire over the curb. It was as ridiculous as my finding the letter that that goddamned panderer had relayed into Allie's hands! But I was back. The buildings unstoppably took on meaning from it. Words came to me—things I've said in honesty about wanting never really to live through again what I had lived through once, about this being impossible. I parked the car in the shadows. What feelings might come when I in fact stood in his building, on the broad white tiles in the high, cool foyer?

I hadn't once in the long years had an actual return of the terror I knew when I might have disbelieved in everything we build over us. But there the building was, and I recalled, as I had on the phone, how much I'd needed this doctor once—and how I needed on my first return for his face to be the same and for him to remember my name.

Then I was in, and the foyer was enough the same so that I felt that I'd come back to something. I moved to the elevator and pushed the button, wondering now how I'd watch the light inside rise through the numbers, and if the elevator would be the same one I rode on that first time over fifteen years ago.

People poured out, and it was time for me to enter the cage, which was the same, only faded by time, with a smell of age, which I found ludicrous, though I was not amused. And the new jolt when we first rose was sharp—so my eye and my heart did carefully watch the light and wait for it in the slow gaps as it made its way through the numbers.

But I smiled, with absurd good humor, as I thought that he didn't listen to me when I told him the twenty-ninth floor was too damned high for acrophobes; and that I was getting relaxed enough to smile was for me a sign again of the healthy stupidity of my life. Then again I was saddened, confused, preoccupied by the thought of all the differences between then and now, as almost without noticing, I did arrive at the twenty-ninth floor. In fact someone had to ask me if this was my number before I knew where I was.

But I did literally watch my step as I got off, and caught a glimmer of a light in the crack at the threshold which revealed some of the great vacant depth of the shaft. So when I stepped into the corridor, if not truly vertiginous, I remembered more things. I was thinking particularly, as I moved down the gray carpeted hall, of how much it had meant to me that he would be like me and of how much it had also frightened me that he would. Then everything began to seem sad and pathetic as a smell in the carpet recalled the past, and I saw more things that were the same—names, partnerships, a reproduction of a Rembrandt face in his trap-door light, then Conlon's name, not chipped, written in the same way, on the same glass door.

The new receptionist took my name, and it was odd for me to see the face after the voice had had such an effect on me. But the feeling was again a healthier, stupider one, and she was plain, middle-aged—also essentially unmindful of my presence. And when I sat down to wait for my name to be called, I got no uneasy feeling from the fact that I wasn't alone. An older man, twenty, maybe twenty-five years ahead of me, sat across from me. Looking at him, I had a sudden, strange thought—that the body, if it remembers who we are, is no better a defense against madness than a golden ring in a poem. But this didn't make my heart sink, and I could open a magazine and read.

After some minutes, I lifted my eyes from the page, and I wondered, as I had the first time, what Conlon would look like—though I was healthy enough now just to feel sad, and furious. Yet when, after maybe five more minutes, my name was called and I got up and headed for his office, I had a very real fear, too large even for my anger, that in his face and physical presence I would see the end of everything.

At his office door it was the same war zone. The smells, and the shades of light and dark, and the confines of the walls were the same. And it was Conlon before me. He was sitting in front of his desk, finishing some notes. I could look at him—look even at the empty space beyond his window, which was infinitely different from anything that I could do the first time that I had come.

He knew, maybe, why I'd come. He just set his pencil and paper aside on the desk and said, a bit awkwardly, from his chair, "It's been a long time, Peter, I think maybe fifteen years."

He stood now and asked me to sit. The years had begun to loosen his neck and had taken more of his hair and had whitened most of what was left. His teeth were an older man's, and he was slimmer and looked smaller, though he had no thin look, or any sign of special physical health. Indeed if he wasn't tired down fairly far into his soul, then I was misreading what I saw—though I should say too that I was again sad, and beginning to be afraid again that he was all there ever was, and that that was nothing much.

"Some of the old things come back? Or something else on your mind?"

Like a deadly switch, his words in a second simplified my feelings down to the rage that made me go to see him, and made me call Barbara, and makes me think of going to see Lemaster, and of murder.

I answered, in a voice that he'd never heard, a voice out of a terrible mask, "The old things, Al, at least had a degree of poetry. I think I'm reading a dime novel now—a lifeless piece of trash that's got a triangle and a go-between. So you don't have any suggestions for a life that's filled with pain that doesn't even rate? Or maybe you don't know what I'm talking about. You see there's this doctor, or someone who for me was at one time a doctor and who in that role performed his task—putting together for me what was decidedly falling apart—but who now disconnects what he so nicely connected and, as this fucking panderer, brings together my wife and an old friend. And actually this isn't complete trash, because this doctor was a rather large presence for me, so his new role as sneak or pimp is a reversal with potential for first-rate pain. But maybe you still don't know what I'm talking about. Maybe I'm assuming all kinds of things here. Why don't you tell me? You're an authority on plot-obsessed delusion."

"Peter," he said, his eyes down and his chin on his fist, looking the very part of dejection, the image of the world's most profound sorrow, "the man is dying. He wanted a letter delivered. I have no idea what it says."

I started murderously, through my teeth, "I don't give a fuck if he's dying. You tell me honestly now, you goddamned liar, just exactly how much idea you do have of what it says. You tell me just what the hell you think you're up to and just how much you knew when you were treating me."

He said, "I knew a few things, but very few."

Then, as driven as I am now by blind lust, I shouted back,

"Jesus Christ, Conlon, you were in a territory so taboo for me that the mere thought of coming across the line against you was like dying. I was sure you knew where I was! I had to be. But I can say it now. Honest to God, I can say that you might not ever have known the first thing about anything, which I tell you was the theme of all my worst nightmares then.

"Or say it's what I made you that saved me—and maybe nothing more. You were good malleable metal. But now what? Now what? Now you deliver letters. You tell me, does a doctor's duty to his patients end in cases like this? Is that little story over?

"Who's that old guy out there? What's his problem? And where the hell will I be if I've got the same problem at the same time of life? What do you think about the fact that you've got me convinced that good doctors are dreams? But then maybe it's your opinion that I'm making too much out of all this. If so, you'd show your serious ignorance of where I was. You'd show you don't know how much we're afraid that we lie to ourselves! If you're content to let me think you're no authority at all, then you certainly as hell *are* no authority at all, because you don't know how much we need authority when we're goddamned down to it."

Then I stopped—in a period that I felt all through my being. He lifted his head, but turned it slightly. He said, with a kind of tentative aggressiveness, "This might kill you, but I want you to know that I'm a human being. If that's too much for you to live with, I'm sorry—but it's a fact."

"I hope to God," I said, "that you're not trying to make me 'mature'—that you're not a good tough modern man telling me I need to *face my end.* I hope you remember what I think of that shit. And I'll tell you what you need if this *is* the case. You need to get real. Nobody, and I mean nobody, not you and not that fuck out in California, ever finally believes the modern message."

"I'm not sure what you mean. What? That we need to recognize we might not ever know what's true?"

"Yes. Close enough. And you know that you can only suggest that kind of shit to me now because I'm stupidly healthy enough to hear it—just the way I know that I can only come after you like this because I'm healthy enough and stupid enough not to need you. I can get away now with saying that your therapy's all just imagination, because I don't *need* magic. I can say, and hear myself saying, that if people couldn't kid themselves about what you are—if they couldn't believe that you *are* a magus—you'd be out of business, because your patients would be goners. I couldn't even whisper that in my sleep when I was here before."

His look changed to something distant and blank. But I pursued him, along my dangerous line, bitterly.

"Worship," I said, "worship, blind worship, saves everything here, Al. And you'd better the fuck not close the church door on anybody who's really alive with pain. When you're dealing with real human beings you'd better not look at them wisely and maturely and say, 'I hope you realize that I'm a mere human being.' I can tell you that it's *only* because people think that you are in fact a priest that they haven't all, to the last man and woman, gone back to the old priest for what they need."

When I'd finished, he had his eyes on the floor again and his face in his hands. He said, "If I were a priest, I'd only feel a degree stranger than I do."

And not believing now in my own sorrow, and not even abhorring this response as it deserved, I thought how unbelievably pitiful it is that what we find in the end is this—and then also that there may be drugs that could work for me even still. My sister is in California, and I thought (as I now have for weeks, with nothing changing, and my lust, or despair, ready to make its second phone-booth call) that I might arrange to see Con—before Lemaster dies, and that it would be a comfort to me if she had good news. But then, thinking rapidly also of the old worn truth about murders almost always involving husbands and wives, friends, lovers, brothers, I broke the miserable silence with a question, "You said you knew things. What things?"

"Just some things Lemaster told me, things it would seem you know already."

"What things, for Christ's sake?"

"Just that they'd had the affair, the times at the Ambassador East."

And when I heard the name of the place, the name that my wife wouldn't tell me, I was still myself, still Peter Roche, and on fire with shame and misery. But the word 'affair' also was particularly terrible. I felt immediately a new dead weight and needed to throw it off or smother. I said, "Which times are we talking about?"

"I only knew of the times before you came to see me."

"Exactly what times?"

"I can't say exactly. I just know that it was over before I ever met you."

I had to know. "Did he tell you if it was before or after my wife and I were married?"

He said, "Honest to God, Peter, I can't say for certain. He said it was over in a week, that it was no go. He'd tried to win her over, I know, and failed. So it may very well have been before. I honestly can't say. At the time I didn't take notice. Also, he told me about it some time after it was over."

So I was relieved, but still in agony and completely ashamed. I now pictured the hotel room, with pain and angry shame. I thought that I'd go to the Ambassador East as soon as I could—even that I might look for someone to take to the Ambassador East—or that maybe I'd just go there to a room and tear things apart. I asked, "What did he say it meant to him? Do you remember that? Did he call it love? What did he say about her—I suppose that she was unforgettable in bed?"

He looked at me and half-smiled, his cheeks still in his hands. He said, "So who needs me to help him look at his own end?"

"All right, fine," I said, "fine enough. But I spill my guts out for you for years and in return I get nothing out of you— ever—except occasional cryptic one-liners. You say that you're a human being—so the hell with it, why don't we just see it all. Why don't you just talk to me, and tell it. Let's have one real, honest conversation."

He looked at me with a weariness that for a second worried and sickened me. It came home to me again for a moment that he really was all I had or that anyone now had; and his age made me sorry again and afraid. But he surprised me—or part of me.

He said, "What is it, Peter? Do you want to hear that she screamed? Do you want to see it all, experience it all so clearly that it will end all your difficulties for you? Maybe you're just tired of life's politics and you want to be so fully assured of its imperfections that you needn't bother to do any work anymore." He put his head in his hands again and looking at the floor said, "Yeah, that's right. Absolutely. Lemaster said she took him places he'd never been before and that she told him he'd done the same for her. I remember it all now. So are you happy?" He looked up. "Lemaster said she was the sweetest imaginable fuck. Is that what you want to hear?"

With an old, ready appreciation for his wisdom, and with a sense that I had to, I conceded to him. I nodded, even while some part of me felt the unbearable pain of this possibility and believed that the real truth that he had to offer was maybe revealed in this calculated jest, that she was this fuck.

I said, "You have to understand, down in your guts, in your balls, that it's him, not just anybody, and that this is my fucking news! I can still count the days, even hours, since I found all this shit out. I can't help myself with this damned unstoppable curiosity. I'm driven by this really useless, really fucking imbecile need that takes me absolutely nowhere, I know it, but right now I can't stop. I'm sorry."

He took his time. He said, "I know what you're feeling—I know, Peter—because I felt it myself—and went with it—the drive to self-destruction. And it got me to an even deader dead end. Only I'd *completely* screwed it up beforehand by betraying and alienating my wife first. The marriage got to be nothing but destruction, one of us killing the other and both of us killing ourselves, which is so nice at age fifty."

I said, "It's over? You're split?"

He said, "Two years divorced, with all the bloodshed. The pain is still incredible. So if you can forgive me for that, for feeling pain, and still listen to me, take my advice and don't lose what you've got."

Again immediately I was afraid and guilty in the center of my brain, where there was now a name and a phone number. But I could think that this advice I was getting came from the messenger boy! I loved my anger. I said, "You realize perfectly, of course, that if you'd buried that letter I'd never have felt a threat to what I've got—or an urge to smash it."

"Peter, that I've been, exactly as you say, some pimp for human anguish, is coming clearer to me by the second." He spoke with contrition and trouble in his voice, sickeningly reversing our roles, making me the doctor. "Yes, I knew that it was dangerous and wrong. Yes, I was afraid that you'd find out, so I became, exactly as you say, a sneak, waiting down your street till you left. It was unbelievable. But dying in agony at the end of losing everything seemed to me maybe to win the man the right to a last request. I tried to be utterly silent. I knew that your wife loved you. I knew that. But yes, I had a sick feeling that I might see you again. If I've damaged your life, I ask you to forgive me for it. I'll regret it for as long as I live."

When he said this, I loosened, with some dull suspicion that I was now failing to despise what I should despise more than anything on this earth, though I promise I'm learning more and more now to forgive, as my own lust makes me smaller by the hour. I asked him about his broken life. I said, "How did it happen? I mean the divorce."

He said, "I had my crisis—and was sure that the best thing to do to fight off my own fear of dying was to make a fool of myself. So I did make a fool of myself, and she found me out—caught me in fact in this room, which I'd decided was a perfect place for a rendezvous. So I'm a cliché as well as a fool."

I was struck hard by the devastating image and idea, the contemporary cliché! and again by his age and look. And as I felt once more the astounding difference between what I wanted from this man and what I was now finally getting—I thought that this *was* really it, the God-Almighty-damned twentieth century, and that it was the actual end of every story that ever was. I had no doctor but myself, no touch of Jesus for a wounded mind. But still I felt curiosity, or a need for this shit. I said, "Your wife came in?"

"She came in, saw all that she needed to see—right before I put an end to what was one of the most pitiful love episodes in the history of man."

I said nothing. Thinking what? Of being now my doctor's doctor? Of the great difficulty of feeling compassion now for the one who made me patient for summer? Of betrayals that took place in this room, which once for me was a final measuring ground of shadow and daylight—of how, if I got sick again, I couldn't heal myself while believing in nothing. I couldn't respond.

And he brought something out of the silence which I don't believe gave me the strength he hoped it would—because it was sentimental, maybe even a lie. "You know," he said, with a kind tone, "John Lemaster wanted to see you recover. He told me he was never sorrier for anything he'd done. This is what we talked about, maybe for an hour once, right about the time you first came to see me. We were sitting over in the park; I remember perfectly. He said it all was sick envy, that he didn't so much want your wife as he wanted to injure you—because he was obsessed with jealousy of you. He was deeply sorry, I promise you."

I turned against this. It was too good to believe—and it didn't help my lust or anger, which I wanted now more than anything. "If it'll help him, where he is now, to know he succeeded in making me feel he had all the power in the world over me, you might let him know. Tell him he's convinced me forever that there's no greater sin than disagreeing with what he says." I stopped for a second. "Tell him he's 'King of the World'—and maybe you remember what I mean."

Conlon nodded and said, "Yes, I do"—which surprised and frightened me. But I was afraid too about how far he ever could see Lemaster or see me or see anything—how much he ever knew about the poetry of life, or the terror. He said, "You know, he was a good doctor."

I was glad, very glad again to be angry. "He may have had moments, but if you can't see that he was capable of an almost unfathomable disregard for human life, then I wonder what you can see. Or maybe I'm blind, but I hate him enough for what I see in him to murder him for it—though I'd end up the guiltiest man alive. The cancer is ruining the murder plot of my life. I've fantasized about getting there just in time to pull the plug."

He said, "If you'd seen him in action, before the booze and pills started getting him, you'd have thought differently. He worked hard at saving lives. He cared. And your marriage was something that he cared about—impossible to believe as that may seem."

"He told me once," I said, "I think I told you, that he became a doctor because he wanted to see the difference between what we expect and what we get. Did you ever notice any of that delightful modern sentiment in him?"

"I know we didn't see the same man."

"My wife suggested that he used strong-arm tactics in their little get-togethers. So do you think that maybe it's more than this jealousy that you've mentioned? Did you ever think that maybe the bastard is the devil incarnate? My wife says he's not that interesting. But did you ever think he just liked to see things break?"

"Jesus Christ, Peter, I don't want to justify the man for you. What I'm trying to do is get you to cool off. You're still enlarging some dramas you ought to shrink. Take it from me, not as a guru, but as an ordinary, mistake-prone man. You don't want to expand anything here other than your forgetfulness and forgiveness. Take it from me as a divorced man."

But now he made me think of this poor quest I've been on so long, this quest for poetry, which became pitifully then a matter of pride for me. "Do you remember," I said, "that the first time I came here I had a prepared, written statement?"

"Vaguely. I think so."

This weak response was as painful and frightening for me as his surprising, clear memory of the story of the bowl. But I went on. "The feelings I had when I wrote that statement are feelings I want to recapture—if in a safe way. I know you think I need to keep the drama down and save myself a lot of trouble. But the magnitudes were so convincing. I was afraid of offending gods with every word I put down; and yet, if I proceeded in the absolute terror of showing or even of having any desire, or of imposing any direction on anything, I had more desire and hope, and as profound an understanding of how things move, or of how we need them to move, as I have ever had. If I was miserable, I was also never alone—which means that I may have been really and not merely human. I'm sure that I knew something, and I want this intelligence back."

I stopped. He waited, not moving in his chair, before his desk and that old high window. Then with a feeling of mixed anxiety and emptiness, worried and feeling a fool, I said, "I should tell you that right now, to recover my life, I'm writing this book about it, and right now I'm too stupid to put the thing together, too confused! I'm trying to find what makes things move, or what's larger than I am, so I can escape my damned limits. I know that I knew it all once—although, like some damned curious blind Greek, I've wondered for a long time about what discrepancies might exist between your remarks on my case and my own story.

"I remember an hour we once had when I thanked you for helping me develop patience. I mean real patience: the kind that waits in terror of *not* waiting—because it knows if it pushes it'll be punished—and then waits with faith when there's nothing known or visible to wait for. I was especially thankful because this seemed to me a key experience for anyone ever wanting to tell a story—as my patience didn't 'make up' anything, didn't goddamn dare to, but just faithfully watched things proceed. I saw myself back then as such a story-writing person. And I'd love to know, for instance, what your notes for that day say—maybe you considered my gratitude for this weird 'virtue' of patience unhealthy. So you see I've come with all kinds of self-destructive curiosity, if I'm so damned confused and weakened that I don't even really know why."

He gave me a look suggesting that he thought it perhaps

important to take care to be relaxed. "I'm not sure what my remarks would reveal. I'm sure I said something about that story you told of your sitting with your father in the bowl. I remember that, and being very much impressed by it, and remarking on it. I used to use it, if you don't mind. But I've changed. I notice other things. I'm not sure really what I said then. But I'm sure I'd have said, as I'll say now, that thinking of murderous possibilities the way you do is going to lead to morbidity in your life, and, I suspect, in your book."

"I've thought of other endings," I said quickly, "other endings in which I don't kill. I just go see him and talk to him, knowing that he's dying and knowing that he's betrayed me, intending to take from me the best thing I've ever had.

"But when I go into his hospital room, I find him very ill, looking like a ghost, yet waiting for me with a smile of thanks. He tells me that he knows I know, that he's been warned—by you or by my wife—I don't know yet—that I'm not just coming to visit the sick. He says to me, as he has in fact to you, that he was never sorrier for anything he'd done. He says that he'd hoped that I wouldn't find out, but that he also hated having these secrets on me. He says that he hopes that I gain strength from the revelation and that my marriage gains strength from it and from my forgiveness. He says that he hopes that I learn what that word means in its fullest sense, and not for his sake but for mine. He tells me that he knows that Allie always loved me.

"Then he tells me that he's terrified of dying alone and that he needs to have me with him, that if he's somehow convinced me that there's a god of nothingness who demands appeasement, I've convinced him that alienation, contrary to contemporary dogma, is neither our delight nor our destiny.

"We talk—have true healing conversations—and end with our differences reconciled. I'm with him when he dies— when he needs me."

Conlon had his chin on one fist and his cheek pressed against the palm of his other hand. He lifted his head. "You're a romantic—you know about the imagination, after all. Go ahead and write what you want—but *don't go out there—*

either to threaten him, for God's sake, or even to make peace. Just let it end in real life however it will, without you. I say this for your sake, as one who knows how important it is just to *forget* some things."

I said fiercely, "He asks my wife to come. Thanks to you, she knows that."

"Would she ever go to punish anyone, or to convert him or to kill him? Would she even go at all?"

I was embarrassed, and ashamed. "I didn't say I liked that ending. In fact I find it sickening and terrifying." But I loved too my pride and the curiosity that kills. "I believe I have the right to see my medical records. I despise talking about my *rights,* but I actually do want the things very much."

He said, "I think you'll find them fairly flat going. Otherwise I might tell you I'd not kept them. But I never had more than what you told me, if I may have placed emphases differently here and there."

I said, "Good enough. I want to know all those differences—between you and me, and any between what you thought, and said."

But I need to say now how he closed his eyes then and bowed his head and looked weary and pathetic. He shook his head, I thought in disapproval or disgust. I thought that he'd try to talk me out of requesting the notes, and if he had I might have given the idea up right then, as I was repelled by it myself. But he said, "Lemaster," then, "Goddammit all; maybe you're right. Maybe he taught her everything she knew."

And I was his doctor, if I had nothing to recommend me but a remnant of idiot health. I waited for him to say more, as he sat now, head down, in his chair before the desk and the high window.

He said wearily, "The plot does sicken some for us." And then, "It was with a former girlfriend of his. My thing."

And if I was utterly confused, with a terrible fear somewhere jerking spastically, far under a dead weight of stupidity—I was beginning to remember her words about the music, and my old nightmares. But these were passing already into the little last-chance sex dream of our time. All roads lead to

Barbara. And poetry succumbs to the Sex Drive. When Conlon said her name, I had a vague recollection that somewhere—some place I wanted most to get to—we can come to understand the poetry of our sorrow. But I was at a distance from everything, my anger, my fear—everything except her image.

I asked with a barely concealed anxiety if she still lived here. And I was thrilled when I heard that she did. Then, helping me clear out of the way every last thing between her and me, the cynical thought occurred to me that it was destiny—that *I* was now human destiny, moving to her charms. It wasn't even weird that Conlon and I were exactly alike, no more than that two different minds in the past could find in their hearts constantly the same God. And that I could take so easily that he had come to his grief, in the smallest sense amused me. I was already gone, so preoccupied when he looked at his watch and said that he had an appointment now, that I almost forgot to say good-bye.

In the elevator I foresaw things. There was a dull transformation; the two most important questions that I had ever asked—if I would get better and when—degenerated into if and when I would call her. Hot as well as stupid, sufficiently diminished in the perfect modern resolution, I'd pursue her with a suicidal, meaningless vengeance. I'd take her to the Ambassador East, and in some room there for several days I'd make love to her till all hell screamed, or didn't. Everything left in me would give itself over to the sight of her and the sound and the smell and the touch—and I'd find out what it all was worth. And if in a moment, as the light came on for the ground floor, I thought still sadly of his thin white hair and his teeth and his seemingly shrunken body—and of how for so long I'd wanted to tell him how much he meant to me—of how that was going to come, at the end of the story—I couldn't care, if I was such a fool, that he was such a fool. She would be enough.

And this is where I am. After the hour, I went back north; and, as I'm sure I'd planned before I heard what I'd heard, I went to Lincoln Park. I drove all the park drives, dull as death, but there was no stopping anywhere. I was too alive with a kind of panicky lust. I turned back south toward the Ambassador East and lost my breath when I came in sight of it. Its presence was unbelievable. I turned away, toward home again, but on the Inner Drive at the south end of the park, I saw a phone booth with a dangling, thick Chicago book; I drove by, but then stopped a little past it, parked and walked back— with a feeling that I was being moved beyond resisting by all the gathered forces of stupidity. I opened the book and, trembling with lust and anger, began to look for her name, at last moving my finger down the column where it should appear— till it did. And I felt the thrill of the chance I feel now. I had the change and touched myself as I pulled it from my pocket. I could see her face and feel, with detachment and a wild thrill, the end of everything I had, as the coins dropped and I dialed the number. And with the sound of the first ring, I felt some very odd future coming on—but it departed into a void when the rings ran on with no break to four and five and six and seven. She wasn't home, and as I wrote this account, weeks and weeks passed and amazingly I didn't try again.

And, though the reasons are strange and I can't claim to have won any peace, I haven't, as a matter of fact, opened the package of Conlon's notes, which came after some three weeks, believe it or not, and which has sat now for two more weeks next to my pile of early chapters, and will continue to, for some time, yes.

But this afternoon—this is where I am at the present second—I saw another phone booth, with another dangling book, and I accepted the fact (learning for the first time the real meaning of the word 'rationalization') that there would be too many times when this would happen, that I'd never stop coming upon these chances to call. So I stopped and found the number, and once more felt in my groin the thrilling loss of my life, running my finger along my cock when I reached into my pocket for the coins. Then that completely odd future stretched out again in the same way when the ring sounded. But this time, after only two rings, it did become my situation completely when an old familiar voice said, "Hello."

I said, "Barbara?"

She didn't know who it was, but her "Yes?" was friendly.

I said, "I don't know if you'll remember me. This is Peter Roche, an old friend of John Lemaster's? A lot of years ago we had a few drinks a couple of times and then the last time there was a fight—for which I offer belated apologies."

"Peter! Of course. How are you? I remember you very well. What's new? My God, it must be ten years."

"Yeah," I said.

She said, "What's the story? Need help? I'd be glad to help."

I said, "Maybe a little conversation?"

Then with a softened, slower voice, she said, "Sounds easy enough. You wanna just come over? I recently received a nice gift of some very useful white powder. I find it helps the talk."

I said I couldn't then. But I wanted all she could give—her drugs, her beauty. I was close to speechless, but I said, "You wouldn't be able to meet me in the bar at the Pump Room, tomorrow late afternoon, maybe about four?"

She said, "Sounds good. I'll be there."

And I said, "Great."

12
HOW THE POETS COUNT

My daughter's in the next room, sitting legs-up in a chair, reading a sonnet of Wordsworth's for school. She asked me to help her understand what it means, and I went over the poem carefully with her and gave her all the help I could. We looked too at the Immortality Ode and sections of *The Prelude*. Then I told her that Wordsworth was a real poet and that he knew what he needed to know about joy and fear, or pain—that I was sure that he was one of the world's experts on these subjects. And I told her what the terms joy and fear meant to him, showing her where he used the words, and how they meant something similar to the poets whom he read, going back literally over a thousand years, and to the poets who later read him.

"See, how, where he says 'Fair seed-time had my soul, and I grew up/Fostered alike by beauty and by fear'? And here, a little farther down? 'Impressed upon all forms the characters/Of danger or desire; and thus did make/The surface of the universal earth/With triumph and delight, with hope and fear,/Work like a sea . . .'

"The beauty helps you relax, and forget yourself. It helps you feel joy, which is a release from yourself. And the fearful things make you turn around in a big hurry and remember who you are. The fear makes you get back home to yourself. So the whole world says to Wordsworth, 'Remember yourself and forget yourself.' He's been thinking that's what he's supposed to do, but now he feels what he calls a correspondence between himself and the world. And this is a large connection.

"The poets make the heart their business. And one plus one in the heart doesn't equal two. Take one from one in our souls, and it equals the fear of loneliness, which we understand when we know it's the same as the fear of meaningless death. Dead zero. But add one to one, one heart to another, or one heart to nature or to friendly time, and it equals the end of our loneliness, which makes us feel we may have infinite meaning. So in poetry, one plus one can equal everything."

I said to her, however, that a number of critics now, who aren't much like me, or like fathers, when you think of it, would say that virtually nothing means the same thing to any two people, or in different places, or times in history. But I said to her that I couldn't be more passionate, or more concerned about her education, when I told her that that was at best a half- or maybe quarter-truth. Then honestly she said, "What about math and science? Aren't they the same everywhere?" And I said to her that words for the heart weren't that much different, or at least that their truth in one place can also be the same truth in any other place.

But I wonder what she would think of her dad if she knew who he was these days. She means the world to me. If I never do have any damned book, I'll let my children tell the story; and I'll try my best every second of every hour to see that the story turns out well, remembering very carefully what it means, in efforts like this, to let life just go on. But, God forgive me, now I've got to lie and keep on lying. I've kept this manuscript safe in a fireproof box—though I've wanted a number of times to set fire to it. But now, since Allie, since me, I've had to lock it, too, so my children could never get at it without my knowing.

My father's life was so powerful for me. There was that silencing authority in his physical strength and basic beliefs, in the fact, say, that he never would have betrayed my mother; and this gave me my sanity. Obviously I know that it helped make me crazy too. I don't forget that I was even afraid to let Colleen and the boys learn about his history. But if the power and weight of his life was too much for me, it also was enough, and it gave me something good not just to be afraid for but to live by. I think again of Wordsworth, and I'd say that the body of my father's values led me to the joy as well as the fear and pain, and that, taken altogether, it helped me incalculably in my reading of all the poets, which is still what matters to me. But now, Christ, to keep my kids from feeling that there's no connection between them and me and maybe someday buying the miserable idea that that's the way it's got to be, I have to hide the truth. I need, for a lot more years than I have so far, to hold my place as *their* king of the world. But what if that girl in the big chair in the next room, reading poetry and running lines of thought and passion across all the so-called differences in the world, saw her father in some hotel bedroom with a woman who was not her mother? What if she saw it?

It all happened according to plan. That's the way it is when two people want "the same thing," though I'll say that moving through that time was as odd as anything I've ever done. The simplifying, overwhelming lust that reduced everything to inevitability was like nothing I'd ever known. Everything was going to work, no matter what. The calendar was easy enough to clear, and the time away from Allie was easy to get. But if there had been difficulties, they would have been overcome. The prayer was going to be answered: Barbara would be there for me, and she would tell me exactly what I wanted to hear. Every movement and gesture would say exactly what we wanted them to say and be exactly understood. We would be funnier than we've ever been before, and more emotionally compelling. Not a single disturbing difference can survive for a second in that kind of heat; and sleep becomes a perfectly mutually understood joke.

So we built up a chapter in no time, as fast as pornography gets written or read. Although for me the room in the Ambassador East, in the way it pressure-sealed my brain against the guilt, and in the way it provided the hot compressed atmosphere for a very complex revenge, may have been more dramatic and strange than I know. Of course there were her drugs as well—to make the talk, the love, run smoothly—and for all I know maybe nothing, not even moves I made in the past, angers the gods like this dosing with fraud ambrosia.

Any capacity at all for critical detachment is comforting now. A week ago I told Barbara that I wanted her more than anything ever, and didn't even smile. But I think now of a young, devoted girl passionately giving her mind to the study of poetry. I say "my Colleen," and measure her beauty and what I'd call her sweet brilliance. A week ago I eliminated her existence in a second. Barbara, in an immediate response to some signs of worry on my face, whispered, "No one will ever know"—which was enough for me. But my daughter's life— body and soul—is really, with our talk about poetry, all on my mind now—her beauty; and the whole story of her life; how I've prayed for her in some way; how I've tried to be there for her and also, so cautiously, to keep out of her way; how I've watched to see that she finds at least at some point in her life the place where the gods play their huge games for believers; how I've tried to keep her safe, never from what she needs to know, I swear, but from the stupidity of modern life and modern thought.

Oh Goddamn Jesus *Christ* my anger at her mother! I want to make her feel the pain! I want to make her stand outside all that she ever wanted and beg for her damned life to get back in. But no. I can reverse that. And I will reverse it. I can say that the vengefulness is as untrue of me as it is true, and that Allie and I can still make a life, and that I'll stop what I'm doing before it's too late.

"I'm so sorry," I said to her yesterday, after shouting at her in fierce anger over something, as if she were to blame for where I am now. She said nothing, just held my hand, and looked at our hands as she ran her other gently over them—

which is the poetry that the vow makes possible—the marriage oath to tend till death the vulnerable body of love.

And I'm not laughing when I say that at one time what I thought I would be doing at this point was recalling passionately the day Colleen was born. I was moving to it, recalling Allie flushed and beautiful, suffering the pain and recovering, telling me that it was easier "knowing how it's gonna end." And even if I can say now that it was just lucky ignorance, really pitiful naïveté about Allie's past, that let me take in the impressions that I took in during those hours, I'll make the claim for that naive eye and say that what I saw when Colleen was born was what mattered for my life.

I was going to mention too, all along, how the doctor whom we chose had a reputation that came to us from a new source. Lemaster was out of our lives by then, and I never got to know if he was capable of making nothing out of a doctor watching to see a baby come out right from her mother.

But I have got to say, as something else keeps moving on, that I hear now from my sister regularly about how he's doing. Con's been living in San Francisco for a year and a half, and I spoke with her about Johnny not long after I'd found out about the cancer. She hasn't seen him, but she's talked to people at the hospital and found out that he was in fact temporarily released but that he has come back and will remain for some time. She's even gone now to the floor to speak to staff, and has heard among other things that no one comes to see him. She's told me that she may stop in his room before too long—even if she feels like an intruder, and feels some terror at the possibility of seeing cancer again so close up—if she continues to hear that no one's come to visit him.

I told her frankly that I might come out myself. "Though, Con," I said, "you know there were troubles in the past—and there might still be difficulties."

I asked her how she was doing with her treatment. She said that she had remembered, when she was pregnant and had to go off the medication, "what Panic Disorder was, God help us"—though it didn't destroy her. She was determined to have the children she wanted, and after my niece was born, without any trouble, she did go back on the medicine. Even with the dosage reduced, she was feeling "perfectly fine." So that news was very good. And things keep moving on.

But I had had hopes that Lemaster would at least have found for us the doctor who performed the delivery. I expressed my regret to Allie, even after the fight and separation from him. "I'd always wanted at least that," I said.

She said only, "It's probably better—this way." But this remark brings so much pain now—like loneliness.

I've been compelled by the idea of the doctor as some good soldier in the field, knowing a great deal about terror, watching with the sharpest, quickest eye what to save and what to kill, and aware of all the other important discriminations, trying to keep the body safe, while the clock moves. So maybe I wanted Lemaster forced to be in Allie's delivery room, to see him admit something, by the reality. Yet God knows I'm sure I had some strong, wise superstitions that if there was going to be any doctoring done it had better be done by someone like Johnny, or there might have been a curse on the birth. But Dr. Alston Shephard was recommended to us by Allie's mother, who told us that he was the best around. "My God, yes; he's absolutely wonderful." And he was a kind and charming man, who made us trust him with his voice and smile as well as excellent mind—which had additionally, thank God, a fine sense of the ruinous effect of sentimentality. He counted his money, not just his babies.

Also not just anything can fill your heart with joy, which might go to school but won't respond arbitrarily, no damn matter its fetishes and perversions. When the line between my father and me broke and his eyes were shut for the last time, I was ready to go mad. Lines can't be broken like that without enormous pain. The heart knows about lines and breaks; but, on the other hand, it knows when a new line begins, and it will follow it point by point. And for me when, after that long time during which I couldn't think about either living or dying, my daughter was born, the miracle pretty nearly overwhelmed the disaster. Gestation seemed to have prayers more powerful than those of disease.

"We can get silly over all kinds of things, hon," I said also to Colleen. "But if it's life coming or going—joy or sorrow—the poets'll know. That's what they do. They watch for these things—and they find 'em in a million places—life coming and going—joy and sorrow. They know 'em everywhere—and so keep the world from being small."

By 1972 there was a women's clinic down the street. Allie took her initial pregnancy test there, and we were asked, "Do you want the baby?"—which may be the perfectly modern question. Drop old devotions and take on a false liberal look but keep the soul of the ultimate conservative: the killer of inconvenience. Would you have to give it your space, time, and precious matter? If you choose not to, kill it, having decided against it with names like 'embryo' and 'fetus.' Would you have possibly to face and accept an odd child? a freak? a mongoloid? If you can use amniocentesis to peer into the dark and detect the presence of monstrosity, reach in and kill it in the dark, before it's real. Nothing that hasn't been seen is real (believe it like sky-bombers who never see anything but clouds and trails of smoke—and hear no final screams as buildings fall). The poets may have said from time immemorial that everything that lives is holy, but that was then and this is now. And think of the depth of the obligation now to say something other than what the poets have said.

Allie answered the clinician with a simple Yes. I said to her later, "I think of my father's cancer and the way it spread like wildfire. God knows, I was no fool pantheist when it came to that. Kill that. Peer into the dark all you can to find out where it is before it comes too close, and kill it before it goddamned moves. But when doctors are performing abortions, the world has changed."

But of course ask me about this now. Ask me if I'm not capable of the great mind-change of our time—of putting the ellipsis in the oath of Hippocrates, right in its center, where its heart was (and so of effecting the final twentieth-century dispersion of the subject and elimination of sorrow and end of poetry). I've said something other than what the poets have taught me, just like everybody else. And yet goddamn me, I'm going on with my old story, the one that runs deeper, and that I want more than my idiot drift around town.

And I'll get back to what I was about to say, which is that when Allie's water broke, we knew what it was. We'd learned almost everything for parents that there was to learn at the time. This got extremely virtuous and absurd. I remember Allie laughing, saying, "Lamaze may give me just enough contempt for others to get me through this thing." But as it turned out, we liked very much the way that knowing what was what gave us good cues, told us when to move and how fast, and helped cut down on the surprises, while making nicely clear to us dozens of things that we would have missed otherwise. I was the "coach," and she was the "primip." Though it's amusing here too how medicine changes. The schooled breathing will probably lose its reputation and become a joke, and so-called "natural childbirth" will to a certainty go from virtue to crime. But at the time, we were sure that the new techniques would ease the pain, get the timing of the delivery right, and help prevent any tearing, which may well have been the case.

So we were as serious and excited and new-righteous as possible when we headed down the Drive to St. Joseph's, with Allie counting and breathing and the two of us timing the contractions on the car clock. She would work through the pain, come to the "cleansing breath," and smile at me, or laugh, then kiss my hand, then maybe curse me, or direct a sarcasm at God. She looked beautiful with her flushed cheeks, and I wanted to do anything and everything for her, which reaction she enjoyed as ridiculous. We were charmed, the way we should be at twenty-five. And the fact that the moment was powerful enough so that we could concentrate very exclusively on what we had on our minds, and yet be sure that nothing would happen in the car, later made me think, of course, of all the drives, good and bad, to all the hours with Conlon, and of the differences.

In the Labor Room, during the long hours, I thought too of the difference between our single-minded rush to St. Joseph's and the complete impossibility of concentration when I made visits to Mercy to see my father. And this may sound sickening, but I became a better reader of the Bible for the painful thinking, coming a step closer to old Joachim in the wilderness, exiled, pathetically adrift, and to the body of knowledge regarding nativity and arrival after delays too long.

Sickening and no doubt enraging; but that absolutely nothing is in fact worth very much and that there's less than zero point in aching for immortality is, no debate, the real heart of the modern message. That accepting this message can be a matter of pride for us is an enormous oddity to me, but so it goes. The idea, though, that severing all connections in order to dwarf things keeps us sane, since it keeps things small, is understandable. No mania. No depression. Or so Barbara said the other day. But I was glad as hell back then for my manic impiety, which wanted only the enormity of poetry, because it helped me feel complete in the moment. No fearful darkness—no beautiful light. And the event was large enough in itself so that I could even suspect superstitiously, for a few mini-seconds, without terror or dead sleepiness, that my father was in a place where prayer for his granddaughter's safety was one of his tasks—a thought which would nauseate dwarfing modernity. But dwarfing modernity gives us no ritual, no structure, no vitality, no nothing.

And that bastard wants to see her and have a few precious words with her. Why? What for? I swear it's as painful to me as anything else I've learned in my life, short of when I was really learning, balancing over the river of fire. I'll say too that it would be simple as hell for me, if I were on my deathbed, if I had Barbara with me and was drugged. I could die sentimentally and lusciously. What I'd see in Allie would be my marriage: the incredible desire for union, painfully split to a rough edge by the desire for escape; the demands and dissatisfactions; the constant effort to make things work and the perpetual failure. The incompleteness of marriage would make me believe, I'm positive, that death was the final end. I'd feel it in the memories of sex that wasn't wild like sin and that didn't give the rush that comes with suicide.

But let him have his complete say. Let him say that I

believe in less than he does. Even if I say what I say about marriage because there's a large element of fear in my commitment, I'm more in love with Allie than his mind could understand. I think of her as charmed forever. I can't imagine that anything in the universe could hurt her. I've whispered in my heart now, God help me, that the first commitment of the angels is to the safety of her life. And the years have taken us incredibly deep. He doesn't know. I give him credit for knowing things. Why? I think I know—but still—Why? She and I have been together in life, not in some unbelievable smooth fantasy, not for five days in a downtown hotel. We've had children together, not hot conversations or pet cats. Jesus Christ, it's poison to think of him. I swear I'll go and unload on him just before I stick the fucking plug up in his face. Who the hell in this life is he to ask for her? And that pitiful idiot Conlon helping out with the scheme! It's laughable.

But right now I'm going to go on with what I want to go on with. I'm going to say that all through the hours of labor there were dissatisfactions, that I was bored, even through the cheers at the end, which were not all true. But I'm going to say also that they *were* all true, and that there were no dissatisfactions. Everything was actually happening. The distortion of Allie's body, her losing her form due to her having to make room for somebody else, was coming to an end. I wasn't just thinking of it. She would in fact be restored because she was in fact remembered. But the accommodation, her sweet housing of the unknown burden would end too, and the curse is that it couldn't end without great pain. On this the Bible doesn't lie.

But in the Labor Room we joked about it. She said, "I hope that damned apple tasted real, real good"—though the sweat and agony, and moments of delirium, were no joke. It was as tough as it gets in a first delivery, and it was as disturbing as hell to see it. One time she just chanted "No . . . No . . ." with her head whipping for a half hour. But I'm certain, even still, that more than anything she wanted me there, in that unforgettable room with her, behind the curtain. This doesn't need to change with the change of our history, with what I am now, or where I am. Only a damned fool who couldn't forgive the heart its stupid confusions could fail to know it. When her head was thrown back, it was my name that she called when she could. It's that simple.

She said, when she could, "I can't believe there ever were rules that made you wait outside. You there, and not here would be such a waste, and this is so good. It's the best part." And the incredible way the pregnancy had started, with the complicated, desperate masquerades and secret passions, gave way to nature's utterly fierce simplicity which, with no apologies, remembered nobody but the two of us in this effort in fashioning our daughter. And if it sounds odd, or it doesn't help me enough, after all, I'll say that Allie was completely herself in those moments when she was very lost, wanting to find me—"Peter, where are you, Jesus Christ"—frantically reaching out, three times tearing the IV needle from her arm.

The nurse, a young, brittle blond, each time restored the needle, which delivered the labor-inducing medication from the drip bottle. Then with lubricated gloves, she measured the dilation. And all day, as the hours went on and on, how far the breach had opened was a question that got answered by this stick with the greased glove, who called Allie "Honey" in an infuriating mechanical tone. She was cast for a quarrel over a dime, and custom had so far killed perception in her that there'd be no coming back—until maybe she was there with her own husband, having her own baby, feeling the pain, and some dead-eyed bitch called her "Honey." I remember her voice with enough anger, and see the curtain closing at her leaving.

But the very question of the breach was so immediately powerful. In the monitoring of contractions and watching the time there was power. In the inducing, in the labor, in everything: the whole and the separate were written as large and clearly as in some great madonna.

And there was enough power in it so that through these sixteen years we haven't lost interest a single day. Of course I'm supposed to reduce this, to drain out the poetic life in it, to bring it down with tough, unmannered prose—honest—to the real nothing of modern life. Postmodern narratological theory doesn't like it. It doesn't like the look in Allie's face. It doesn't want to hear her say, "This makes us real, Peter. This makes us real. It gives us our life. It shows us." And I can't say what, for moments out of the common dullness, I felt: that in a world that may be the home of gods, or angels, this was the integrating opposite of disintegrating, metastatic disease. That's far too neat a story.

But I thought in a quiet moment too of how we drove out south on the Drive to the Museum (the temple to Science and Industry, which has lions' faces every ten feet around its endless cornice and is gryphon-roofed and held up by angels and caryatids and goddesses of grain, and shows carved Greek letters naming the Theos Geometriou, along with the scenes from Olympian stories, at the door, and inside has all the famous names inscribed on the walls). Allie was maybe four months, and we went to see the line of embryos and fetuses, these names, suspended in lighted bottles against black backgrounds, along a wall which interestingly has hanging in the face of it a warplane of the Luftwaffe, camouflaged but marked with the broken cross, which must have met my father's eye how many times in the air?

I remembered what I could of a heart beating at twenty-six days, of a tube of a nervous system which buds in the eyes, then of the response to touch, then of lips that will swallow if touched, of a skeleton beginning, of an ear, of a completed heart, of a grasping reflex, of growth so fast that if it kept up its pace for a lifetime it would end in a body weighing more than the earth. And so of Albion, the Human Form Divine, the Book of Urizen and the pounding hammer.

Dr. Shephard was from the old school. He wanted Allie to use drugs or gas after transition—said it would save her pain and let him work more smoothly. Such things as the episiotomy and the sewing up, he said, go more smoothly with anesthesia. But Allie said, "I want to feel everything that happens." He told her that not everything that happens is so beautiful or glorious, that "a lot of it just means raw pain." He tried to convince her that she was getting lied to by the Lamaze people, at least as far as the delivery's end was concerned. But he heard her when she said, "Lies or no lies, it's what I want." And he respected her, just asking her with a smile not to call the doctor a bastard when the baby was coming. He said he'd had a fair amount of that in recent years.

So she went without anesthesia to the end, and as the pain, over fourteen hours, was exactly what he said it would be, Allie's mouth once in a while did get as raw as the pain—though she never called the doctor a bastard, I think. And I was exactly on the edge, often enough, for those moments that seemed to resolve the nice little battle of unknowables that has tortured our brains for so long now. Is the development of life up to the last expression of cerebral potential completely the result of random violence? Does the remembering, self-replicating capacity of DNA, in combination with nature's inevitable perpetual variation, show life has the best pace for growth? Does this suggest some kind of providence? Or is it all accident, to the outer reaches of space? Is human intellection to be regarded as part of or as separate from natural history? What difference would the answer make?

It's of course a matter of that extremely odd pride, as well as a keen thrill, to maintain that we're only the result of a history of violence and accident, that this history has no goal and never will, that this is both locally and universally the case, and that what gets called man doesn't exist at all. But even in the automatic, phony voice of the blond nurse there was something, when she said, "It's here," and that she could see the head coming. And for me it meant, *for* the time, that disease was not the final word, that accident was not the final word—since everything didn't just seem to be but, in fact, was moving toward the end that I thought beautiful and good.

In fact what nature had done (and to hell with custom and self-destructive speculation) was so much more remarkable than my dreams that, with what I could see with my own eyes, with that miraculous structure of the cerebrum, mucous-covered, softened and collapsed for the passage, I received, without disturbance, the structure of the room, of the hospital, of our duties and devotions, of the life we want—for that time.

It was all undeniable, and delicate, but enduring, like this new baby—which under the guidance of a decent mother and father (surely, for God's sake, expressions of natural history and indications of something) would become more and more beautiful as the years passed.

Allie's tears of ecstasy and pain, her inability to stop pushing when they told her that she had to resist, her spasmodic cries to God, were the heart of the right message. Everything else was a lie or a stupidity, even if the words, "It's time to go," also, somehow, stupefied me. I still couldn't hope without permission. But, as we raced down the strangely peopled corridor, wheeling the bed, I also could remember Lemaster, who was new enough to believe in breast-feeding, having said to me once that the pap, astoundingly, was filled with medicines that kept the baby safe in the first few days and weeks of life—which was remarkable to hear coming from him, even if for him things remained accidental, period, from beginning to end.

But oh, Allie, it keeps coming back. Why on God's earth would you ever have let him touch you? Why him? Why? Why for one second would he have been in that place? It ruins so much. I swear to God. The pain. And now I'm hurting you. I was born to hurt you. This has been coming forever. It would have come anyway. God knows what road I'm on. He's not the cause. You're not the cause. In the gaps that come when I can't think where I'm going with the story of my life, Barbara's appeared for longer than I've known anything.

And now, so wonderful, you and I talk less and less. I'm sure that you know something very strange is going on in my life—that you don't know me now. I've seen Barbara twice more, just at her apartment—so now less drama, less tension. Sure. I'm fouled up beyond belief. The sex is far more small-time panic than pleasure, I promise you. I don't know what my goal is. Maybe just to have as many or more goddamned days of it as you had with him? Sure as hell I'm counting, but this only makes me feel more profoundly the idiot futility. It's not like those measures down in, not close, and not useful, not anything. But who in this godforsaken hell life does he think he is, touching you? And asking for you now? I remember touching the cool wet towel to your forehead and lips, with so much love, the love I've had all my life, and the things you'd say between contractions. I've wanted to talk about all this now—the curtained room, the rush down the corridor. I don't know if it's right. I don't have the feel. But this birth is something that I want to save.

You told me, when we were alone behind the curtain, "It's OK. I just think about what we get in the end. That's what helps most. There's this girl I've seen in Shephard's office. I've talked to her, and she doesn't want it and feels completely trapped. She's as serious as death, Pete. You couldn't convince her of anything. The way she'd laugh if you mentioned miracle would make you so ashamed of yourself that you wouldn't speak for a month. And the pregnancy hasn't been one long sickness for her the way it is for so many.

"I don't know. I think about my luck. Then when I get scared I think I'm wrong and she's right. She can get to you, I swear. But then I think everything she says is just an unbelievable mistake. It's easy for me to say it—and at the same time feel compassion. So many things get solved by what's happening to me. It's coming. It's definite. And I'm not trapped. But I feel so sorry for her."

And when I heard you, I knew that if I ever wrote a book, I'd let you say this in it. When I saw you then have to suffer through the next grip of pain, with your cheek and neck pressed against the pillow, already soaking from your sweat, I knew that you could write a book yourself on waiting.

I heard you say, "I'm glad I don't know if it's a boy or a girl. How's your guilt? You gonna be disappointed if it's not a boy?" You smiled over this in a pain-free moment, with your face so calm and flushed-beautiful in the quiet light that it could make me believe in world peace. You said, "I hope it has your face, the same features, the green eyes, even if one's as blind as your right eye." And I'm not supposed to bring these things up. But I want to—and I'm sick to death of being shamed into compliance with another way of looking at the world.

Barbara, who has another way of looking at the world, tries to convince me now that you two were seeing each other after we were married. I'm sure she'd love to have me think my daughter's features and green eyes, with the bad one, astigmatic, on the right, are just like all the proofs of anything in the world, that is, suspect. Barbara gives me drugs and tells me that for Lemaster it may be cancer now but it was probably AIDS in the beginning. "Dying in California; no woman to speak of: what does that tell you?" She loves to tell me I'm the most naive human being on the face of the earth. She's got theory after theory after theory and long lines of cocaine to bring her up and a nice pile of antidepressants to bring her back down. So she has a very active heart, and she gets mine to beat along with it.

But I was with you, and to hell with these side tracks, when you were raced from Labor to Delivery. They kept repeating, "Don't push!" But you told them, when finally we got to Delivery, under the ferocious, ice-blue lamps, and they had you spread and strapped down, that you could not stop. You were right there—where the violence of decision doesn't want any more sweet life in the dark. You knew it all, in that cold hollow of a room, like an empty pool in winter. And with your nails dug into the back of my hand, your back tortured, your teeth and jaws clenched, in absolutely all of your strength and violence, you pushed for your life.

The clock on the wall caught my eye; and I could think as Shephard snapped on his gloves and asked quickly for the small, glittering blade, how the clock was coming into the life of this baby and how it would spot now the beginning of our long time of caring for someone passionately, dangerously. It made no noise, but I could think of hearing the spinning red second hand loud; and in your wild groan as you pushed again with enough violence to tear open the earth, there was the sound of simplicity beyond doubt, or profound enough to make me forget my own need, over months and months, never to breathe without caution in a dark room.

But that there was a light and that the doctor was saying now "Go with it. Push! Push!" and that your hands and nails pressed into me so hard that I was cut in several places but nothing hurt—was all enough. He told you quick to look in the mirror, to lift your head—now—and look in the mirror so you could see what was happening, and there wasn't the remotest need for apology. I know, though, that I prayed away hexes and cackling furies—even if the only thing that I could hear in fact, as I looked in the mirror with you, and saw the blood, the fluid, the smeared, yellow disinfectant, was "It's Here Now! It's Here! Look. Can You See? It's Your Baby! Here It Is! And . . ."—the doctor now suddenly lifted and turned it to us—"It Is—A Girl!" To which you said, "Oh, Pete, it's Colleen. It's Colleen."

But then there was no sound—until they cleared her nostrils and throat and she made the first small cry, as an answer to that moment's frantic prayer. And immediately I was leaning down, holding you, trying to keep you from trembling. But Shephard asked me, "Peter, do you want to cut the cord?"—which out of the dark was such an unforgettable rich blue; and I stepped over to do it, though I could barely take the scissors in my hand. And the shining red blood spilled out on the blue cord as soon as I cut into the soft, strange-textured flesh. But the scissors was as sharp as it could be made, and the work was done and the wound clamped in seconds—after which they took Colleen up and brought her to the incubator to get her warm and clean and wrapped.

The placenta was removed—so no danger of any bursting poison, which is something not spoken of at moments like these; and Shephard (unlike doctors we've had since) was not impatient when you winced in pain as he sewed you up. As he had said, a local anesthetic would have been very useful. But you endured the pain in the excitement, when they said from the incubator that everything looked fine. No marks. No deformities. Twenty digits, and everything in the right place. A slight jaundice, but no cause for alarm. Seven pounds, thirteen ounces on the scale, and twenty-one inches long.

"She looks so light and small," you were moaning, really frightened.

But, my Lord, she'd already urinated and was hollering

like a banshee. And only one thing was left to be done—the name-tagging—spell it with two l's—before you could hold your baby. Then there it was: the end of something that had kept pushing on, right along with my own healing, and also beyond us both, and which even in my most profound stupidity, has power to move and convince me. It was the union of fact and dream—like the healing—and it seems still to be right for my story and to justify whatever great push I might give to it. And I will be damned if I'm embarrassed over it, or over the real picture of you later, when in a soft light you unfastened your cotton gown and gave your nipple to your baby's hungry, sucking mouth. Neither of you had to learn what to do, or learn anything about the need, after separation, to come back close together. Heartbeat to heartbeat, you were at the point of the Madonna, an artistic topos which for centuries moved the world, but which now embarrasses it to bleeding hell.

Barbara said to me, "It was painful for me to see you fooled the way you were fooled." It's a drama! Jesus Christ, it's been some days since I've been back at this, and it's a drama! Babylon winning over Jerusalem. I'm so lost and knocked dull, but—I'm sure so very believably—I can feel it now, the heat, big time. No brain left, I live comfortably in the moment at the Pump Room bar. It's the history of my small fear and my cock. I won't disappoint. I'll tell it. I fall into it now hour after hour and masturbate to it, which is about right. And I come when I think of us beginning with the drugs.

She was there waiting, dressed sharp in black and very ready, as it turns out, to help me with my revenge against Allie and Lemaster, whom she had come to despise. In that famous room, with all the glossy pictures of the stars rising on the paneled wall, she looked very good—alive and dangerous and ready. She knew the bartender and had him pour a champagne for me when I appeared, right on time. Just a word to him, before she turned and waved to me—and God I think of this—offering me the warmest smile, which measured up, as I say, perfectly and thus oddly to all my breathless expectations. Then, when I was really there, she stood up to give me a friendly kiss as she placed her hand on my arm and let it run down to my hand, which she held when she said, "It is so good to see you. I really can't believe this. Sit down and tell me the story. You look great. You look the same. I've ordered champagne to celebrate your victory in the fight. I never had a chance to say how much he had it coming."

I said, confused, hot, not knowing any more how I got where I was, but taking my glass and touching it to hers, "I'd be perfectly happy to give you the chance."

I didn't remember that I was in a haunted place—with a room above me, a weight on my mind. I was nervous to the point of breathlessness. I forgot this whole story. This whole book, down to the collapse of all those foolish expectations, when I pulled open a locked compartment. Everything was just gone—not only the half-memories of the gods' tyranny over me but the day of liberation, that victory over Lemaster that ushered in my time of grace and ease, my time of forgetting of victories. And then the memories of a child's birth; and even the smaller story of the revenge, which drifted off into murder. With Barbara holding my hand, maybe since I first could think in this life, I did not care where I was.

We made sweet talk of everything from living to dying; so stuff came up. I gulped too much champagne and it got in my nose and made me choke and laugh. Recovering with a dumb smile on my face, I said, "So what'd he do to you?"

She laughed. "He was a bigger shit to me than either of my two husbands—and that's saying something."

"Married twice?"

"And divorced twice, and that's the end of it. You still married?"

"Yes."

"To the same woman—is it Alice?"

"Yes. Allie."

She took my hand in her two hands, and, lowering her eyes, watched herself lightly run a finger along one of my veins. She asked, looking up slowly, "You still wanna be married?"

I said, "Yeah."

"Too bad!" she laughed, but the smile faded away as she kept on looking in my eyes.

I said to her, "Any children?"

She dropped her look and smiled again. "Thank you. No."

"Well maybe that's good. I mean when it's not working out for the parents, it can mess 'em up."

"I got pregnant twice with my last husband. I thought maybe. And then like an idiot I thought maybe again. Then like a fool I went to this religious doctor the second time and took some big shit from him, which believe me I did not need. So I called Lemaster and got another name and he sent me to some Buddhist doctor—I swear. I don't know. And that was all. I knew I did not want to be Mama. Anyhow, so you and Alice—Allie—gettin' along OK, raisin' kids and bein' squares?"

I said, "Yeah," and let it all pass. She had a great laugh. We were both laughing. Then we had more champagne, and I said, "So come on. What made you say he was a bigger shit than both of your husbands, which I take it means he was a shit of some enormous proportions?"

She put it to me simply. "I'd say he loved cruelty in all of its forms, though I'll give 'im credit and say he was maybe a little nicer when he was drunk. But what was it with you two, or do I know?"

"I don't know—do you know?"

She said, "I think I know."

We both laughed and had another sip of champagne; and I—without any sense of trust- or confidence-breaking—said, kind of giggling, "Alice . . ."

She didn't laugh back; she gave me a sympathetic sad look and said, "Schmitzy, another bottle of champagne here for me and my pal."

And we both laughed over this. I started again, "Alice, you see . . ."

But she stopped me, and said in a soft voice, "I know."

So we touched glasses and drank "To each other." Then I told her that I had had no idea at the time, and she was puzzled, wondering if generally I fought my battles before I knew I needed to fight them. I said, "Pretty smart, eh?"

She smiled. "Pretty smart, baby, for a fool."

Then I said, "What all do we mean?"

She said, "We mean close your eyes."

So I did; and she leaned over, gave me a soft kiss on the mouth, and leaned back, but left her hand in my hand.

What is it Pater says? It's not the fruit of experience but the experience itself that matters? Or some such honest crap. Sentimental intensity, cheap thrills without devotion or belief. No yesterdays, no tomorrows; no lines drawn except for purposes of beauty. So much from one of modernity's daddies—I think of his name and have always compared him with my real pater! But how could marriage match the hard gemlike flame of adultery?

She asked, "What d'ya say we get outa here?"

I said, "That sounds like an excellent idea, but maybe I've got an even better one."

"OK."

"What d'ya say we stay?" I lifted my head slightly.

She gave me a warm smile. "So ya wanna keep it going?"

"I'm not sure again what we mean."

She held my hands more affectionately and brought her face, her mouth close. "Honey, he told me everything. You see he liked to have me feel it—so he threw Allie in my face a good number of times. I guessed why we're here. I thought the second you told me the place, having heard it enough times."

Her cheek was on my cheek, as she put the last words in my ears and kissed me, and the smell of her perfume was beautiful, and good for the sweet talk.

I said, with the oddest conviction that everything was working, that I'd stay absolutely comfortable in a dream, "Do you mind the mixture of vengeance? I promise it's not all there is. I've wanted this for I don't know how many years. I didn't think of anybody else. I thought of you. I think of you when I get afraid of things, or when I feel empty. I don't know why especially then. You're just my comfort."

"Tell me you've ordered a room." She was amused.

"I've ordered a room."

She laughed. She said, "Let's go."

Then I put my arm around her and didn't feel the earth move, or think to feel the earth move; it was breathtaking, but easy. If the world saw, I didn't care. And at the elevator I didn't care, with her arm around me too. It was effortless, even if as grimly intentional as all bloody vengeance. I felt so oddly easy about the way it kept happening and happening. The light in the numbers rose toward fourteen, and nothing stopped us. I was getting my prayers answered—Good Lord, I could almost laugh—and I was wider awake than I can remember. Knowing that it was unreal made no difference. Maybe it's when we're filled with good desire, moral, that there's terror in the elevator, terror and clumsiness with your true woman. There's terror and misery when it's marriage and, with your life, you want it to work. But the gods don't bother a damn when it's modern romance. They let you feel complete. They don't—and it's so odd that they don't—come in and crack your brain in two, or get you talking to yourself, if you're off line like this—even if you're very much on line: vengeful and determined to get what you want. On the contrary, they make you feel great. They're happy to let you order a room. It's incredible. They let you get so fucking stupid that you believe that you've found the metaphorical key to life in a flame, and they let you seal your faith with a clinging kiss.

And now, just with the thought and the remembered taste of the kiss, my words are rushing with grace and to the right end. I'm not drifting, or fighting sleep or the fear of emptiness, because I'm not building but demolishing my life, because I'm not with Allie but with Barbara. And if there will be a murderous fall, I don't care. I just think of Barbara, with us doing a comedy entry, buffooning at the door, and then of her giving me a soft, long serious kiss, saying, "I could use a little vengeance too," and leading me in by the hand.

It's enough to make me furious, in some small way—how easy it was, in that warm room, with its tasteful elegance, unthreatening even in the rich moldings and the humming in the thin cream window blinds. But after I ordered drinks and they came and we'd been drinking and laughing (I had all the time in the world and so did she), I said something that I actually for a moment feared—God forbid—would damage the bright, expansive moment. Why? Maybe just another thrilling jump into nothing. I said, "What's this I hear about you and one Alexander Conlon, M.D.?"

But there were no bumps in this road. She burst out laughing. She said, "Did he tell you, that poor old rat?"

"He told me about an awkward moment."

She laughed again. "Have you ever seen her? I mean Mrs. Al?"

"No."

She reached in her purse casually and pulled out a clear, capped vial with a white powder, and a small mirror, then set them out on the table in front of us. She laughed. "Fat! I mean rotund. Hindenburg! And poor Al! I feel bad, but it was so funny. It's so funny when I think of him with her. And ugly and mean, too. He needed help; I'm sorry."

And I could even think of Allie's words when she said, as the hours and months passed with Conlon, that I'd come back to a good safe place. I could think about how I couldn't talk about him or even mention his name or the good sense and balance he stood for, because I had that much hope and was that afraid. But I was laughing with Barbara, and I wasn't afraid. I said casually, "I was real crazy—back when I first met you. I mean real crazy, and he actually helped me."

"Howwwwww crazy?" she said, but was serious and relaxed and sensual as she ran out two lines on the mirror and took a straw from her purse.

"I didn't trust buildings." I was laughing, but watching her. "I thought for almost a year that I was in danger whenever I came under a roof. I mean it, especially at night this was true."

She had set the mirror on the table and was laughing hysterically. She put her face against me and was shaking.

"And I counted on him. I mean that too."

She said, as she sat up, "And now you've come to me." But she wasn't laughing. She took her straw and bent to the mirror and took a line with passionate hunger, then rolled her head back and closed her eyes like a maenad.

It had me instantly in a place I'd never been in before, and I can pour words out now like a stream, thinking of it. I fantasize all day now about how she then silently, standing for no refusal, put the straw in my hand and lifted the mirror up to me and placed her warm hand on the back of my neck to bring me close to the line. It was a dream older than I can remember, and I took in the line with her same passion and closed my eyes with a feeling of utter completeness, with the simple "I do" that I was never able to say. Then we were kissing with complete passion, and she began to undress me— but stopped and went back to the vial and laid out two more long lines, having me take mine first and then taking hers with the same passion again—before she had my chest bare and was placing her lips on it.

Then she stood and took me, with her arms around me and head bowed, to the bed. But she went back to the table and picked up her things, which she brought to the nightstand and, kneeling down, set them out very carefully where we could reach them. She stood then, slowly, and began to unfasten her dress. But every move had the power to end any potential disturbance in this untouchable perfection. It was an old chapter come completely true; and without second thought, in the euphoric warmth of the cocaine, I read to her the blazon on her blue eyes, her light brown hair, her breasts, which in light and shadow were dreams of an aesthete. And the gods were gone; they did not care. There was even a clock radio with digital numbers on the nightstand with the vial and mirror—incredible—and she set it on a station she knew and got us uninterrupted soft music—without enraging Apollo, or even worrying me.

But even in the bed in the dim light there was more to say. I had to say, as we lay on our sides facing each other and I was touching her hair and cheek, "You know he's dying? That he's out in California with cancer?"

She closed her eyes for several seconds and her face appeared lost, but she was running her hand softly along my side. Then she opened her eyes, but was looking at nothing. She asked me, "What am I supposed to feel?"

I answered with tenderness, with the warmth of the drugs, "I don't know. I don't know what he was to you, or did to you."

"He used to say things about you. He used to say your wife should never have wasted her time on you." She kissed me warmly, then looked passionately in my face and ran her fingers across my cheek. "He wanted her, Peter. He kept after her after you were married. I know he made it with her. He did it to hurt me too. I had to listen."

But I knew what we were doing now and what all we wanted, and with the drugs I took all the available pleasure. I said, "He told her once when they were here together that he'd kill me if it took that."

She slowly dropped her eyes to my genitals and began softly to stroke my cock. "I've wanted this. I wanted this back then. I wanted it that night. I thought you were gonna kill him."

I ran my hand with the pleasure of the sex and the drugs over her thigh. "I still might."

She smiled and kissed me warmly but broke off and turned to the nightstand. Her turning didn't hurt the moment, rather offered only a richer promise. She needed even to sit up and turn on the light to run the lines out carefully on the mirror. She said nothing, just finished the business seriously and then handed me the straw as she put the mirror out for me. And I felt warm and sentimental—and intrigued by the face in the mirror. Then when I'd taken my line completely, I handed her the straw seriously, in what was becoming a ritual manner; and she bent over the mirror, which I held steady for her, till she took the line and then with her finger caught up all the particles of dust and wiped them on her gum over her teeth. Then she replaced the mirror, turned the light back off and lay back with me to wait comfortably for what would come.

I said, "He took her virginity too, when we were seventeen."

She rested her face on my heart and just said quietly, "I know."

And I believed her completely. I said, as if to my closest friend in the world, "Among the times I keep going over, there's this one. It was at that time. We were on the wrestling team. I hate to say this—or I love it—I don't know—but he was the best I ever saw. I mean this—I thought, and sometimes still think, that the record of his victories proves how right it is to believe in nothing. He never cared about them. He had freedom and speed. God, I wish I'd known you then; you might have helped me. I was the opposite: all knots and exhausting anxieties. I used to do everything to get myself ready—hoping so much for a victory that I ended up turning my world into dry bones."

"Tell me"—she placed soft kisses on my heart—"tell me about the one time."

"I set dates on my bedroom wall, days when I'd conquer my enemy and win a little kingdom for myself. But of course when the time rolled around, the enemy actually showed up. I put threats to myself on the wall too: they seemed eventually to map out the damned course of my life. But no day was like this one day. I had it scarred on the wall, and told myself that I'd have no damned life left if I didn't turn it around this time. I begged Allie to come—because I felt like nothing could move me like fighting to win my love. It was a romance out of the middle ages—just like a good deal of my insane life! But it was just before that that she'd been with him! I didn't know it. And she was actually out there sitting with my father, watching. Of course I didn't win; I could barely breathe. Just thinking of myself pinned down and defeated and seeing him after winning his match, triumphing before the crowd with his fist in the air, looking up at Allie and my father. It's so painful to think of him as a lover, or of me as a lover. My fear and defeat."

She said, just above a whisper, "I want you to be a better lover for me, OK? I want you to have your vengeance today. I want you to write this down on the wall." She began slowly and lightly then to fondle me. She went down with her mouth on my cock and caressed me. She had me hard and then lay down on her back. She said, "I want us to think of them and be better lovers."

And too stupid to feel my night terror, I did see the two of them as I finally moved on top of her, and with a calm glance at the clock, entered her, whispering to her her name. Then for a long time I was lost in her, and it was nothing less than I expected. No need for masquerades, no desperate gestures, no real care for the clock—while time went on and my great empire spread. I called her name over and over, and she told me that I was a far better lover—and neither one of us smiled or laughed. But thoughts did come. After a time I thought in split seconds of her abortions and that as far as I knew we'd done nothing to protect ourselves. But this in the moment became only another stimulus. I said a silent prayer of thanks for abortion, a prayer which was in fact what brought me peacefully to the end—which then, however, brought back soon enough the feeling of incredible oddity. And this feeling remained through the sweet and drugged after-fatigue.

She said to me, "You're a winner," and bit me lightly on the shoulder. I smiled back but was beginning to remember where I was—hearing that faint hum in the blinds—as the oddity got to be too much. But we slept then for a long time—till I knew the clock must be saying something dangerous. I opened my eyes and looked, and saw that I was right. All the time in the world had shrunk down fast enough.

I tapped her lightly on the shoulder and, pointing to the clock, whispered that I had to go.

She looked at the clock and said, "I guess you do," giving me a kiss. "Do you mind if I just stay?"

I said warmly that of course I didn't, but I was up already and gathering my clothes. And I was dressed in under a minute, which amused her. She smiled as she watched me put on my coat. The way I jerked myself into it and then tried to straighten my hair before the mirror made her laugh. She said, "Come here for just a second, and bring me my purse, OK?" I obliged her, and she had me sit down next to her so she could comb my hair. Then she held up our little mirror and asked me—"Back to normal?"

"Yeah."

"Look me in the eye, OK?"

"OK."

She held my face gently in her two hands and said, "I want you to promise you'll call me again. Promise?" I nodded. Then she gave me a light kiss and said, "Don't worry." I nodded and kissed her back, then took her hand—but stood to go. She held my hand tighter, just to turn me back slightly, and said in a soft voice, looking up comfortingly, "No one will ever know."

I said, "OK," and let her hand go and walked to the door and left. Stupid and rushed enough to forget then where I was, I knew when I came out into the ten o'clock sounds of the street and the touch of the air that something might happen sometime to make me remember—the Ambassador East—and that I'd know my revenge then as the poets know revenge—which is to say like a nightmare. And if the Drive in the summer night stayed fixed to the ground and was even spectacularly beautiful between harbor lights and city lights, Barbara was no comfort anymore.

Right now, too, I don't fantasize. I don't want it—and every bit as much as I say I don't want it, if this refusal doesn't amount yet to a revolution. Allie just said to me an hour ago, "You're so far from yourself these days, I don't know what I'm married to." And I said, "I'm comin' back. I've just had things on my mind. It'll turn out. I promise. Give me time." She said, "What is it—maybe five, six weeks now? I'd blame myself. My life. I do blame myself. I can't live with myself. But I think there's more." I said, "Don't blame yourself. I'm learning to deal with things. I'm trying to forget things. It's not you. It's me. But it's coming around. You'll see it." She said, "I'm so sorry." I said, "Please don't be." She put her arms around me and began to cry. "I'm so afraid I'm losing you." I said, "You're not. That's not it at all. Please believe me." She said, "Promise?" I said, "Promise."

And two days ago my daughter got her interpretation of

Wordsworth back. The English teacher, while apparently not understanding all Colleen intended, wrote a most kind, enthusiastic comment. "I can see," she said, "that you love poetry very much. I'm sure Wordsworth would appreciate the warmth and intelligence of your remarks. This is the best paper I've had in a long time." And I said to Colleen, giving her a fatherly hug, "The poets do count on good hearts."

13
THE JOURNEY ACROSS AMERICA

Whatever it was that I had with Barbara Dern, it's over—a story without real drive after all; though I wouldn't laugh at Sheehy's *Passages* as a bad book. Three months, with fairly regular cocaine use for a time. Christ knows, if it had gone on much longer, it might have come to some utterly miserable conclusion, one that would maybe have told me something I wouldn't forget—something only the lost know about easy, false comfort in the gaps and the true nature of prayer. But it's over, and things have happened which are so much larger that even the drugs and the sexual revenge, the betrayal and thrilling alienation of Allie and of myself, the incursion into Lemaster's old territory, the exciting taste of Barbara's almost complete despair, which would be enough for most of us, are dreams blown back in the wind. I ended up on my knees in Lincoln Park in the middle of the night, spitting to get the taste out of my my mouth, crying, making promises. But in a way incalculably different, as different as *Passages* is from the poetry that constitutes and destroys the heart, I make promises now to the gods, that I'll never see, for

Peter Roche, either the slightest sign of victory or the slightest sign of defeat in the death of Johnny Lemaster, which came unbelievably on the morning of April 4, nine weeks ago, almost to the hour.

It's different—so different from when my father died. I don't feel the exact same things. But fear translates, no matter what modernity says. Without Johnny, as I suspected, or maybe, yes, even hoped, built things don't stand up for me either; and I've had days when I needed to get far enough into the open air to keep safe from what might fall.

"The feeling of the disease," I said to Allie last night, after it was quiet, and we were alone, "—it's always different. It comes to me now only in these flashes. But it's the same."

She said carefully, "I remember my mother having dreams right out of hell after her sister died . . . for some time . . . she couldn't sleep. Then it just changed for her . . . after she'd dreamed out all her dreams."

I haven't called a doctor because by some absolute miracle things are getting better. I'm not on my own, though; I'm with Allie, and I am waiting again on time. But it's only in a whisper now that I can say so. I wouldn't be so incautious as to talk about this right now with Allie. And yet I am again certain and will say, fast, that only a radical fool thinks that things don't happen for him when he just waits. I feel released from doubt on this as the days pass, and as it's now morning—though once again I wouldn't express such confidence after dark.

Not long before Johnny died, I got a letter from my sister.

My dearest Pete—

I went to see Johnny this afternoon. Still nobody comes. I feel such sorrow when I think of his life. God knows how he got where he is now. It was definitely AIDS first and is now cancer, everywhere: I get a feeling from talking to him that he was using needles on the street! It sounds so unbelievable when I say this. But it doesn't matter now. He's got very little time left. His face is someone else's. It's unbearably cruel. I see him still as so beautiful. It's all still with me—the thousands of hours and days he was over at the house and you two playing ball. I can't think of a day from my childhood without the sound or the picture of you two in it, close as brothers. But it's Dad all over again, Pete. I don't know what he weighs, but he's gone. It's so hard for me to look at it. I can't find things to say. But I know he's glad I come. I bring him flowers and things, and he doesn't make me feel stupid or insulting. But I feel that even right now I'm wasting time. You need to come now if you can come. It can't be more than a few weeks, or maybe even days. He talks about you all the time. He doesn't want to say something that will make you have to come, but I'm sure that he wants to see you. And I want to see you. It's been so long, and you need to see Francine before she gets any bigger. I'm sure Johnny doesn't want me to say this, Pete, but I know there's something in this visiting of the sick and dying which we all need. I'm sorry. I know you know this! I remember—very amazing, dear bro—your telling me when you were young that when you grew up you wanted to be a saint! I'm not sure what happened between you two, but if it asks sanctity of you, I think that you should come. And if I didn't tell you that he has no one, and that he wants you, I'd be hiding something I shouldn't hide. Please come.

> Your loving sister and friend,
> Con

When Allie read the letter, she said, "Please don't, Peter. For my sake—for our lives—don't bring things up that are better forgotten. If you have to, yes, go to him, and help him. But promise to think of what's best—for what we are."

I said, "I promise. I promise you. But I need you to come. I know I need you to come. There'll be other problems in this that I won't be able to solve on my own. I'm not thinking of punishing you, but of my own need. It's been a long time, but I think I could be heading into one of those bad times again. I have trouble even seeing myself board a plane. A night flight couldn't happen for me without you."

And if she could have wished for an altogether different world, she knew I was telling the truth. So she agreed; and we made arrangements immediately, with the feeling, confused, but complete, that this was something to which life had led us. And in the late afternoon, we headed out to O'Hare Field for a sundown flight to San Francisco, which made me think, among other things, of Assisi and the saint who gave up his riches and wrote canticles to the sun, who tore the mind of Italy in two and divided it against its own violence, and thereby, I whispered in my heart as I threw coins into the toll bin, added an honest chapter to the history of the world.

I knew how much trouble it would mean for me if I thought it, but the ideas of this disease now really came to me. The picture of Johnny making homosexual love or of Johnny at the world's end, binding his arm to find a vein, very very frighteningly brought me some degree of satisfaction. I thought quickly of some homophobic revenge graffiti that I saw carved on a bathroom wall, something that mentioned AIDS and God's plans. And the breakdown of his immune system, plus the spread all through him of rampaging cancer, in extreme metastasis now, were things that I wanted, so that I could ask him questions now about his real expectations, desire, and sorrow. I wanted to say, "This is it, John. This disease—it's another fine image of modern irony. How do you like it?"

I'd read things. I remembered thinking with violent satisfaction that the disease worked *exactly* like the principles of modern thought—as it throve on geographical variance, the terrifyingly swift, extensive mutation—even in single patients—with the radical indeterminacy crushing our hopes for a protective, eliminating vaccine. Seventeen mutants of one polysemous virus in a single human host evolved over a terrifyingly short time—and nothing to say that that couldn't go to a hundred. Or that the virus won't move soon into all communities of men and women. Also no discoveries or clues yet. Nothing known, not even a beginning of an understanding of so much of it. And I couldn't say *kill!*

I wanted to hold a medieval death's head up to his eye and say that when there were plagues before, people at least knew the use of terror—and that the very unmodern saints,

blessed beyond their own blessed fear, went in, in self-cruci-
fixion, to care for the sick and dying. They knew, I wanted to
say, that such times were certainly not times to stop praying
for the things that we must pray for—that they were times,
rather, for everything in the heart to stand up in anger, without shame, and then finally find ecstasy in the heart's absolute
defeat.

I wanted to tell him that this is the story of life—this
hoping and praying and then passing selflessly beyond our
hopes and the limits of our lives—and then tell him passionately that I loved him with everything in me, and that because
I loved him with absolutely all my heart, I felt more sorrow
than I could express. Yet I knew how unforgivable it would be
if I mentioned sorrow to Johnny when I saw him now.

But also Barbara was right! She knew. "I'm telling you,
dear, it's certain. It's AIDS," she said. Though that Johnny,
like a different kind of Byron (one who maybe had his wounds
but never studied or sang about them), would try everything,
wasn't surprising. My anger, when I read his letter to Allie,
was so stupid and blind that I forgot nearly all compassion—
though in truth I never really wanted to take any vicious
comfort from hearing about his hard drug use—as the drug
use didn't surprise me and I was deeply ashamed that it didn't.
But I watched Barbara that time take some satisfaction in her
speculations. "You are such an innocent boy," she smiled, and
busied herself coyly with the paraphernalia of a moment without a future or a past. But if she was actually right—if he had
the disease—would this shame her or make her sorry that she
ever dared to theorize? "I'm not your kind of crazy," she
said—and sat with me and made me forget what it was that
she meant about me—though I was always taken by how well
she knew me: by her understanding of how crazy I was.

But now again, heading to see Lemaster, I was unbearably ashamed that he'd ever get hurt. I felt sudden indignant
hatred for the fact that his opening himself up to the penetrat-
ing point of the needle—the cock as well?—only ironically
made him host to the deadly alien virus. I hated the irony, in
my crazy way, even if it was an irony against Johnny, against

modern life. I felt this terrible sudden anger that any sorrowful opening up of the isolated self—so that it could taste whatever ambrosia it might need—would find such a poison as AIDS.

Yet now I was doing it again! I couldn't leave the pure absurdity of AIDS alone but had to make it into a *reason* for my poetry of sorrow. Also I *was* turning Johnny into another Byron. And that I couldn't leave him alone either, but had to make him into another true poet on the far edge of poetry— another one who would never really despair but always longed secretly for the beautiful rose and the end of his proud aliena- tion—made me ashamed enough to clear my head of all no- tions and let him be the absolute death of poetry. I'd let him be this, the death of it. And I'd clear my head of ideas—if sickeningly and contradictorily this clearing of my head made sudden room for thoughts of him and Allie and put the blind- ing notion of homicide immediately back in my mind.

When we got to the airport, it was a mad rush down endless corridors. Our gate was at the far end of United, one of O'Hare's longest terminals; but in the rush I couldn't get nearly mindless enough so that the fast walking and running could work out the dread. Sounds of the page calling a name in indecipherable tones, readable business intentions, dis- guised trysting, sex drives, reunions of families, farewells, men and boys and girls and women in uniform, vacation and recre- ation mania, contemporary moves of one kind or another in this the great contemporary brain had me reflective for some seconds at a time, when we walked. But I didn't need convinc- ing—as I felt vertigo, and terror about my taking off in the air for California—that mine was the real story. There was no need to argue that, in comparison to me, everyone in the world's busiest airport was in an unknowing daze—though Allie, I knew, could read me well enough and tried to say just the right things, with her thumb, as she ran it lightly over the back of my hand, which she held very carefully in the ticket line and as we sat in the waiting area, listening for the an- nouncement to board.

It was so much motion so fast, the arranging, packing, rush over and then the walk-run down those hard long corridors, and now the plane's docking and our readying to board. But this didn't make the fear what it was. My whole life made the fear what it was, and yet I was praying for this life wide awake—but praying also that I would be forgiven for presuming to live it and even to exist at all. I don't know all the arguments. I don't know modernity's full panoply of philosophical objections to the fact of my life, or the illusion of it. I just am certain that I know how, in the profoundest sense, to be sorry for it, as for a crime. And unconsciously I was chanting that I would never argue for it or defend it as, holding Allie's hand carefully, I waited for the announcement to board—which came too fast by the clock I was watching in my guts and brain.

And whatever hospitality of heart that I had to extend to hideous water snakes, I was willing exactly now to extend. Whatever crossbowing of strange birds through the heart— and I knew there was much—that I needed to repent, I was willing to repent. In my frightened humanity, and shifting now in wild contradiction, I could read Coleridge's astounding poem of the Mariner as the plane faced west and the sun stood out before us, the shade of evening behind. This wonderful poet, I could think, knew the whole world about prayer: the delicacy in the achievement of it, the unfathomable need for it, the posture on the knees, the closing of the eyes, the bowing of the head, and yet the sounds, the words, the simple acceptance of the world as it is and the simultaneous unstoppable expression of desire for change. Coleridge the nightmare man, the friend—I loved him. He knew the world as all story and prayer, and yet he also begged forgiveness for his life—for every sound he ever made.

I had my eyes fast, for seconds here and there, on the structure of the plane. Anything that struck me as insufficiently authoritative passed in a vision instantly into my body (if mind and body differ), and I was sick from it. The rivets on the spreading, flexible wings, the sooty residue and dirt around the dark cavern-mouth of the jets, the give and diminutive measure of the tires, all had me wondering what would hold.

And then the timing—the waiting through nothing, nothing, nothing—till there was the sudden, if slow, motion.

Allie's hand was in my hand; she felt the sweat and pressure of my grip, and in speaking to me chose her words with great care.

As we moved, she said softly, "The food helps me. Somehow when they bring the food it helps. And maybe a drink or two—but not six. Maybe some nice warm Manhattan or something." Her words, her voice and her smile, helped me (though I couldn't think this) till the bell sound came and then the captain's voice, his hello, his introduction of himself by name—Captain Tom Ward—and his clear indication of our procedures, our expected air speed, the weather in San Francisco, got me relaxed enough to smile and breathe and then even to think and talk, and to manage the readying for takeoff. But I thought that if I could see the pilot, or were in charge myself, I'd feel better still.

And I can insist that it was the going to see Johnny that made the difference; or that it was my damned life, summed up in this event, and roaring in the event, that made me need to sit at a window and measure moment by moment the distance between myself and the ground. My damned life with Johnny, the insufficiency of my love, was the reason that I watched for every sign. It made me consider and indirectly then fear my consideration of the measure of thrust when we first jolted and then roared down the flat, straight, concrete-ugly runway. This was the takeoff, and nothing could be more true. Nothing. That I feared and so hated him; that I had immeasurably painful visions of him in bed with my wife and so wanted him dead; that I recorded forever his every victory and watched like some bird of prey to observe any step back that life might make him take—these were the reasons that this moment of liftoff into the air was the misery that it was.

Apologies! I know with my whole life that it is as great a sin as any to speak like this of reasons and causes. I know. I promise with my whole life, in this roaring agony. But we must believe that the madness we suffer for believing in causes is caused by believing in causes. Johnny can't tell me I'm crazy unless he's crazy like me. And as in some absolutely inarticulate way I said that to myself, I could breathe—even as the plane turned and seemed to fall, and the sun and the ground disappeared, and it was undemarcated sky and no distance everywhere.

The plane seemed also, suddenly, to slow to a stop as it leveled off, and then it was really all my fool life coming up in me—the measuring of distances, the desperate attempt to domesticate all time with some explanation of motion, the fear of the air, of empty space, the need of orientation, the need for a structure that will hold. Then the sun was lost again. The oddity of flight patterns had us turned east before we could head west. Then another air pocket, but the fall was slow. And when the clouds were gone, I could see the world again—my world, in fact—as we were making a wide sweep over the shore above the Drive. But the water and the land were too far from me to be part of me. The world was not one. The Baha'i Temple was small and the harbor unreachable for my sick heart. A thousand perspectives on all this, and now an aerial view which set out the land and water and sky in a spectacular, clear arrangement like that of Father, Son, and Holy Ghost in Masaccio's Crucifixion. I wanted to see it all as a sign of the Holy Trinity, but I was so far away, so terribly high in the air, and small, and locked in my damned self that I couldn't, even in my sick fear, make anything larger than it looked. Everything was absolutely small, and then gone, as the plane, in another odd, loud, rising motion, turned away into the just lingering sun for the voyage across America, to Johnny.

So high in the air, I couldn't hate him as I did and be the poet I wanted to be. I was as frightened as I needed to be, but I couldn't dare to reach any conclusions, or make any act of faith, or have any vision. I just held Allie's hand—though I remembered times when I hadn't been able to do this either, and thought that if I showed too much affection now there would be real trouble again.

But Allie was right about the drink. It helped me forget just enough so that I could give my mind to something. "The crime of birth and death" and the blade "like a looking glass" from Yeats's "Dialogue" came to mind; and I was just relaxed enough to be able to think of how, five miles high in the air, I was measuring everything, and of how this showed me what I was. Then the dark finally came, and I could see points of light below me, like stars on the ground, whose distribution and orientation, whenever they gave a clear indication of something, were a comfort to me.

I held Allie's hand—but then thought how I was going to see the one who set my life on fire by sleeping with her! Goddamn life—I could kill! The sorrow. But then—in this plane—I thought of my burning, miserable life as an evidence for faith. I wanted to say—Look at me, you goddamned pack of fools! Jesus, can't you see, when you look at me, how much we need faith—how goddamned sorry we are without it? Then it helped me to think that if I had what I needed—the right faith for my life—I could be Allie's tenderest lover. And I grew calm, and felt the peace.

I looked at her and said, after a time, "I love you."

She said carefully, with a smile that spread gently with her care, "I love you too."

I looked out to check all the lights in the dark. "I think this second—that I could save myself—and not be sitting like this—claustrophobic in this goddamned miserable tube—if I could want *never* to harm him, or for harm to come to him, especially after all the news that came to me. That for me was like the final stage of something."

She said, with her eyes turned away, "Do you hate me that much?"

I couldn't look at her now, to bring her back to me. I was still so afraid in the air. I said, with my eyes down, in a quieted voice, "When we were fourteen—when I first met you—I knew what I wanted for my whole life. At level after level now, after all our years, that's maybe a lie. There's a level where I'm angry at you—maybe forever. And another where equally I'm ashamed of my anger—and of myself. But in the last place in my dreams it is always you. Always. Never different. And that's my life—though I'm so crazy that it makes me very afraid right now to say so."

She smiled, carefully, and held my hand, with her fingers lightened. Then time passed; and as the plane kept steadily on, I grew easy and thought of other poems. I thought of Blake's perpetual Eden in the mind—"the Eternal Man's bright tent"—and of how much I liked the idea of such a named place, a place forever rediscoverable!

But now, as if to shut me up, to murder Blake, or extinguish even the trace of stars, the plane jerked hard and fell again. The captain's voice came on to tell us that there would be turbulence for perhaps the next half hour or so, and that we should fasten our seat belts. The stewardesses smiled, and for a brief moment this helped me more than Allie's gentle touch (which I suddenly could not acknowledge). And I thought with the slightest, safest degree of furious repulsion that in a death fall from the sky I might look for Barbara's face—though even here this had a horrible useless feel to it, and I could think it about as good against death as a night with one of these stewardesses. And then I was able actually to think that I might get the words "I love you" out again to Allie in that nightmare moment and that I'd chant these words over and over as my last prayer.

But the pockets of air weren't too deep, and there was no real storm to climb over or sink below—though pulses of lightning seemed constantly to electrify and light the clouds, and at times there was again the sickening jerking and falling of the plane and then the noises and vibrations and inexplicable sudden turns of the airfoils that made me wish it was over—that he'd died, and there was nothing I could do. I wanted out, and could see myself hypoed by one of the stewardesses to stop my screaming or going for the door. But more time passed, and after a half hour or so, as the captain predicted, the weather changed; and then there was no more change for a long time in what became a very smooth glide toward the coast.

I couldn't sleep—not at all, but for great stretches I could feel this wide-awakeness as an intense pleasure, which I held back on; and the calm was perfect for thinking. And although I could believe that the slightest overconfidence on my part could even make the plane fall, I thought that maybe my experience and understanding of hell—Blake's Ulro—might *be* as useful for a right reading of things as a mystic's journey to the Gates of Paradise.

Our humanity, uncrucified, stupid, locked in this tube of a structure, floating five miles high in the air, was for me instructively lost. Wide awake, I could understand where I needed to be, because I was precisely not there. The sickening, relaxed, dangerous plane ride was moving through a place which was not home. And home I knew, perfectly, was this same place in the air, but without fear, without any fear, and without the dread sense of distance or the desire to see Johnny a corpse. But of course to the end he would despise this knowledge too, and even the slightest traces of desire for it; and this made me angry enough to feel again for a second how I feared every sudden sound or movement in this life.

But the meal was a comfort, when it came, as was, all through the flight, that talismanic limited number of smooth strong drinks—so that time passed on eventlessly enough. And Allie held my hand in just the right way and talked to me in tones that did not once make me think of killing anyone. Then, amazingly, the bell sound came, and the pleasure of not having watched any kind of clock for some very good length of time made me feel that the descent, now announced and in fact already underway, was a passage really to some shadow of heaven. The captain's voice, the smiling stewardesses, made me feel a kindness toward the world; and the sharpening pain in my ears just composed me, the way such things will when we know their cause and limit. And so it went, till the plane seemed once more to stall and the turning of the airfoils created the familiar blasting noise and there were sinkings that stretched out—but always long and slowly enough for me to get used to them and find pleasure in them. Then the safety-belt strapping went on in a routine manner as we heard that the night weather in San Francisco was what it always is. And I thought of Coleridge's *Rime* again, as the plane at last did roar down undisturbingly toward the long double-lit runway past the control tower and then reversed its jets in a hurricane roar and touched its adequate wheels to the surface of the smoothed ground.

It was something. I felt now alive with fear and beauty! Awake, capable of poetic grace—and of appreciating it against a whole life of fear—as I walked with Allie out of the tube of the plane and down the enclosed ramp-corridor to the waiting area, where, for the first time in a long time, I saw my sister, who had with her our little Francine. It was so good. Con looked beautiful, and I was very interested in Francine, blinking as she awoke in Con's arms. Allie was hugging Con. "My God, Connie, she's you, another one with the old classical beauty—I can see it—and the green eyes. Let's pray she'll never know she lives in California." And so it went as we moved on to Con's house and still when we got comfortable after unpacking and were having Irish coffee around the stove with Con and her husband, Tom.

But things turned of course to Johnny finally, and I felt immediately a profound and beautiful guilt. Yet I wanted again in all violence for him to hear me out before he died! I wanted Allie—yes—to have to listen to his name and feel the pain of it, right now in front of me. The pleasures of anger make us forget our own infidelities, the silencing fact that we've done maybe worse things ourselves (and the *real* question might have been what Allie would have done, or wanted to do, if she'd known what I'd done with Barbara). But it was life as in this new kitchen, with its butcher block and hanging stainless steel cutlery and cool stone tile, talking with family, I was beginning to be afraid of everything that I heard or said, of every selfish desire that I had and then of every self-eliminating concession to Lemaster's possible lie of a life.

Con went on innocently about the sorrow and the pity of it all. "I just remember him as so powerful and beautiful. It breaks my heart to see him. I cannot believe I'm the only one who goes. The unfairness and sadness of all of it. There were moments, Pete, when I could see the same Johnny and get that sense of humor. But not now. I'm so glad you've come."

I don't know, really, what Allie felt hearing these things. Was she torn by guilt and old affection, or by bewilderment at such a sad report about someone for whom she had now only a neutral feeling, or dislike, or hatred? She said little as the night went on, and then finally just "Good night," touching me on the hand and leaving me with Con to get what was left of the story.

But I couldn't keep it up much longer myself, as I was almost unbearably disturbed by my own curiosity. With her voice breaking, Con told me there was no requirement now for a visitor to wear a mask and gown. "It's past that point. You can just go in now." And I couldn't ask for another picture of his condition. In that new, cool room, I was warned that I'd better stop it all, and was feeling terribly that the night now was the only thing possessing any right to exist. Yet like a fool I put a last question. As I passed out of the kitchen, I asked, "How are you doing with your doctor, Con? He's so different in his approach from mine."

She said, "Better. I can even say much better, though I think you know that sometimes it seems dangerous to use positive comparatives like 'better.' "

I felt warned not to comment and just smiled, tapped the doorpost and went to bed.

Allie's eyes were still open when I lay down next to her, but somehow I could hold her without danger. So there was that relief from bitter loneliness. But after a minute—not even a minute—I started. I said, "I *hate* him. I hate him even when he's dying. Christ forgive me the anger. I can't help it. But you know I don't want it. I've got no right to it. It makes me goddamned sick to death—so fouled up that I'm scared I'm gonna die."

She turned her face close to me as she lay now on her side. The room was lightless except for a glow from the pool lights out the window. She whispered, "Talk to me."

I said, "I watch my heart and breathing right now, thinking they could fucking stop any second. I still think of finding you out, catching you in the act, and swearing I'd never see you again as long as I lived. But then after a week of this, coming back to you and promising I'd never mention it or think of it again as long as I lived. I mean this more than I can say. And I know—I know we've got the patience and faith to ride out anger and guilt and whatever shit comes our way. And because I know it, I keep breathing . . . though sometimes I think it's wrong even to goddamned breathe."

She said, with a look of terrible sadness, her eyes suddenly lowered, "I'll help you forget, Peter. I'll make you happy. I will. The ways aren't unknown."

"I always want to tell you so much about what I understand, A," I said to her. "But I . . . Maybe . . . though . . . the other craziness too—the crazy raving violence—has something in it for us—for getting us started hard enough to make it to the end. Maybe people who aren't crazy like that, who don't think of every kind of vengeance and then don't repent hysterically on their knees, begging in the dust for mercy—or at least in some quarter of their nightmares don't go through all this—are just gonna be what they are: uncommitted pieces of shit who don't know the first thing about a vow. Have your vow and you live forever; lose it and you die. Nobody who doesn't feel this has got anything. It's everything."

"This is the use of memory," she whispered to me, in a voice that now was breaking with that new sorrow, and pain.

I spoke to bring her back—and to show her I knew. "I swear I'm learning it all again fast. I haven't in years felt so strongly about what I want—if I'm lying here terrified of what I'm saying. I don't wish my way on anybody, Jesus. It's sick. It's as morbid as a monk's cave. Thinking that I'm rediscovering my convictions *because* I'm lying here terrified of what I'm saying. But it's real enough—it's made me see, maybe, a purpose in my life—just some cautious telling of our story."

She never moved away. She kept her face close to mine. But now I could see tears. She was crying now, and swallowing her pain. She whispered to me, in her broken voice, "Promise me—that you'll remember . . . I've feared so much lately—so much—please don't just unsay it—that I'm losing you. And your book, or at least the book you used to show me, never brings in the you I'm losing. I wonder if all of a sudden you won't tell me you're leaving me. Going after some thrilling, life-changing experience. Is that what it says in the chapters I haven't seen?"

She was crying now with her head on my shoulder. And—though it was a miracle that I could move at all—I was back like lightning in Lincoln Park at midnight. The self-disgust came back, the same foul taste. In this small, dark room with the clean smell of the pool now moving in the window breeze, my mouth was polluted—and then weirdly my arms were like dead parts now separated from me—a sensation I had had once on drugs, but had been stupid enough to laugh about. But I held her still and kissed her with my dirty mouth.

Then, though it was truly dangerous for me to be taking any steps in any direction now, and what I needed was sleep, hours and hours of sleep, I said something that for me was as true as my fear. And I believe it now more and more—beautifully dangerous terms—because I think, not just that I push things this way (and I say this now at 9:30 at night) but that they move this way too. I said, "It's still my war story, A. It's about a soldier who goes to war, learns what for him can't be learned anywhere else, and comes home. It's about me, and about my coming home. I know you must have noticed some good things lately—though this California episode makes it look like I'm as hungry as ever to reenlist and go up on the front line and get killed. But I promise you I'm not. I promise you I remember that person you love, and that I am him, and that I love you the same way you love me."

I held her tight with my odd guilty arms, which I knew, however, weren't too guilty for cleansing—or most of life is even stupider than I suspect. And everything that I said now seemed to pass unnoticed by the eyes that watch, who have a proven zero sympathy for mere sentimental desire.

But she still hasn't seen the chapters that I have locked now in the fireproof box (along with Conlon's narrative, or notes, or whatever it is, in that unopened package). I don't know how or when I'll show her this. And how in God's name can I publish this—this book which now becomes what? Dangerous to me, to my children and marriage, while remaining disgustingly undangerous to the modern mind? A weapon to hurt Allie with? A real and unreal revenge story? Too alive for me, and too dead for my time?

But I can't care either way—though such crap nonchalance seems to me now as I write this (the time's pushing midnight) about as dangerous as any of my moves along the edge. But Jesus Christ I've got to be able to talk about the places I've been, about the degrees of things—the idiot vestibule down to the ninth circle in ice. How many people out of a thousand would tell me to leave all this unsaid, unknown? But I'd say to them that the place of my dreams that night, and the meeting with Lemaster the next day, and his death and burial, and the dangerous, ecstatic plane ride home convinced me of things as only last battles ever could. And when I slipped past the gods that night and at last fell asleep, arm in arm with Allie, I knew, though I wouldn't say it, and barely can now, that my life might be worth something. I believed that with what I understood, I might help the people I loved—that my story might keep them from falling out of poetry's and loyalty's way, even if it showed me very dangerously both a fallen husband and a fallen father, and also a potential madman, an apparent antique simpleton and false contriver.

I was awake and the sleep was out of my eyes before the sun came up; and when it did, I was as aware as I'll be on my deathbed of the way things come out of the dark in the morning. The quiet of the half-visible pear trees in Con's backyard, which appeared to me now like an enclosed garden in the Middle East, didn't mind giving way to the green and golden-spotted arrival of the fully visible, comforting trees when they came. The early dawn-smell and lacquered green of the oleander were incense and church for the wild parakeets that drank from small puddles by the side of the blue-and-white-tile pool, which was as still in the half-light as the idea of a pool in Paradise.

But, touching my fingers to the window screen, I thought back instantly on how I hadn't been able on the plane to look for more than a second at the pages of a *House and Garden,* because they terrified me—the fruit bowls and paneled rooms and greenhouse walkways and wildflower gardens and mansions, or right modest award-winning cottages, and the upholstery patterns, or monochromes—everything textured and illuminated (with light and shade in sensuous ravishing embraces) so that thingness was as pleasing and terrifying as murder. I had to put it down or die. And in flashes, after that, I thought of the question—that question roared in the ear of the little King of the World—"How does it feel . . . ?" (which seemed now something that I'd just dreamed of too, in a dream whose story had just been silently moving away but now scurried out of the reach of all understanding). And I turned now from the window back into the still dark bedroom and got out of bed carefully, ashamed to stand erect and making it my most intense morning prayer that I wouldn't think of my body or my clothes or bring on some hideous devil by looking for a second too long in the bathroom mirror.

I sat on a chair and watched Allie sleep. She wouldn't go the first day and perhaps would not go at all, though whether she went or not, it was clear that we might spend the rest of our lives considering the alternative. He wanted to see her and have a word with her before he died, and I thought with my head down, how much I was damned if I did or I didn't cooperate with this. Nothing in my life could be more important than the defending of my rights in this case, and nothing in my life could be more dangerous than such a defense. I knew this, as I heard more birds in the back garden and sat slumped in a greater and greater light, and actually thanked God that my body was still there. An alarm went off somewhere, and some quick hand reached out and won ten more minutes of sleep. But it was time for Tom to get up and head off to work, so I'd go see him and leave Allie sleeping—and dreaming God knows what faithful or unfaithful dreams.

But somehow I was able to whisper to myself that she had been mine from when we were fourteen. I was able to do this and to feel, as she slept, motionless, what the end of her life would mean. And I could feel this, this meaning, because I'd been absurd enough to believe somewhere all along (and it's gotten and gets me right now into terrible trouble) that we might have what the poets sometimes say lovers have, or what they always keep in mind when they say anything about love. Call it, as it's been called, no matter what the historical conditons, some kind of answer for death, some feeling of rightness that comes with a correspondence of souls and that's larger than sheer, brutal mortality.

I'd say too, at the risk of my life, that this is what the world wants, that this is what it goes for, no matter its infrastructure or superstructure or ideological, hegemonic, or hierarchical mediations, or the nature of its damned discourse. It goes for immortality in every kiss, every touch. But I promise to God I'll be careful to say this against a picture of the pathos of her aging, of the horror of death in the awkwardness of her mouth hung open in sleep. And I'll remember her liaisons with Lemaster and mine with Barbara—the sorrow, the disjunctions, the fury—and how, as the sun came farther into the room and I left, these things made the upcoming meeting with the enemy, friend, and ghost all that it needed to be to make me afraid to desire even to open my eyes or breathe.

In the kitchen, in that early morning light, Tom made me coffee, but I had no taste or appetite. He'd had a thought. As it turned out, he could take me now to St. Francis, the hospital also named after the saint who spoke with the birds, which was all the way across town, but really not that far from his office—so things would work nicely, and Con and Allie could take it easy, sit around the pool, maybe later go shopping. So all of a sudden it was set, if I wanted to get there now.

I asked for a minute, went back to the room, made a quick stop in the bathroom, taking no look in the mirror, and then knelt down by the bedside. I tapped Allie's shoulder once, twice, till she opened her eyes; and I put my hand on her neck, rubbed it, and told her Tom's idea.

She closed her eyes again, in the still soft light, and nodded, but reached for my hand and held it as if she wanted never to let go.

I said to her in a quiet voice, "It's time."

And she let go—which made some of my enormous trouble (born of my insane hope for our love) move away. But I thought then, feeling all that I felt, that if I made the slightest mistake in any of this dangerous action, I'd learn why it is that in heaven we will not know each other as man and wife.

It was something's motion, and I was caught up in it. The speed of the departure made me think that I was—God knows—not much, or was almost nowhere but in this strong motion. It seemed that I might be dead before I knew what was happening—though I somehow had some sweet powerful lines of Hopkins' on my mind and could think (though I felt I might get an ax in my back while I wasn't looking) of Hopkins' choosing with the utmost care to say, in his poem for the blacksmith Felix Randall, that "This seeing the sick endears them to us, us too it endears"—and to speak of the "Fatal four disorders" all contending in the body of someone once incredibly powerful whom he'd watched over, and pardoned, as the man lay dying over months. But I was saying nothing to Tom, and I thought that the car might just be rolling vengefully against lines of poetry down a San Francisco hill into crowds or buildings, and that I'd die absurdly with a fragment of Hopkins on my lips.

Suddenly Tom announced that the hospital was very near—"Just a block or so—just a few minutes." And what I've thought of so incautiously as my life's pilgrimage seemed more ironic than any ever ridiculed in any cynical piece of literature, as the inclines of the hills got for me steep enough to throw the car back over, or propel us down into an end that was just complete damned terror. But even as unobtrusively, in shame, I gripped the edge of the seat with one hand and the door with the other, I had to accept this possibility of meaningless terror rather than think what, in deepest secrecy, I so much wanted to think: that there were two ways for this built world to fall. The one I came to know when my father died, and now another. In secret I wanted to think that Johnny's bitter laugh was as necessary for the preservation of the structure of things as was my father's careful, treasuring eye.

And again when I'm sitting here on still another night, not just writing but goddamned feeling what I say, and measuring every word in actual degrees of peace and terror, I think I may know something. The sheer vengeance raging in my blood against my poetry—against a faith in the music of Johnny and my father wrestling in an eternal ring and making the world—all of it makes me think I may have something. You can't just talk yourself into the things I feel. I can't just *tell* the world, as it lives in my brain and life, what its story is. It's a lie to think so. Real prophecy is only real wisdom about the way things go. And, God almighty, the things I talk about here have *something* to do with the things that happen in me. My blood listens to the names I say, and it moves with what it hears. It hates poetry. And loves it more than anything on earth.

Tom was gone—and I was heading under a ferocious sun toward a painted image of the tonsured Saint Francis, with his arms spread, his hands spotted with the stigmata, as in the Bellini—where he stands in ecstasy before the cracked and grooved rocks, the cave and skull, and the ten thousand things and colors of the world, which Bellini saw with a Venetian eye. Beyond the entrance, even in this hospital which, typically, was a thing of rambling additions and complexities, it was axis and terminus. I was moved to the desk where I mentioned Johnny's name and heard "Yes. Lemaster, John F." and was told where he was and how I could get there—all things that tortured me—the movement and sounds.

And that he would actually be here and that I'd be making my way along the circulation, torn by construction, the dust sealed in plastic sheets, the noise and fluorescence, and then up in steel elevators to his actual room was so strange and yet so convincing, that I could think—while feeling for split seconds a tremendous weight of something pressing against the walls of the corridors—that history wasn't the series of accidents it's now made out to be. And right now, as the days pass and I continue to see my health return (something that I not only couldn't help but wouldn't dare try to help), I'm almost fool enough to think so again—though I'd better keep silent enough about this if I'm going to take things to that door, and that room—or I damn well will feel again what I felt when I got there and came in and stood before him.

There was an orderly, brutal symbol of today's youth,

with a number of gold neck chains and a blank stare, who wheeled into the elevator the bed of an old man, sick, near death, whom no one ever, for the love of life, should have pained with tests. But it was straight business, I could see it and think it, as the orderly, without turning or looking, asked me, "What floor?"

When I said "six," he made the 6 light after he hit his own 5. Then it was the harsh fluorescent illumination on all of us and then the jerk and whining progress of a hospital elevator, which the ancient, emaciated man had no mind for at all. Sightless, open-mouthed and grotesque, he was a figure in a mythic history, now suddenly wheeled away to the nowhere that I feared whenever I came into the presence of John Lemaster—or forever, as I was in fact always with him. And in all truth I once again could believe anything and nothing, as in this motion, and on this course plotted by I know not what, I saw the light finally sign "6" and felt the cage rock on its cables to the portal.

The door opened, and I stepped into the light and open space. Signs with numbers and arrows pointed for me like connectives in a sentence working toward a meaning. I was terrified and ashamed to read it, ashamed to think even for a second that he might be in a specially marked room, or that I wasn't masked so he'd be safe from me, from the disease I might bring, or be. Ashamed really to think of anything— scrambling any sentence now that might dare to form in any region of my mind, as I somehow made my way down the corridor, following numbers and arrows with a guilt large enough to end my life.

It was now. If I was ever to be a saint the time was now, when every sound of every step I took seemed to make another stab wound in the body of John Lemaster. But I wouldn't need to kill him if I could walk in and see his face and take my satisfactions—the satisfactions of a complacent, totalitarian reading—and the revenge of a life of goodness on a pagan enemy, who ferociously went after the construction of my life—for what reason?

And then, shocking and unbelievable, it was there—the

actual end, the door, before which in this motion I felt immediately that I should make the sign of the cross. On a white slip the names of medicines, and of the patient. I wondered—with a scream in my mind like the battle cry of warriors trying to drown out their terrors with enough sound—what final words would he say?

The door swung quietly to my touch, and the room light defined a bed, a body stretched out. His face. Oh God love him forever, his face! It was his, but so different. With the power in the motion, I stepped into the room, silently, more ashamed of myself than I've ever been. He was sleeping, which made me feel far more terrible and wrong. And, Jesus Christ Almighty, it was no sleep that would heal him. The head was arched back on the pillow, and the mouth was hung open in a face so pale and drawn that it could not be his—though it was. There were the marks; the figuring; the cuts of mouth and eye and cheek, if too deep and soft in some places and in others too hard and dry; the dark color of his hair—though his hair was pitifully thinned. What was not Lemaster still found opposition in what was. But this disease immediately broke my heart. I had tears for it that would drown all intellect. And now, especially, my God, because he slept, I was in an ecstasy of reverence for his life. I wouldn't have made a sound if it could have saved me from fire or the tiger. I couldn't look at him for more than a second because this would have been punished, I knew, by all the powers of heaven and hell, whom I promised, with my head bowed, that I felt nothing, nothing but sorrow. I wanted in my complete compassion to call his name, but I was sure that I had no more right to this than I had to disconnect the lines running to his wrist and chest and neck.

I sat in a chair beside the window and ran my eyes over the white slats of the blinds, counting, losing count, catching blue bars of sky among the angles, and feeling on my face the light breezes as they came in and died off. The noise of power systems below, in the mechanical well, kept the rest of the world silent, except for some long-separated but rhythmic bleeps from a monitor by the side of his bed and the slow, regular unfolding of paper from a graph printer, which was writing now the last chapter of his life. I couldn't look. I couldn't believe this was happening; his dying shattered one of the deepest beliefs of my life. Yet as I felt the pain of this ending, I thought that I might lift my eyes for a second to see if it was true, thinking that if it was, and I saw it, I would be shocking and effacing myself enough to prevent more punishment.

So I lifted my eyes, and when I did I could see, terrible, his eyes slightly cracked open, blue, looking back, and his mouth closed, his face wearing a look of understanding—but an understanding which, as ever, did not confirm me. I felt, unbelievably, anger, and then even greater shame. But I had the strength, somehow, to sound out his name. Just louder than a whisper, I said, "Johnny," and stood up and pushed the chair over, an act, I am tremendously relieved to say, that kept me bent over as I stepped to the side of the bed.

His head was turned away—and whether I should make any further sound or dare to touch him were questions that some great wisdom of mine simply stopped. I waited for him and would wait forever and not move. But with furious perversity my eyes traced the lines running to his body and then watched the graph needle move on the paper, and noted changes. But the weight loss, so terrifying in his neck and shoulders, and the unbelievable bruised pallor and deadness of his skin, were enough so that I closed my eyes and again waited, with no hope, I promise, except to hear him say, at some time, something that would make me feel less ashamed. That he had lost his power and weight, his beauty, his form, were things that I knew I should never have been allowed to see. Not for my eyes ever the sick purple of veins swollen at his temples and spread across his pale bone of forehead—even if seeing these things assured my betrothal to sadness. For he wouldn't want any part of my sadness, or of anyone's sadness, and—as I knew—he was the sworn enemy of betrothals.

I waited. But I couldn't help that for me it was sadness upon sadness. The days or hours that he had left numbered so few that I was broken by the sorrow. I felt that the world was as small as dying alone. Johnny's history, his record—things that meant so much to me, that I enjoyed so much, now seemed reasons for a mound or a tomb, and flowers. And that his death also gave me what I "wanted" made me sick enough of myself so that I could see myself visiting the grave and not feel tainted. Just sorrow. For moments, just sorrow—as I hated myself enough.

Then, in this story which happened and happens, there was movement on the bed. The sounds in the bed-metal and mattress were the sudden sky-shattering lightning and thunder for the storm in the mind. And when he turned over, he made death come as close and appear as large as it possibly could for me, though there was soft daylight in the room and beautiful sky blue between the slats of the window blinds. But his voice, which seems even now to bring the comfort and threat of actuality to this story, made me believe, and with unforgettable kindness in its tone allowed me to believe, that the further I pursued the course I was on, the further I would come to what's real—if never to any meaningful end.

"Peter," he whispered. Through a mouth heartbreakingly shrunken and dry, and with a voice that didn't belong to him, he sounded out my name.

I let my face write out the unmistakable language of sorrow, as I saw his poor terrifying face purpled and whitened by diseases which I hated with a hatred that is life for me. Then I did reach out to touch his shoulder and then his hand—his skin moistened from sweat—and I found, maybe crazily, enough sense of privilege so that I could answer him. For the millionth time in my life, with Johnny Lemaster, I felt I was in the presence of a king. But I didn't think it was wrong to respond, or to believe that perhaps he did think, for seconds here and there, that something depended on our friendship. I said, "I'm sorry."

He closed his eyes and managed to curl his mouth, almost (I believe this) as if to say some things never change—then whispered, "Don't be."

But none of this hurt me. There was, I'm certain, such kindness still. And I thought that it would be all right to say, "Con has been keeping me posted. She said you'd mentioned me. Please forgive me, John. She thought you'd like to see me. Can you hear me all right? Do you want me to be here?''

He turned to me his remarkable blue eyes, which the powers of life hadn't yet forgotten, and said clearly, "I want you here, Peter. I didn't want to make her ask you."

"She said that to me." I stopped, ashamed, as God knows I should have been. But I felt then that there was a miraculous chance here for the best possible friendship as I understood it, as I dreamed of it. I told him how Con wrote that she couldn't remember a day from when she was a kid that didn't have the two of us in it, that she'd mentioned that she could still hear us and that I was thinking then of how we turned on music to play catch. I said, coming closer to him, with all my affection, "I remember us in the driveway, John—listening to 'Honeycomb' and 'Corinna' and 'Travelin' Man.' Do you remember that feeling when the music was playing? I don't know if we really threw the ball better. But the feeling. The lightness on our feet. I remember it was fine."

But he seemed now not to be listening, and I actually began, unbelievably, to think why. He waited, though, till I was finished to ask me, "Are you writing?"

And again I'm sure that he had suddenly a very earnest and kind look in his eyes. I'm positive that he wasn't unwilling or afraid to admit then that he cared; and I can say now again (even scream that I've known all along) that he always did lead me to believe that I should do this, that I should write— though he was never willing to let me think I knew any truths worth telling. No change in this ever—I knew. But I wasn't too ashamed to say over again to myself that he wanted me there. He wanted me, for God's sake! Yes! And I honestly didn't think he'd be offended when I said, "I think I may be coming toward the end of a book. It's about us, among other things."

He moved his dry, thinned mouth a fraction toward a smile. He looked back into my eyes. "Will I be sorry in the end?"

I said, and God knows, feeling with an insane bravery that I could throw words in the teeth of a dying man and have hours before I paid, "You might remember some of the things I remember." And I actually thought: maybe even care about them in the same way—or maybe appear to me to be the man I've heard about from others sometimes—this doctor whom I haven't seen.

There was silence, and his look changed. I became sure that he was asking me, with his eyes: Will you try to make me feel some sorrow that I don't feel, Peter, goddamn you, and take away from me the ability to die in peace! But I heard him whisper, "I always knew you'd write a book, Pete. You had it in you. I knew it from high school." Then—after he caught his breath, a struggle for him—"I figured that I should do something back then to help."

But with this he stopped; and if he was in terrible pain, I still found a way to say something to him, feeling immeasurable anger and shame and love. After an intolerable interval, I broke the silence with words that came like a burst of tears. "If you knew what I felt for you—if you knew how damned I feel, John, even suggesting to you that I dare to mention your name on one of my damned pages—God knows you'd feel sorry you were responsible for such a crazy sense of sin." Then, almost whispering, "But, Johnny, if it's wrong for me to regret what's happened, or to say that I feel tremendous sorrow over what's happened to you, then I'm wrong. You don't know how much I love the way you spit in the eye of tenderness."

He had turned his head away. A long time passed now and nothing happened. He had closed his eyes, and I turned my eyes down again, inexpressibly sorry for what I'd said and incapable of looking at him in that silence, broken so horribly now by the return of the sound of the graph printer and made tolerable only by the mechanical hum from the well, which still also brought a steady light to the room. But I couldn't even contemplate the color of the walls, let alone make this some hard square room of attention. There were times—three, four—that I could see he was tensing severely in pain; and I knew, without daring to call it wrong, profoundly how *wrong* it was that he ever should suffer this unbelievable punishment. But then at length he returned, as he did all through that day till the end, when I knew everything about the walls and had thought all I could think—including the idea, so utterly detestable to him, that the miraculous fraction of strength of his essentially departed body was that of a soul still here. I'd shamelessly gone that far, even though I came to know better than ever, during the course of the day, that I'd misspent a lifetime speculating on the sources of his power.

He whispered, "Will you be curious in the book about how I got here?"

I answered slowly, "Yes, I'll be curious. I am curious." Then very carefully, "But don't misunderstand me, John: that makes me sick—so sick that I distrust all curiosity about anything. If I never find out the cause, I'll be content. If I do find out the cause, I'll be completely ashamed, I promise. And I promise you—not of what it was, but that it came to me— that I got to know it." But I wasn't sure he heard me. He wasn't reacting, and truly against every lie I ever told or will tell, I wanted him to know what I'd said.

I kept on thinking (not out loud, words seeming utterly obscene in the moment) that I had no theories that didn't shame me, that I had no real ideas at all about the fifteen-year gap—none, and no desire to fill the gap with any ideas. I thought I'd kill my curiosity for my own relief if nothing else. But God damn life, he still wasn't looking, which I couldn't stop reading as a hard, knowing refusal to make peace, at this last opportunity. I was angry—I couldn't stop it—and then terrified of what might happen because of my anger. So in a perfectly complete moment, I said, my head low and my voice quiet, "I swear, if you want me to destroy the book, I'll destroy it."

His eyes opened, and he looked at me; the look seemed to say that I was as large a fool for these words as for any I'd ever said. But then as time passed and he didn't say a word, my inevitable anger came back from wherever in heaven or hell it keeps itself, and I kept considering. I thought with anger that if I came in a disguise, if he thought that I was someone else, he'd let me be who I really am, and he'd show me that he could really want someone who was so ready to show him his love.

But I asked God to forgive me the thoughts. I couldn't believe that I had them—that's how much I knew.

But still I couldn't stop. I actually opened my mouth. "I want to tell you so much that your life—I love—who the hell on earth knows for what reasons, and who cares?"

The tears were in my eyes when I said this. I put my face in my hands when I saw what appeared to be a kind response—from my great king. A strange half-smile again. And in the long succeeding quiet, with my eyes closed, I heard nothing that made me believe that the words I spoke were recorded, against my right to live, in any book of judgment. So I felt no overwhelming compulsion to leave for fear that I'd be punished for presuming anything, or that for my sins I'd have his dying face drive me in terror, soon, over the cliff of my own ambition.

I was gone in the present, dead-alive in the moment, and I could forget about how I had so carefully to step, to position myself. It was all right, in what I saw now was a light green room, with the white blinds hanging in air some, and then falling back with the action of the breeze. The moment, in plain actuality, seemed as small as the things in the room—though no doubt it would stay with me for the rest of my life. And I saw clearly now the pills on the bed table, the paper cup, the button for the nurse call. I looked at the face again, hard still as it was to do so without utter shame. I could gaze at it for four or five seconds at a time, the light in the pallid flesh and the spread of shadow in the hollows of his eyes, and think of the trespasses of this absurd disease upon his beauty and of how I might ease his pain with a cool dampened towel, or help him with his razor, or make some other gesture that would amount to nothing more than a simple kindness.

But again now, Jesus God Almighty, it was long, over-long silence as he withdrew completely into himself. And I hated the wait through it, not knowing what he was thinking, or where he would come from. I suffered tremendous shame because I was actually growing homicidally impatient now with a dying man, and hateful because he seemed not to care or even notice that I was there. I was that insane. I had far too much time to think. And I remembered exactly where I was. I began to think now, too, about how high I was in the air, about the possibility of panic—which had its magic way of making the reality of panic come closer and closer as passing time grew nearly long enough.

Yet I couldn't help dangerously attending to things in the room—the tight oblong dimensions, the ceiling height, or thinking about the limited field of his last days, and counting and measuring it all. For several minutes, in the most suicidal perversion, I thought of his taking her virginity—which I *know* he was claiming was an action intended to help this book! In high school he wanted to help! And certainly I knew as I sat by his deathbed all that time in silence (and can remember as my pen marks the page now, near midnight, with the sound of the wind a factor) what insanity might come with wanting to murder a rival.

Then—unbelievable—it was the best irony and circumstance, and laughter. I'd waited for so terribly long now, and become aware that a single inch one way or the other is either suicide or murder, and so felt the meaning of silence like a poet—and now *he* was the one who made it all too neat—who became the storyteller. He never turned to me or moved. After that interminable wait, in that room, his voice just broke the silence with the perfect question, which erupted into the air like the terror of first gun-blaze in a fire fight—though he managed it only just above a breath.

Out of nowhere he whispered, with his whole life (though I have to say this now almost laughing), "Did she come?"

Instantly I had more words than I thought. They came like panicky machine-gun fire in that moment of night terror. But before I could open my mouth—absolutely impossible to forget—the enemy came out in full force, all his numbers screaming and moving. He was pulling his head forward and pressing his hands to the mattress, stiffening his arms, turning to me! It was shocking (though I felt I was in a ghost story, or monster tale, in which the unkillable beast keeps coming back) that I could hate so much his dying face and that I could want to kill him and riddle holes through everything like him. But I knew enough of what he was.

He said again, as if he had every goddamned right to the question, "Did she come?"

So I went for his life, as I hated his pitiful thinned hair, his shoulders shrunken and his chest, visible and shocking white under the neck of his thin blue gown—that chest that I can now see, collapsed atop a proportionally distended belly, which was still pitifully small. I fired into his despicable protruding bones, his white, bruised flesh seeming ready to discontinue and just be torn away by hand. "You liar," I said, knowing all that I needed to know to make me actually rise up, though I spoke in a normal voice and remained still in my chair. "You're no different from anyone else. You want what we all want. But you goddamned lie and pretend that you don't. Every miserable piece of dirt who thinks like you, says one thing and lives another. All liars."

But if I dared to keep looking at him, I knew that it would be too obscene to use more words. Yet I kept right on considering. I thought, in utter violence—Yes—I've read your mail! I wish somehow I could have stopped it in the air before it ever arrived. And I've spoken with your absurd, pathetic messenger. I've interrupted some things. Why not? You with her is my whole soul on fire! Who are you to touch her? Any of the times that you dared to touch her, from the beginning—about which I know—who the fuck were you? Who in hell do you think you are, calling for her? *Nothing* gives you the privilege. Do you think I'm filth for reading your things? Then what are you for sending them? You want to make marriage insane. Do it, and you make murder nothing. So do it, and I swear I'm good for the kill.

Once I'd let my mind go on like this, there was for moments nothing that could wake me up to what I was doing. But I'm writing this down furiously, nonstop now too, and I know damned well that my pace will slow down—and can think what it means, remembering how the sun went down that day in San Francisco and how there was the noise of the birds in the night and the sick misery of being indescribably terrified again of the dark. And I'm wise enough to regret even writing a word, or even living as long as I have. I'm that sharpened. But I also think, now as I do stop, how if I wait, with the quietest possible prayer going on somewhere inside me, that time will move me on, to the next word, the next sentence.

In the hospital room I began crying, with my face in my hands. But the release of tears didn't help ease the pain—which came the second that I knew what I'd said and thought, and with the instant return of that fear which I try to make so much of—yet which I have got to keep saying means absolutely nothing.

I looked up and saw him leaning back now from exhaustion, but smiling. It was enough to make me want to spit in his face, which in my suicidal desire I wanted to come immediately to its death mask.

But then he spoke, and I knew in no time that I had to listen. He was smiling, looking off, and he whispered, again with the unkillable determination of a ghost or monster, "I never know what you're saying. I know that you want to make me afraid to die—which is your problem. You call me a liar. But you want to make me cling to some false dream. I'm *not* afraid, Peter. I'm *not* afraid. Don't waste our time. I want to see her for reasons you'll never understand."

It was all too much—these irresistible provocations, which could make me move out far enough to end his life, to rise up, when I knew now that I needed just to retreat.

Insanely I said, "You goddamned *liar!* You did it to separate me from her and kill me. She was me and she is me, and you wanted her to give herself up so that I'd be dead. You wanted her eyes to close for you and for her to touch you and kiss you and meet you in the fucking Ambassador East so that you could tear me apart. If it's a comfort to you to know it—and I know it is—I *have* died with what you did. But I've come back."

All this noise had the gods immediately in the room, like the batwings of nightmare. I was at an end—the conclusion of a book; and I knew how much of a crime I'd committed. But still I read in his words an utterly dishonorable toying with language and life, and found in my discovery of this dishonesty a terrifying satisfaction. I wanted to say that it scared me beyond control to see someone like him so pitifully dishonest—that it made me think that someone like me might be right about something, and how much that frightened me. Words were so much *there* that unstoppably they came up out of me into a silence that I knew with my life I should have let be. I said, "But goddamn you, you don't understand fear—even now, for Christ's sake, you don't understand it. You think fucking bravery is the key to wisdom. Fear has taught me things—things that aren't dreams. This building we're in stands, and if it falls it's not a joke. Don't make it fall with glib words; you'll prove yourself terrifyingly to be a goddamned fool. Can my words bring your mind to attach to that?"

He had his eyes closed now and seemed to be very weak, or bored, but he had enough energy to say, "No."

As someone who goes an inch too far and falls can keep screaming from the edge of a great height to the bottom, I was not going to stop till the end. I said to him again, "You liar! I won't ask how you got here. But I'll say that it was a romance. I don't need to know. I could care less if you made homosexual love a million times. More power to you. And I don't care if you contracted this fucking plague through some poisoned needle. I promise you that I'd be far too afraid to take any such filthy satisfactions. I'd never condemn you for such things. I wouldn't care. I swear an oath to you. But I care that you'll deny that it was a romance—for which madness of caring I'll also ask you to forgive my life. I know exactly what you're saying. I despise your answers to me, your assertions that you can't understand me, and the violent fucking lie that you want to see her for reasons that I couldn't understand. Jesus! It makes me want to scream at you that your goddamned blood is filled with this deadly poison, to get you to respond in anger, to feel my anger and my love, my incredible love for *you,* to get you to feel a love for life.

"I know exactly how good for me the things you say are. The things about my wanting to make you afraid to die. I know exactly how much I have to listen to you and exactly how much you have to listen to yourself—for the sake of your own freedom. Don't take me for a fool. But you liar, *you know* what I'm talking about too—the love and the anger and the fear and the sorrow, even the hunger for eternity. Either way—needles, sex—it was a romance that got you here: a sadness, John, and a need, which I know and you know were profound—though I swear I want your forgiveness for saying what I say. I'll want and need the memory of your forgiveness forever. I know that you'd rather die than say things like this, let alone shoot off your mouth. But you need to know that I feel exactly the same way as you—that I'd rather die than say what I'm saying."

He hadn't moved all the while I was speaking; and I was relieved (just as if I'd fired a gun at his head and when the smoke cleared discovered that I'd missed) to think that he hadn't heard my words. I thought that, possibly, when the price was fixed for my having gone so murderously insane as not to leave him alone, my words here would be forgotten. I truly knew how much anyone should be ashamed forever of words used to insist upon eternity. But for a long time again nothing happened, and I once more became stupid enough to hear the mechanical hum and that faint scratch of the printer. And then—God knows I was this suicidal—for seconds I was insane enough to theorize again, with tears in my eyes, that this tight green room had isolated something like the workings of the soul of the world and that nothing could happen here that wasn't an indication of what was always and forever.

Then my eyes dropped to his face, and I couldn't think. I didn't dare theorize about how any life could be left there in that terrifying bruised, shrunken body, my brother's. This dying was too perfect and complete a departure for the self-ishness of my sadness. So I cleared my mind of any slightest protest against its finality—keeping myself safe in a trance, while time prepared in the lengthening silence whatever it wanted to prepare.

But the first sound to come out of the silence was his voicing of a fundamental challenge. Out of nowhere the powerful first move was his. With his eyes still closed, he asked me,

"Why would you be certain that not being afraid is such ignorance? Why do you know this?"

I looked at him laid out as if in his casket, and my terrified, enfeebled convictions, disenfranchised, without rights, still helped me whisper, "Because I'd be a fool if I didn't want you somewhere other than where you are now."

And again, miraculously, he responded. "But you wouldn't deny that you want me gone."

I moved on another fraction of an inch, my heart complete with human feeling. "Oh please, John, please don't make it so simple. I could say that you want to see *me* gone. I could say that as a lover *you* were cruel. I know about it. I've heard. I know that you weren't above the use of force. And, Christ— *everything* for you is just here, just now. But still you're no saint! With you it's just no responsibility. No children. No existence. No vows to anything. It's all just moves. So the cruelty—and God damn you, don't deny it—don't drive me more mad than I am, and, pray God, don't satisfy me by making a still larger fool of yourself—the cruelty comes as no surprise! I'm trying to preach to you. Yes. I'm trying to convert you. I'll go to a very deep pit in hell for it. I'm going as I speak. I hear the goddamned sounds of it. But the cruelty comes as no surprise. Believing in nothing, you're left with just yourself and nothing to give that self up to. The end is selfish violence. I've come to violence that way, your way. I've come to a number of bad ends. I do know some things. Give me credit."

He was smiling again, and still would show a mind for me heartbreakingly sharp. And now—I don't know the time—it's not yet evening, but there's a slight rain falling and an unusual darkness, but no wind, only gentle sounds—now I'll say that his astounding, miraculous energy was in part *due* to my presence: that the fact that I was there is what kept him strangely vital during some of the last hours of his life—though I would let this observation sleep if there weren't a rhythm in the rain. But, as I hear it falling softly, I'll say that it was *because* of me, and against me, with great quick power, and with that smile that I could have killed him for, that he said, "You want credit. I want no credit. I loved her in a small way. I loved her again in a small way. And again. These last several months I've loved her in a small way. You don't know what that is."

He stopped, but it was clear he wanted to say more; and if he was the dark beast of my life, I still waited to hear him.

He whispered, "I said to you once I never meant to hurt you. I believe you're a good enough writer to know that was true." Then he stopped again for a second, tensing, but continued; and with incredible new power, he brought on for me the pain at the heart of my life. He said, "You call me a cruel, forceful lover." Then louder, "But there's something else you know. You know I was a good lover. I never tried to find a thing. I was in it for laughs. I'm sure your book is all laughs, isn't it? Don't you try to make me afraid. Don't dare do it." Then the monster was turning all the way to me again, saying with perfect clarity and violence, "Think instead about how I made love to her. Think about it. Think that if there was force, I was simply playing the games she seemed at the time to want to play. Think about how much more there was, about how much you never got told and never will. Stop on it and feel it and watch what happens. You'll only write what you need to write when you know it well. And remember I am not one goddamned bit afraid to die."

But it's not so simple, the idea that for my freedom, for laughter, I should contemplate my life's undoing. Where I am now—several paces out from dread—I know this. And even in that room I could think that it wasn't anywhere near so simple. I could almost mock outright the idea that I would be freed into a fuller life by the vision of my wife-to-be in bed, in ecstasy, with my lifelong enemy! that I'm supposed to taste this *jouissance* of betrayal like ambrosia, and be freed of the sick embarrassment of my marriage! With the cutting of every line extending from me, with the rupture of my miserable identity, I'm supposed to know the real free-play in this story of my life! And I'm supposed to believe that this notion is itself no goddamned *line!*

I told him exactly what I knew. I told him I'd heard more. I told him about Barbara, and I can say that he looked at me

as if he'd gotten his own life-giving medicine. I remembered
everything that she had told me about his meanness. I said to
him, "That makes two witnesses." I said that she'd found me
infinitely more gentle and asked what we were to make of
that—that she'd said he experimented with every form of cruelty, that he threw Allie in her face.

I can hear my voice now. I said, "I don't mean to remember too much—but every now and again in a small fucking
way it's maybe not too bad to tell the truth. You tell me I
won't write. But I do. I write day after day now, and I don't
fall asleep over my work. Work and no sleep! Do you know
what that means? Do you know what it takes to keep a writer
awake? Do you have an answer! I swear you don't—you
don't, and I swear that it's as important a question as there is.
It's *the* question. And I'll tell you now that the plot I'm following takes me right to you. It makes me crazy enough to talk
like this. And maybe I'll pay with my life for unfolding it. But
it brings me to tell you that I love you, and *yes* to tell you that
I'm afraid not to listen to you, no matter what you've done,
or afraid not to undo myself, or not to untell my story! That's
something! I believe in it. It gives me life. It's me *and* you. It
keeps me awake! This is what does it! Keeps me awake! And
yes, I want to hear from you that you love me as much as I love
you. Is that too much?

"Jesus Christ, I've heard from more than one witness too
that you were a great loving doctor, John—somebody who
watched to see that people won all the life they could, down
to the last extra second. I don't say this to hurt you—and I
believe perfectly that you don't say everything to hurt me. I
say it because *more, more* than I ever could want to kill you or
harm you at all, I want to find that place where we can make
peace. Please, John, just let me love you and remember and
count all your beautiful victories, even if you can't count *one*.
Let me be the memory. Let me whisper somewhere, if only in
a half-sentence, that our story is not utterly goddamned incomprehensible. I promise you, the satisfaction will terrify
me."

And if the words he said now were as combative as they

had to be (and *because* my life hangs on an edge and can fall, I know how much they had to be), I can say that the smile that he wore was again one of kindness. I know it, if I can feel, as I suggest that there was this trace of kindness, that I ought to shut my mouth finally and forever.

He told me that he was utterly helpless, and that he knew how that for me this was some tremendous moment, when someone gets to be this helpless, how that it meant for me the beginning of something. "I know you," he said. "I know how crazy you are." Then he said that when he told me how far the cancer had gotten on my dad, he was getting ready for this, for his own dying. He said that his life was all over and that if my experience made him someone important, he could not listen to me. "I cannot care if what I am means something to you—if you've put me somewhere in your world. I won't go. I want to go nowhere. If you have to build some factory of sorrow, and madness, and fear, Peter, don't make me work in it. I try to free you from sorrow. I saw her marrying sorrow! Goddammit, I want you to write about something else. I know you could."

When he finished, he was utterly exhausted, or in pain, and his eyes shut tighter than ever. Then some moments of silence passed, with it nonetheless getting clearer that something was coming. His hand was shaking, and he bit his lip. Without moving, he whispered to me, "Push the button"— then half-lifted his arm and hand to point, but he had no power to locate what he sought.

I touched the call button immediately, and the light on the wall went red, but the unbelievable reality of what was happening left me sick that I was ignorant of what now to think, or feel. I didn't know. And if we're incapable of conviction even in the face of this kind of pain, it must be understandable that we can drive no stories home. The incompleteness (I even felt a dead reluctance to move any more) left me wondering whether I was right or wrong about anything I'd ever brought my mind to. Then like a wheel, like an angel, the nurse came in and asked me to step outside into the hall, where (though there was all the rapid movement of white and the PA calls for doctors sounding and sounding) I felt immediately an enormous silence, a silence so impressively deadly that it let me know truly how much offense and pain my presence there gave to the gods, whose names were as impossible for me in the moment as any comforting expectation.

And I almost laughed that so much that I'd dreamed and thought of had come true. It seemed by far the safest thing almost to laugh—though I knew that I'd better look neither right nor left down the corridor, and that if I actually did make a sound it would be remembered. So I waited, and now necessarily without thinking about what it means to wait (though the time must have been close to an hour and I guessed once that it had to be now early afternoon) till the nurse finally did come out again and said that it was all right to go in.

With concern, she said that the pain came now like the clock, every five hours as the morphine wore off, but that the morphine was still "enough for it, at least at most times." There was a black, wheeled drum not far from the door. She opened it, and dropped into it a sealed bag with the syringe and closed the cover. Then she reminded me, as she tried to make her face a sign of complete kindness, that there were "no visiting-hour limits for cases regarded as terminal." I nodded then to this actual person here before me, now wheeling away the black drum, promising to return; and I took a cautious step, and another, and then touched the door as carefully as I had before—when I found in the real correspondence between what I thought that the world would do and what it did, a tremendous threat to my life.

And I am crazy enough to feel, this second, how much I needed not to be pleased by any such correspondence. But he was there again, and he lies before my mind's eye now, wearing—I'll say against the danger of any slight satisfaction—the undeniable signs of a need for the most intense love possible. His body in that merciless white light still reminded me perfectly of who he was, with the terribly contracted lines and drained color, the pitiful remainder of weight, the revolting thinned hair, the look of incredible age recalling still the beauty and power of his young manhood, which, with him gone now—God help me it's so unbelievable—I cry tears for in anger and protest—and which I thought of then with thoughts that dropped from me like distinct bombs in tangled concert falling from a bomb bay!

He was in a deep sleep, with the morphine; and this would last for several hours before he'd come back—as he had when I got there in the morning, now perhaps six hours ago. And I began (I think of Tennyson, "you so dishallow the holy sleep"), as soon as I sat down close to him, tenderly to call him a damned pitiful fool for not knowing what it meant for someone to need him as desperately as I did. I made silent speeches—cheaply, disgustingly, while he slept!—discoursing on my conviction that anyone who ever insisted on fundamental changes within our time and space always talked, when asked for actual exemplification of his abstractions, about nothing but Johnny and me.

I asked him, now that he was sleeping and I didn't need to fear his answer, who in God's name he thought I was. I said, you love to think me the pathetic last Christian, the absolutely pathetic last married man, and of course the best possible proof of the insanity of all my so-called values. But, I said, the undeniable truth is that *no one* ever was as stupid as you make me out to be. I said that the book you have on me is the wrong book. I said that no one alive, for Christ's sake, is naive about marriage, about God, about how life goes—and especially no one on earth is fooled by words or governments. Nobody! I said to him, where then in *hell,* John Lemaster, is the fool you spent your whole life trying to wise up? With tears in my eyes, as I took another real look at him sleeping (and the violation of it sickens me now, the intolerable thought), I told him, startlingly, about something that I'd written in the Advanced Studies Program all those years ago—in that time, and that exact place, in which sunrise and sundown were the beginning and end of the world—that place where I had at least days of a real, convincing spiritual life.

I said you'd probably laugh till you cried, but it was something on the true and necessary *fear* in Milton's builder

God, who raised the walls of heaven in self-defense but made them also strange miracles of beauty and life. I said, god damn you, Johnny, every word in the poem, and every word I wrote, had for me—I know this—what Milton wanted them to have: the conviction that there are actual overwhelming magnitudes, glorious spreads of beauty and divine power. But I thought how the idea of God's sporting fear, the idea of his memory, of his choices, of his destruction then of everything that he'd chosen and feared for, of his Sabbath, would all do nothing for this near-dead man, lying here now as the dark came on, and who would just let the sun fall and the light disappear without the first sad thought—even if he knew that this was the final day of his life.

I was sure that it was madness to think him larger than Milton, especially as I longed, if terrifyingly, for Paradise, wanted it in this room, which I definitely studied now and found soulless and small, perhaps ten feet by twelve feet, dirty light green, cracked, and hired because hospitals had to make money. The stipple plaster ceiling even had a cobweb, and every expense was no doubt cut in procuring the accouterments. So in the hospital of Saint Francis there wasn't much true hospitality—which is nothing less, I'll argue, than the free gift of space, time, matter, and self to the alien wayfarer, the widow, the orphan, the sick, and which in the Bible (no *doubt* a code for all poetry) is commanded more regularly and forcefully than any of the Ten Commandments.

Business, for Christ's sake, business! In Shakespeare it means seeing the limited life-space and life-time of the other and giving for the other's safety, some, if not all, of your own limited life-space and life-time. It's knowing, in and through your mortal fear, where to be and when—and then being there, at the right, necessary time, as a prevention against the other's death, or injury, or pain. God almighty, I thought, if this is small, this beautiful and glorious business (which is impossible without a combination of fear and faith: faith in regainable Paradise and simple fear for the things of this earth) then I concede to modernity, with its goddamned passion for the radical separation of all phenomena. If hospitality is small, then let the goddamned historicists call me a miserable, pitiful fool.

But this is what I was bound to pay immeasurably for—this kind of sad thinking; about this room and about my friend and enemy—all this sad desire for self and selflessness, poetry, to be larger than his death, and larger than his monstrous vitality, which I hated. I don't know what he wanted me to say. I won't assume with satisfaction that he wanted to convert me; I don't need the dangers of any satisfactions. I wanted to help him in a tight spot. That's what it was. I wanted, I suppose, fully to convert myself to my own faith. And here was the room, ten feet by twelve feet, the last place where he would be; and I was here doing business. Shakespeare's business—that's what I wanted to devote myself to, with some not too small portion of the devotion that knows that the kingdom of heaven is only an inch away from the tight, miserable world. And even if I'd killed him, killed a king in his sleep, I'd have wanted to do it in the name of a selfishness so tremendous and insane that it would have made into an absolute fact the great loss of Paradise—the ultimate, original sorrow.

But now the afternoon was waning, darkening; and eventually in the coming dark I thought of Barbara, of how once in bed, beautiful, deep in the sweet sentiment of cocaine, she said with a smile, "He'd tell me that if I wanted to kill myself I should do it—that as long as I kept on seeking small pleasures from brief moments of happiness and cheap thrills from danger I'd never know anything. And that that was all I ever would do."

I was her sweet sentimental friend. I asked her, "What did you tell him?"

She brought my body close to hers, into the charmed circle of her beauty, and said, "I told him that that's all there ever is." Then she took me softly into a kiss that was as graceful as any perfected delicacy of tenderness.

And even before he woke up again, I believed (and far more than I wanted to, I believe right now, writing each word here) that the only thing large enough to convince me of a world of spirit is the tremendous diabolical vengeance—the hell—that waits in silence for any movement of hope, or sound of prayer. I had for the moment nothing else. That's all there is. But still with a diamond of earnestness in the dark black of my mind, I was saying to the god of randomness and absurdity how sorry I was, sorry for my life, as the sun had gone down enough to leave the light-well gloomy now, and the walls significantly destabilized.

Then motion and sound. Louder. A heart-shattering groan, to which I could not respond. I was paralyzed, afraid to move out for anything—though part of my fear was that I would be punished for hatred of his monstrous strength, a hatred which I still felt somewhere inside, and which constituted possibly enough of my life so that I *would* die without it.

The groan wasn't that distinct death rattle. I knew this. I dared to know it. But (a last brutal irony) the sound was his sound, and this was his moment, his proof—the still identifiable, distinctive mock on identity. What could I say to it? to this sound that I knew wasn't the death rattle, but which was the sound of a pain always greater and more real than any wish of mine to relieve it (so indeed still his; and still his point proved)? and to the eye which was going nowhere till it found me?

It stopped on my face as if it had never seen me, but, in this nightmare moment, was still capable of an absurd evil wish. The blue I wanted to call beautiful, the blue gem I wanted for human life's treasure trove of sapphire and for my most intense memorial passion? What could have been more important than what I wanted? I wanted to say that he meant more to me than my life. I wanted to love him so much that I could in absolute fact bid him the casual good-bye that he wanted from me all along. "Oh, is he dead then?" To ask it like this and walk away—but to find the strength to be casual like this in a love more powerful than the most compelling, honorable, sacred absurdity.

In other words, I wanted again what great religious poetry has always said we want—a love that would set me free of the world. I don't care how embarrassing this is! I don't care. I wanted again for him really to find my eyes and for us to find something better than anything we know in this world—this godforsaken small cracked heartbreaking inhospitable room. But my shame and terror then were too quick for me. Thinking what I was thinking, with that sound still in the air, was, is, a crime against the real universe, against the universe of that blue eye, which would add itself to no accumulation in any dear gem-trove in the mind, and which despised equally the possibility of any faith in the sacred worth of its own uniqueness. It was ice. And his response was, and is, beyond any power of mine to domesticate it. He came back into the ring of the world with a demand. When he found me in that last, graying light, looking at me as if he had never seen me, but as if he desired still to tear me apart, he opened his shrunken mouth, and set his teeth.

But now I don't lie. I just say—because it's true—that with me immediately then was the thought that it was his father whom mine, laughing, threw against the wall of the bowl, and that it was Johnny who held on to this whirling figure on the lightning-fast rim of the world while I sat there in that unmoving center, at peace. I almost wish it weren't true—wish that I hadn't thought this. The drama cost and costs me that much. But I can take comfort in the brutality of his demand, as I did that night when the beauty of the birds' singing in the bushes by the pool made me run to this sheer brutality as to my only salvation.

The shocking, paralyzing sound of his moans was in the air. Then suddenly he was breathing fast and tensing in an agony that made me want to seek all new grounds even for the idea of dignity, to put hope off and, dead cold, to submit honestly to metastasis, as his eye widened on me but made me instantly, bitterly ashamed that I'd prayed Hail Marys at my father's deathbed! That I'd opened my mouth for any such thing! How could I find in myself the nerve to make that situation worse by asking for intercessions "now, and at the hour of our death"? The insult, in the beauty and hope of the prayer, to the veracity and honor of this monstrous terror was too much. But I was too insane to love the beast. It is my fate,

I am sometimes certain, to die from terror. With his eyes wide in pain he found me and stared at me. Then he opened his unforgettable shrunken mouth, which, if it was not scarred, will be scarred in my dreams, and made his demand. He whispered to me, "Bring her here."

This book, this book, as he knew, will only be worth continuing if I make nothing of this, or consider it proof of nothing, or if I let it ruin everything that I've said—which I am immeasurably pleased to do. But I could not find it in me to let him have his way then, in his death agony, in that last moment that we had in the world. I couldn't bear it. I was somehow still insane enough not to let him have his way. Hours later, in the dark, I wished to God that I hadn't had the strength to resist. But I did. I stood up, heard the roar of the furies, working always to undermine the built world, and heard my own voice say, "No!"

Then I saw my hand extend almost like that of a priest making the signs and gestures of a final blessing. Then it was an actual stepping away from his wide eyes and tense fast breathing—to the door—and the corridor, where I heard my footsteps shattering and exploding on the tile—and to the steel elevator, which I so very nearly did not believe would come safely to the ground. Then quickly I got out to find some place where I could settle and shut myself in, for good—some place past the stigmatized, tonsured saint, upon whom I could no more look back than I could divide the world, as he did, against its own violence. Or no more than I could say a word about hospitality.

I walked frantically past one phone—it was too close to the hospital—and on to another, some blocks farther away. There I called Con, who asked me how things were. And when she received no clear answer, she promised that she and Allie, whose presence instantly I could not imagine, would be over in twenty minutes to get me. Still somehow in the world, I told her to look for me on a bus bench at the corner where I was.

I had twenty minutes to think, and it was too much. So I walked quickly, without intention or hope, farther away from the hospital, just glancing at structures, not pushing my faith in anything, and reducing my steps to a mechanical insignificance, a kind of idiot rosary, hoping in silence that this old method wasn't now punishable. I'd done what I had done, and there was no repairing the situation. He had so little time to live, and maybe I could have done something; but even as the early-evening light shone brighter than any down in the well, I couldn't allow myself to think, in any noticeable sorrow, that he had so little time left: to presume that there was such a thing as urgency. So when Con did come (and in an instant Allie—her hair glowing in the light, burning in the window glass—had to be made into another person, whom I could not see, or know!), I just got in the car and let it pull away and leave. But I'll say now, still feeling the immeasurable relief, watching my pen follow what I'll call the trail of it, that this was not the end of the story.

And I use those words because my pen does follow, quickly, a kind of trail of pleasure and relief. And it is without question the same relief that I felt later that night, after the dark had fallen and I was alone with the birds, whose songs made me feel the terror of hope, in my room, which seemed to border on Paradise, and to be ready to my infinite peril to open up on it. I made a decision—and the relief came; and I can say that and feel the satisfaction and not fear having to pay. I tapped on Allie's shoulder, one, two times, and woke her up. I said, when her eyes were open clearly on me and she knew where she was, "We have to go." She seemed to know what I meant, but I said, "We have to go now. He told me to bring you to him. I can't not do it. Please, Al. I'm afraid that I'll never get out of the trouble I'll put myself in if I don't do it. If he's got any time left, even tonight, I'll be thankful as long as I live."

Then in all the magic running action and consequence, she put her soft hand on my cheek and got out of bed and stood before the moonlight and took off her nightgown, to begin dressing, but perhaps also to let me see her; and in the passing seconds, in which I could forgive her everything past and now coming again, I could watch. Truly as I wished to live, I believed that if I let her have her time with him now—as he needed her and as perhaps more than I ever could know, she needed him—I could watch her and feel the life in my desire.

She was beautiful, and for those seconds I could think it, as I felt the immeasurable relief of what we were doing. I saw her breasts in the moonlight, beautifully shaped, with delicate nipples, and the slope of her back, down to the buttocks, sweet with its woman shape and so fine and smooth that it would be the envy of girls. If I could forgive her everything and unsay what I said to him—and this remains true to this second, even though I know that later that night she was alone there with him, listening to him, touching him, and this causes me indescribable pain—the feeling that the room, along with the built world, was safe, would be strong enough. And her beauty could fill me with living desire. I loved her as I watched her; and when we left, I put my arm around her and walked with her, with that feeling of lightness that's the most beautiful grief in the world. And it's an absolute truth that our going where we were going, for the purpose that we had, made it possible for me not to have to change her into someone whom I did not know.

I told Con I'd called to see what was happening and that the nurse said I'd better come. So Con told me where I could find the car key, and I went and got it, and we were gone.

The San Francisco night was cold as always, but the fog gave way to the stars, and I felt that the pace at which I drove had to be exactly right, not to give some new offense—not too fast, not too slow. I had the world, even with all the steep hills, set right enough under the stars; and I could glide on the streets, not feeling the slightest hatred against Lemaster for anything—nor too much sorrow, listening to music on the radio: soft music which put everything in distance relations that composed the world. From hilltops, the city lights and the bay and bridge lights were only remarkably beautiful, and I could feel that this whole act was pure enough so that the relief would last all through the dark hours.

Allie would be there with him, offering words, her touch, her presence. They would share utterly profound secrets, secrets maybe beyond anything that I could ever experience in that way. I'd said that I wouldn't let it happen, and meant it with my life; but the best thing for my life, and for this story, which cannot end too easily now one way or the other, was that I was letting it happen.

At the hospital Saint Francis was not transfigured, but, in my eye, beautifully adorned by the spotlight above his head. I pulled the car up under him, not too ashamed to feel that I understood what it meant for him to give up all his riches. I wouldn't call this a chapter in the history of the world. But I could call it a little flower and think again of how gifts and tributes of flowers are used in moments of love and sickness and death to enhance or keep safe our sense of the beauty in time. Flowers come, so there is a measure of goodness.

Under the wounded, open-hearted image, I knew that the relief I felt might be the relief of suicide, with its erotic anesthesia. But I didn't fall for the temptation. I only said to Allie, as relief and pain were nonetheless unquestionably one, "I will see you," and kissed her gently on the mouth.

She looked me carefully in the eye. "Remember, I'm with you. I'm here, not there. I'm doing this because it's impossible not to. I know it's unbelievably wrong for me to say anything negative about him when I'm going off for this, but I've got to have you know how much I love you, and how odd I find this, and how much I think this is more than anything else a measure of how little he ever found in his life—though when I say that, I know something of your crazy guilt. I don't want to say it again. I better just go. I'll be right back if for any reason I don't need to be there."

I was looking back in her eyes and felt, when I kissed her, that the kiss, as it was a tearing like a wound, would help me and never be forgotten. Then she was gone, and I watched her move past the desk and down the corridor till she turned for the elevators. I pulled away but didn't need even in the dark to get far from the place. I found a parking spot from which, under trees, over the city lights, I could view the bay, and I entertained some vague, unremarkable thoughts about the destiny of America, a country not insane enough maybe to stay married to its great task.

Then I thought with the tenderest passion, a passion that I prayed Johnny would somehow know I felt, of a day just before the day we went to Silver Beach, *the* day before, it must have been, when Johnny and I went to Warren's Woods, where the sign at the gate read "The Forest Primeval," and adventured in a beech grove so beautiful that it would spread out in dreams at the hour of death.

I saw him barefoot on an Indian bridge fallen over the Galeen River, agile, making his way over bark and branches to a low spot from which he could plunge and enjoy the river. And I saw myself watching uneasily the way the river moved, disliking the mud, afraid any dive would injure my head and struggling on the trunk of the Indian bridge just to reach the point that I didn't want to get to—where I'd hear him laughing, calling from the water for me to come on in. And I did dive in, laughing but uneasy, afraid of what I couldn't see in a river that I'd taken fish from. But it was joyous, and we kept on diving or basking in the sun as our bodies told us what to do and where we were. And then I cried thinking of the last thing we did or didn't do as we left that day, still laughing. I had somehow in my pocket a coin that hadn't been lost in the river; and when I saw all the names carved, thousands over the years, in the soft bark of the beeches, I said let's carve ours and put the day. But Johnny refused! And I cried now, thinking of the way he just shook his head no, and like a fool prayed that he'd know that I was outside now crying—now, while he was with Allie!

And then somehow it was Lincoln Park and my midnight there, and I thought how impossible it was to believe that Barbara ever would call for me at the end of her life. So I thought about how much more Allie had with Johnny. But I knew that the excursion with Barbara was a nonstory, an extravagance, even if it moved me like life, day and night. So I thought that it could be something of the same going on for Allie now in the room up above me.

But there was no comfort for me, as she was up there with

him, in having had my own time of infidelity and heart-pounding revenge, though I thought that I could understand revenge tales now and that mine was one, and that the gods came into it as they did into the tales of the sick Greeks when they had bloody sick vengeance and marriage stories on their minds and were building their nation. This moment of waiting now, at a distance, was my civilizing expurgation—always a part of those stories. But I thought that it was good for me too to know that if I'd caught them back then I might easily have killed them. If no such sickness, then no marriage, no task, no nation. But then immediately I knew again why I had to wait outside now and let them have secrets that I'd never know—let him die in her arms, let her kiss with ultimate tenderness his closed eyes, when he was gone. And so it went as time passed. I found, still, relief in the pain, hour after hour. And though I knew that the time's passing meant that she was needed up there, I even slept, for a while, the kind of sleep that I'd now come to beg for—and which I'll know tonight, I think, when this chapter is done.

I dreamed uneasily of that time when my father died, and of how the same gods chased me then, only for not all the same reasons. And if in my dream I could get no one to listen, I still tried to plead that all of it was important, that my father and Johnny were the hub and the rim of the world—which shows maybe how much conscious desire prevails even in dreams— or is it just in stories of dreams?

Then my eyes opened. It was daylight. And I saw that Allie was with me. I was startled that she was there, and I knew that it was time for questions which I couldn't bear to ask. She watched me coming awake and touched me softly on my shoulder and then on my face. Before I spoke, she said to me, "He died just after four." And no gods ever would have stopped me. I woke up to that light and broke into uncontrollable tears. I reached for Allie, and she took me in her arms, and we both sobbed violently as we held each other in the car.

14
TEARS WHEN WARS ARE OVER

Flowers come, and so for sad eyes there is a measure of goodness. There will always be some garland bound for broken hearts. Some weeks after we came back, Allie and I walked quietly, arm in arm, as we looked at the Conservatory's Easter flowers, the wealth of colors, and then the whites of the lilies' horns set so powerfully against dark and darker green leaves. And so many different faces, types, languages, in the crowd with us, people from all over the world, living in this huge city, bringing their interest in flowers to this quiet bouquet for the spring. A composition of place for all our meditations was the gathering of pink and yellow petals, petal dropping delicately over petal in the blown globe of the Charm Hydrangea, winning praises in four tongues as I lost myself in the sight of it. And the virgin white of Sister Therese. Then the blue stalk of the boy Hyacinth. The Snow Bush with petals of white, showering white-green leaves running in long trails. The unbelievable pastel green and baby-blue lavender of the Foch. The coming drops of blood along the gray arms of a Flowering Judas. And everywhere, enclosed in green darker than black, the pure white lilies' horns trumpeting the Resurrection.

I prayed for my friend and brother as I walked arm in arm with Allie. I laid upon my memory's grave for him these flowers which helped me pray. And I believe my praying for him, the crime and insult, is something that he'd finally forgive. I didn't seek and couldn't help the moment, and I'll pay for it with my own pain—and try to think out loud now along the lines of that pain as it comes. I'll listen to it as I argue dangerously for what I believe. I'll recall how I truly could not contemplate bringing flowers for the memory of a lost life, and in praise of him, before I'd come down far enough from my night flight home—though in perfect honesty I can think of no better use in our time for the beauty of flowers.

The voices that arouse the same responses in my mind whispered inside me that the day Johnny died was something close enough to the day my father died. As I've said, I became afraid, with the same kind of fear, that built structures could fall at any instant for no detectable reason (though again the duration and, consequently, degree of the new fear were different: the new being measurable only over seconds, minutes, at most hours, rather than over months and months—and with the real difference indicated most clearly, perhaps, by the fact that I'm still alive to say a word about it).

I've tried when I could to figure out the relations between fear and belief. I know that I need to be profoundly afraid in order just to bring the world into its distinct, familiar shape, to hold it firm, and that I need to believe that it will last in the shape I see, or else I'll go insane. This is the fear that is life, for all of us, and that modernity hates. In its fantastically naive hatred of God and of our care for ourselves, modernity won't respect the godlike terror that needs, and so instantly builds, a lasting world. And I know that this naive hatred is wrong. But I know just as well, and in the same way, that I need to let the world go, and fear go, and all shapes go, and God—or the world will fall just as fast and as maddeningly as it would if my fears for it came true. This is what I learned in a weird school, or what the voices whispered, in those minutes and hours after Johnny died.

I am in fact amazed that the voices know exactly that the world needs Johnny as much as it needs my father; know even that the world could in a way do without my father if it just had Johnny—that is, that it could survive nicely with no intensity of caring at all, like a stoic's equanimity or the state of nirvana. But without doubt—and I know that I continue radically to contradict myself, to make choices when I shouldn't—I want more now. I want more than just to know that the world only stands firm for those who aren't too afraid for it and don't overcarefully watch it! It's wrong to say this now, but I don't want, with Johnny, just to live hard by being unafraid to die. I want, still like a pitiful anachronism, to seek the *fullest* possible relations between fear and faith.

This is, in moments, the way it works with me: to fear intensely and caringly enough that my fear could be called love, and then to love so much what I'm afraid for that I stop feeling afraid.

But I can hear the new priests now. Hear them say, "You—you're the kind who still has some kind of crucifix in his brain—for whatever reason. To get beyond fear, you want to begin, not as you should, by denying you are someone, but with desire and love and words made flesh, and then to die in the flesh for what you love in the flesh! Amazing! Our sense of our limits in space and time, of our territory, our 'humanity,' the junk that makes us crazy enough to kill anything different that comes our way—you say—can engender compassion for everything different everywhere. So you want the limitations, the confinement, the incarnations, the fear, the sorrow. You want it all; and you say you get told by voices that there's something to this, that Golgotha is what you call a place—an eternal place. I'm afraid these are sins for which you have *got* to be sent to hell."

But I can't really talk like this now. I can't. It disturbs me—this second—to sound even slightly like a Christian. Disturbs me maybe further in than I know—and reminds me of how I felt when I decided, with Allie, to have an actual burial service for Johnny—no matter that a burial service now is as sane as anything else.

When the plane took off from San Francisco, I knew with every movement of that aircraft that I'd better keep my praying as silent as I did after I learned again the absolute necessity of silence—after I tried a prayer, just whispered a name, by the side of Johnny's grave. I'll say once more, too, that I know from the return of the terror, to what degree structure, like a phallus, needs Johnny's vital laugh. You have *got* to laugh, or things come screaming down. But I can't speak of how well I learned this. I'll only say, quickly, that because I couldn't laugh at my precious life, for two hours in the air I was right back in hell. And that I came as close to believing that the plane would fall as I could and still live—again coming just awake and to safety as we do when we're about to die in a dream.

But I also heard for a second the small man, the small adviser who'd kept me safe from cutting blades when I might have used them on myself. Do you know who he is? Have you met him? Do you believe that you can speak casually about the complete dissolution of the self, the laughing away of identity, before you've met the little man?

And I want to put in quickly—and God knows maybe I'd rather go mad than not finish what I have to say—that it was again sundown when we came into Chicago and that again the flight pattern, as we circled in a delay, took us out over the lake and that more than ever (as I felt the joy of returning to the ground) the lake, so delighting and murderous, and the land, with the Gold Coast and the miles and miles of green, holy parks, and the history of the architecture of the world—all under the royal blue sky-dome—made me cry in my heart ecstatically for sweet poetry. And Lake Shore Drive was the relation of poetry and story.

But with this I've gone on too long, said too much. I know by a certain rush in the brain. This second I dread, I swear, to think of finding any answers—to think I've understood the causes of things. The vengeance against me works this simply at times—like a machine. And though I should not say so, I'm trying this second, by instinct, as I did when I long ago walked along the shore without any purpose, to stop the pain that comes from taking this story too much in a single direction: toward poetry, and the scattering of flowers.

We went to Johnny's apartment after he died and before we buried him, to see what personal effects there might be, or no doubt curiously what last pieces of a life story. And (although I have to hush even this, and I know that, when I entered Johnny's place and when I left it, I had some very very dangerous moments of satisfaction) I take honest comfort from the fact that there possibly has never been a more complete discovery of nothing.

He'd been living in a run-down one-story duplex, half of a nondescript fifties box on a treeless street lined with the same thing. Wet junk and paper here and there in a cold rain made me dangerously heartsick at his not having found a place where anyone cared about anything. An unbelievable rusted car was there; and broken, brown-metal lawn chairs, with shell-shaped backs, tumbled in an absurd group: disjunct things that no one ever would arrange. But there wasn't even much of this kind of satisfying, miserable evidence. It was all just nothing—a row of mean, flat-roofed boxes, all filthy cream-white brick, with sodden tar and gravel roofs and torn, wrinkled, tar-stained metal flashing, and regular broken window screens. But then my being there with Allie made me for the moment feel unbelievably sad again for him—till she opened the tilted mailbox and we saw a letter addressed to John F. Lemaster, M.D., and I was utterly silenced by the shame that I felt for ever trying to figure him out—so much so that I wished the name "Allie" meant nothing to me and that I'd never thought anything about the value of my damned marriage. But blessedly, Jesus, the letter was insignificant, a form notice from a utility company that his payment was overdue.

He had no money, no family, no friends. And when we opened the door and went inside his place, we found only the silent cancellation of the drama of his letter to Allie: no signs of drug use, of the life of someone who'd been stabbed in the streets. No indication of love partners. No pictures on the walls other than a conventional shot of the Bay on a calendar, which was turned to January, with no dates circled anywhere. A television set but no telephone, no radio. A pair of blue jeans, a pair of khaki pants, dirty running shoes, and a nondescript assortment of T-shirts and shirts. No books, and no more correspondence of any kind in any of the drawers—no letter from anyone tucked away. Canned soup and canned fruit in a cabinet, along with a box of rice. An empty liquor chest, though there were a number of circular stains where bottles used to stand; and in the refrigerator literally nothing. The place and the furniture that no doubt came with it—the chairs, table, couch, bed—were musty-clean. And that was it. This was the place of no relation, no touch, no memory, no desire, and no evidence. And I was, and am now, too relieved by it to ask who in hell would choose to live in such a totally disconnected void.

But when I was almost gone from there, I did think for a second, with sudden anger (and like a *fool* I'm stopping now on my nowhere walk as if to look at an interesting stone) of the neatness and satisfactoriness of the end that comes with diseases like cancer and AIDS, which like to work together to take hope and rip it apart every place that it might dare to show its face.

"Goddamned fucking plague," I said to Allie, as we stood before a cheap, empty closet and I looked out the single front window. "What it does is bring hope down to streets like this. There's a satisfying truth—something we can hate with satisfaction."

Or so I was crazy enough to think. And I didn't finish with this. We were going now, quietly. There was nothing left to do or say. But I came out of the door crying suddenly in my heart that this wasn't right for the one I knew! not for my friend! The painfulness of this dead-end place, this lifeless embodiment of emptiness! I had already in my heart's memory the soft texture of the petals of flowers, the beautiful colors. And I knew that the poets, after paying homage to the end of the world—after ripping apart the world and our dangerous confidence in our knowledge of it—the illusions of causes and effects, our whole understanding—will whisper a real name, the name of a friend, a sweetheart, a hero, a brother, or king, to recall to us who we are, and bring back the world, saying that despite the large amount of truth in paradox, zero is not all of the holy.

"Christ Almighty," I cried to Allie.

She held me fiercely tight and whispered in tears, "He never should have ended up here. Never here."

But even if I was and am, with my poetry, a complete *fool,* this place still brings me comfort, as it helps me to *stop* looking. When we left, passed finally beyond the cheap and broken door, with nothing to show for the trip, my figuring him out was over.

And I cannot get angry—or God knows not at Johnny—when I think of what happened after the utterly sterile up-to-date burial service (and don't we all know some version of this sane improvement over the sick past?), which would no more let us see what happened at the grave, or throw in a handful of dirt, or a flower, than it would suggest an unsafe thought against money or the world. And if this is easy, cheap criticism, so much more pitiful are our times. But the idea—and here it goddamned is—the idea, as I said, that we'd have a memorial service of any kind for him seemed immediately to us both to be a profaning of something tremendously more important than dull modern health. It was everything—the whole beautiful, terrifying problem! That we'd choose a stone and have his name carved on it—that we'd dare possibly to have it say John Francis Lemaster, M.D., and cut into it the years of his birth and death, seemed not just to me—with my haunting, pounding memory of a day when no name or date was carved on a tree with a coin!—but to Allie, to be deadly wrong, repulsive.

"It makes me as uneasy as that apartment," she said, looking away, "that we'd have to decide how to close him in."

How much she understood this because of what she'd learned in bed with him, or in her heart when she went through every dream of giving herself to him or every memory of what they'd done, or because of any last words they'd had, I considered for a moment with violent savage anger—but then stopped considering—because immediately I knew that I had to.

Still, we did it! We had this ceremony, and had a stone cut—with his initials. We had to. We had to do this also. I am sure this is understandable, if not forgivable. And two days after the disinfected service (five minutes and a few dead words from a collarless, sport-coated chaplain in a coffinless, hygienic chapel) which maybe, for all I'll ever know, Lemaster would not have objected to as a final word on our millennia of dreams, I did go to the memorial garden. But it was possibly the perfect next and last place after that street that I saw stretching out in the rain without the slightest sign of decision or desire.

Inside the gate (no massive rusticated masonry, or pure platonic forms for defense, and no recall of such things), there was indeed an encased map, its careful maintenance forcefully guaranteed in the covenant securing perpetual care. And I almost laughed tracing the line to the gravesite, or felt utter shame and disgust that I would think that that contract and this map were good things—and that maybe the gatehouse did recall the dream of a dream of a fortress.

But beyond this the place was almost perfectly safe—an utterly treeless expanse which was in a few spots broken and colored by flowers, but which showed no pretensions to eternal memory or fame: not a single classical mausoleum, no crazy, unhealthy magnitudes of any kind, no obelisks, and if names, no other words carved on anything, no poetry, and no statues, stone wings of angels, or thought of them. And no slight trace or analogue either of the symbolism of service in military graveyards, the rows of white crosses which march on the eye and drive it back to drown in the sea of the heart. Whatever kind of sickness came up once with the words for gravesite services, or for the solemn funeral mass (which Johnny and I served often together when we were twelve and thirteen, memorizing *et lux perpetua lureat eis et clamor meis ad te veniat,* and which found me somehow terribly vulnerable to its beauty and Johnny somehow not) had been wiped out from this place as cleanly now as smallpox from the world. And am I the last one to visit a grave? Who does this now? Who would be insane enough to think of it?

But there were still the directions from the map, lines that I'd scribbled down and followed now, marker by marker, toward the end—which movement made me feel as if I were torturing someone whom I'd imprisoned and bound down hard—as if I were holding a knife to any part of him that I wanted to lop off, threatening to dismember him if I didn't hear exactly what I wanted to hear. But after the last marker, at the third crossroads, I could put away my scribblings.

Outside the car, there was only cold wet suburban San Francisco air, and everywhere that same gray neutral cemetery, where the stones lay flat—except for indistinguishable stumps here and there. The wide space never was anything but this miserable cold glare, which reached finally to chain-link fencing irresolutely stained with some dull, disordered creepers, extending a vague protection along several long stretches of roadtown. But I knew that by any reach of the imagination, this moment was not the horror it would have been if I'd placed him in some poetically right place and felt any touch of poetic satisfaction (and my mind insanely now does go to Calvary Cemetery, to the wall, and the urn elevated on a cross-emblazoned column, dividing the sky at the end of the city, the last corner of Eastlake). And when I took the first steps in the cold air to what I knew, from the transcription of the map, would be right there, not far in front of me, I was maybe as safe in this almost complete nowhere as I would be on the plane when there was for me still some possibility of silence.

My walking, the steps and sounds, in the dead, glaring dampness, made me regret any pitiful dream or hope that I'd ever had. And then after just so short a way, and another sudden, indescribable feeling of terrified remorse that I'd actually done this, chosen a gravestone for him, I saw my work. In this world empty, for a million miles, of trees, of mercy, it was actually there. I saw it set now at the head of a fresh-turned grave—so incredible: the small flat granite plate with the initials "J. L." But so strangely, I felt with a relief that will save me high in the wind, that this put an end to any pleasure I might ever feel in the world's bringing itself out just as the lines and colors of a map say that it will. And, trembling, I was more grateful now—more than I'll ever be able to say—for the dullness of this place, the unending images of lost desire.

Yet even here—I might cry out for myself—like an insane mourner from some completely insane time and country. Over the noise from roadtown, however, voices as loud as any I'd ever heard, right with the thought, told me to take any prayer book I might open in my mind and get out. So I was hushed. And the very idea now that I'd get angry about his life ending in the way it had made me feel something even deeper than my insane kind of shame. I was still here, and he had arrived—having made the perfect last move of his great life as a wrestler. I was telling stories, lies, and he was the exemplar of honest silence. How on this earth did I have the nerve to come to this place? I could feel the question spreading over the whole gray waste, over the unpretentious flatness—and then was sure that I had no right even to the little space here that I took up.

He wasn't here. He wasn't in this world, or any world. He was gone. And I was unspeakably ashamed that that was so hard and terrifying to believe. I was too ashamed of love to love him, even slightly—and so more luck to me. To the extent that I would love, I would pay. And not for a second could I complain here, or even think, that sacrificing identity on the cruel altar of modernity—playing Lemaster's game with the self's stability—*leads* us to this kind of non-place, where even a name's initials are too much for the goddamned intolerant truth. I could never whisper that there was nothing for me in this modern "memorial garden" but a final life- and book-destroying sleep; that for me this place was the end of language, language which kills but also, out of love, gives the most honorable burial to all things. I felt here that I had no rights of any kind. With incredible good fortune, I could pray for nothing, standing in my fool footprints, on that wide place devoid of any comment on or memory of the gods.

And for such a long time, I didn't say a word. Not with my writing those letters in stone sounding the sentence against me, moment after moment. But again, now, the shame of poetry!—that so helpfully destroys the world so we can stand by the side of a grave and think of nothing—and then, against all this that it's done for us, *will* whisper a name—so, for better or worse, we'll remember who we are! And after more good time with the world all gone, as some godforsaken wind blew through me and brought the rain of our tears, I began trembling, breaking and slowly crying. It was time, even if the truth was laughing with Johnny in the river and the sun! My eyes came again to my sins cut in the stone, and like a murderer, I made the sound of it. I'm sure I did. Crying in this place that was not mine, I sounded it out, in a whisper, "Oh Johnny. Johnny—No. God. No."

Then I was terribly awake. I knew that there was some prayer, even if silent, some prayer. But then so fortunately for me—so fortunately that it saved me locked in my pitiful self thirty thousand feet in the air—I learned again—and stopped—and let my eyes just sleep and my body not wake to any pain. Or maybe it wasn't sleep that I felt—maybe just quiet. Then more and more time passed—without my adulteration of the silence. And eventually I left as I think he might have wanted me to, just moving off when I felt that it was time, and passing over the roads as if I'd never see them on a map again.

But it wouldn't be all of it if I didn't, necessarily by my own logic, want for him to have been her true lover and my true enemy. He had to love her! I couldn't accept that he had no love, even if ironically that meant so much more pain. And because without question I *am* incurable and suicidal, I did finally ask Allie, as we sat waiting to get on the plane, what his last words had been.

We were alone together on the waiting chairs. She looked at me carefully and said, "Peter, they were nothing. I mean, there were no last words. He was laboring terribly in his breathing. He whispered at one point that he wanted your book to be truly good. But that was so early. For the last hours he never said anything."

"Did he tell you that he loved you?"

"He told me he was glad I came. He told me that several times."

"Did you hold him?"

"If I didn't, Peter, I wouldn't have been human. I held his hand for a long time. I had to. And I wanted to because the moment was what it was."

I started to ask her more, but she put her fingers to her lips. And I knew from the silencing feeling that I had when driving out of the cemetery that she was right in this, and that she must have known somehow, miraculously, what could help put me back together. I also could hear then the roar of the jet engines, and was worried to death about the sensation of lifting off from the ground. And no doubt, when that liftoff finally came, I had more trust in the silencing of my questions than I did in the pills Con had offered me (though I took these too, regardless of how much they might affect my heart). But now—God save me please—only this last thing to add about that flight: that absolutely all the wisdom that I could ever lay claim to was summed up in the way in which, in that terror, Allie and I spoke, or said nothing, or touched or let go of each other's hands, and trusted some completely magical alternation of noise and silence. And I'll always think that the first wise move was her touching her lips as she did.

But it's four days since I said this—and there's a new development.

Barbara used to appear for me, with wonderful enticing colors in her lips and eyes—just the right soft pink and soft blue. I remained perfectly startled, when I woke up to my vanity about how it would all work with her, by the fact that she'd actually graced me with the presence of her body, which more than anything else could at the time, and for long moments, helped me not to think about the fact that the story of my life was getting lost.

The soft liaison had been the perfect repression of a real

nightmare—or a very sweet circling of the final zero point of the death drive. I did drugs with her and carried on when I had no doctor and was going nowhere, and the pleasures of it without question gave me a kind of animation.

"When I'm alone," she said once, "I like to have a hundred different pictures of you in my mind. I run fast from one to another when I lie back and play with myself. So I need to study you with kisses in a hundred different places." She laughed then and passed me a joint, and began, giggling, but with delicacy, to kiss me.

I said, "If I wanted fame and fortune, I'd get inside your head and write your story. The world would gobble it up, and I'd write it like wildfire."

But how much could I discriminate, as I regained my senses, between this easy, gorgeous movement with Barbara, this kind of luscious, druggy answer to the problem of falling into bottomless holes, and the hard work of marriage and what it did for me? This seemed to be a question that I could answer always in favor of my marriage—just as I could still believe in an honest attempt to make words match things rather than in the lies that I told Allie, or in cocaine.

But now it's happened. Allie knows. She waited till I came down far enough from the air—several months—and she didn't throw it in my face when we talked about how much there was between Johnny and her. She waited long enough so that I'd know that she didn't care to put things together like that: balancing powers through mutual accusations: the old story. I'm certain, in fact, that she timed her revelation so that it came when it would work best, helping me to forget things and to stop wondering forever what might have gotten said when she was with Lemaster in the end.

There's also the enormity of the fact that Allie knew about Barbara and me even before we went to California and that she handled and kept on handling everything with the forgiving love and restraint that she did—and even in my dreams this could help me like that finger to the lips. But things had to come out.

"I have to let you know," she said night before last, in an

odd voice, "what's made me afraid to ask what you've done in your book since I last saw it. I know you so well. If the smell of your hair is slightly different I know it."

We'd turned the last light out and were in bed together. I couldn't see her fully, and now couldn't look. Her voice wasn't hers. But I knew, because I knew her like my life, that she had the sick feeling any decent, true human being would have when she made her incontestable accusation: "I smelled traces of perfume sometimes."

I couldn't touch her. I listened with deliberateness and uneasiness.

"It was so awful. One afternoon when you told me that you'd be out for a meeting downtown—I waited outside your office and followed you. I felt so small and ashamed. I knew what was happening—but I didn't know. I couldn't believe that I wanted to know, following you in the car! sneaking after the worst possible suspicions. It's so painful—how much I hate this kind of thing—wanting some end of my life. . . . But I kept telling myself that maybe you were heading for the meeting as you said. Yet I knew that was wishful thinking."

She wiped the tears from her face and eyes, then took a deep breath so she could keep on, though now in a breaking voice. "You don't—you shouldn't—even if you've done things yourself—even if you understand it all perfectly—you shouldn't forfeit your right to anger. I was so angry, Peter. I knew. I can't say that I knew who it was. But I knew when I saw you pull down that street what I'd find."

But when she said this, right on the brink of the recognition, I knew, in my insane sense, how much I loved her. I knew perfectly that we'd be able to do it again—to stay up hour after hour sleepless, talking about what happened. I knew, after so many simple discriminations, what my affair meant to me and didn't mean to me—and exactly how much more my marriage meant to me. And I knew my life with Allie was an answer to the problem of terrible, painful gaps. I knew that it could fill voids that I hadn't even yet seen and was ignorant of because my experience hadn't caught up yet with the wisdom in the words and stories of our language—because I didn't know yet what all the poets meant by the word "loneliness."

Struggling, with an effort to get me to see what was going on—to get it right—she said, "I can't tell you the feeling I had when I saw the door open. When I saw you and her. I knew it and couldn't believe it. But I could believe it. It's what I mean, when I say . . . so painful. And the feeling that I'd gotten what I deserved or looked for. I had the crazy feeling when I recognized her that something had been going on for years. I felt that I knew all along—that it wasn't surprising when I put certain things together. Then I thought, like a complete paranoid, that it had been going on in fact all these years and that you'd been seeing her without my knowing—and that made me feel completely lost."

I was afraid to touch her. I knew I couldn't. I said, "No." And I knew that this answer was true and that I could touch her—that it would be possible for me to love her for my whole life—if that isn't an inconceivably ruinous, repulsive thing to say—something that makes Johnny's truly good book impossible.

Then quickly, she said, "Peter, you've got to tell me I'm wrong—about how long you've been with her—crazy and wrong. I know it's over. I think I know you better than I could know anyone. I have to think it couldn't last. Tell me that's true. Tell me that it had to end quickly. If it starts so far back that it has no start, I don't care. If in some ways it never ends. If it's always somewhere in your head. Things like what we have go deeper. I've got to believe. And I know. The things we have. And truly I don't care what's happened to me—or that I was fool enough to have to have things happen to me, with him—or to want things to happen to me, even destroy me. Or that you haven't been able always just simply to believe in what you had, but needed her. It's not what we are."

I touched her arm, so ashamed, and feeling that maybe I should never touch her again in my life. But now the unbelievable pleasure of having this secret out was helping me say, "It's over. It's been over—some time now." Then after a moment, I went on slowly, "I guess I had to seek it. I had to. I was always such a good boy. I had to find out the difference between one experience and two. I don't blame you—not ever."

She looked at me with an expression of understanding, and sadness. I turned on the low bed light now, and we sat up in our bed and faced each other.

I said to her, "I get so scared—when I can't produce—when instead of things flowing, there's a gap or a hole, a silence; and then I want druggy dreams—and so I fantasize—about things that mean no work—no trouble. And if the guilt of pursuing the fantasy is painful, so much more the need for the candy and dreams, and on and on—so it goes round and round, in an unreal circle. But it's no life, Al—just a useless chase. I know this, even if there's a pseudolife, a drug life mixed in with it. You know what I feel. You know how much I love you. You know how much you don't need to ask me to be sorry. And you—Christ—you knew about this thing before we went to California! You didn't hurl it in my face. You didn't even defend yourself with it. I would have made a weapon of it. God help me. I hope knowing how much I love you helps you. I hope it helps you—in the deepest places where you're afraid—even more than knowing how incredibly sorry I am."

She was crying and trembling now, and she put her head on my shoulder, wetting my chest with her tears and mouth. She just whispered, "I trust you. You trusted me—our life—in San Francisco. I do everything not to lose you. I know what to do in my life because of the way I love you."

Utterly sick and ashamed, I said to her, "No better way."

She whispered, "Because of what I did, I've always been so afraid that you can know too much—and end up hating yourself. I didn't have to be unfaithful to find out how much I needed you. I think we're never stupid—never—that the same way we know all about heaven when we're in hell, we're also experts on hell when we're in heaven. Everything we are travels both ways—so why not be happy? It's not stupidity. Our happiness is not stupidity."

I held her when she said this, and held her tighter as she sobbed. I lifted my eyes into the soft semidark—and wondered if I'd ever suffer the feeling of brutalizing anger again, praying I never would. Then after a time, when she was calm, I turned out the small bed light. Then, though we stayed awake, we just lay back for several hours, letting what we'd done now to repair things keep out the world's wind and rain. Then sometime before morning we made love and, finally, fell asleep, having found a familiar sweetness in sorrow.

But now!—in that morning mail!—God Almighty!—a packet of things from my office came to the house. Included in it—excruciating as sunlight shining directly into the eyes—was an envelope—a familiar blue stationery with an unmistakable blank in the corner for the return address. It was Barbara. And I knew what it was about. But beyond this, I was curious as bleeding hell. What a laugh! Just feeling this intense, suicidal curiosity for a second again now goes so far against the work that Allie and I had done that night, setting marriage against nightmare, that it darkens again the tone of this book for me. But I wanted crazily to see what Barbara had to say because I knew that she was sending me some word *on this book*.

I'd loaned her once some of the opening chapters and some other notes about Johnny, the childhood memories, and she'd said to me, when I'd told her that I couldn't ever see her again, "Some day—I'll let you know what I think." This was it. It had to be. Jesus Christ, maybe now too she had something really sarcastic to say about Conlon, some joke more powerful than the power of all our blessed science. Or maybe she just wanted to see me.

And right now this is where I am. The letter's been for some days in the cabinet with my packet from Conlon. But here—this second—the two envelopes are right in front of me.

Conlon's narrative, or diary, or set of disparate comments—I have not looked, though I've been given the "right" to. Who the hell is he anyway? Yet even as I say that, I think of what happened with him and Barbara as the last unbearable thing. I can hear her laughing at him, and somewhere it terrifies me like the old night wind.

Even if he's a fool, I think of him as someone I could go to. You can't change doctors and feel safe. But still as I'm not with Barbara, drugged, forgetting who I am, I sometimes, in grotesque flashes, see her dancing with Conlon—with him having chosen the music. And I may *not* be down long enough from the terrifying air, not stupidly safe enough from poetry, to be able to think of my doctor as as large a fool as I am. But I *don't* think of him as a fool. He was a good doctor. He seemed to sense the worth of poetry.

I hope too that he *does* undo my story! I feel there'll be even greater authority in what he says if he disagrees with me—maybe even if he says that I'm incurable.

And Barbara! The idea of pleasing her thrills me. It goddamned thrills me—even if I honestly never believed a single word she said to me, her "most naive boyfriend of all."

If she hears notes of despair she'll be pleased—I can see her smiling—and I'll be pleased. I can't say that if she hates it I won't give a goddamn. I know that she'll *hate* any sweet remarks on marriage, on "the happy-ever-after story of Alicia and Pietro."

To hell with it. Let it burn. Just forget it. We can forget things (Allie says, "for the love, and the comedy"). But I want to know from my doctor if I'm right about myself—or if I'm doomed to die insane. I'm sick for this perfect all or nothing. And I want still to get "real" and let Barbara's words enter the story. Let her make fun of everything—so I don't have to be ashamed of myself for being alive, for being constant in any sense, for being terrified of this new drug "crack," of which she is not afraid.

But I don't want to die. The ancient story is true. You can go on seeking knowledge till you die. You can take the wrong drugs till you die. You can run from marriage and constancy, from your book, *till you die*. So I'm going to burn these things. Trash them and forget them. I'll burn them together and then when I've come back enough to myself, I'll come back to this story.

But I won't disappoint. I read them, of course. Barbara's first.

She addressed me in the way she often did when we were together.

LaRoche,

I always knew you were very beautifully crazy. I liked this, even though I was sure you'd vilify me, or villainess-ify me in your book. I'm interested to see how often you're afraid—since you say my picture comes to you when you are. Think of me, my love, whenever you're feelin' scared. The little townhouse here, as you know, has no yesterdays and no tomorrows—just me. But I don't like the way you always keep me out when I come into your sentences—though I suppose that is the story of your life, or wife. The stowwy of youw wife. And chiwdwen.

I loved my father too, by the way, till we decided, after he caught me and this boy doin' dope and doin' things, that we'd never speak to each other again. I was just bein' myself, and the boy was just a boy like you.

And maybe I'm the doctor. You went to Alex when things weren't standing up, and he came to me when things weren't standing up. I laugh to think!

I hate all the religious shit in your book, though. And why did you never tell me you liked masquerades? I wanted to get into masquerades with you so badly it was like an obsession. But why didn't I tell you? I don't know. I didn't think you'd like it. But I did think it really. I knew you. Damn me. I miss you.

Lemaster was a complete prick to me that time after we first met. I asked him. I said what is it with you and your friend Roche? He said to me I wouldn't know in a hundred lifetimes. He said I might as well just forget everything but day-to-day little doses of my own stupidity. But I outlived him, didn't I? And we'll see whether it's you or me who lives longer and has a better time. Love you.

Your friend,
B.D.

I glanced at some pages from Conlon's file, only ten pages in all—one from the beginning, one from the middle, and one from the end.

In October of 1972,

The patient, Peter Roche, showed symptoms of acute anxiety, marked by a particular neurotic apprehensiveness regarding the safety of standing structures. Mr. Roche's initial reluctance to enter treatment and his anxiety about the nature of therapy are pronounced but apparently not at this point inhibiting. Exaggerated sense of the stature and the importance of the accomplishments of his father and of a particular long-time friend seem to have led to a serious crisis of self-esteem. (One of these figures—the friend—as it turns out is well-known to me. The relationship between Mr. Roche and this friend brings out extraordinary feelings in both of them. It would be perhaps difficult to locate the more problematical difficulties with self-esteem.)

In July of 1973,

Mr. Roche has shown marked signs of improvement, confidence in the nature and current direction of therapy.

In October of 1974,

The mutually agreed-upon decision to terminate was based on clear evidence of patient's increased well-being. Mr. Roche has gained critical distance from the long-time cherished illusions about the mythical power of certain others, illusions which were fostered at the expense of his healthy feelings about himself.

And now time has passed, and it's done. Three weeks ago I burned both the papers from Conlon and the letter from Barbara in a trash barrel outside my house. I was lucky—the reading, and the burning, of these pages proved manageable; and I won't complain. I didn't douse the letters in fuel, or imagine the two of them dancing to the music, and then fucking to the music, as I destroyed the pages in the trash barrel. No bell, book, and candle. No real anger—not at Barbara, for what she said, or what she was, or is. I even hope that she *will* outlive me and come to some wonderful godlike, or goddesslike, wisdom in her golden days. I pray please let it be so— though I fear that it won't be. And I forgave Conlon for being a man, a man who once needed for his life, for his sex and power, a series of small doses—and who at least went to "the best" when he believed that that was all there was.

There is no end to it. I'll think of Barbara and of masquerades as long as I live; and I'll be glad for the simple narrative in Conlon's report—with its beginning, middle, and demythologizing final end. I say this even though I don't want either his health or Barbara's decadence and, crazy enough still, have my own story to tell.

I was really very lucky in my curiosity—not that there weren't things in these pages that could terrify or kill me, or that it did me the slightest good to hear about Johnny's feelings, or troubles—but because it turned out that I simply wasn't going to die. Maybe the finger to the lips, Allie's hush, and her forgiveness kept me safe—preserved me for the writing of my own comic story, which, because there *is* an understanding of heaven in hell, of beautiful lightness in the gracelessness of dead weight, she wants me to bring to the end.

More time has passed now—thank God. I told Allie carefully, truthfully about Barbara and Conlon, and about the drugs. It didn't shock her. She said, "I saw no signs"; and we both could believe easily that my interest was pseudoerotic and that it just died of boredom.

Concerning the Barbara and Conlon thing, I'd had an inexpressible fear that Allie would say something that would strike me as too hopeful and that this would drive me from her. But after I'd burned the pages, and more time passed, I told her. She understood why I hadn't before. I told her too about the letter, and she was glad there was no terrible religious drama in the fire. She could even say, "Barbara Dern's beautiful and funny, Peter. That she got into your head shouldn't torture you till you die. She's a sort of queen, really—of something." And she wasn't altogether surprised to hear about Barbara's affair with Conlon. "She seemed to have a thing for doctors. She hung around with that crowd for ages—good Lord."

But sensing, I'd say, how much trouble there might be for me in the demythologizing of Conlon himself, she said now, "I know how you can smell the rat of cowardice. But, as you say, there come times when we can't do it ourselves. So what happens—when the safety net in our mind is gone? There's just more. More safety. Even if you've been so curious about the net that you're sure you can't trust it anymore—there's more. And you don't need to be your own doctor. There's more outside you. If the time ever comes, you'll find what to believe in."

I said, "What about going too far? You've said yourself . . ."

"Who was it," she said, "who said, 'I might have to believe in hell, but I don't have to believe anyone's got to go there'? Anyhow—I lied. Or at least I know that that kind of misery's not for us. You talk about 'the best,' and you're right about it. And you'll believe in it. The safety beneath us never stops. Our kind of faith, anyone's basic faith, is faster than the fastest criticism, which *never* gets at the truth of life as we live it. I know your terms. You worry about some a-political, a-medicinal, a-marital dead end. But it's not gonna happen. And forget the threat of triviality. Like it or not, you're too much of a damned poet."

She fixed me a cold beer when she finished, and we sat on our back porch and rocked in the swing.

And now more days, more safe days have gone by; and if I can manage somehow to be sick with guilt for burning out from my life some potential for deadly tragedy—for burning those pages—I have been for all these days, for hours and hours, in conversation with Allie. And we've made a plan. We're going back to a place where we've been before. No second honeymoon—but just as good (or even better). I've gotten a room for us at what was in 1968, when we were there, the Conrad Hilton—the tremendous old place, once the Stevens, now renovated and called the Chicago Hilton, which looks over Grant Park to the Drive, harbor, and lake.

I've booked us a room which gives us views of the museums, the Planetarium, the Aquarium, Soldier Field, and south to Mercy and the University and north up the Drive. It's a view we had also in '68, just days after the infamous Democratic Convention. In fact, the massive cleanup was going on the entire two days we were there. Allie was attending an Americans for World Peace conference. So perfect for that time—God! She had this wonderful room—very likely one of the ones from which McCarthyites had flashed signals of support to the protesters gathered in the park. She'd whispered over the phone sweetly—after we'd talked and understood each other perfectly—I remember it almost as if it were now—that "the world wouldn't fall apart" if I broke the rules and joined her.

I think back now on how absolutely crazy I was getting in the car, knowing that this would be the day, finally, that I would lose my virginity. And on how impossible it was, moving down the Drive (afraid of nothing except maybe some stupid delay), to see anything, to gaze at anything on that road which always gave me so many things to see as I sailed by— things which I could look at really even on my worst days. I remember that I couldn't listen to the radio at all and that the beautiful women on the beaches only came to me in the briefest glimpses and just made me more exclusively hot and insane for where I was going. Maybe, too, I knew it all that much better—the sun, the air, the sky, the sights of midsummer, the music to which I could not listen—*because* I knew so crazily what made me turn away from all those things and drive to see Allie: this crazy, absolutely imbalanced desire to lose my virginity (a desire which was no more a matter of some structure of discourse than was the world's adoration of the Virgin) and to lie naked in bed with her for hours, for as long as we wanted.

So with these old times in mind, we're going to go back tomorrow to the Hilton, to our room over the park—and we'll have enough sweet passion together to carry us to places that we want to go.

I'm not afraid to say this, even if I know that audible predictions will work like black magic and ruin anything. What we want to happen is going to happen, and even if it doesn't, the desire—deeper again than dreams and tears and sex fantasies—will find satisfaction in seconds of peace and confidence. And I'm talking about seconds that mean so much! that will let us rewrite our histories—unwrite the letters that Allie wrote near that time; unwrite her time on the beach with Johnny; make us both virgins exactly as I'd seen it then; unwrite my times with Barbara, my phone conversations, letters, years of druggy dreams of her, and my revenge story and all of Allie's times with Lemaster. We'll have seconds when we can forget these things. We'll know what it means to forget them, even when we can't.

I can say this, even though I've had more intelligent superstitious dread of making statements than most people—even though I think of twentieth-century thought, which laughs hard at what I say, as the manifestation of a very mighty god. And think of a laughing Johnny Lemaster, in that he went beyond even any interested destructive criticism, never wanting to prove anything at all, as being at one with the greatest God (though I know too that at the far deepest level there's no greater terror for me than to assert this—to put Johnny Lemaster in the presence of God).

I was too afraid of the dark once and too ashamed of safety in the sun to think even for a split second of terror or safety, and now am close enough to this madness again to remember it. If I forced my way back, so what? You cannot force what isn't forcible. You can't learn what isn't learnable. You cannot just make up things like the feelings of this crazy return.

And I do remember now—from that time in '68—my fear

of accidents on Michigan Avenue and how I didn't look over at the park then, even though I knew, and perhaps because I was so preoccupied knew with even greater intensity, that it was haunted immediately by history, history right there in the present, too soon, like a frantic ghost looking for its grave on the day of its death. History, as they say, in the making. Kennedy and King murdered. And doubtless these men were great enough to bring on the enormity of murder. Listen to their words! And the war was doubtless goddamned enormous enough to bring on the deliberate, new, modern, godlike tearing apart of self that was that protest, or at least part of it; while part of it also, as extremes met, was a military buildup of its own kind, with the Yippies and the Mobilization in violent Platonic formations during their training exercises, which brought on the words "Shoot to kill"—words which were not the slogans of any convention, as this "convention," or "confrontation," was almost altogether fresh and new. And the police who beat people on the street, and were pigs before they heard the term, weren't ready for the shit they got. It was all wild, true poetry, and the spirits were still right there to see and feel.

Anxious with fear of an absurd accident, I turned to look for parking, somewhere! I was thinking only of what was coming to me, of what I would be when it began, and when it was happening, and when it was over, and of what I'd know about Allie, who'd give herself to me and let me undress her and look at her, and who'd open herself up to my mad intentions, which would die there inside her exactly as I hoped and prayed they would. I parked, and then I couldn't trust my feet, or the cars on the street that I had to cross, or, in some incipient way, anything in the world. But at the same time I was afraid of nothing. It would all happen. I knew. And when I came into the enormous, balconied lobby and saw all the people from the convention of Americans for World Peace, I was thrilled beyond myself by the actuality of this moment, and guilty because of it. I remember enough of this now, can hold it well enough in thought, so that our plan will include the recapturing of something crucially specific.

It was a time of special grace. I was so filled with desire; and looking around the wide, cool lobby, up into the marble columns and along the peach marble balustrades, I was preternaturally confident that everything would go the way I wanted it to go. But there was pure joy in this too which ran counter to all the crazy driving desire.

The elevator was there, the bellboy heard me and pushed the button, and the elevator took me off the ground, only to make me nearly weep for peace. And this feeling of incredible peace still serves me as a standard of truth, against which I can measure any insulting lies about what we are, or any bogus notions that suggest there's nothing divine in that hell-bent desire which gives us the most focusing drive and energizing courage we can know, but which also leads to complete abandonment and the gift of self (and so even more complete courage) in an act of love.

And I'm not only saying these insane things at this time but planning to go back to the place with my wife and rewrite everything—the wedding, which I had one way in my head and then lost to brutal irony—and everything else in our histories all through. It's insane, but I feel a certainty, a liberated joy of certainty, that what we *need* for our lives is in fact ordained for us and right and possible. What we need in order to live is some conjoining of memory and time-free joy. And in the light of memory right now, and happiness, I can see her face after I came down a corridor to a spy-holed door and sounded on it (with that feeling of grace: the fearlessness and yet the crazed hunger for her face and no other) and she was actually there.

Each one of us in the world, I believe, remembers a kiss that is like no other, but which is not just the best for one but for both lovers, and which remains for both something to think about till there's no more thinking. Allie and I remember and talk about ours at times still after twenty years. We know exactly what we mean when we smile at each other after one or the other recalls it. "You know the one," she'll say. Or I'll say. And we won't need to add another word.

It was unreal—the tenderness and taste in the lips, cool

and then warm, and that holding each other close together which lifts us off the ground and eliminates the weight of everything except what we love to feel with our hands and body—the roundness of the breasts, the pressure of the thighs. And then the shared desire for more and more, until it's all broken by the desire to go further, to go to bed together, which (and for us it was the first time!) must still be embarrassing and will need diversions and delays.

So we laughed and walked giggling arm in arm to the window, where there was a pair of rose-colored satin chairs, turned out for looking at the park and the lake. And after a few minutes, when we'd come quietly together again, we were sitting up so that we could look out, but also feel the beauty of the cream room behind us. We had a conversation which I can think of now with easy pleasure. The conversation turned to events of the previous few days and had its moments of young, heartbroken, simple political emotion, mixed with the taste and poetry of that kiss, and with the lightness and weight of the embrace and our desire to get into bed together and stay for as long as possible.

As we looked out the window, holding hands, waiting, I said, "I've thought at times, Al, as I've been driving down Sheridan Road and through Lincoln Park and down to Grant Park, with these names—Lincoln, Sheridan, Grant—about the Civil War—I mean sort of like some freaked-out 'history buff.' Right there—can you see it?—the statue of Logan, down there, on the top of that hill? Can you see the thing that looks like a spear, in his right hand? It's the Union flag. Did you see the picture the other day of the kid who'd climbed up on the horse's back and hung the Vietcong flag over it? I won't ever forget it. It tears me apart—two ways—I swear to Christ.

"Just the names of the parks and roads—on some days they honest to God work for me—I mean like great music. The memorial sculpture too, even if I'm embarrassed as hell now to say—I really oughta keep it to a whisper—that I'm moved by the human figure—St. Gaudens' two Lincolns—you know that one where we sat that night? It all makes me think about and feel sometimes what it might have been, back then."

"You'd have to whisper your affection for the figure," she said, "if you were in my sculpture class—very, very softly."

"Do you know what came down the street there—starting about Twelfth Street—in 1865?"

"I could guess."

"A hundred thousand walked with the caisson in the rain. It was the last stop before Springfield. They put it on huge ten-foot wheels. Down to Lake Street and back. Then the train pulled out backwards."

"I saw a picture somewhere."

"Sometimes—when the lake and the skyline put me in this mood—it's like somethin' goes off in me. I'll think of horses breathing—always in winter so I can feel the colors most and see the steam of the bodies and breath, and men getting ready to kill each other, six hundred thousand dead, Jesus, for the sake of keeping something together, or ripping it apart. It's close to that crazy now, too. It's so unbelievably damned alive out there."

"I hope some day I won't mind remembering it," she said.

I said, "It's *certain* things. I believe it. We're made for remembering and making a lot, or sometimes too much, out of *certain* things—particular things, and not just anything. If we're awake at all, these things take us and tear us apart—interest us—with this way of appealing to our *need* to exaggerate all to hell. I'm convinced it's the way it is. Even if my last four history teachers want to equate things like Lincoln's love of the union with something like his trimming of his beard. You know, so that nothing would ever get privileged—God forbid. But then even to that—trimming a beard—I say OK—because the particular things I'm talking about, to the right eye, are right there in a single goddamned hair. But let a poet make the equation. And the same with this time now. Put it in the hands of the same type who was crazy enough to give us Samson, so we'll know what the hell it was—what about it had greatness or power—and no more miserable trivialized shit."

Her mouth turned sad. "It was just too much last night, when I looked out. Enough's happened one way or the other so I just cry, and keep crying. This war. What more does anybody need to know that something's wrong!"

I looked out. "It's so impossible now to feel it all at once. I mean, to think now from both sides. The unbelievable new guilt—the one that makes you love the Vietcong flag!—*is* enough to make you hate your father and not even laugh at yourself. Then you go to the other side and think about some *real* threat to everything we've always been, and you think Hoffman and Rubin are about as amusing as your own gravestone [I pick this up again now, having left it for some days, and I want to pay tribute to Abbie Hoffman, who, I read, has died of unconquerable sorrow, and say that I love his name and would pray for him, loving to laugh still at the way he changed that name in order to fuck so-called American justice]. I can't believe what went on here. A hundred thousand people. We won't be the same, and that's good, but it's more painful and terrible than anybody I know is saying."

"I think people are too ashamed to admit how confused they feel—unless they're really lucky enough for things to be simple. Or maybe it's too painful for them to talk about the way they're torn in two."

"I can still see that cop beating that guy with the camera. And the fact that he was going to take a picture of a girl beaten to the ground. Jesus Christ. Yet I keep thinking of those people *training* on the other side. But I think of all that America is, how great; and then I know how much of what those people who'd tear it apart—how much of what they say and believe—is right and more beautiful and appealing than anything that currently is. I know it because the fucking unbelievable fence around the Amphitheatre was barbed wire, and because there were rifles on every roof, and every goddamned manhole cover was sealed. It's enough to make you wish that the plot to spike the water with acid had been a roaring fucking success. Daley, or my father, on LSD!

"But for me that it's all come down to it here, in the Civil War park, with my crazy memory or imagination of horses and men and the feel of the weight of the bodies, the colors coming out of the mist! I swear, Allie—it's so ridiculous—but

I've trembled, thinking about the damned Civil War. I'm sha-kin' when I look at things like the lake and shore and the parks and Soldier Field and the Field Museum at the end of that long stretch on the south Drive. It oughta be embarrassing as hell to say this. And yet lookin' out now, with the history right there, makes it less embarrassing. Being here, with you, in this mood, makes it a lot less embarrassing."

I stopped and thought of how I was just a half hour before; how crazy and distracted. I smiled. "I *promise* you, A, when I drove by the park a half hour ago I wasn't thinking of any of this. I just thought of how much I wanted to be with you. I couldn't even look. I thought that something might go wrong, if I looked. And see how I keep on talking like a fool!"

She sank down from her chair onto the floor, put her head on my knee and kissed it. She said, with her eyes closed and her cheek on my thigh, "We won't be fooled by 'em. No Chi-town coppers. Nobody from the other side either."

She briefly kissed my inner thigh then; and the irresistible warmth made me come down with her to the floor. I said, "I don't think so," and kissed her mouth, the flesh of her lips, and the shadow.

I'd never tried to see her unclothed or asked to see her, as much as I'd dreamed of it. But I didn't hesitate to unfasten the buttons and the clasp of her skirt, pale cream in the pale cream room; and she let it happen, without the slightest sign of timidity—even if we'd waited for so long for this to happen. Then leaving her skirt just loose, I unbuttoned her blouse, the buttons leaving the soft lace, and kissed the tops of her breasts, and she held me against her gently, letting her hands fall then to my shirt, which she began to unbutton. And she touched her warm lips just slightly to my shoulder and neck.

Then it was time, with the ghosts from the park still so powerfully in the air; sweet grace and desire, it was time, as simple as the sadness and terror of war, to give ourselves and take each other.

And our plan for tomorrow is to go back, knowing the real impossibility of ever again being so crazy and full of grace, but confident that there'll be beautiful moments, strong enough to hold up our thoughts and determination for as long as we need.

And I say, no matter what, that she was a virgin. I say it again with complete contempt for the stupidity—for the pathetic dullness that hasn't learned yet that it's the lake and the parks, the sky and architecture, the masses and shadows, the wars and the desire and grace, the men readying in winter dawn to kill and show their colors in the mist, the loudspeaker voices of Hoffman and Hayden and Daley, the idealism and the beatings—all colored by an unforgettable kiss—which reveal the truth of how much she gave to me then.

The real Allie and the real me—our stories move on—against the priestly deconstructing, subverting, dismantling ambition of late-twentieth-century intellectual intention. I say this even though I buried Johnny with a ceremony and a marked gravestone, and have only been free for a few days from the sick fear, the absolutely unspeakable terror in the air, which were mine because I did it. It's too rare that we go back to the edge of our lives—and then come just enough away to feel the meaning of health and freedom against the roaring memory of the right definite dread. It may be more dangerous than I know, but I have to speak—on an occasion this rare.

She was so beautiful. I can think of it now and not be in danger, as if for a second at the end of my pilgrimage, come in safe, and feeling no disappointment. It was beyond the craziest, sweetest expectation. The fall of her auburn hair making a soft frame for her face, and spreading on her shoulders like a quiet wave's end on the shore. Her pale face, like a mysterious face from an Annunciation, helping me understand even more. She was afraid. This, after our long wait, which we had somehow, against the idiot age, the intelligence to prolong, was the beautiful, incontestable truth. It could be read in her eyes, half-opened in the shaded light. But it only helped us understand the moment—when she let herself be seen and knew unforgettably the painful joy of letting it happen, against her own shyness.

She let me look, and whatever I know of the meaning of praise I know from the seconds that I took to look at her breasts, with the darker rounded areoles and the nipples erect for hungry love. It is impossible that she was not proud. Her firm, tight waist was something to be proud of, to keep hard, except—and I could look, and see—where it turned softly into the curves of her thighs. And now I could lay and press my stomach and thighs against hers. It was our time, which my body understood, even if there were seeds in me of more trouble than I knew. I kissed her, as I lay down with her; and there was the taste again, cool and then warm, and the softness. I let my tongue run over her teeth. I held her more tightly now, on the course that was irreversible, for she was just as passionate and crazy to taste my mouth and run her tongue and lips over my face. I whispered to her, "This tells me where I'm going in my life, Allie. It helps me understand everything. You know I love you."

She said, "I love you so much," as I entered her, "I love you. I love you," in a soft chant, "Peter."

Then it was utter passionate intercourse with wild extreme words which had nothing in them of mere hot love talk, if they were the same words and just as easy to say. We said that we were in heaven—everything crazy and utterly embarrassing. But with her, in this moment, I wasn't afraid of any height in the air, or of any structure falling. I knew for the whole brilliant time that I absolutely was born, like everyone else, to keep myself and give myself away—both, and both crazily. And these convictions, magnified insanely in this passion, were as truly right as there is true grace in being unafraid. For hours in that bed—and we stayed till the following morning—we made the completest possible love—at the Conference of Americans for World Peace, over Grant Park, with ghosts of wars and every conceivable kind of hope and fear in the air—and with all of man's magnificent handiwork spreading out below from the Art Institute to the University and saying, in each of the homes of the Muses, that the simultaneously keeping and giving thing that is radical love, the life, the living naked body, the marriage of flesh and bone, is what's true.

And when I'm with her tomorrow, I'll tell her that this is

what's true. I'll say that our marriage is the truth—with everyone dead or gone, the damaging information and surprises dismissed, or forgiven, or burned and forgotten, all of which shames me and will tear my words apart in time. But for seconds, nothing will be closed but the closed moment, which still will be enough: sufficient to carry us through the rest of our lives.

We're going to see *Romeo and Juliet* at the Blackstone, and I'll have enough of my mind and soul alive to know what Shakespeare, as he gives us the superintelligence of suicidal teen love, means by his pearl in an Ethiop's ear. But if the critical mind of the age finds all of this assertiveness cheap and repulsive, what must it think of the last memory I'll speak of now, which is another that sets a standard for me, against which I can measure the dangerous stupidity of our time?

We were naked, closed in each other's arms under a thin blanket, when the first predawn light made me think how much it would mean, on this morning, to see the sun come up over the city. I touched away Allie's hair from her ear and whispered that it was time, if we wanted to see the sunrise; and after a second she opened her eyes without any sign of desire to forget what we'd done, though I know that there had to be some profound sorrow. She smiled, consciously held me tighter, if she was still half asleep. Then she sat up slowly, her eyes closed again, with the blanket pulled over her shoulders.

She opened her eyes and looked out over the park toward the horizon. "Oh, you're right! It's just coming over the edge!"

She let the blanket drop from her shoulders, and she took my hand. We both got up naked to look out the window. Our room, ten stories high over the empty, silent park and Drive and water, seemed to be exactly as quiet as it should be. The unbelievably powerful city was still partly in a mist, which the sun would burn away by the time the noise began. But in the low fog now, the classical temples along the south shore were the dream of Greece that the unembarrassed architects who designed them were dreaming; and Navy Pier, with its huge vault and odd towers, could have been reaching out into an Eastern Mediterranean bay. It's not too much to say either that the moment gave me another vantage point for the under-standing of Paradise, and any poem of Paradise: Milton's Michelangelo's, Masaccio's. We were wonderfully drained, and maybe wanted just to lie down and hold each other and rewrite books on rest and calm. But it was so good to be awake and looking out on the harbor and houses of collections and fish and ideas of the stars—as the sun fired up into the river and off the buildings' glass (see Lake Point Tower truly in burning gold at dawn!) and stained beautifully the low clouds on the horizon with incredible orange fire as the first powder blue of the sky set them off.

I didn't know as much about Paradise and love as I would a few years later, when I couldn't dare think back on a high moment like this, or take a step away from deep hell, every move then being too much. I was too far in, at that later time, not to feel the paralyzing shadow of dread. But then after that time in starless hell, I moved out again; and I was in the state of grace, which is sublime, and which for me has existed most really, in fact, just past the reach of absolute oracular terror. And without saying a word about what will be and what won't, I'm right now, for these seconds, at a very precise right distance from misery and dread—a distance from which I can still listen safely to them both. And just out here, in the state of grace, is where we enjoy most what we know to be true and good, like love and life.

The tears when wars are over have more in them than all the sacred names of French intellectuals, who haven't yet accounted for a single specific grace or grief in any of the world's poetry, and who are so far and stupidly safe from madness that they can call madness a mere historical phenom-enon, a disjointed word—and are as far from any understand-ing of structure as anyone is who never for a second has had the slightest doubt about a post and beam.

But I had something in the back of my mind that morn-ing, as I'd seen a number of detailed advertisements over the previous few weeks. I knew that in a few hours, north of the park, inside the breakwater south of Oak, a huge crowd would gather for the spectacular summer air show—which for us would be that much more understandable as we would come across from the Hilton exactly at the time we would, walking in the park among the horde of groundskeepers, who stabbed every leaflet in the green grass with a spear point.

We pulled the drapes and slept peacefully again. Then later, when we'd dressed and eaten, we went out and began our walk at the far southwest corner of the park—with the Hebe fountain, where the goddess cupbearer offers for the gaze the flesh of her thigh and breasts, and wine in any instant that the immortals wish it. What a complete oddity here, I thought—if I loved Mr. Rosenberg of San Francisco for his whimsy. But I couldn't believe either that it would take more than a moment, with almost anyone who came to drink at the drinking fountain, to start a company of sorrow—who all would see that they longed for what was held in that tipping amphora, and so come to know Hebe like a first love and want her in their park.

The long row of elms vaulting and shading the promenade which led to the steps to Logan's hill, and the gardens, which were not destroyed by the throngs of protesters or police in battle lines, made me think too of the satisfaction that the cupbearer could bring in her heaven to our unkillable thirst—think it and feel it so unsentimentally, as I saw Logan now high up in the wind, the tail of his black horse blowing back like his hair. I gripped Allie's hand tightly, as we came to the steps, and clenched my jaw to hold back tears, which would have made conclusive something that should never end. I put at the gigantic black horse's hooves a young girl, one I saw there in a picture in the paper, with long blond hair and an Indian dress, a beautiful frail flower child. I climbed the steps thinking that there might still be shreds of the red banner depending from the staff tipped with no flower but the war eagle, and read with an utterly confused, pounding heart the names Champion's Hill, Vicksburg, Corinth, Atlanta, and the dates, thinking of the clumsiness of flight from tear-gas-firing police, who'd hate my looks.

This was that time, so confused, no matter what doctrinaires of either side, who've never been afraid enough for a "confrontation" with the gods, might say. And down an alley of apple trees with a central garden and lilacs, across from the Spirit of Music standing on the round world, her breasts bared, with a harp, and from Buckingham Fountain, where police had just beaten and held people down in the water, offering what new life?—there was another half-oval stone bench, punctuated by twin flame-crested Doric columns. Though now, as if we were to understand from this second presentation that he'd come past all beginnings and endings, only his name is cut by St. Gaudens in the block, and he is not pacing forth but sitting in the eagle-backed president's chair.

I think now too, as I write this, of the Chinese students here who gathered around his statue these last few days, in a show of solidarity, while in Beijing tanks have rolled over the Statue of Liberty; and who had hung a banner in Chinese characters, which I cannot read, but which I'm sure translate into a simple admiration for his name, read like a prayer expressing hope for the future of the world. And God knows I've been moved even by a radio commercial which brings back the picture of the death train, carrying him home, and, advertising the Lincoln points of interest in the state, says to parents to teach their children who he was.

And if in love I've told my children who my father was, I'll tell them that Lincoln would have known in his terrifying sorrow the divinity of the muse of history and how to recognize in fear and compassion that union demands a poet's understanding of the enormity of sunrise and sunset, and of the words "and" and "but." And now I've just seen a column in the *Tribune* which, considering the slaughter in Tiananmen, the picture of the bloody deconstruction of a man's brain on the cover of *Time,* rips a contemporary critic who had kind words for the Party (perhaps because no signifier of theirs ever tried to touch a signified: "No one died in Tiananmen Square") and called our love of freedom and human rights narrow and "culture-bound." And so no sorrow, just sleep.

And that morning, as we moved on to the park's end, past the harbor and the Chicago Light, the Pier and Lake Point, to the beach—the places Chicago's mind runs to from its crimes and its flatness only surreptitiously relieved by money, or a dream of money—I thought passionately of what I'd seen in the advertisements for the air show. Or I thought about one plane that they said would be there, the image of which, so I could understand it, I set in my heart against the image of my friend John Lemaster, who could do more to make me ashamed of my desire to see the plane even than a picture on one remaining leaflet of a sixteen-year-old Vietnamese girl, whose name was given, though sadly I have forgotten it, and who was disfigured beyond hope by napalm, which couldn't be torn from her face.

We arrived on time and found a place comfortable and uncrowded enough, and lifted our heads first thing to see the inevitable Blue Angels—but there was indeed unbelievable spectacle in the silver screams and roaring American thunder of their presence when they came as low over the crowd as their terrifying brethren had over the village of that girl, and in Euclidean Platonic formations that either held to the inch or exploded into elemental fire—as everyone in the huge crowd knew, watching with perfect fixed attention. The Angels weren't what I came for, but in the state of grace I could feel, as they swept by, the meaning of presence so perfectly well that for me the groundskeepers, the morning after my first time with Allie, were stabbing that girl's body one more time.

And I've thought of this time, and this air show, for I don't know how long. I knew I'd include it. But, Johnny, I didn't know truly how much you'd be here to challenge what I say. I thought of you so much, that day, not even knowing that you'd been first with Allie, because you were for me so far beyond any holy French philosopher, or the protest, or the movement. You were always the true complete absence to any spectacular presence. There's no word for you. I knew it always and wondered immediately what you would think as tears came to my eyes when the announcement came over the loudspeaker that heading our way from the south, coming low over the horizon now at a speed of four hundred and fifty miles per hour, was what I'd come to see. But I will say as I want to, and because it's true enough so that I can say it and not even ruin my plans for tomorrow: lovemaking is a book that we've been given to read, and everything is in it. And first lovemaking, which was ours, John, not yours—I'm sorry—took me beyond your reach, into the presence of a glory that, breaking into the sky over Soldier Field and Grant Park, mixing so beautifully, in the highest form of art, with the echoes of the cries of protest, gave me intonations of some harmonious voice of eternity.

It was his plane, coming with a noise so much more terrifying than the choir songs of the Blue Angels that the crowd, infinitely hungry for poetry, knew that this, and not the Angels, was what it would remember. Those who knew already what it was could picture, as I did, the vision of American squadrons breaking low over the English Channel in the dawn light; for this was the Second World War, when we were guilt-free and could speak, to the everlasting relief of our souls, of heroes (but I was that much more alive now as I was tortured by guilt, by the cries of the protests, the hopelessly disfigured face and body of that Vietnamese girl) and could thrill like boys to the name: the P-51 Mustang! And this is exactly what made it more: the mad pain of guilt, the feeling, as this perfectly preserved memory of thirty years came over the trees now with a power and screaming ferocity that made me weep for its presence. I couldn't hold back my tears. Because of the guilt, the plane was *there*. Because of it, it came from some eternal place, from which we receive sudden messages of eternity. It was too true—my night with Allie was too true—beyond the reach of Lemaster—as this plane now rose beyond the reach of the earth—rising, completely blinding and deafening, the color and shape and sound, intact and gaining speed in a pure perpendicular. And I imagined what in those moments of hatred and violence and sacrifice and grace—those moments of terror and pure courage, in the face of the Luftwaffe, what feelings he must have had! The weight and the lightness. And I will say, without, for this second, a trace of shame, that the worst that can be said of eternity is that it is unreal. For real or not, it gives without question the highest possible grace to our lives.

15
THE KING OF THE WORLD

This is my story, and I've always known when it's not been right. Every miserable time, I've heard protests in my brain when I've lied. The falsifying book-shape has put pressure on me that's let me know perfectly sometimes what my poets—pagan, Christian, it doesn't matter—mean by the dead weight of cares. But when I think too of the black magical and true connection between what I've said and what has then actually happened, I am very afraid that ending this thing, this "life," just may be like heading toward a death.

It's not just that, like everybody else, I've got something in me that beyond the policing lie of a neat ending will never stop wanting the wild life—drugs, extramarital sex, affairs, candy, fantasy. Or just that I'm crazed with modern guilt and so feel an absolute obligation to destroy myself rather than commit the unpardonable sin of bringing something to a close. It's much more, as I've tried so many times to say, that I *know* that to structure things, to bring them to a conclusion, is to threaten the very possibility of keeping the world safe from falling. I promise, it's that Johnny Lemaster will always be my friend, in ways that will outweigh anything I'll ever read or write in a book.

But the world is *not* perfect. We've got to make use of things, bend them to a reflection of our own intentions—or die. We've got to choose, to close things, or we'll just sleep (and ultimately there's no ground for choosing that lies short of the mad life of the Chosen People in the desert, wandering for forty years, praying on the rocks and sand, which, viewed insanely, were poetic, not just loosely metaphoric). There's no poetry without hard facts either, without truths. And we won't cry sweet saving tears, without a hard *understanding* of the truths proffered. It wasn't until I'd lived and known enough, that I cried reading *Romeo and Juliet*. And it takes even more than understanding—it takes belief for us to cry like this. Nothing happens until we are dead cold certain that something matters—Romeo's life, or his losing it in the dark.

But we don't have to go completely mad to learn all this. At some edge of insanity, when maybe the fear of a world-collapse comes closer and closer to an actual *belief* in such a collapse—right here—our faith in patience might begin. And right here, where houses do teeter, is where poetry and metaphors are born. Possibly a faith also in silence and noise. In shutting your mouth completely—and then in the most careful whispering of what you want—which leads to a clear perception of and faith in the enormity of quiet prayer, a key to poetry. Or to a clear understanding of and faith in the power of light and dark—which lead to a true poetic understanding of the people whom we love or need or hate, and of their stories, and of how much it matters whether someone is here, in the light, or lost in the dark.

And when Allie and I did go back, as we planned, to the place where we first made love, it could not have been more tense, alive, beautiful! We left just after nightfall in the rain, and I remembered in a second of terror my love and fear of music, and of hope. But sounds from the radio went to just the right places in my heart for the swing out South Boulevard. I knew it as I came round the corner of Calvary: as my car lights swept over the classic, Christian stone memorials, the columns crucified with the Irish Cross, and, the next moment, past the wall of boulders out onto the darkening lake, which could have been then the memorial crypt of the Ice Age.

It didn't matter again either what force I might have used at any time to get to where I wanted to be; the soft rain and the lights at night, along that edge (which has often been the setting for my dreams) were enough. And if a nice ready feeling of completeness is only possible most times with drugs or in adultery (and to make the pulse really beat, we'd get the pay porno film in the hotel room rather than go to *Romeo and Juliet!*), I could say to Allie, "They're strong enough maybe even to beat irony: I mean the similarities between what I wanted when I began my damned book and what I'm getting. And even the differences are maybe too poetic and beautiful for irony to make anything out of them."

"It's a very nice and odd feeling, isn't it?" she said, "getting what you wanted."

I smiled, and looked at her. Then the wind was powerful enough suddenly to move the car out of the sharp curving lane, but the music was in my hands on the wheel, and I didn't think—as I brought the car back in line on southbound Sheridan Road. I didn't make plans either for the elimination of trouble spots in Rogers Park—the architectural, commercial hideousnesses, the roughnecks and punks. I just listened to the music, and talked with Allie, and waited to see the city, after we turned at Hollywood, with its trillion lights shining in the rain.

If I could have planned this, I would have—the high buildings cut off at top by a low, sharp-lined ceiling of clouds (though the moonrise was visible now in part to the far southeast); and this gray-black cloud-ceiling glowing everywhere, reflecting the uncountable lights from spectacularly present, huge, sharp buildings and lower halves of giant buildings which glistened in the rain. It was absolutely a peopled heaven too; for every star in these constellations, as I said—no damned shame!—was an apartment with vulnerable people struggling in it in the same way we were.

"And who've been made stars for the night," Allie said,

"by my insane husband, whom I do love—even if he tells me there have been times when he couldn't think of me and still live." Then quickly she said, "Look how wild *that* is tonight!" and pointed to the huge Alaskan totem which stares wide-eyed into the road from the beach park at Addison—Kwanusila, the Great Thunderbird, gigantic, its colored spread wings and the grotesques below transfigured by misted iridescent spotlights against the black trees. The pole in the passing second was eerie, remarkably there and not there, like a face in the dark with a flashlight under the chin. But this vision, and the moon low over the empty harbor, adding in this dark more strange glow to the lit, compressing ceiling of clouds, were enough so that we could even talk about them and not diminish them too much.

As a city boy I didn't know wild animals, except as they live in the zoo, which we saw signs for now. Looking tenderly at Allie as she looked out, I said that I was sure there was a place, "—some place, A, in which I'd start carving poles like that, even if I'd never heard of totem poles before."

I thought too of the great lighted totem at the center point in front of the Field Museum, at the end of that beautiful long perspective on the south Drive. And of its story of Big Beaver—and of how the magic power of the mysterious animal was assumed by the Indian family. And then of how once in the House of the Great Apes I brought my face up to the separating one inch of glass—"Do you remember how they have it? How you cannot believe it's safe?"—and of how right with me a tremendous ape brought his, and of the instant terror and indescribable respect I felt as I stayed with him, eye to eye with his utterly strange might and grace, our faces only inches apart, for some seconds.

I went happily on, thinking out loud of the animals in the zoo, as we wheeled south past Fullerton. And of people at the zoo. How we gaze at what's caught in a cage but wish, every one of us, that the great animal that we see had more room. "It's really sad," Allie said. And how we all wonder if a great cat, sleeping, lying utterly motionless, showing no signs of life, is dead—but then catch that subtlest sign of his breathing.

Parents pointing and pointing for their children. Then how our hearts stop when a great Bengal finally does move and rise. How we want then so badly for it to talk, until it does talk, breaking the silence of its utterly graceful, sad pacing with a sound so deep that none of us ever could forget it. And of how *anyone* in the real presence of such power, speed and innocent grace would want to carve a story on a long trunk and could understand the prayer for our oneness with the Thunderbird, the Beaver.

Where we were, on the Drive, at the near edge of the huge city now, we enjoyed everything that we said to each other. And the buildings everywhere, still so spectacularly delineated, lit, glistening—looming and then stopped by a bordering of darkness as terrible as a drowning—let us know in the music and the rain that mere dead fidelity or some heart-shattering split wasn't in our future. Or that our kisses in the half-light of the bedroom later on would let us write again a poem's ending with us both still there, body and soul, in a close embrace.

And why not the presence of everything? I know what I've said about choosing, selecting, but really I have no objections. Only let it all be placed along Lake Shore Drive, and let me think of it all with Allie, in the music, with the car wheeling by gracefully on a glistening night—just after I've been so frightened in the air that I couldn't contemplate the contemplation of a sound.

The museum of the Historical Society was announcing with green banners (like the blue/gold mummy banners for Egypt at the Field Museum and the burnt red banners for Gauguin, flying at the Art Institute—showing too the figures from Gauguin's universal myth—alongside slow, billowing notices of "The Human Figure in Greek Art") a display of the multifarious American Street. Let it be there, along with the designs of Frank Lloyd Wright for Johnson Wax—and I'd call Wright, as he'd call himself, one damned good poet of the lake shore.

I should say too that the total, awakened, dangerous care of Wright's design (working from the armchairs to the last outworks) and the cantilevered horizontals in the small house at Sheridan and Fargo, time after time save Rogers Park for me, like a magic gemstone. These and the perpetually forlorn and falling House of the Congregation Sinai, with readings from the Torah announced always in tilting letters on a tilting marquee.

And God bless forever Wright's friend Burnham (the villain in postmodernity's explosive story of Chicago), who knew that some lunatic like me would need huge spaces voided between Michigan Avenue and the water. Who *gave* the city poetry and water, so it wouldn't have only money and madness.

The commonplaces, too, especially at night, can still wound me with desire: the giant rusticated stones and burnished columns of Sullivan's Auditorium, and the replicating Chicago windows in white terra-cotta of the Railway Exchange Building, the precious Wrigley with its floodlights at the river setting off the whiteness and the delicacy of its form (sweet moon flower) so we'll know why we don't want war ever again, the hyper-clean glass and I-beams of Mies's millennial curtains—which Allie and I did read now, talking respectfully, free of dead-headed polemics, about "less is more," as we passed south inside the breakwater at Oak. And I swear to God I was back, for a brief moment, at that place where the air show had twenty years ago put a sound and a color and moving form and power in my mind to accompany forever the terror of the disfigured body of an innocent girl.

The embarrassing days of Vietnam Age brotherhood, peace signs, brother, the repulsive exaggerations of *Apocalypse Now,* Allen Ginsberg chanting the news on radical radio stations, the absurd stoned tripe of Woodstock: "People, people: don't drop the brown acid, OK, people?" It's no wonder our kids can't stop laughing. But obviously this wasn't all of it. Mace in the air makes Burroughs in Soldier Field forever oracular. And there was something too right or wrong to be embarrassing in the haunting, driving rock sounds of "The End" and in the terror of helicopters cutting the air over the Mekong and in the true ecstasy in winning, for seconds, A

Little Help From Our Friends, with three hundred thousand mad souls moving back at the same time, in an extremely goddamned sad world, toward the Gates of Paradise. And I thought with a damned far better wisdom of the powerful Beat poet, who has understood Blake, intoning over his harmonium, "And-in-the-world-todayyyayyy," which used to make me think, back then, of the Bible and the Apocalypse.

I've said that there were times when I wasn't allowed to think anything good about my relationship with Allie. I meant this absolutely literally. If I'd thought something good about it, my fear that the bearing walls of any place that I was in would give way, and that I would be killed, could in a second have become a positive belief—which right there would have ended my life in the world as we know it. But I have to add, quietly—if not so quietly that Allie can't hear me—that I'm absurdly proud of having had this experience. And if someone said to me that I lied about the way that things get discovered along that edge, that cliff high on the mountain of the muses, or that the truths discoverable there aren't really big enough to withstand goddamned facile conventional reductionism (the two-bit bravery of an age of thin, humorless Falstaffs who'd stick the leg of dead honor several thousand more times), I'd say to him, "Look, you son of a bitch. You go there, and you come back and tell me what you think. Until then, shut your fucking mouth."

But maybe I've made enough things clear so that I do have a right to say some of the good things about my relationship now—while the structures of the built world seem safe to me (if still, even after months, precious and rare against the background of a known threat).

The Hilton was recently renovated "to the tune," as they say, of some one hundred million dollars. If I'm damned sure that murderous uncountered capitalism is one logical extension of that reductionism that I so violently despise, just as cannibalism is the final extension of pure materialism, I don't mind thinking about the part that money plays in keeping things up. It's good business, and I was glad I had enough money to be where I was and to have tickets to the play and reservations for a dinner—one can always use a touch of class when trying to repair a marriage and rediscover a life.

So we chose the balcony restaurant, perfectly elegant inside the peach marble balustrades and under the shining columns, and asked for window seats, out which maybe we would see ghosts, and ordered a beautiful meal and wine (though we wouldn't want to drink too much and have to fight off sleep at the play) which all tasted as good as confirmed hope, or a sweet kiss. The glasses with sparkling ice water, and the crystal lanterns with white flames on all the tables across the room, and the light-reflecting silver under the crystal chandeliers—all spellbound me into a sweet civil mood which gently refined conversation with the waiter and took me back for a second to any of the unsleeping ages that had the wisdom to put service at the heart of a meal, to bless it with a grace, to pour down libations and offer, at the sacred cutting of the portions, the best parts to the gods.

Smiling, I lifted a glass of white wine to Allie, and with a gesture infused with all these odd, graceful reveries, offered a toast, "To my dancer, and soul's healer—since she was fourteen, and till the end of my life."

It touched her. She said, blushing, with soft eyes, her face softened and beautiful, "Peter, tonight I'm where I want to be. It means more to me now than then. I feel better. Happier. But I never thought this wouldn't be. Never once."

I looked into the warmth of her eyes, seeing the red-brown color in her hair, different now, and the beautiful flesh and shadow of her mouth, "It's what you say goes deeper than dreams. The truth of the drive of the heart."

She lowered her eyes—thoughtful, and happy. Her dress was a dark blue silk, which I would set in her portrait now against the peach marble in that shining colonnade. She wore a fragrance of rose, which she'd been given by her sister.

So many times I've tried to say what I mean by that place which is just past the end of war, but not yet free from the echoes of the last battle thunder! That place is my statement, my main point, for God's sake. Even a fool will pay good money for lakefront property, because even a complete damned fool can sense in that location the powerful relation between being and nothingness. A madman, who might hear voices, gets too much of being or nothingness, or of both. A poet, who might hear voices, certainly gets too much of both: being and nothingness roaring in him louder than the whole history of philosophy. But a fool on his godlike days and a madman in moments of respite and a poet in moments of tranquility, all know to a lesser or greater degree that driving gracefully on a road between these two things leads each one to his own Jerusalem.

I've never fought in a war. I've just been to these cliffs in my mind—and discovered there, on the far edge, that mental chaos and death, when you're truly alive with fear, come like lightning if you choose either to be *or* not to be (and knowing this misery brings you straight to the real Hamlet as nothing else will). I couldn't move an inch in either direction. I became absolutely helpless—and this was maybe the key event, this coming to helplessness, as I knew from then on that what happened wasn't moved by me. But later, after the fear subsides, there's a place you come to—when you're still wounded, not yet overhealed and stupid, but also not paralyzed by the terror of either the need to exist or the need not to exist. Conversation helped me get there. Help for my helplessness, which made me think there's nothing more important in the world than a good doctor, who can put you on the road again, give you a chance for friendship with your own name as well as your own ignominy and annihilation. And in that place, call it the place of first peace, I got to know for a while what to believe in.

"You can become lost, though," I said to her, "without someone to lift you up. Someone who knows the worth of your happiness."

"When you finish your story," she said, with the perfect smile for her portrait in blue silk, "we'll go to Italy. I think Italy would be the place."

At *Romeo and Juliet* we held hands in the dark, listening, watching the stage-lit action, aroused. We knew how all partings are sweet, complex, dangerous, bitter—and in what ways they are so. Or in what ways some partings are good. And that Romeo's love of darkness makes beautifully suspect the quality of his nonetheless completely convincing love—and of all love. And that when the light named Juliet breaks the darkness and speaks the name Romeo and thinks of him and only him that this all should be read along with that forgetting of names so radical that it must be worth spending a whole lifetime trying to understand—and which you love with your life and weep for when you hear the names, the word "story," so dangerous and beautiful, in the ending of the play—the last mysterious word of which is in fact the boy's name. Allie and I knew and have talked of these things.

We knew too that knowing all this is what makes you come alive and not sleep for a second during the play. And I mean come alive as no two hours' traffic among the new poetry's things, which lie out beyond old dread "Hierarchy" (how much better to understand hierarchy as *proportion* and to understand proportion as a radically innocent term) and which are scattered in the any-which-way of no-grammar, could ever make anyone come alive. Or, that is, anyone except the one who in living violence is trying, in the way of a grammarian, to figure out the key to such poetry. And this quester is the *only* reader of it not sleeping—not sleeping profoundly like the eyes of the average reader, so utterly desperate for poetry after the seventy-year mandarin starvation, but here still without a prayer, going for a short unfriendly time over the lines of poets who still invent, for violent killing, a straw man (who does not exist and never did or will) who, as *only* a straw man will, believes absolutely in grammar and syntax and God and not in poor words as fair attempts, best attempts, to characterize unnameable fire.

And maybe now I could say that Lemaster would have loved the porn film and a good laugh. God knows what he'd have said about *Romeo and Juliet,* maybe nothing, maybe something about the futility of exaggeration. I've sometimes imagined him saying, "First I'd ban poets—the way Plato did. Then I'd ban Plato."

But I see the sculpted figure of Shakespeare again, seated

now among the flowers in Lincoln Park, beside the figures of other poets and storytellers and musicians. The words cut in the block: that he was not of an age but for all time. And then more words in the block (the Protagorean *anthropon metron,* also in the logo for "The Human Figure in Greek Art"): Man Is The Measure Of All Things. Words which should and do embarrass me, as does my love of the human figure in the first place.

Allie and I didn't throw our money away on Marilyn Chambers and Johnny Holmes (now dead of AIDS too, Christ). We held hands crossing the wet, black street, talking particularly about the enormous differences that those few minutes here and there would have made for the star-crossed lovers and how (with their time's slipping out of control only enriching for us the sweetness of sorrow) we were glad that for the sake of the play they weren't given those few minutes or seconds that they needed.

Tears were brightening in her eyes then too, and I kidded her, which got her laughing. "Damn you," she said and laid a soft fist-blow on my shoulder.

Then back in our room, after twenty years, we sat in chairs by the window and talked.

"It's even nicer," I said, "with everything so new, and expensive."

"I'd imagined for some reason," she said, "that the bed in this room would be turned in a different direction. I'm glad to see it's the same."

"Back then," I said, "what did you think really—when you called me?"

"I was scared and happy—both," she said. "Scared—and very happy . . . and scared . . . knowing what I was getting into."

The lights were on at Soldier Field for a night game; and with the lamps in our room down low, we had a remarkable view of the stadium, on fire in the dark. Bright as an alien invasion, it must have been visible from the air for a hundred miles. Far from it and encased as we were, we could still hear the crowd roaring.

I said, "Something good must have happened in the game." And suddenly with all passion I thought of my father's eighty-five-yard run, to the national championship, and then of the pain of my losses in the ring—and of the one that I'd suffered at that meet that absolutely I'd lived for—of how I'd learned about freedom, not from motion, escapes, any conquest of weight, but from imprisonment—under the absolute undreamable death sentence of the referee.

I whispered, staring over the lights into the dark sky, "The painful moments—if we could just forget . . ." Then— perhaps because the mind will think of the worst to keep us passionately aware of what's best, like mothers who imagine their babies killed—I thought of what Johnny and I really were looking at up in the crowd on the day of that meet—of who Allie was then, of what she'd just done. And of course it was a damned certain thing that I would think of this now. But she and I for a thousand hours had been talking, and still are; and this remains such a good sign. When she's there, when she talks, the reality, the sound, a hundred times wakes me up from my damned luxurious self-torture and dreamy violence. It makes it clear—I can say it—why action and being (children of the sun god, I thought, looking out still on the dark sky) can be so far holier than any uninterrupted thinking. And so we learn.

In the low-lit room, she said, "We won't die, Peter, if we forgive each other. I think that we like to remember, we love to remember, because it seems like then we won't die. But we won't die if we forget." She put her arm around me and reached her head over to my shoulder. "I remember when I first saw you. We were in church, and I couldn't keep my eyes on the Mass. I promised a nun once I'd become a nun. I remember thinking to myself when I watched you that that was one vow broken. And I swear if I ever did forget you, then I would be dead. So I forget what I need to forget, and I remember you."

I held her. I loved her so much again for waking me out of sleepy violence! But I was thinking how I'd planned things for this book that didn't work out: how I'd planned to have us dance together in a ring and have that dance beat away memories of my having been defeated in a ring by someone who wanted more than anything else to keep me from moving. How I intended to say that we feel things so intensely in the ring that the ring does come home to us truly as a symbol of eternity, and that my good times in the ring, my moments with her there in the dance, were going to be enough. But I had had to change that, and I couldn't honestly rewrite now what I'd changed. So of course I heard him say how he made our wedding insane (which sometimes for my life I am happily ready to believe, because it saves my marriage from shame) and wondered—as a mother thinks of the dead stare of her child, lying in the bloody street, hit by the car of a drunk—which of us it was that she was dancing with at our wedding dance.

But I swear to God she can read my mind! She said, "If you want to know what I thought of him on our wedding day, I'll tell you. What I was doing with you that day was past the beginning of my forgetting of him, which I promise you wasn't hard. I'd forgotten him even when I was with him. But I thought of one thing that day—which should tell you something. I was certain he'd sneaked out and not paid. I saw a ticket he'd signed with a false name. I know he just walked out. It summed things up for me, and I promise I just closed an already closed door in my mind and said another good-bye for good measure."

But now, when she'd said this, I turned my eyes from her in pain. I had to look out at the black sky. I even wished completely that the cloud-ceiling had stayed low and not drifted away and broken open to a handful of stars—lights that I now quickly turned from. And the dome of the Planetarium out on the water shining now in moonlight was deadly.

But she was with me, and talking. She said, as she touched my cheek with her warm hand, "You need to know this. I know what you need. And it's you I'm talking to. Not just anybody, but you. No lies. No chameleon escapes. You need to know that this is what I remembered—that you would always be you, and never once a cruel man—just as much as that I love you for the pain that being yourself causes you. It goes to my heart. I saw it in you from the first day. And I've never been bored for a second, only scared that it would be too much.

"And it is. You scare me. You scare me every day. I wonder if I ever could be enough for you, or how in hell I can avoid being too much: not right for someone I think's the best I've ever known and who at the same time might die if he had the slightest idea of this. You're crazy, boy. Don't worry about not being crazy enough. Even if you do think that yesterday connects with today and tomorrow and have children whom you love, and in your daily life show no sign at all of being crazy, and are incapable of cruelty. You need to know that I know, no matter what I've ever said, that I can count on you *and* that you're crazy *and* that I've always known and loved all of this and that it keeps me happy, worried, and passionate every day—from the beginning to the end."

She sat down against me on the floor and rested her cheek on my thigh; and I ran my fingers tenderly through her hair, thinking in the half-light that when you go to Barbara, sister of Eros, and her candied masquerade truly it is because you have no answer for death. With this queen of something, you do break time and the surface of yourself (if never your adamant selfishness) so you can't know the pain, or the joy of sacrifice, or of real, murderous honesty—and so won't have to be responsible and cannot be civilized. I knew that Conlon could give away his life, break up his marriage for Barbara and so suggest terrifyingly that maybe he never had any real faith in the civilized self, his purported leading vision. So go then to Babylon. To maintain your identity is to miss the best chance. So be a masker. But I thought that I would certainly have killed someone if I'd heard a sound of this when I was helpless and went to this doctor.

And now suddenly I thought again that there might be meaning to life's motion! I looked north to the Art Institute and saw in my mind some of the things inside—the cool marble and parquet floors and the magnificent collection of late medieval and Renaissance armor—the steel halberds and hooked spears (the dark emptiness inside the nightmare helmets making room for the mind to move in and find in this steel a reflection of our eternal violence and desire)—beautifully lit, glass-encased on the cool floor, just one turn from the placidity of the row of smooth, sandstone Buddhas, come from where they come. Then Shiva dancing with Vishnu (another word pointing to nothing), who holds together the structure of what is, and Brahma calling to the zero end—in that corridor over the garden court, where Allie and I have often sat and had a meal and beers and listened to music till the time ran down and we rushed to see the hand of Abraham in Rembrandt's *Abraham and Isaac* or the red blood dripping from the chest of a ripped medieval Christ, or a horned bull that scrapes the dust in the mind of Picasso, till we heard that it was finally time.

And now, in our room, her cheek was pressed warmly against my thigh. Her hair spread over me as I lifted the rich auburn in waves and let it fall. The game had ended, and the stadium lights were out; and in the dark out over the water, new stars were shining with the brighter moon. I could look at the hazy red lamp at the pinnacle of the Planetarium and see the silver moonlight spread down over the dome.

And what might two twenty-five-year lovers see out a window in Michigan Avenue's beauteous wall of buildings? I could think it would be something so lost that we would be led by it only to our isolated selves and our inevitable death. But then, because of Allie's soft touch and the caress of her fingers, I came out of prison, and could move—and move us both out past the twelve-cornered Planetarium building (each corner with a gilded insignia of a phase of the zodiac) to that farthest point out on the peninsula, where we went sometimes in the summer to look back on the spectacle of the city's shoreline lights.

I thought of the terrible beauty in the history of the mind's mad love of the stars. As the Planetarium's builders and planners no doubt hoped they would, names came to my mind and ideas larger than the names. Crazy men who found out in their heads that the circle was the true, deep symbol of eternity. Plato, for all he said about the dangerous madness of poets, was crazy enough himself to believe that the circle's beauty dictated itself to heaven. And Ptolemy, another sad one who knew a good deal more about where the world would go than he gets credit for lately. I love Kepler (what could be sadder!), who after decades of sick love for circles and geometric solids was forced to admit the monster presence of the irregular ellipse. I could think of these things and not ruin or fear them, as if music were still sounding deeply, and without trouble, in my heart. I thought of Goethe's remarks on the understandable terrors that the whole world had to feel when Copernicus (whose huge figure sits at the end of Solidarity Drive—the road to the stars named after another embarrassing objective in our prayers for human time) said what he had to say, and of all the smart guys now who are dull-witted enough to find what Copernicus said easily amusing. You can hear them laughing at the words on the red, interested arrow, pointing to a pitiful, minuscule spot on the Planetarium's beautiful map of "One Hundred Million Points of Light," saying to us "You are here." Amusing museum.

The huge Field, too, another home for the Muses, as Allie kissed me, was conceivably the haunt of a goddess. Every type of relic of human passion now silent in the dark; the day's ten thousand eyes brought down now to the two of the night watchman, who may or may not have been interested then in things that have met me like replicas of my dreams. Beautiful, terrifying ancestral masks handed down through great ages of Indian sadness for the sad hope of right ritual communion with the powers of heaven. Case after case in the huge dark rooms, lit only by spotlights in the glass; the right dress for hunting, for the dance, for burial; cups and bowls and knives, pointed weapons, shields; the sounds of drums and chants and of the excited telling of stories, the mad Shaman's voice, explaining the creation. And for the memory of every citizen of the city, every lover of power and terror, the huge bull elephants fighting and spearing in the great hall; the skeleton of the dinosaur standing, as he stood seventy-five million years ago, over the equally terrifying skeleton of his prey. "You are here." "You are here."

And back through the tunnel under Lake Shore Drive, in the kingdom of Neptune, past the doors sculpted with low reliefs of every conceivable form being devoured in the mouth of some other—in the Aquarium's black, twisting vaults, like caves of the sea, there's still more of interest. Shining in lighted cases, in the dark vaults, astounding beauty and monstrosity in colors that couldn't possibly have names, turning and then gone—presences and disappearances of utterly lethargic, floating and then awakening, darting loners and schools. None really going anywhere, ever, and none caring. Such unbelievable hideousness and beauty. Nowhere is color more powerful, making the smallest forms magnificent. And the enormity of the giant squid hung from the ceiling, looking at the sharks, around whom people gather over and over in clusters, wanting to see the war-flag fins and the rows of teeth. "Do you see that!" "Look!"—coming from interested parties, who all laugh when they're frightened but safe. And again and again in the spectacular light, in coral gardens, or among representations of the wreckage of ships, that stillness that has to be death, until shockingly it moves.

But the near impossibility of speaking like this—Oh Christ Jesus how it infuriates me! That I'd talk tough, that I'd be one more up-to-date idiot who in crisp clean unadorned "real" prose (what a fucking laugh!) talks about street shit; or that I'd be one more really strange surrealistic goddamned bedazzling cliché, or that I'd try my damnedest and for my life to forge a new incomprehensible philosophicolinguistic backwards-forwards upside-down challenge to the hegemonic logocentric discourse of the West—Jesus God Almighty this makes me sick enough (I promise you in blood) to want to die.

Poetry as remote philosophical linguistic experiment—just what we need when even life readers and professors of literature do not (because they goddamned cannot) read *any* of the poetry of our time. And the self-justifying arguments that point to an unbroken history of unpopular difficulty in all true poetry—as if Milton were not far easier to read than any little item in any one of today's little magazines; or as if the announcement at the beginning of the Great Age of Irony, those seventy ungodly long years ago, that poetry *had* now to be difficult, were not responsible for the fact that virtually *no one* reads poetry now, and so that nothing is understood by anyone as it needs to be understood; and as if a purely philosophical language, which will have nothing to do with the structure of that disgusting "illusion," the self, could ever speak of love, or sorrow, or the anger of Achilles.

All I have is that I nearly went crazy, and that for some months I couldn't think for a second about my death or my life, about night or day, the structure of the world either staying as it was or changing even slightly, having my eyes or being blinded (and I mean exactly what I say)—because these things screamed with terror, and in one second tore apart the world, if I took any position. I had to trust authority with an absolute trust, and yet I had to remain completely hopeless because hoping meant for me immediate unspeakable terror. Too far, for me, was a goddamned fraction of an inch in any direction.

But after the utter helplessness (and I mean if I tried for one second more to hold out alone, or made the first move toward trying to do one more thing for myself I'd be torn cord from cord in the brain) there came better days. Days when I was given seconds to say to myself with total passion, long enough before the night would start a revenge, that the sun was a saving god. And then even better days when the sunrise and sundown were the stridings of gods that I could love in tears and with words. This was the place. I read poetry then with a hero-worship of the poets. I said, "They've been here." And I knew absolutely that I was right. They spoke to me, and I understood. I'd been to school, and I knew something. And because I so nearly went crazy, there might (as there might in the words of a war veteran) actually be some honor in what I say here.

The edge of the moon, the pinpoints of the stars, the shining on the domes and octagons and temple columns of the museums and the empty harbor, the magnificence of the buildings (one second the obscenities of earth-ripping pandemoniac Mulciber, the next second pylons in the Gates of Paradise or the living walls of Heaven)—only the dull (one of the most terrible words in poetry!) can't see it. And my hands running through Allie's hair were the hands of a dream lover, a virgin Romeo from a page of poetry—touching her cheek, feeling the flesh and bone, running with special gentleness a finger over her closed eyes and tracing with care and passion the borderline of her lips.

I felt the wetness of her tongue and, moistening her lips with it, ran my moist finger off the border to her cheeks, and moistened my finger again in her warm mouth to wet her face, as she pressed her mouth in tight against me and kissed me. And I could feel that I was near the place, with ghosts and the heartbreaking city night lights and gigantic shadows—and the waves spraying at the breakwater, the bronze and sandstone Shivas poised dancing in the silence—the place exactly far enough from terror, where joy begins, and confidence in the beauty and power of the ground you stand on is enough to let you move out past the breakwater in the dark.

And as lucky as I was to love nothing when I stood by Johnny's grave, I was lucky now, further out from the shadow of the presence of the largest conceivable terror, in the quiet of that room, to love Allie completely in the moment she asked me, "Do you still love me?"

It's so hard that she needed to ask. It's unbearable. It shows that working, forcing things as brutally as the madman who inscribed the sixth commandment, is inescapable, that Urizenic mania as sick as an evangelist's is needed to keep the one vow that we still remember to swear, from degenerating into another twentieth-century joke.

Yet for all the sadness that I felt instantly when she asked me, sadness because I knew that vows meant work, praying for rain in dead hours of sleeping affection, I was so happy to say "Yes"—and didn't look over my shoulder to see what Johnny Lemaster's ghost thought now of my book. Rather I knew that love, like any beautiful spot of light and green enfolded by forest darkness, was approved by the gods. And call this book a true love story—a working out of a life sworn to patience, informed by a history of sporadic but real mad pain and terror, cognizant of the sanctity of its experience of helplessness and of the power of the gods of sunrise and sundown, and which found its metaphor at last (as did the poems of so many mad poets who wrote comedies, divine or otherwise) in the unashamed celebration of constant love: the dangerous beautiful sun shining in the sweet civil night.

But the truth is (and if we want a reputation for courage and originality we'll say it) that Ulysses Grant was only a boozer and a grafter, and not that he drove the world to Appomattox; and that Abraham Lincoln needs to be revised down from the poet of our great task *here* and of the fourscore-and-seven-year history of eternity, to the measure of a closet racist. Values are only values: the bastard children of an accidental synchrony, existing even in their own small circle only for one spasmodic generation and absolutely inconceivable to all strangers. And the sacred dictum that honesty writes only to diminish things will be paradoxically the rallying point for the future of the paradoxically Great Disunion.

But maybe I can say that when Allie kissed me on the thigh and brought the warmth of her mouth to my cock, I tightened my finger hold in her hair and, knowing in my hand and finger how far back was the place where a hint of pain brings pleasure, pulled her back so I could see her and she could see me—so we could dance quickly a return to grace and freedom, looking at each other, with open mouths, as I let her hair loosen through my fingers. She was glad to feel the almost hurting grip, as passion loves the moist lips of sorrow, and to be let go. She unbuttoned my shirt and pressed her cheek against my skin—kissed my chest with the side of her wet mouth. And I wanted her warm mouth on my mouth so I lifted her up to me, for the happiness—for the happiness that is her life, to be mine. Then we stood together kissing passionately, pressing ourselves hard to each other and then lightly running fingers, fingernail traces, over the skin of each other's face. We lay down with some embarrassment, even after so many years, but I unfastened her dress to her lower back, and my hand stole in to touch her stomach and side, and my finger ran down beneath her silk to stir the rush of heat and blood that came when I found her moistness—which I left traces of on her thigh and then took to my lips and tongue before I kissed her.

The lights were soft enough, and the shadows, the gods in the shadows, helped us make crazy love. What we'd learned—if that's the way to say it—in all our years together, we turned now to the use of grace and the most reaching, intense passion. I knew her places. She knew what I loved to see and hear. I tasted her, with my eyes closed as she ran her fingers through my hair. And we used a dancer's false hard strength and lifted each other and wrestled in the ring of all our sadness and desire, of all our time together here, which poets say over and over is not long.

I could scream that any work I've done here to reveal the life in a vow is work that the world had better learn to do again. But I've screamed enough. I'll just say that after so many years my night with Allie was still as tender and passionate as could be. She whispered to me, from where she'd gotten—please to wait for her. We called each other by name. Chanted each other's names in each other's ears. In the joy of pure patience, I whispered back as I kissed her ear that she had time, that she should take all the time she'd need. And I kissed her closed eyes as she showed me a brief strained hard smile. Then in relief and joy she pressed her head back hard and tensed and held me, pressing her fingers with all her strength into my shoulders as she came hard in my arms, sobbing, saying that it frightened her and that it was heaven. And having known again patience and desire—I mean what I say—and all the mysteries of the body, light, heavy—in the half-light—the taste of kisses, the words, names, whispers, I came with her, and my breathing changed to a low heavy moan, the wordless end, as I'd planned. Then after a time we laughed and joked and were embarrassed by what we'd said—joked about that, enjoyed the body's incomparable pleasure after the end of passion. We held each other in the best comfort, and searched out with our limbs the best way to make complete the embrace we would travel in to sleep.

And maybe I could say that these are nearly the last words I'll write about my Allie, for just saying it makes me feel so tenderly, with compelling sadness, the terrible fact that there will be a time when one of us will be alone. My living partner in a love story, who has let me know day after day that, as she's taught me, she's learned from me the secret worth of things. It won't matter which one of us it is, the sorrow will be the same.

And as a mad terrified beautiful poet said, let sleep visit her with gentle wings of healing—while I'll go on in my own insane way—say what I thought in the early-morning dark, when in our noiseless room an alarm in my head went off (because I desired to hear it, and set it to end this whole thing), and I opened my eyes.

I disentangled myself, but, as I saw and felt her in peace asleep, I whispered a prayer for Allie's life and joy, for her rising to meet the greatest possible number of days in the deepest possible happiness. And as I sat up and bowed my head, I thought of what an absolutely complete life of pain and joy it takes to understand the terror and ecstasy in the request that we be forgiven as we forgive. As I felt my limbs again, but also the deep warmth and comfort of sleep, and love, I cried into my hands (after so much work on this book, over so many years!), tasted the salt in my tears on my fingers, and knew, even if I'm sure that it takes a whole life to know what these words mean!—what the words mean in the Our Father—"as we forgive those who trespass against us."

Then because I knew that it was time for this, time to bring this thing to an end, I worked my way further out of sleep. I dried my eyes and thought, as I knew I would, of my daughter, Colleen—who'd cried an infant's cry in one of my dreams, which were almost as deep as my intentions, which for so long now *have* been to hold her at the end of this story, as I held her that one night, not long after she was born and maybe a year after I'd begun to see Conlon.

We were on Greenwood still, and so I had before my eyes

the walls and ceilings, rebuilt by faith, that had been subverted by a loss of confidence so terrifying that, *ironically,* it taught me the language of poetry and the Bible. I heard the sound of Colleen's crying breaking into my sleep; and I was able to think that Allie had nursed her just a short while before; that Allie could use sleep now; and that if I got up and held Colleen and rocked her on the porch, I could get her back to sleep.

And when I felt my limbs distinctly again, as I began to wake up, I was thinking with joy of poets and night watchmen sounding the All's Well, and again of the difference between myself then and myself not too long before—when being half-asleep and half-awake had left me terrified of any slightest choice of either sleeping or waking, needing sleep so much but having to keep my eyes open and on objects or lose my mind in instant nightmare. The idea that back then I'd respond to my own child's voice crying! that I'd even move, or think of an outcome! The dark would have gone wild with devils working on my walls! But now, where I was, I could contemplate the joy in the difference.

Devils not there, I could think too of the potentially tragic pride that I took now in Colleen's every move forward, which we were watching these days hour after hour with nice maniacal parental care—think of it and lay flowers before images of the same gods of darkness who threatened me before for any single good move that I might make. I knew that they would define the limits (now out further) of my building of Colleen's life and so keep her safe both in me and, God knows, from me. And now that she sits cross-legged, at sixteen, beautiful in the big chair, recalling the white flower of the East, and reads poets and has the soul to begin learning the words, I'm so thankful—just as I am that she loves the guys, and begs for the car and works like a fiend when she needs the money, and cries hysterically over what she sees in the mirror.

And when I saw her through the bars of the crib, crying, I could feel the worth of my being there in a way that let me understand the meaning of light shining in darkness, as I hadn't quite ever before. The house (as Tennyson or Spenser might say, thinking of what?) was for me built now to music, and I could think as I held her of the milestones that she'd passed, the smiling and the rolling over, and of the safety in the weight of her body. And when I looked and saw her eyes shut again, but still felt the jerking and hard breathing of her crying, I wanted so much to rock her back to peace, with whispers of healing words for her ears. I thought in the dark, with unbelievable joy, of her presence here and her future—a future which, the other night at the Hilton, in the chair by the window (so close to where I wanted to be), I could contemplate in its actual coming round! And this book has in the most important sense corresponded with the coming along of this beautiful young life, her mother's daughter and mine—though, irony of ironies, I could never be ending this thing if I actually had the feeling that I've always wished to end it with, some perfected conviction. Too deadly. Lemaster knows.

But on the porch, when I took Colleen out to rock her, I knew I'd come to the place! I cannot possibly sink far enough into it now—not and write this. I have to be far off—far—in the vocabulary of the human soul, which the poets have discovered. I'm lying miserably as I try to put myself there by saying I'm there. But I don't lie when I say that I've known again so much lately—been so close, looking out the other night at the last stars in the dark. And I can't wait forever to say amen.

We were on the third floor on Greenwood, high as the elms, and there was wind from the lake—but I wasn't afraid of what was coming. Holding and rocking Colleen, I even had the freedom to imagine Yeats' great gloom in the mind and to imagine fear of the future—but in delight—as I embraced Colleen and all the silence and air. I had no differences with anything, and so thought in sweet peace of Yeats' bellowing noise, politics in the world, the utter deracination of hatred.

Yet I could pray. Unembarrassed, I could pray for my daughter. I put words in her ear that didn't wake her but which could be heard. I whispered to her, "You are so beautiful. I'm here with you, sweetheart. My little sweetheart. I love you, and I'll always love you. I'll always be here for you." It was midnight. Time for the owl of death. But I whispered, "I promise you, you'll get to know what can be known from the ice, the world in an ice storm, and the first spring birdsong, in tears the fire in the colored leaves. Sweet perfume of baby skin. I love so much how your sweet body, only out of the dark so long, brings me into a world of cares. I watch you so much. I dream so dangerously about what you'll be. Like some vicious tyrant in a book, I want the time to come right now when you'll be formed just as I desire. I hate your slow infancy, and I'll hate your childhood. I'll hate your backtalk when you talk. I'll hate your life. I'll ask you what you mean and where you've been and who you think you are. I'll say no to everything. I hate already that there is some boy in the world who'll take you from me. I hate him. I think he's no good. You'll have to come home early if you go out with him. But you'll show me with your life how wrong I am and make me love you and trust you and see that you're better than what I wanted. We'll talk to each other. I know you'll be a dancer like your mother. I won't kill you. I promise you. I say, my little sweetheart. My little sweetheart. We'll go to the parks along the water. I'll show you the places. I won't tell you. I'll let you guess. I'll say do this, or you're in trouble, and I won't mean it."

And the other night, sitting in the hotel window, looking out over the dry fountain stones just coming into a softer dark, the cold beautiful hard grays and slate blues of predawn coming out, I was so sharpened and so close to where I wanted to be that I wasn't afraid to die. Everything was becoming mine as, in the way the saints say, I became nothing. Or closer and closer to nothing, as I still owned a magic gemstone of confidence—or call it the little ship which, if it doesn't go down in complete madness, sails deeper and further than the waters of nightmare and dreams. A few car lights out on the Drive—so few that a city boy could take them, as they disappeared, for the few falling stars he'd seen in his life.

And on Greenwood, holding my little girl, rocking her, thinking how I knew what the walls were and how devils in them, who would emerge at sudden times with faces as hideous as any ever dreamed, were driven away by singing angels, who were in the wind and in the walls, ready to break out and show their faces and wings—like angel-fancies in Gothic cathedrals bursting from the walls at the joints and high corners. But I say this and for me now it's a lie. It's just sculpture for me right now, not poetry gone wild! Buildings don't rise for me, as they have, on the wings of the Resurrection. But with Allie, just days back now, after so many years' labor on this godforsaken book, I was burning, and music was in the traces of bending light coming over the gray water. And I remembered that Colleen's eyes opened, that we smiled at each other—she only so long out of the dark, needing me—and that I heard angels in the wind, as I rocked her and whispered to her, "Let me tell you a story."

What in her would understand my words was only sleeping then. I still for my life don't want her to read now in this book what kinds of things woke me up over the years. It scares me to death—what she might think or do. But the end of this story (and I thought and think of her beautiful mother), she knew truly there as I rocked and held her and smiled and she read my face. She was my audience—she knew before she could say a word. I thought the end for her life was nothing I needed to force—or the end for this book. And I thought it again, crying at the hotel, remembering how I whispered to her, "On the other side of the lake—it's gone now—but there used to be a park. We would go there, in the summertime."

Then I turned her—and I can't find the enchantment, the chanting that will put that small body and everything that comes out of the dark and heads on, in my hands again now—propped her so she sat up on my lap with her back against my stomach. And I looked at the walls and out the windows at whatever lights still were shining after midnight on Greenwood. And with a feeling unlike any I'd ever had in my life—even at the foot of the altar, in full ecstatic belief—I thought that everything I'd learned showed me how to hold this infant body, how firmly, how loosely—how to touch or let go, and where life ends for her and death begins. I knew it as her mother knew it forever. And angels' wings, faces—the sounds of their voices! Do you know what it means to be able to replace instant screaming nightmare chimeras in the walls with these powers? I cried unbelievably the other night thinking of it, remembering. I cried from a place so deep—Jesus God—where? Is it nothing? Just anything can make your heart tear open like this? The infant didn't know the end? I'm wrong! Her mother's wrong! We're both dangerous and obscene!

But I was with her there, and she stopped crying as I told her my story, rocking her, only just out of the dark, still so dangerously light that it made me think of all the terrible possibilities that could end her life. And she didn't know the prayer in me? My hands and my healed-insane heart gone wild with joy, my eyes looking at angels! The end wasn't something that would go straight to the heart? I whispered, very softly, "It was an amusement park." And she knew, because she'd embraced them all sleeping with her, who the Muses were. "There were rides, and we went in the summertime, across the lake. It was called Silver Beach."

Now I'm struggling! still fighting off the death of sleep after thousands of hours—which only screams at me that I don't have a structure, even a few steps from the end! I'd be awake! I'd be alive if I did! But the other night at the hotel I was crying, while Allie slept there, and I prayed, for her, for myself, and, because the building's holding firm made it possible, prayed further for the whole world, like a saint in ecstasy. Yet I remembered too the weight and balances of the self, and how incapacitated my heart had been for showing any kindness when I feared for what my eyes could see, feared so much for built things. The ego's shame. Though I knew again too that somewhere in their dark cells of self-forgetfulness the saints forever need candles.

And rocking back and forth with Colleen, that night just so far and just so many days, hours, out from my worst fear, I held her and talked to her, and she knew the end. I thought, as if there were music playing, of the Silver Beach rides—of the wait before any ride began, then of the sound and motion, the terrible sublime exaggeration in the clanking of the roller-coaster chain as you came higher and higher to an end—to a view of miles of beaches and the widest lake and sundown over the water—and then the last pause and the bracing and gripping which were no help for the wild dying plunge, which ran mercilessly, and to our unforgettable delight, through the echoes of our screams. I said to her, "You should have seen us, or heard us—Johnny and me—after we got off, after we'd done it—shooting off our mouths as if they'd never stop. It was hilarious. But you know. I'll take you—but you know."

I whispered, "And I know you'll remember this—the way I'm rocking you now, when you go up on the Ferris wheel with all the colored lights and the music, as we whirl around, losing and gaining weight, looking out over the whole world, and I rock the car on the crazy rockers made so that crazy people can scare themselves to death. You'll start to cry and scream, 'Daddy, stop! Stop! I hate you!' And I'll laugh and let the music and rhythm and the smooth sail down from the top delight you, and I'll hold you tight as we go up again and around. You won't forget, little girl. You'll remember where you are now—because it's one of the things that we never completely forget.

"My friend Johnny. You don't know him. I'll tell you about him. But you'll already know. And you'll have certain friends whom you'll never forget, no matter what. But Johnny went too, you see. He was with us that time. He and his dad. We were on the bumper cars. I remember the rubber smell and the craziness. The mole-mound shape and red color of the cars—how they were spaced and jammed. I can hear him shouting, 'Hey, Petie, watch out for me! Here I come!' And how we were smashing and bumping, and laughing because we'd crashed so many times that we didn't know which way the road went! It was so much fun! We were still shouting at each other when we ran out after the ride was over, but he had his arm around me and we were laughing and holding each other because we were such great friends. But some day you'll know—you already know—why I can't even believe, and why it's wrong of me to believe, that he ever wanted to love the same things I did."

And even now I put these words down crying. I was

crying when I whispered them to Colleen—but felt such joy that I can't ever live it again. The words were so powerful—so true in my mouth, heart—in the air—the power and honor and truth, sturdy as the walls standing in the power of angels—but with the meaning of the Crucifixion, holding the body of things as I held this small body, only so long in the world and light, with such a journey to go and so much need.

I knew that I was cradling the truth. And the tears I was crying as I looked out over the park and lake the other morning in the dark I cried because I wasn't afraid to die. Me too, John, not afraid—for my time and in my place.

I said to Colleen, "If it kills me, sweetheart, I'll say—as wrong as it is—I've still got to tell you—that I remember him in the Maze of a Million Doors. The fun house. I remember being ahead of him and that I was thrilled because I was never ever ahead of him in things. But I saw him, and he was frightened too. We were little boys. We were ten, and we were both scared sometimes—and laughed together. Waiting for him in the slanted room, hunched up near where the erupting floor rose to just under the ceiling, laughing, laughing as he'd laugh, I saw him quickly pushing doors, almost frantic, and so glad to be out finally, because no one had been in with him. And you'll know what it means when I say that I should leave my friend Johnny alone—and never, like a gossip or a murderer, lord it over the absent or the dead!

"But we are all afraid, and we all laugh too in the frightening hilarious slanted room, and in front of the mirrors—the mirrors which make you a sad, sad giant or a tough little midget wrestler; or warp you back to yourself again, which seems every bit as funny and surprising. We laughed until we hurt in the room filled with mirrors, and our dads came in the room after us, and we took them all around. We were all laughing so hard. Johnny said, 'Dad, you're little and I'm tall!' I remember this—though I'm almost afraid to say it. But you'll know why I do. And you'll know why—you already know why I have to take this also to the very end—down the last long dark corridor, through the sudden, surprising air blasts, which make you scream with laughter, and spooky lights and sounds in the dark, which scare you. We all headed down it, laughing and holding each other till we came finally to the door—there were cracks in the frame which let through the light—which opened into a tremendous wooden bowl, a huge dirty wooden bowl with enough room for over a hundred to sit around its rim."

We knew it would be there—but it's always different from what you thought—but still huge! Huge when we stepped in! I could see it now, feel it now!—feel it in tears. Write words awake, in total passion—from the place. In the place! Where you feel so much and care so much, that you aren't afraid to die, even if you hold the world so dear that it makes you weep, makes you prefer it to heaven and never-ending life. I was so close just nights ago. I wrote this ending then, with the morning looking over the city and lake; with the sun bringing more of its endless differences of light, forms enchanting, miraculous, in the first dawn—and for seconds nothing of any shame.

I told Colleen how tremendous it was. I said that I held my dad and that when we came in, there were some riders there already—a few hard ones—two tattooed sailors with their tough girls, some teenage boys with cigarettes in their sleeves. I remembered how we sat by ourselves and waited to see who else would come through the door. And it was every conceivable kind of body and face—farm families, college boys, hard angular men and fat ladies, the girls a boy would think he'd run off with for a time and ones he'd think he'd stay with forever, with ponytails and clean white blouses.

And I said to Colleen, feeling perfectly courageous and yet ready to let everything go—for her sake, "This is such a terrible thing to say, terrible—but Johnny—I'm sure that he wanted his dad to be the best man there. He'd had hard times with his dad. He wanted this to be a different time. I know. I know that it meant so much to him. I could cry for him! But love him too, as maybe really he wanted me to love him—though for your sake I'm afraid even to say that word! He makes me so afraid even to say that word! He makes me so afraid, and I feel everything that he wants me to feel, now, in joy. I'm so glad that it didn't work out—because it stops me from saying I love. You'll see. You'll see. It makes me go into a silence that you'll know. I pray for it. I pray for it with all my heart.

"But this bowl, with all these people—with the contours of every disposition in light from utter ferocity to the beauty of girls who'd make the world lay down arms forever—if the world ever had enough sense to look and think how delicately it would have to kiss such lips! This bowl had in its center a small raised circular plateau, like the hub of a wheel; only here maybe, because the wheel was so huge, the flat hub reached for a diameter of some five feet, and rose maybe a foot and a half from the floor. And there was an object: to get to this center—and remain still, while everyone else in the bowl had to spin so fast. You see, it moved—but you know. And an invisible man somewhere up above, who looked down, pushed a button and made the bowl begin to move when he saw that there were enough people inside the door and that it was packed enough and noisy. And I know, sweetheart, now, in a way that makes me think that we're not born to die—and I'll be a good father if I always believe this—that we're placed always in some tight bowled circle, with nothing visible over the rim, so that we'll want and will fight for the center place—so that we can stop our spinning out to hell and gone."

As I write this now, I hear Allie and Colleen talking in the next room. And I think of how at the hotel Allie heard me crying and woke up as the sun broke over the horizon and came to watch the world come back with me and heard me tell her that I knew the end, that I'd written it, and that as she knew it had to be, it was about what we all know from before the day we were born. That it was me whispering these words to Colleen as I rocked her on the porch on Greenwood with the built world standing still for enough time, in the strength of angels, so that I could hold and rock her—the beautiful person—the rare body—(who's outside the door now, sixteen, asking for money, getting asked by her mother what for!). And that I tell her that our fear of hell, our fear of going there ourselves, or of seeing anyone at any time cross the empty space from hell and move toward us in our small inner circle—

the sense of those bounds, the fear of wild crazy spinning motion, just over the edge—this anxiety so completely condemned now—can be the beginning for effort and beauty, which can be sacrifices, and are the things that we sacrifice. And then that sacrifice and mercy make the small place where we exist into an everywhere and into all time because with them we erase enough of the difference between ourselves and all hell and gone—if we have still to stay in our small place, to have our possessions and a loving eye that watches them and measures their worth.

I recalled that I said, "Johnny, my friend Johnny, was laughing, sitting with his dad, and I was with my dad, and we were all laughing—when the motion suddenly began. The bowl—as you know now and will always—was spinning and we were aware of the time and of our dead weights, which soon enough we had great difficulty even lifting an inch off the wall. I remember that Johnny and I tried to free our arms and that we couldn't. But I saw a sailor move out into the empty middle space. Everyone watched as we screamed going round and round. And he almost made it but flew back and was caught in a contortion against the wall. But if you knew your grandfather, you'd know what I'm going to say. But I haven't told you. Yet I'm going to because I should. He took me, love, under his arm—while the sailors and college boys kept building out bridges with their bodies off the wall. I was so scared. I looked at Johnny. He was with his dad. But we were moving out. See he was—your grandfather—the strongest, like a hero from an old book."

And I cried tears of ecstasy as I said this. I wept in this place, as I was loving so much, and as the gods gave me room—in the place of heaven—so I could be here and not here—so I could hold Colleen tenderly in my hands. I said it to Allie. I said it as I wrote the end of this story, and the lake was on fire with light, and the city almost the living golden walls of heaven.

I said that I whispered as I could, tenderly to Colleen, "He was like a hero from some age long gone by—the strongest of all. And you see he had me under his arm, so powerful, as we went out into that empty space. The others tried to push us back, hold us off—but they couldn't stop him. He tore down their bridges and, laughing as hard as he could, sent them one after another out back to the whirling rim. And we kept making way. Foot by foot as he held me under his arm and balanced himself with his other arm and powerful legs, moving out steadily, till it got easier and easier and easier. And then we were there. And we sat there. I sat on his lap, and we were still and free while everyone else kept whirling. It was all ours. And I saw Johnny way back with his dad, gone nowhere, whirling, with a tortured expression. But then he set his eyes on us. He looked hard as diamonds and then by himself started to move off the wall! He was coming! He wanted it so much. He was trembling violently. And his dad then started to move, and they were making some way! I saw Johnny's face looking up, and everyone was watching and yelling, screaming to them to come and take our place—as you know."

And I know she knows, gone now, with the keys—to wherever she needs to go, leaving me here now to finish this, with the sound of her mother's footsteps in the next room. And we drive on to our ends, each one on a pilgrimage to that place where the gods give us just enough room so that terror and pity could be delightful forever.

And that was where I was—there—when I whispered to Colleen at midnight on Greenwood, as the wind began to move high in the elms. I said, "It didn't happen for them, sweet love. They kept coming. They came right to the edge of the plateau of the inner circle. Johnny's father held Johnny so tight now, and then he reached up to get his first grip on the center. But my father—and I know you know what to think of this. I know you know where to place yourself when I say that my father with all his unbelievable power tore away that hand and then hurled my friend Johnny and his father—I can see them, I'll always see them falling—back into nowhere. And I hold you here on my lap as I do, and I whisper to you what he roared then into my ear, with all the people shouting so loud. He was laughing, and with a power come from eternity, he roared into my ear, 'How does it feel to be the King of the World?' "